Links of a Chain

Monica Genya

SPEAR BOOKS SERIES

Sugar Daddy's Lover *Rosemarie Owino*
Lover in the Sky *Sam Kahiga*
Mystery Smugglers *Mwangi Ruheni*
A Girl Cannot Go on Laughing all the Time *Magaga Alot*
The Love Root *Mwangi Ruheni*
The Ivory Merchant *Mwangi Gicheru*
A Brief Assignment *Ayub Ndii*
A Taste of Business *Aubrey Kalitera*
A Woman Reborn *Koigi wa Wamwere*
The Bhang Syndicate *Frank Saisi*
My Life in Crime *John Kiriamiti*
Black Gold of Chepkube *Wamugunda Geteria*
Ben Kamba 009 in Operation DXT *David Maillu*
Son of Woman in Mombasa *Charles Mangua*
The Ayah *David Maillu*
A Worm in the Head *Charles K. Githae*
Twilight Woman *Thomas Akare*
Life and Times of a Bank Robber *John Kiggia Kimani*
Son of Woman *Charles Mangua*
A Tail in the Mouth *Charles Mangua*
My Life with a Criminal: Milly's Story *John Kiriamiti*
The Operator *Chris Mwangi*
Birds of Kamiti *Benjamin Bundeh*
Nice People *Wamugunda Gateria*
Times Beyond *Omondi Mak'Oloo*
Lady in Chains *Genga-Idowu*
Mayor in Prison *Karuga Wandai*
Son of Fate *John Kiriamiti*
Kanina and I *Charles Mangua*
Prison is not a Holiday Camp *John Kiggia Kimani*
Confessions of an AIDS Victim *Carolyne Adalla*
Comrade Inmate *Charles K. Githae*
Colour of Carnations *Ayub Ndii*
The American Standard *Sam De Santo*
From Home Guard to Mau Mau *Elisha Mbabu*
The Girl was Mine *David Karanja*
Links of a Chain *Monica Genya*

Links of a Chain

Monica Genya

East African Educational Publishers
Nairobi

Published by
East African Educational Publishers Ltd.
Brick Court
Mpaka Road/Woodvale Grove
Westlands
P.O. Box 45314
NAIROBI

ISBN 9966–46–956–7

Typeset by
Jarodi Educational Institute
P.O. Box 38986
NAIROBI

Printed by

Sunlitho Limited,
P.O. Box 13939,
Nairobi, Kenya.

Chapter One

"Susie!"

Susan Juma's footsteps came to an abrupt halt outside the elevator door. It was quarter to six in the evening and she should have left the office an hour ago; but then when had she been able to make it home before six o'clock ever since she started working at B.I.O.? She turned around slowly.

"Yes, Anne," she said.

Susan and Anne Kariuki, the floor secretary, were the only ones left in the hallway. Almost everyone else had left before five. In fact she herself had left, only to return; unobtrusively through the back entrance to get her umbrella which she had forgotten. Unobtrusively or not, her presence was noted and everyone seemed to want her attention for one thing or another. She had already made six unsuccessful attempts to leave. This attempt wasn't looking too successful either.

"Sorry to bother you Susie," Anne said, "but the boss wants to see you urgently."

Susan's shoulders slumped wearily. "Now?" she wailed, thinking longingly of the casserole in her oven. She would never make it home before seven now. Not in the Nairobi rush-hour traffic.

"Right away he says," Anne informed her. "I'm glad I caught you before you left."

"Wish I could say the same," Susan muttered under her breath. "Stupid brolly! And it has stopped raining now. What a day!"

"What was that?" Anne asked.

"Nothing," Susan said. "Nothing at all." She reluctantly walked back down the hall and entered an office marked 'Private'. Life at B.I.O. had always been tough. Needless to say Mwatata was one of the tougher ones. What heavy burden did he carry that weighed him down so much? Susan's expression changed. Perhaps she would find out today.

"What's up chief?" she queried. "Where's the fire?"

Mwatata slowly turned around. Susan noted that his hair seemed to have more grey in it than it had the last time she had seen him. With shock she realised that he must be growing old. He was already fifty-seven and couldn't go on forever. Funny how some people seemed immortal; Jackson Mwatata was one of them. However, right then he did not give any sign of being immortal. He simply looked like a frail, tired old man.

"Close the door Susan, and come and sit down," Mwatata said. "I would like to talk to you." Susan obeyed. For several minutes Mwatata was silent. She didn't try to prompt him or disturb the thoughtful silence. Mwatata would speak when he was ready.

"Several months ago, Eric Were was killed," he said and she nodded. "What do you remember of the case?"

"Eric Were; died on January 27th, 1990; age 55; occupation, Kenyan Minister of Labour; death by drowning; discovered off the coast of Mombasa by two fishermen — Sammy Hussein aged 40 and Abdul Hamisi aged 28," Susan said. "His throat and neck had marks on them indicating foul play but his assassins were never found."

Mwatata regarded her thoughtfully. "Barely a month later, another prominent politician died," he said. "What do you remember about that?"

"Simon Odera; died on February 20th, 1990; age 68; occupation, Minister of Science and Technology; death by poisoning; collapsed at a party hosted by the Vice-President and Minister for Finance, Mrs. Janet Musyoka. The poison was strychnine, thought to be administered through the drink he was taking, by a bogus waiter who afterwards disappeared, never to be seen again. The suspect was never brought to trial." she said.

"Very good." Mwatata permitted himself a small smile.

"And the last similar case?"

"Godfrey Mwema," Susan recited. "Died on February 26th 1990; age 65; occupation, Minister of Education; death by strangulation;

discovered in the bushes outside his country-side home by herdsboy Hilary Onyango aged 11. His assassins were never found."

"All your details are correct, but I shouldn't be surprised really. I trained you myself," Mwatata smiled again. "There were rumours, of course, after these three assassinations," he said thoughtfully.

"Of course," Susan agreed. "People were certain that the same person or group of persons was responsible for the killings. There was a public outcry and demand for the culprit or culprits to be brought to justice. However apart from the fact that all these three men were politicians, there was never any clue to link the three murders. There was similar *modus operandi*, but no clues whatsoever to suggest that the same persons might have killed all three ministers."

"There was mass hysteria," encouraged Mwatata.

"There was pandemonium," agreed Susan. "There was fear of a coup attempt. Kenya certainly does not need a coup attempt. But why are we raking over all this?" she inquired. "I thought it was being handled by the C.I.D.?"

Mwatata regarded her reflectively for a while. "I have been following the case," he said. As you know, the Criminal Investigation Department did not uncover much. And I have been talking it over with Bakari. He doesn't like the look of it either."

George Bakari was the head of the C.I.D and he was Mwatata's closest friend. They were almost like brothers. A strong, hard man; he had risen to the top solely through his own efforts and remarkable brains. So far as Susan could tell, no case had ever buffled him.

"What does he say?" she asked curiously.

"He is convinced that the deaths can be traced to the same source. But, as you say, there is not *modus operandi;* absolutely no connection. And that buffles him. No matter how much a criminal may try to vary his methods, he must always have a certain similarity; especially the more successful ones."

"But surely if I was a criminal would I try not to leave any clue that could help to trace me?" queried Susan. "I would stab this man, strangle that, then shoot the other and so on."

"That makes sense in theory," Mwatata conceded. "But it is not at all usual in fact. Another thing is; if they took such care and precaution to cover up the fact that they were involved in all three deaths, why the non-existent time lapse? Why kill them all in the space of a month? Why not give enough time before the next murder so that chances of connection are slimmer? No; it looks like they didn't really care whether or not the connection was made. They were in a hurry to kill them all; but why? And if they didn't care whether or not the connection was made, why cover up their moves so carefully? It just doesn't make sense."

"Alternatively, it could have been three different sets of people, each with a target and separate motive for killing that particular man at a certain time," Susan suggested.

"All of a sudden, one after the other, just like that?" Mwatata asked. "Well it's possible but not very plausible."

"You're right, it isn't," Susan agreed.   "What other ideas do you have?"

"I don't have any," he said. "Nothing at all. That's why I called you in here. I don't know why but I just have a very bad feeling about all this and I needed to talk it over calmly and rationally. If I could just get an answer I would be able to relax a little."

"What else does Bakari say?" Susan asked eagerly.

"He hasn't got anything to say. But he is very worried as well," Mwatata said. He sat back and stared up at the ceiling. Susan also sat back and sighed.

"You're right," she said. "There is something wrong." ·

Mwatata nodded. "It seems like there is more to it than meets the eye," she continued. "I would have to think about it a little more."

"Alright," Mwatata said as he nodded in agreement.

"I suppose you could ask Chain about it," she said guardedly. "He might have some ideas."

Mwatata looked at her sharply. "I intend to," he said. "He is having a small party at his place this weekend. I thought that it might be a good time to ask for his opinion."

"In Kitale?" Susan asked.

"Yes," Mwatata motioned with his head. They both lapsed into silence. Yet this time their thoughts centred on the man called Chain, whose opinion Mwatata regarded very highly.

His name was Christopher Andrew Mathenge, and he was an enigma. After having worked for B.I.O. for fifteen years he had suddenly retired four years earlier, at the age of thirty. Now, at the age of thirty-four, he lived the life of simple farmer in the suburbs of the relatively small town of Kitale. He was millionaire several times over, having inherited huge sums of money and invested it wisely.

No one knew much of the man who had started working as an under cover agent in high school at the tender age of fifteen. He lived the life of a recluse – rarely, if ever, mixing with former work-mates. He had few friends and preferred living alone in his Kitale home. Yet the stories told about his exceptional talents lived on. The toughest cases had been cracked by him. His name was spoken in hushed tones of awe by the most senior agents at B.I.O. And yet he had opted out and refused any suggestions that he might one day return. He trusted only two men in his life; Jackson Mwatata was one of them.

But what was B.I.O.? What was this place that professed to be able to separate the men from the boys? The wheat from the chaff? What organisation was this that demanded complete loyalty, dedication and talent from its agents?

B.I.O. was a relatively unknown branch of the C.I.D. In full, it was known as the Bureau of Investigative Operations. It had its headquarters in Nairobi the capital of Kenya. Its function was more or less the same as that of the Criminal Investigation Department, only its agents were highly specialised in their work. Their training was intensive and they were nothing but the best. The equipment and technology found at B.I.O. was among the best in the world, albeit being mostly imported.

Its agents had infiltrated all levels of the government and infrastructures of the country. And to add to that, all major corporations, chain-stores and businesses had also been infiltrated by B.I.O. personnel. None were spared, and no one knew about it. Nobody had been able to figure out how quickly and effectively espionage was dealt with; how knowledge of illegal activity was obtained almost immediately; how nine out of ten cases of bribery were reported and punished; or how major plots never had a chance to become more than dinner-time conversation. These quiet, ruthlessly efficient people had given up their lives, passions and careers, to work for the government and to uphold justice and integrity in the small African nation. They vowed to rout out evil as soon as they possibly could. That was B.I.O.; that was the dream.

But how did one find one's way into B.I.O? How did one become a part of this top-secret organisation that only a handful of people in the country knew about?

There were recruiters working on a full-time basis to lure young people into B.I.O. Top athletes, brilliant science students, promising public speakers, talented young artists or just people with originality, personality and charisma. Usually during one's last year of high school, the recruiters managed to do a major convincing job. The first stage was being absorbed into the C.I.D. After that, if the results of training were satisfactory, the switch to B.I.O. occurred. Intensive training and testing followed. After that there was specialisation depending on one's talent, and then, of course, the assignment.

Susan was a confused teenager when she was first approached by B.I.O. She was unaware of anything; had no idea exactly what she wanted from life. She had tried living the wild life but had found it unsatisfactory. She had tried it all; drugs, religion, alcohol, music . . . but nothing seemed to help. A recruiter named Jones had discovered her playing inferior college basketball with single-mindedness and surprising intensity. With finesse, grace and talent, she brought her team victory after victory by using sheer determination to win. The thought of working for the C.I.D. appealed to her and she agreed to join them. Her determination to succeed made her a valuable asset. She kept going long after everyone else had given up and she had an insatiable appetite for action which she had managed to channel into her work.

Mwatata regarded the girl silently. She was one of the best field agents he had ever had. She had successfully solved difficult cases, time and time again and she had a quick, sharp mind. Mwatata wondered what Chain would think of her if he saw her. It was no mere coincidence that the two hadn't met. Chain had repeatedly refused to

6

see her because he wanted no connections with B.I.O. whatsoever. Any B.I.O agents, brilliant or otherwise, were anathema to him.

"Who do you think wants these successful politicians dead?" Mwatata asked suddenly.

"There are several possibilities," Susan replied, "one of them being political opponents. It's not unheard of for desperate politicians to kill off their opponents."

"One opponent, yes. Even two over a time span of three to four years," Mwatata said thoughtfully. "However active your imagination is you can't convince me that one politician suddenly decided to do away with three enemies at a go. It's utterly impossible. For one thing the three men represented different constituencies."

"Quite true, but you are still acting on the premise that one man is responsible for all three deaths," Susan argued. Mwatata lifted an eyebrow. "It is still possible that the three deaths were caused by three different people," she said.

"For what possible reason?" Mwatata asked.

"The political one still runs true," Susan said. Mwatata looked skeptical. "Yes it does," she insisted. "Look at it this way. One man decides, at the beginning of the year, to kill off his very successful political opponent. He can see no alternative. He hatches out a plot and executes it. The opponent is dead and the country is in uproar, but in no way can the murder be linked back to him. He joins in the public outrage, shouting harder than everyone that the murderers be brought to justice. He feels that he has an unattainable position."

A second politician is also anxious to get rid of an opponent. Suddenly he devices a brilliant plan to kill the man now, while the country is still in turmoil and people are likely to link it with the first murder. That way, the first murderer is blamed for both murders and the second murderer is safe. He does not exist at all in people's minds. And then of course it happens again, involving a third murderer. It could have continued indefinitely, you know."

"It's possible of course," agreed Mwatata.

"Of course," Susan shrugged.

"But highly improbable," Mwatata finished and they were both silent. There was a perfunctory knock on the door and Anne Kariuki entered.

"Some people to see you, sir," she said breathlessly.

"It's after office hours Anne," Mwatata said irritably. "I don't want to see anyone."

"I think you will definitely want to see these ones sir," she said firmly as she threw open the door. Four men entered the room. Two were B.I.O. security guards and one of the other two was being supported by the other. He wore a long grey overcoat which fell open to reveal a patch of blood on his shirt. But that wasn't the most interesting thing about him. The interesting thing was the knife firmly embedded in his chest.

Chapter Two

Susan and Mwatata stared in silence at the group for a while. They glanced briefly at each other and resumed their perusal. They both knew who the two men were; the stabbed one was James Otieno, who was a notorious drug dealer. The other one was his younger brother, John.

"Call Raymond," was Mwatata's only comment. Raymond Abdul was a doctor stationed at B.I.O. He usually worked far into the night in his laboratory in basement of the B.I.O. building.

"I have already called him," Anne said quietly. She ushered the four men in and ran back to her desk for a tape recorder. She returned with it almost immediately. All conversations with third parties not connected with B.I.O. had to be recorded and filed.

"Mr. Otieno has something to say," she said, inserting the new tape which she had brought.

Dr. Abdul entered the office hurriedly, his first aid kit in his hand. Otieno was laid down gently on a sofa. As the doctor examined him, Susan and Mwatata glanced at each other again. Successful drug dealers like Otieno never sought out the police, the C.I.O. or B.I.O. There was too much at stake. So when they decided that it was worth it to risk everything, their reasons were usually very important. Very few of them knew of B.I.O., but what they knew they feared. Whatever Otieno had to say had to be very important. More important even, than his drugs business. More important even, than his life.

"Not good," Dr. Abdul said in a low voice. "He needs to go to a hospital. If the knife is removed, chances are that he will die. My guess is that it cut through several major arteries and veins."

"No hospital," Otieno whispered hoarsely. "I have got something to say first." His breathing was shallow and his face was turning a sickly grey.

"Alright," Mwatata said calmly. He brought over the tape recorder. "Anything you say will be kept in confidence." He switched the recorder on.

"They are going to kill her," Otieno said.

"Who?" Mwatata asked. "Who are they going to kill?"

"The Vice-President," came the astounding answer. "They are going to kill Mrs. Musyoka."

There was a general intake of breath around the room. Assassination of the Vice-President so soon after the other assassinations would be too much for the country. The repercussions would be terrible. It would be a disaster.

"Alright," Mwatata nodded. "Who is going to kill her?"

"A minister," Otieno said. "I don't know who. John . . . tell them," he gasped.

"There are a group of people who meet at our hotel everyday. They have been meeting there for the past two months," said John emotionlessly. "We have seen them as they arrive in limousines, park at the back and go in through the back entrance, heavily surrounded by masked guards. My brother heard, on the grapevine, that these people could have been involved in the political killings and decided he wanted no part in it. He told the link man that he was pulling out of the deal."

"Who was the link man?" Mwatata asked.

"A man called Njogu," John replied. "He is the one who contacted my brother and set up the deal. No need looking for him, though. He's dead." John's emotionless tone had not changed.

"Go on," Mwatata urged.

"Njogu was the only one we ever saw," John continued. "We cleared out the hall they were to use and locked the doors. They came in through the back, did their business, and left."

"What made you change your mind about the deal?" Susan asked.

"We became ostracised," Otieno said painfully. "Our contacts all of a sudden stopped doing business with us and we couldn't understand why. A close friend finally told us." He stopped, his breathing very shallow.

"He told us it was because of Njogu's people," John said, his voice still very flat. "The rumour was that these were high government officials plotting to distabilise the government, and that we were being paid highly to keep quiet about it."

"We admit to running an illegal drug business," Otieno said. "Next to what these people are plotting it seems petty and insignificant. We are very proud of our country. It may not be the best in the world but it is stable and prosperous. It is a safe place to live in. To think that there is a powerful group of people sitting quietly somewhere and plotting the downfall of the government is horrifying. The death, the violence that could come out of its scares even the most hardened criminals."

"We decided that we could not be party to what was going on," John continued. "We asked Njogu to tell his people that we were backing out of the deal. For one thing, if the rumour was true we would be in very serious trouble if we were caught by the police. Secondly, we do not support anti-government activities and thirdly, our business was suffering because of them."

"Njogu said that the group had requested one more meeting, and at double the price," Otieno said faintly. "John was not in at the time and I decided to accept for two reasons. One of them was of course the money. Greed is really a terrible thing." He coughed painfully. "Another was that I had suddenly thought that if these people were really highly-placed government people I might be in real trouble. To make sure that I didn't talk they might decide to frame me and have me put in prison or even kill me. So I decided to prepare some evidence against them, for my own sake."

"What evidence?" Susan asked. "Have you got it?"

"I decided to record the conversation. I have it on tape," Otieno said. "After the meeting Njogu came to tell me that one of them wanted to talk to me. I almost fainted with fear; thinking that they had found my hidden tape recorder. When I entered the room, there was only one man. He locked the door and then quietly stabbed Njogu to death. Soon after he drove the knife into me, turned around and walked away."

There was complete silence in the room for a full minute. Everybody was immersed in their own thoughts and nobody said a word. Finally Otieno broke the silence.

"He must have thought I was dead," he said. "I blacked out and fell to the ground."

"When I returned to the hotel and opened the door to the room, I found both Njogu and my brother lying in a pool of blood on the floor," John said. "I saw that James was alive and managed to rouse him. He insisted on coming here.

"They are planning to kill the Vice-President," Otieno said. "I don't know who they are but there is a Minister there. I'm not sure which minister it is. The others addressed him as 'Mr. Minister' whenever they talked to him."

"Why do they want to kill Mrs. Musyoka?" asked Susan. "She's very pro-government."

"They are the ones who killed the other politicians," John offered in way of explanation.

"Which other politicians?" Mwatata asked sharply as he and Susan exchanged a look.

"Were, Odera and Mwema of course," John said impatiently.

"Why were they killed?" Mwatata asked.

"It is all part of their sabotage against the government," John replied. "They are going to kill politicians who are pro-government to stir up the people and also to eliminate the opposition. At the same time they are going to kill anti-government politicians in a bid to make it look like the government is ordering the deaths as an act of revenge to oust those who disagree with the constitution. People then lose confidence in the government and the distabilisation begins. Killing the Vice-President is just the climax of the whole bizarre arrangement. From then on, it will be a free-for-all massacre of leading politicians and government supporters. Then they are to step in, overthrow the government, and take over the running of the country. Using violence, they will quell the riots and impose calm on the nation."

"It can't work," Susan breathed in astonishment. "There is no way that they can overthrow the government. It has been tried before. It's just impossible."

"It has been impossible as long as the army, air-force, navy as well as the police have been on the government's side," John said. "But if the distabilisation works then all the armed forces will also lose

confidence in the government. There will be hysteria, pandemonium
. . . All in all, people will be scared. They will be willing to listen to
anybody who promises to make it stop."

"It can't work," Susan said again. "It just can't," she said in
disbelief. "It's impossible."

"Nothing is impossible," Mwatata said. "Although it is highly
improbable, nothing is impossible.

"What happened to the tape?" Anne asked suddenly. Everybody
turned to look at her. "Do you still have it?" she asked Otieno.

"Yes," he whispered hoarsely. "In my pocket . . ." John moved
swiftly to his brother's side and retrieved the tape. He handed it over to
Mwatata. The latter stared at it in silence for several seconds. Abruptly
he turned around and stopped the cassette recorder. He removed the
cassette inside and inserted Otieno's tape. Then he rewound. Everybody watched as the tape rewound. The seconds went by with
agonising slowness. It seemed an eternity to those watching before it
finally stopped. Mwatata then pressed the play button.

For the next few minutes Mwatata listened in horror as the plans of
a maniac and his agents unfolded. What had seemed highly improbable
a few minutes earlier suddenly became frighteningly possible. The plot
was complex yet simple, and it seemed guaranteed to succeed.

Silence once again reigned in the room. The previous periodical
silences were nothing in comparison. Conflicting emotions flew around
the room, the prime one being helpless fury. Nobody spoke, nobody
needed to. The tension was tangible, thick. It could have been cut with
a knife. Frustration was also present as nobody knew what to do to stop
the plot from developing. And finally, there was the fear. The cold,
clammy fear that enveloped everyone as they slowly accepted that the
plan was feasible; an in fact was going to be executed. After that came
the realisation that they were the only ones who knew. The only ones
who had access to this information.

Mwatata slowly sank back into his chair. The tape ran itself out and
stopped. Susan looked sharply at her boss. In the last few minutes, he
seemed to have aged even more. Mwatata looked like a tired old man
with no idea of what to do next.

"We will have to call an emergency meeting," he said "Get together all the personnel that we can. Discuss it . . ."

"I'll get on to it first thing tomorrow," Anne said, efficiently. "As early as possible. You can use board room 7." She seemed pleased that something was being done. She was perfectly willing to leave the whole affair in Mwatata's hands.

"No," Mwatata said. "Not tomorrow. Today. I don't care if we're here all night. Track down all senior personnel and our best field agents. Call them all and make sure they get here."

"No!" Otieno almost shouted. "For God's sake no. No senior personnel. No agents. We don't know who is loyal and who has been bought."

"What are you saying?" Susan cried as another cold shaft of fear raced through her.

"I'm saying that you can't trust all the field agents and senior personnel at B.I.O.," replied Otieno. "Some of them are planted."

"That's IMPOSSIBLE!" Susan screamed. "That's a lie! No one could infiltrate B.I.O.!" Mwatata sank even lower in his chair, his face drawn and wrinkled. He seemed to age completely. But he didn't show a single vestige of surprise. In fact, it seemed as if a terrible truth had been confirmed for him.

Susan couldn't believe her ears. Nor could she believe her eyes. She stared at Mwatata in horror. So that was what had been worrying him? That was what had been plaguing him in the last few weeks. An infiltration of B.I.O. was almost too much to contemplate. That could mean the very highest government circles had also been infiltrated. She spun around to face Otieno.

"How do you know?" she asked. "How can you possibly know this?"

"Be realistic," Otieno said. "How do you think we have been able to avoid getting caught all these years?" he coughed. "We pay large amounts of money to connections to get information for us from B.I.O. They tell us when a raid will be mounted, when a colleague has turned to your side or when an agent comes to us posing as a buyer. They make sure any informer dies before he can talk about us. And they are everywhere."

"Can you tell us who they are?" Susan asked, more calmly.

"That wouldn't help," Otieno said. "We only deal with the small fry. The very junior agents. They, in turn, refer to the senior personnel. We don't know which of the big shots are loyal to B.I.O. or to the other side."

"How long has this been going on?" Susan asked.

"At least five months," Otieno replied.

Susan looked helplessly at Mwatata. She had no idea what happened next. Mwatata stared sightlessly ahead.

"Okay," he said. "What's been said in this room will be kept in this room. This amazing story has got to be kept to us." He looked around the room. Susan he could trust. As he could Anne, who had been with him for a long time. Otieno didn't look as if he could last much longer. Raymond had been with him for longer than he could remember. As for John and the two security guards; they would have to be kept under surveillance. He decided to put the two very impassive looking security men under a thorough screen and then brief them on what exactly to do. He counted seven people other than himself who knew this terrible secret. This was not good.

"Anne," he said sharply. "Call an ambulance for Mr. Otieno. Raymond, you will go with him and make sure that everything is alright." He turned around as Anne hurried to obey. "Susan, take these tapes and leave the building. I want you to call Bakari. Meet him somewhere in town and give him the tapes. Have him put them in a security box in a neutral bank somewhere. After that, bring him here. We all need to talk. Use a call-box to phone him. All the phone calls made from this building are logged and I don't want to make anybody suspicious.

Susan walked over to the table and grabbed the tapes. She quickly thrust them into her jacket pocket and walked to the door. As she opened it she heard Mwatata call out. She turned around inquiringly.

"Please hurry," Mwatata said quietly.

* * * * *

Twenty-five minutes later, Susan turned frustratedly back to the tall building that housed B.I.O. head quarters. A barrage of fruitless phone calls had not been able to locate George Bakari. She had called his office, his house, and his friends to no avail. As she approached the gate, she saw an unusually large number of police cars and C.I.D. officers as well as B.I.O. agents walking around. The guard at the gate recognised her and let her in after a cursory glance at her identification card. Nobody noticed her as she walked towards and into the building but she was immediately stopped at the reception area.

She had left through a secret back entrance, not wanting to explain to the reception as to how she had gotten back in without signing in at the desk. But the night receptionist wasn't there, now. The reception area was filled with agents demanding to know why she was there. They inspected her identification but seemed reluctant to let her go up the Mwatata's office. A tight coil of unease began to develop in her gut.

Finally, a senior agent agreed to take her upstairs. Although she argued that she could find her own way up, he was adamant that he should accompany her. She fell silent as she wondered what was going on and what Mwatata would say when she turned up for his meeting with an outsider.

As she rode the elevator she worried about Bakari. Where could he be? He usually was available but at the moment nobody seemed to know where he was. She felt the tapes in her jacket pocket. Where could she put them and they would be safe?

The elevator door opened. In surprise she was met by a large number of agents milling around the floor. But this floor was private. Something was definitely wrong.

She and the senior agent were stopped as she listened to him explain whom she wanted. Their inquisitor studied her sharply and then turned round.

"Follow me," was all he said. Susan and the senior agent followed him to Mwatata's door. As they reached the room, the door was thrown open and Susan was ushered in. She stepped in and stopped in horror.

There were seven people in the room. Mwatata, Anne, Otieno, his brother John, Dr.Raymond Abdul and the two security guards whose names she didn't know. There was blood and pieces of human flesh splattered all over the walls which, were riddled with bullets. The seven people all lay slumped on the floor. Every single one of them was dead.

Chapter Three

Susan's feet were worn out from continuous walking. It was almost nine o'clock and she had been desperately walking around the city as fast as she could go. All thoughts had been suspended and her mind was completely numb. Strangely enough, when she did thaw out enough to think, it was childhood memories that crowded and clamoured in her brain.

Solitary walks around the park, solitary lunches, solitary games and solitary laughter. Not being close to anyone because it was unsafe to do so. People couldn't be trusted. Just when you needed them they moved away, flew out of the country, took off to a party, entered a boarding school, enlisted, went on far away business trips; or died. People promised and promised, but couldn't deliver. They gave with one hand and snatched away with the other. And they always wanted more, more and more!

In high school there were crowds. Large, noisy, bustling crowds. These emitted shrieks of laughter, applause, approval, dismay disdain, envy, malice, pride, joy, tears and amusement in a chorus of loud, blurred voices. Faces in the crowds were indistinct and unremarkable. It was easy to slip into one of these crowds and lose yourself; even lose your identity. As long as you contributed to the general screaming and frenzied energy, no one remarked. No one noticed. Members were always being dropped or added to the crowd. No one noted the number come and go. There was no pain, and everything that happened, happened to the crowd; not to the individual. You were no longer an individual and the phrase, "safety in numbers" began to take on a new meaning.

Then came fame. Doing something better than everyone else so that you no longer blended into the woodwork. Suddenly everybody knew your name. You would pass by and strangers would point at you and whisper, "there goes . . ." You were no longer a faceless part of the crowd. You were forced into individuality and pushed into the limelight. You were exposed.

Promises were made but rarely kept. Another side of human nature was uncovered; superficial love. As long as one was famous, one had a multitude of friends. The crowd you were once a part of then dissolved into a party of "hangers on" and "close" friends. There was light-headed laughter and a heady feeling of power, generated from the popularity. People stumbled over themselves to do your bidding. Money and compliments flowed like fine wine: lavishly. Every little gesture was noted with sharp eyes and bated breath. The crowd had forced you up onto a pedestal so high that it might have been made for a king: a god. They pushed you up there for daring to be different; for daring to excel. They made sacrifices and they worshipped. And they waited for you to fall.

And fall you did; eventually. The slightest stumble sent you crashing down. Deep down into the abyss of despair and misery. The crowd then nodded in satisfaction and walked away. The most cruel of rejections, yet the most common.

It was almost comical to see the turned backs, hear the snide remarks, and feel the studied hatred. You would have laughed hilariously, if you hadn't been so busy crying. Great, racking sobs of self-pity and self-recrimination for daring to believe, for trusting, for venturing out of your protective cocoon. And for being deceived into reaching out for the glitter, and finding that it was not gold.

Then, of course, came the principle of sink or swim. You had a choice, you see; the course of your life depended on you. You could either sink into the deepest depths of oblivion and stay there forever or you could fight your way back to the front. Whether or not you stayed there, again, depended on you.

There was a quality of steel in some people which prevented them from giving up and which kept them going no matter what. If you were one of them then you shrugged away the pain and the disillusion. You dried your tears and started over. You determinedly ignored the sneers and degrading remarks. You disregarded the pointed fingers, the whispers in every corner; the delighted giggles. You once again closed yourself up in your half-forgotten shell. Then you worked hard to achieve the level of success which you had before. And when the crowd came back as they invariably did; pushing and clamouring for attention, you stared glassily, unseeingly, ahead. You refused to acknowledge them completely; you allowed no one to get close. You did what you should have done in the first place; you closed in on yourself.

Life was easier that way; never needing anyone, and nobody needing you. Never letting anyone get close, never letting anything touch or move you. Going through life in a haze, driven on by a fierce desire to succeed and protected by a hard outer shell which was seemingly impregnable. However, nothing is perfect. One day somebody manages to break through the barriers and stir you to life. A totally unlikely person is able to move you to affection and trust. Before you can blink, you become very attached to him. A man with innumerable good qualities. A man with strength, power, a sense of justice, duty and selfworth. A man like Jackson Mwatata.

He had been Susan's friend and mentor for a time and now, just like the others, he was gone. The familiar pangs of pain started creeping through Susan's veins and she quickly stifled them. Now was not the time to think . . . about him. It was time to move on.

Twenty minutes later she was sitting inside the brand new Twentieth Century cinema hall. It was minutes after nine. The film was a kung-fu thriller which had most of the audience totally engrossed. Susan saw faint images flickering and heard voices as if from a distance. The scenes playing themselves over and over in her mind had little to do with what everyone was watching. They consisted of a blood-splattered room, and dead bodies. Blank faces; still bodies; lifeless limbs. She could hear disjointed phrases.

Suddenly she sat up. 'What about Chain? Did he know?' She cautiously felt deep in the pocket of her overcoat. The tapes were still there. Then came the question; 'did the men who killed Mwatata know of the existence of the tapes? And how had they known about Mwatata? How had they realised that Otieno wasn't dead and where to find him?' The most frightening of all was whether they knew about her and that she had been in the room when the tape was played.' Perhaps they were outside the cinema this very minute waiting! Perhaps they were sitting behind her waiting for a chance to shoot!

She resolutely stifled her paranoia when she realised that things weren't going to be improved by her falling to pieces. She had to get her act together and decide what to do. She had two choices. One was to take her information to the head of B.I.O., Mr. J. F. Kimani and leave it in his hands. The other was to pursue the whole thing herself. But even as she thought about it, the second idea didn't sound plausible to her. There was no way she could do anything by herself. And again there was also the possibility that the men responsible for killing Mwatata also knew about her. This she digested and acknowledged in a cold, detached area of her mind. If she died, the information would die with her for they would soon be coming after her. She had to tell somebody else.

Yet the first idea didn't sound any better. It wasn't impossible that telling Kimani could jeopardise the whole situation and be an act of suicide. Kimani would never believe that there were rogue agents at B.I.O.; that not everybody there was completely loyal to him. And furthermore, B.I.O. agents were all that he had at his disposal. Nobody knew who was loyal and who was not. Someone who was completely trusted could turn out to be a paid informer. If the news leaked to the killers, that was the end of her. No, she needed to tell someone else. Someone completely removed from B.I.O. and its environment. Someone she could trust with her life. Trust. That five letter word that meant so much.

She didn't know a single person who she trusted at that moment. But she knew someone who Mwatata had loved and trusted. Chain. The best, the greatest, the toughest, the most precious, the idol, the legend, the infallible Chain. If he was good enough for Mwatata, then he was good enough for Susan. She had no other choice.

* * * * *

Half an hour later Susan was standing in a queue outside one of the telephone booths opposite the Hilton Hotel. Her palms were sweaty and her breathing erratic. She still didn't know whether or not she was being followed. She had quietly left the cinema hall without any sign of movement from anyone else. Once outside she had walked rapidly around the block but hadn't recognised anybody who might have been watching her. And yet she still couldn't be sure.

The phone booth she was entering was sound-proof after one shut the door, so her conversation with Chain would be private enough. That was if she even got in touch with him. She had two private numbers; one for his apartment in Nairobi and one for his home in Kitale. Both of the numbers were strictly red phones for emergencies and only three people were supposed to have the numbers. These were Chain, Bakari and Mwatata. But a few weeks previously, Mwatata had given Susan the numbers, making her commit them to memory. They were to be used only as a last resort. Well, if this wasn't a last resort situation, then Susan was likely never to encounter one.

She thought again of the rules in using them as she entered the booth. One was to dial the number and wait. Nobody was to pick up the phone, which was locked in Chain's study, except Chain himself. The phone rang three times and then the caller cut the connection. After that a second call was made, to be picked up after the fifth ring if Chain was in. If he wasn't in, the caller disconnected again and rang for the third time. This time, after the third ring, the answering service came on and one could leave a message.

She carefully pulled the door shut picked up the phone, waited for the dialing tone and then dialled the Nairobi number. She followed the procedure carefully, replacing after the third ring and dialling again. Then she crossed her fingers and waited. Chain would have to do the rest.

After the third ring her heart almost stopped beating. Then came the fourth ring, then the fifth. On cue, the telephone was picked up.

"Hello," a male voice came on.

"Chain?" she cried out.

"Who the hell is this?" The voice was flat and uncompromising.

"Chain!" she said wildly. "Don't hang up, please! Only two other people had this number and one of them is dead!"

There was silence on the other end of the line. Then the voice said, "You haven't told me who this is."

"I'll tell you in a minute," Susan said trying to control herself. "But I have to make sure that I'm talking to Chain. George Bakari was one

22

of the people who had this number. You have another red phone in Kitale which is almost unknown. What's the number?"

There was more silence at the end of the line. Susan couldn't tell if he was debating or if he was even going to answer. The silence lengthened. Then Chain rapped out the answer. Susan heaved a sigh of relief.

"My name is Susan Juma," she said. "One step away from you, on the table next to the phone you have two photographs in ebony portable frames. One is of Bakari and the other is of Jackson Mwatata, the other person who had this number."

"Who gave you the number?" asked Chain.

"Mwatata," came the reply.

"Okay," agreed Chain. "Who is dead?" he rasped out.

There was no way one could soften it. And there was no time for platitudes. "Mwatata," she said emotionlessly.

Chain drew in a deep breath. Counting the seconds, Susan waited. "When?" he asked.

"This evening," she said. "I need to talk to you. Something is up." "I'm in a phone booth outside Kencom, opposite Hilton Hotel," she said."

"Okay Susan," he said. "I want you to replace the phone and walk round to Kenya Cinema. There are some phone booths there. Wait for fifteen minutes and then call me again." There was a click, and Chain was gone.

Susan replaced the phone and looked at her watch. It was quarter to ten. She slowly left the both and started walking to Kenya Cinema. She was filled with conflicting emotions. It had been too easy. Chain had asked for no verification of her identity and had seemed just to take her word for it. 'Was he going to agree to meet her; just like that?' He had been an agent, one of the best. 'Wouldn't he be in the least bit suspicious of someone who called out of the blues and asked to meet him?' In his place she would have asked a lot of questions. She would have tried to verify that the caller was really who she said she was. Yet Chain hadn't asked for any identification. He hadn't seemed to question the fact that she might not be who she claimed to be; Susan Juma.

At ten o'clock Susan got into an empty phone booth near Kenya Cinema. Quickly she dialled Chain's number. He picked it up on the first ring.

"What is it that you want to tell me?" he asked without preamble.

"I can't tell you over the phone," she said. "I have to see you. It's very important. Please."

There was silence at the other end. "You seem very anxious to meet me, Susan Juma," he said.

"Look, this isn't a feeble attempt to get to know you better, you know," she said scornfully. "I'm not that desperate. And Mwatata's death is something I'd never joke about. It's not a lie. He is dead."

"I know," came the surprising answer. "I called B.I.O. headquarters. They confirmed his death. You didn't think that I would just accept your story on principle, did you?" he quizzed.

Susan was silent. That was exactly what she had thought. She should have known that she could expect something better from Chain. Something a little bit more. But did this mean that he was willing to see her or not?

"Can you give a clue as to this fantastic story that you are trying to sell me?" he inquired in a polite voice. "Or are you making a play to pique my curiosity?"

"Listen buster, you may think that you are the reincarnation of a Greek god but let me tell you that you come in a poor second, or third, or even ninetieth. The closest we ever came to having a god is a man called Jackson Mwatata, who at this very moment is probably lying stone cold at the city mortuary, blissfully unaware that his best friend has a major narcissism problem." Susan was really angry. "But I didn't call to discuss your hang-ups, pal. Either say yes or no."

There was silence at the other end of the line. "Well, if you're trying to come on to me you're sure doing it in a strange way," he said. "Wait!" he said as she drew another angry breath. "Don't get mad for nothing. You have been on that phone long enough. There's a row of phone booths opposite Nyayo House, near the General Post Office. Get into the second one from the left and wait. I'll call at ten thirty on the dot. Be there."

Susan started to speak but Chain hang up before she could say anything. In frustration she slammed the phone down. What would she do? There was no one else to turn to. No one else who could help her.

At ten thirty Susan was standing outside the designated phone booth, twisting and untwisting a handkerchief in her hands. She was unsure of what to do next. She waited for five minutes and then resolutely entered the booth. She called the number but there was no response this time. She hung up and went back outside. Where was Chain? He had promised to call, would he break that promise?

By eleven o'clock Susan was crying openly. Great, sweeping sobs racked through her body. Chain was not going to call. He had decided that the answer was no. What was she going to do next?

Suddenly the phone rang. She ran and picked it up. It was Chain. "B.I.O. agents aren't supposed to lose control like that," he said. "It must be some kind of story. I'll meet you at the Carnivore Restaurant in an hour." The phone went dead.

Chapter Four

The Round Table. That was what they called themselves, and every member was a knight. They were therefore the Knights of the Round Table. Nothing really original in that. The legendary King Arthur had headed one, centuries ago. The only difference was that King Arthur already had a kingdom and was only trying to protect it whereas the present Round Table members were still trying to conquer their kingdom.

The knights were only nine, carefully selected. They were in fact hand picked by King Arthur the conceiver of the whole plan himself. His right-hand man was a twenty-seven-year-old man Nicholas Tanui. He had adopted Tanui seventeen years before, and knew everything there was to know about the young man. Tanui's name at the Round Table was Mordred, the rebellious knight, and his function was execution.

The other seven members of the Round Table all played a very important role. There was Lancelot, an important Cabinet Minister in the Kenya Government; Galahad, an engineering student at the University of Nairobi; Tristan a brilliant scientist and brain surgeon attached to the Kenya Medical Research Institute, KEMRI; Perceval a well-known and respected judge; Gawain a Texas oil baron; Bohert the successful president of a French company, and Balain a popular bishop, well-known and well-liked.

Lancelot was in charge of propaganda, Galahad was in charge of university student manipulation and Tristan kept all medical records of people in high places and was in charge of extortion. Perceval was protection for the group, while Gawain provided money, Bohert had the trained personnel and Balain gave much-needed support through his 'flock' of followers. The whole set-up was the mark of a real genius; King Arthur was a genius in every sense.

26

The Round Table met every Saturday morning, at 9.00 am, in the basement of King Arthur's posh home in Spring Valley. The room they met in was air-conditioned during the hotter days and gas-heated during the cooler ones, making it the ideal room to live in. In the centre of the room was the round table at which the knights sat. It was a big, polished ebony and mahogany table, surrounded by identical stately chairs. These chairs were elaborate coastal carvings of pure ivory and teak; resplendently ornamented by designs in gold and silver, intricate chains in turquoise, beads of emerald and ruby and padded by big, oriental made Chinese silk cushions. There were nine of them.

At the centre of the table was a big map of Kenya; framed in gold. The geographical features were all correctly drawn out. The only problem was the political boundaries. They were all wrong. Instead of eight provinces, there were six subdivisions. These were labelled 'kaya', which roughly translated means village. What was supposed to be Nairobi Province spanned a much bigger area encompassing the towns of Thika, Kiambu, Ngong, Machakos, Narok, Gilgil, Kajiado and Embu. Central Province was non-existent, and all the others had been 'modified' to form six 'kaya', all equal in size. The previous boundaries had been almost completely eradicated, and all the divisions had new names.

Nairobi became Topiah, with Nairobi city as its capital. It would be headed by King Arthur himself. Lancelot would take the coastal area, renamed Sarasota, with Mombasa as its capital. Galahad would take the north-western area, renamed Shomei with Lodwar as its capital. Tristan would take the northern area, renamed Griar, with Mandera as its capital. Perceval would head the central area named Drystan with Isiolo as its capital and Balain would take the last area, the south-western area renamed Verance, whose capital city would be Kisumu.

No real names were used at the Round table. They weren't needed, although, with exception of King Arthur, all the members were well-known personalities. They drove up to his house every Saturday morning and met in the basement to discuss events of the past week. After the meetings, which usually lasted two hours, the Knights played pool or drank some coffee in the lounge upstairs. Sometimes they played tennis, squash, or badminton on the courts outside the spacious double storey house. At other times they drove down to a nearby golf course to play a few holes. All in all, it was a relaxed, leisurely group which met each week to plot the downfall of the Kenyan Government.

The huge ebony and mahogany table was usually deserted on Thursday night at eleven o'clock. In fact, it was very unusual to find anyone sitting on the magnificent chairs at that particular time of the night. Almost downright impossible. However, this Thursday night, the lights were on and the chairs were filled. The Round Table was holding an emergency session.

"I don't disagree in the least with the first two killings, previously this afternoon," said King Arthur. "After all, I ordered them myself. But what on earth did you think entering a room and proceeding to spray its seven occupants with bullets from your machine guns and leaving all the seven of them dead. Not that I was close to any of them so their death is really no loss to me. However, you did succeed in killing a very important B.I.O. official which will not be taken lightly either at B.I.O. or at the C.I.D."

Mordred looked around. All this had been addressed to him.

"It couldn't be helped," he said. "All of them had to go."

"Perhaps you could explain to us just why they all had to go," suggested Arthur.

"The man I employed to kill Otieno at his establishment made a mess of it," Mordred explained. He didn't wait to make sure that both Otieno and the other man, Njogu, were dead. As it turns out Otieno wasn't. His brother came home and found him. Instead of rushing him to hospital, they both rushed off to B.I.O, which means that Otieno had a story to tell. We couldn't be sure how much he knew so it was imperative that he died. However, when we reached him, it was too late. He was closeted in Mwatata's room with all those other people. We didn't know how much he had told them, but he must have told them something, because he had been there for quite some time before we arrived. We couldn't take any chances. He had to die, and all the others had to die with him." Mordred sat back and looked around the table.

"How did you find out that Otieno wasn't dead?" Lancelot asked.

"We have some people planted at his hotel. They informed us that Otieno and his brother had left the building," Mordred replied.

"How can you be sure that they didn't talk to anyone else but the people in the room," Balain inquired.

"We can be sure because they were followed from the hotel to B.I.O. headquarters," Mordred said. "They never stopped once; never made any phone calls or talked to anyone."

"What about inside the building?" asked Galahad. "They could have told the receptionist or the guards or someone . . . "

"No," Mordred answered firmly. "They didn't. The night receptionist is a girl called Faith Karanja. She is on our side and she informed us that Otieno and his brother arrived, and demanded to see Mwatata. She called over two guards and escorted all four of them to the elevator. She got in with them and took them to Mwatata's floor, where she handed them over to the secretary Anne Kariuki. They hadn't spoken at all."

"What about other people on the floor?" Galahad persisted. "They could have heard the story and left before you arrived."

"No way," Mordred said positively.

"You seem very sure," King Arthur said.

"I am," Mordred replied. "You see, there are six elevators in the building," he explained. "Four of them are for ordinary use and two are very special. One of them only goes to the twenty-second floor which is the last floor. J. F. Kimani has his office on this floor. It's express, and makes no other stops. The other elevator plies between ground floor and the eleventh floor where all the senior agents have offices. The elevator is express from the reception to that floor and back. It is impossible to leave that floor any other way, apart from the elevator. The stairs leading to the floors up or down have been blocked and to go from floor twelve to floor ten one has to take the elevator — that is the ordinary elevator. And then, anyone going to that floor must sign a book and indicate the time. There are two guards there, round the clock. When leaving the building; all personnel must sign out with the receptionist. The same goes for entering the building again," he paused.

"Now the elevator book shows that nobody used the elevator to go up after 5.45 pm, and the reception book proves that there were only two people left on that floor when Otieno and his brother went up; Anne Kariuki and Jackson Mwatata. After Otieno went up, Anne called the reception and requested that Dr. Raymond Abdul be sent up. All in all, by the time we arrived, the only people on that floor were Otieno and his brother, the two guards, the doctor, Anne Karinki and Mwatata. They talked to no one else and no calls were made. All telephone calls within the building are logged. So we assume that Otieno hadn't finished telling them his story."

There was silence among the members of the Round Table. Then one of them cleared his throat gruffly.

"Excellent work, Mordred!" King Arthur exclaimed.

"A fine example of detective work," Lancelot said. "Very well done."

"Well now, we couldn't have chosen a better person for the job, now could we?" Gawain asked looking very pleased.

"Mordred is doing better that the special police in my country," Bohert added. "A fine job, if I may say so."

"Tristan, Perceval, any questions?" asked King Arthur. The two men shook their heads.

"It seems that Mordred has covered everything that needs to be covered," Perceval said.

Tristan nodded. "And very well too," he added. "I don't believe that even Scotland Yard could have done a better job than he did."

"Suppose you explain to us how you did it, Modred," King Arthur suggested.

"It's not hard to get into B.I.O. once you are aware of the procedure," Mordred explained. "I took two of our best hit-men and machine guns. The guns were inside our coats. We went in through a side entrance which doesn't have searchers and is mainly used by personnel. We presented the guards there with fake C.I.D. cards and they let us through. At the reception area we removed the machine guns and held everyone down there hostage while I went through the books. Once I was satisfied, two of us took the elevator up to the eleventh floor; went to Mwatata's room and sprayed it with bullets. I checked to make sure that they were all dead then we left the building. We parked round the corner, changed coats and put on dark glasses. As the C.I.D. and police cars came zooming in, we followed and in the general confusion, we managed to get the receptionist away for a few minutes

30

and questioned her. Then we left." Mordred's monologue had come to an end.

"Well, that seems taken care of," Balain said. "Let us hope that B.I.O. decides not to make this public. It will interfere with our plans for the next two deaths if the public goes crazy over this one."

"Yes, it was an unfortunate occurrence," Lancelot agreed. "Unplanned for events are the greatest annoyance. They always throw things upside down."

"The thing that could really develop into a major headache is if B.I.O. decides to turn on the steam and investigate the case thoroughly. We might have them snapping at our heels for a while. One thing they cannot stand is one of their own being murdered. They turn out in great numbers to retaliate. They might stumble over something or other and that would really be unfortunate. We cannot afford to let them come anywhere close. We cannot let them make any move that we're unaware of." All this was said by King Arthur.

"Well now, Arthur, how are we gonna be able to do something like that?" Gawain asked.

"We have many of our people at B.I.O.," King Arthur answered. "We shall have to get more regular reports from them, on a day to day basis. Mordred, you will have to handle that." Mordred nodded. "Report on all levels, from the highest agent we have there to the cleaning maid who is on our payroll. Increase their pay and keep a sharp eye on them. We have to know everything that happens every single day," he concluded.

"That will be done," Mordred said calmly. "I will organise it in the morning."

"If anybody appears to be getting close to us, them eliminate them," King Arthur said emotionlessly. "We have gone too far to be stopped now."

"Are we still meeting on Saturday or should we lie low and wait this week?" Balain asked.

"Yes," said King Arthur. "We shall meet on Saturday as usual. We have still got a long way to go before thinking of lying low. We shall give our reports on Saturday. In fact I may have some new information on your oil fields, Gawain."

"Will you now" said a pleased looking Gawain. "Well then, wild horses couldn't keep me away."

King Arthur smiled. "They say that B.I.O. is a whole lot more dangerous than anything - wild horses included," he said seriously.

"Well we've got something that's ten times more dangerous than anything they might have," said Gawain. "We've got Mordred and he's the best. That's a fact."

It was a plan that just couldn't fail; at least, Gawain couldn't see any chinks in the armour as yet and he was no fool. If this plan succeeded he would be one of the richest men in the world. Gawain hadn't thrown in with this lot for the fun of it. He didn't want political power or prestige. He wanted oil.

Vast reserves of oil had been discovered across north-eastern Kenya. In fact, two-thirds of the country was sitting on one giant oil-well. These reserves had been discovered by Gawain's company and he had been given permission to prospect for oil in the area. After discovering vast amounts of oil Gawain's workers had managed to put a lid on the discovery and quietly told Gawain about it. He was a shrewd man and he knew that if he told the government about the oil he was going to have to give up all rights to the precious mineral. Under the present Kenyan law, all the oil would belong to the government. He couldn't let that happen.

Gawain had worked out a contract with the Round Table which enabled him to keep almost all the oil profits for himself if they took over the country. Ten per cent would go to the government, some would pay expenses incurred and the rest would be his. He couldn't have made a better deal.

King Arthur was speaking. "If there are no questions, gentlemen," he said, "then you are all free to go. We shall meet on Saturday as usual."

The Knights of the Round Table stood up and once outside, each got into his respective car. When they had all entered, each car took off silently and slowly. They carefully timed twenty minute intervals between them before driving out. Soon all of them had left except Mordred and King Arthur who stood on the porch quietly talking about the day's events. They watched the last car leaving then turned around and went into the house. They locked the doors and quietly joked as they made their way upstairs. It had been a long day, which had held many unexpected complications. However, neither of them was unduly worried. But then neither of them had seen the teenage boy, across the street, watching the seven expensive cars leave the impressive-looking house yet again, from his bedroom window.

Chapter Five

Carnivore Restaurant never changed. You grew into it, got caught up in it and then grew away - eventually. There were always the same frantic faces, and swaying bodies. What else could one expect at a discotheque? The same desperate souls, searching, for what they knew not.

Susan made her way through the wildly pulsating bodies. She was now calm and steady. She had taken a cab from town and was prepared to take one back again if Chain didn't show. She was ready to tell him her story if he did, but she convinced herself that she could find help elsewhere if he refused to help her.

She caught sight of him just as she was about to give up her search. He was sitting at a table alone, obviously waiting. He fitted the description and looked exactly like he did in the photographs. She walked up to him and sat down.

"Hi," she said trying to sound cheerful although she was not. He looked at her intently and then smiled to himself. She wondered what he was thinking.

"So you are Susan," he said. "Jack talked about you all the time." A shadow briefly crossed his face. "What will you drink?" he asked her.

"Whatever you are drinking," she replied.

"Scotch?" he asked, making a face. She nodded and he ordered one for her. They sat in silence for a minute and contemplated each other.

"So," he started, "what is your story, Susan Juma?"

She looked at him uncertainly. Now that the time had come, she didn't know how to tell it. 'How would Chain react? Would he laugh her off or be angry with her for wasting his time?'

"Someone is plotting to kill the Vice-President," she decided to jump in with both feet.

"Someone is what?" Chain asked. "I'm not sure I understand you correctly."

"Mrs. Janet Musyoka, the Vice-President of Kenya, is on someone's death list," she said.

"Impossible," he said. "They couldn't get near enough and even if they did; there is no way they would be able to get away with it. They would be caught for sure. The risk is too great for anyone to even contemplate it."

"It would take a fool to try it, right?" she asked dryly. "Well, fool or not someone wants Mrs. Musyoka, and wants her badly."

"Do you know who?" Chain asked.

"No," Susan replied.

"Do you know how?" he asked

"No," came the answer.

"What do you know then?" he asked with some irritation.

"Not a lot," she admitted. "I know that someone big, probably a minister, is plotting to take over the country. He probably has two, or more partners. They are the ones who are responsibe for the recent deaths of the three prominent politicians."

"Okay," he agreed. "How do you know that?"

"I have a tape," she said quietly.

"A tape?" he inquired.

"A recorded conversation that took place at a meeting attended by this 'minister' and what I imagine are his cronies," she said. "They addressed him as 'Mr. Minister' and all seemed to be under contract to him; under his pay."

"Go on," he said.

"Well, they talked quite freely of their plans to assasinate Mrs. Musyoka, mentioning the plot two or three times. It seems that the hit-man; or at least, the man in actual charge of the operation is someone who they refer to as 'Mordred'. He, in turn, refers to the minister as 'Lancelot'."

"The Arthurian Legend?" Chain asked, in surprise, immediately recognizing the origin and significance of the two unusual names.

"Exactly," Susan agreed. "These two, Mordred and the minister seem to be of equal stature. Mordred could be an assassin hired by the minister but is definately superior to the others at the meeting. Both of them referred to a 'headquarters' and orders coming from King Arthur and the others."

"What others?" Chain asked.

"They were never mentioned," she said. "Neither by code name nor directly. The whole meeting was evidently a culmination of many meetings and a general winding up of their work. Those who were directly responsible for the killings were told where to pick up a bonus in cash and tentative plans for the next meeting were made — where they were to discuss Mrs. Musyoka's assassination. Then they talked briefly of a takeover planned to take place almost immediately after her death." Susan stopped talking and sat back, looking drained.

"Nobody is going to take over this country," Chain said very gently. "It has been tried before." He sat back and stared at Susan. She was an amazing girl with an amazing story; simply amazing. 'Did she really believe all the drivel that she had been spouting out?'

"It has been impossible as long as all the armed forces are behind the government," Susan said tiredly. Where had she heard those words before. "This group is planning, in fact has already planned and started, a process of destabilization which will make everyone, including the armed forces, lose confidence in the government. There will be no-one to support it. The group simply has to make a lot of promises, which people will only be too eager to accept and believe. It's a brilliant plan Chain," she said sadly. "And what is even worse is it's possible." Tears started trickling down her face again. She never even noticed them.

"How did you know all this?" Chain asked softly. "Who gave you the tape?"

Haltingly, Susan managed to tell him about John and James Otieno. She told him how the brothers had suddenly appeared out of nowhere and blown her life out of control. The unbelievable story that they had to tell and how nobody knew what to do. How they had handed over the tape and how everyone in the room had listened.

Then she told him how she had left the building. "Twenty-five minutes Chain," she said frustratedly. "Twenty-five stupid minutes.

When I came back they were all dead; stone cold. Irreversibly gone. My life was shattered. I didn't know who, and I didn't know if I was also part of the list. I didn't even know if I would be the next one to die."

"Where were you going?" Chain asked. "Why had you left the building?"

"I was taking the tapes to George Bakari," she said. "Mwatata asked me to run out and phone him, meet him, give him the tapes and ask him to put them in a security box somewhere."

"But why?" Chain asked, perplexed. "I don't understand. Why Bakari? Surely the next move would have been to call a meeting of top B.I.O. personnel? Get J. F. Kimani and other top officials. Bring them together to form a strategy. Bakari isn't B.I.O., why him?"

"Because there is no B.I.O.?" she whispered. "It doesn't exist. Perhaps it never really did except in a few fevered minds. It's just a dream."

"What?" he asked looking more confused than ever. "Susan . . ."

"I know," she interrupted. "I'm not making any sense. But it's true. There is no B.I.O."

"What exactly do you mean," he asked carefully.

"I mean that B.I.O., the great, has been infiltrated," she said. "That's what I mean."

He studied her closely for a few minutes. Susan touched her face and was surprised to find moisture there. It had been a long time since she had opened the floodgates like this. She wondered, again, what Chain was thinking.

"Come on; let's go," he said suddenly. The next few minutes swept by in a whirl as Chain paid for the drinks and stood up, pulling her up with him. He hurriedly weaved through the drunken, swaying bodies around them, dragging Susan clumsily behind him. She wondered what he was up to but was too tired to care. She might have felt excited that Chain had listened to her if she wasn't feeling so emotionally drained. In a hazy, still functioning part of her mind she acknowledged that Chain seemed poised to take control of everything. But then the name Chain was synonymous with 'control'. He had turned out ot be everything that they said he was.

Long and loose-limbed, he seemed to gracefully glide above the ground. He was tall, six foot four at least, had a very light complexion and extra-ordinary dark hair. His eyes were light brown and gave away nothing of his thoughts.

"Where are we going?" she asked when they were finally in his car which was rapidly pulling away.

"To my apartment," he answered shortly.

She sat back and tried to think about it but her mind seemed as though it had cotton wool in it. "We hardly know each other," she said obliquely.

He didn't answer. Didn't even turn to look in her direction. He had a grim look on his face and he seemed to be concentrating intently. She hoped that he would be able to absorb all the facts. She hadn't yet succeeded in understanding all the implications. She wondered illogically if he had anything to eat in his apartment and after a little while, she decided to ask him.

"I hope you have a casserole," she said conversationally. This time he favoured her with a look, eyebrows raised. "I'm hungry," she explained. His eyebrows did not falter from their position. She sighed and tried to concentrate. "I didn't have any supper." She explained further, "I couldn't go back to my apartment because I was afraid that . . . that . . ." Her voice trailed off.

He turned back to his driving. "Why don't you get some sleep?" he suggested. "I'll wake you up when we get there." She stared out of the window. It was his turn to sigh. "Susan," he started, and she turned towards him. "I can't promise you a casserole, but I'm sure that I can get something to satisfy you," and she nodded gratefully. "Now, get some sleep." She nodded again and closed her eyes.

When Susan opened her eyes again she was totally disorientated. She had a floating sensation, as if she was being carried. Indeed, as her eyes started to focus, she was able to make out the ceiling. To her utter surprise she realized that she actually was being carried, and by Chain, no less. He was opening the door to his apartment and doing a brilliant balancing act, in her opinion.

He opened the door and stepped inside, still effortlessly carrying her. He locked the door and moved through the darkness until he got to a light switch. He turned to put it on and then looked at her.

"Hi," she said.

He smiled and put her down on a chair.

"Shall I make you an omelette or would you like a ham sandwich or what?" he asked.

"Omelette please," she answered, adding, "with cheese, if you have it."

"Fine," he said. "Let's go into the kitchen." He led the way into the kitchen and switched on the light there. "What did you do with the tape then?" he asked as he got down an frying pan from the shelf.

"What tape?" she asked, still not fully awake.

"The one that you were taking to Bakari," he said, patiently. "The one that the Otieno brothers gave you."

"Oh it's here," she said as realization dawned. She removed both the tapes from her pocket.

"What do you mean?" Chain asked incredulously. "You have been walking around all night with them in your pocket?"

"Stupid, isn't it?" she asked wryly. "I haven't been thinking straight today. I just had no idea where else to put them." She handed him both the tapes.

"What is this other one? " he held up one of the tapes.

"Oh one of them is B.I.O. property," she explained. "Remember Mwatata used to tape-record every single conversation which he had with outsiders? Other senior personnel are also supposed to do it but they usually don't these days. It's a rule that has just died out of late."

Chain nodded and put both tapes on the shelf. Then he prepared the omelette and two cups of coffee. He sat her down and urged her to eat while he got a cassette player from the living room. He plugged it in, and inserted Mwatata's tape. For the next thirty minutes or so, Susan relived the last moments of Mwatata's life. The colours were vivid and the voices real and she felt like she could almost reach out and touch the people, as they spoke.

After the tape ended, Chain inserted the other one. There was total silence as both he and Susan listened intently. They concentrated hard, trying to imagine what the people looked like; who they were. As the voices droned on, it sounded as though killing the Vice-President was something that could be done any day of the week. They made a *coup d'etat* sound chillingly simple, and the worst part was the everything sounded so convincing.

The silence stretched out after the second tape had ended. Then Susan turned to Chain.

"What do we do now?" she asked.

"I'm not sure," he replied. "As far as I can see they found out about Otieno, followed him and killed him as well as everyone else who might have heard his story. But they don't know about you. At least, they haven't been following you and if they knew that you had been in that room, they would have definately followed you and tried to kill you at the first opportunity."

"That's what I thought too," she said, then stopped.

"How do you know that I wasn't followed?" she asked.

He grinned. "Because I had you followed," he said. "After you called me and so obligingly told me exactly where you were, I put some men on your tail." He smiled at her outraged look. "Don't feel so bad, my men are the best, you know. They can't be caught tailing, not even by a B.I.O. agent. Anyway they tailed you until you got to Carnivore and they didn't see anyone else following you. Believe me, if there had been anyone else, he would have been spotted at once."

She nodded. "So where does that leave us?" she asked him.

"We're going to have to call Bakari," he said. "At least with him we have a chance."

"No," she said flatly.

"Why not?" he asked. "It's because you couldn't find him earlier today; isn't it?" Chain asked, and she nodded. "I know where he was, where he is in fact," he said.

"Where?" she asked.

"I can't tell you," he said. She turned away and he sighed. "Look, I really can't. It's not my secret to tell." She stared broodingly at the kitchen walls and then turned back to him.

"I have told you my story because I trusted you," she said. "Because in my mind you were the only one whom I could trust. If I had wanted to tell Bakari I would have done so. I can't stop you from telling him if you really want to, unless I kill you. But telling him would be entirely your decision, not mine. It's one decision I can't support.

"I trust George Bakari implicitly and so did Jack," said Chain.

Susan shrugged. "You probably know him better than I do," she conceded. "Up to this evening I trusted him in all respects too. But it's stupid to trust everyone. Bakari had a number. If he couldn't be reached anywhere else one was to ring that number. He would definately be reached that way. It has always worked in the past. But not tonight. Mwatata would have been shocked if I had told him that I couldn't reach Bakari. It has never happened before."

Chain sat back in his chair. "What you say makes sense. In your position I would probably agree with what you say. But I don't have to guess or follow blind trust in this case. I know where Bakari was and why he couldn't be reached at the number. So I'm going to call him. He won't be available until 3 am so I'll call him then." He looked at Susan and added, "in the meantime you need some sleep." "You can use my bed. I'll sleep on the couch. Chivalry is not yet dead," he ended and raised a slight smile.

Less than five minutes later Susan was in Chain's bed with the blankets help firmly under her chin. She had done all that could be done so far and it was true that she trusted Chain. It was also true that she didn't trust Bakari. However, it was heartening to hear that she hadn't been followed and so was probably not yet on the death list. Yet somehow she still felt very uneasy.

Chapter Six

Susan couldn't sleep. She tossed and turned fitfully and threw off the covers. Then she pulled them back on again as she started feeling cold. Finally, she gave up the struggle and sat up. Her watch, which she had placed on the bedside table, read 2 am.

It wasn't as if she was being assailed by doubts or fears. Not really. In fact, not at all. The main problem was that she no longer felt in charge of the situation. She felt as though she was coasting along; leaving all the decisions, major and minor, to someone else. She couldn't remember a single time in her life when she had let someone else make the decisions for her. The feeling was alien and not quite comfortable.

The door opened slowly and Chain came in. He switched on the light, not seeming in the least bit surprised to see her sitting up in bed. After a slight hesitation, he walked over to the bed and sat down.

"What's wrong?" he asked.

She shrugged. "It's not something that I can easily put in words," she tried to explain. "I feel as if I'm in a car, driving along a road. The road is covered in mist and has many twists and turns. Every now and then there is a land mine but I don't know where or when. But the worst part of the whole scenario is I'm not the one driving. Someone else is and that unsettles me because it has never happened before. I have always been in charge."

He pondered her words for a few minutes and then said, "That could be a bit scary, I suppose."

"Yeah," she said wryly. "Well, life is hard; then you die." Her expression was as cynical as her words; cynical, hard, and scared.

Chain looked at her thoughtfully. "Look, nothing as serious as this can be classified as 'life' and left like that," he said.

"Why not?" she asked.

He sighed and said. "I have decided to tell you where George is." She looked at him in surprise. "I know I had decided not to tell you but I have changed my mind. I'm going to need your total co-operation. We have got to have complete trust in each other."

"Sounds good to me," Susan said.

"You'll never be able to trust me, to have complete faith in me if you question some of my decisions," he argued. "For us to succeed in getting anything done we'll have to have blind faith in each other. There can be secrets between us."

"So, where is Bakari?" she asked.

"I'll have to start from the beginning," he said, sighing again. "Bakari has a girlfriend. A mistress if you like."

"A what?" Susan asked. "What about his wife?"

"Emma doesn't know" Chain said uncomfortably. "She has no idea." There was silence. "Look, we don't have the right to judge. I don't judge him, yet I don't understand him. It seems he has some fascination for a sixteen year-old kid in high school. Her name is Elizabeth. But I don't have the right to moralise and neither do you."

"Oh, don't I?" Susan looked distinctly angry and liable to get ting even more upset.

"Well he is with her tonight, anyway," Chain added hurriedly. He intercepted the look of utter disgust on her face and ploughed on. "Not in that way," he said. He sighed and looked thoughtful for a while. "She er . . . found out that she was pregnant a little while ago. He panicked and brought her here to stick with me. They decided to get an abortion and he arranged it for today. He had it done and then took her home. That is, to her parents' home in Meru. They started off a bit late and I doubt that he will be back before three. Anyway I can't risk calling before that and missing him because he is supposed to be with me."

"But why couldn't he just leave your number with his wife or answering machine for urgent calls?"

"Because the urgent call number is supposed to tell you exactly where he is. If it gives you my number and you call here, I'm supposed to produce him, right? But I can't, because he is not here," Chain explained. "He told Emma that he and I have got some urgent out of town business to attend to and got me to back up his story. She never uses his urgent call number. She has never had to. When he's . . . er . . . with Elizabeth he has got an apartment in Kilimani estate where they meet. It's owned by a fictitious character called David Kamau. The urgent call number gives you "David's number where Bakari is supposedly holding a meeting with Kamau. So he has never been out of contact before."

"So this time he just left the urgent call line blank. No explanation no nothing?" Susan asked with some sarcasm.

"He had to, he had no choice; understand?" he said.

"Oh I understand all right," Susan said. "I understand he thinks he is brilliant and that no-one will ever find out about his Juliet. And I don't see why you don't understand his little — shall we say — deviation." After all it's typically male." Susan was looking distinctly angry and disgusted now.

"We don't have the right to condemn . . ." Chain began heatedly.

"You mean I don't have the right to condemn him," Susan cut in angrily. "I do. I have every right because I'm not male. I understand him and I condemn him." She nodded decisively. "But he's human and is not infallible. I can see why you didn't want to tell me, but I'm glad you did. I don't think I'll ever like him again but at least I trust him. Or rather, I trust you, and can be comfortable with whatever you decide . . ." she ran out of words and stopped.

"Haven't you ever done something that you knew was wrong and later on regretted it?" Chain demanded.

"Why?" she demanded in turn. "Are you trying to tell me that Bakari regrets cheating on his wife? Regrets abusing the trust of his children? Regrets interfering with the academic life of a girl young enough to be his daughter? Regrets seducing and misleading a teenager? Why should he regret it? Isn't it every man's right to do exactly as he pleases and say 'to hell with the consequences'?" Susan's anger was burning out of control. "Yes I've done a few things I'm ashamed of," she admitted. "But I have never done the same thing twice; not knowingly anyway."

"There's not much that I can add to that," Chain said wearily and hopelessly. "Except that Bakari's personal life is none of our business,

44

whatsoever. He can help us prevent a national disaster, and that's all we're interested in. The rest is irrelevant to us."

Susan forced herself to relax and turned to look Chain squarely in the face. "You were right to tell me," she said at last. "And you're right again, his personal life is none of our business." She paused, trying to phrase her words properly. "But I'll never be able to like him again," she said. "I'll never be able to look up to him and respect him as he undoubtedly deserves to be respected. I'll never admire him, ever again."

There was silence in the room for a while. "Never is a long time," Chain said at last. "If we pull through this, perhaps between Bakari and me, we can persuade you to change your mind. He really does deserve your respect and your admiration. But for the moment we are both going to have to settle for your trust. It's vital."

"What time is it?" Susan asked quietly. "Shouldn't you be calling him?"

Chain glanced at his watch. "Yeah, it's coming to three now. Why do I have the feeling that we're not going to be able to get any sleep tonight?" he asked with a sigh. "We shall use the red phone in my study. Come on, let's go."

The two of them went to Chain's study. It was full of many small gadgets, the latest technology. Computers, videos, walkie-talkies, stereos, radio receivers and other paraphernalia, and, of course, the red phone.

Chain sat down on one of the chairs at the table and gestured towards Susan to sit down on the other. In swift, practised motions he connected the phone to an amplifier and switched everything on. Then he dialled Bakari's home number.

The ringing signal, when it came, was piped through the amplifier and into the speakers. It sounded unnaturally loud in the quiet room. Chain glanced towards Susan and held up a crossed-fingers sign. Susan smiled back reassuringly, although she didn't feel in the least bit reassured herself.

As the phone was picked up on the other end, Chain opened a drawer inside the desk and pressed the 'record' button on the cassette player partially hidden there.

"Hello," said a femal voice.

"Hello, Emma. It's Chain." His voice was completely relaxed and natural.

"Chain!" Emma exclaimed. "Do you know what time it is?"

"Yes I do and I am very sorry," Chain's voice was alert and awake. His whole attitude was one of confidence and sharpness. A B.I.O. agent at work if ever there was one. "I know that it's almost . . . daybreak. There is no rest for the wicked, you know. Has George made it back yet?"

"Yes, he has just got in," she said.

"I know he is not going to be very pleased but could you please get him to the phone? We thought that we had wrapped everything up but it seemed too good to be true. It seems we missed out one or two vital things," Chain said.

"Still trying to save the world?" Emma asked resignedly.

Chain's face grew a bit grim. "You'll never know how true that is," he said lightly. "Sorry for waking you up and keeping George out all night long."

"Don't let that bother you, Chain," Emma said. "My mother always warned me not to marry a detective. Hang on, let me get George for you."

There was silence on the other end of the phone. Chain looked at Susan speculatively. She could tell that he was wondering how to phrase his next words. All she felt was relief that Bakari was home and that the little deception had worked. She didn't want to see Emma hurt. There was a slight noise as Bakari picked up the phone.

"Chain," came Bakari's gruff voice.

"George!" Chain's voice was warm and jovial. "Sorry to drive you out of your warm bed but we have got a serious problem."

"What's wrong, Chain?" Bakari was alert and awake. Obviously he wasn't used to requests for help from Chain. Especially not at that particular time of the night. His interest had been piqued and he was waiting to hear what the problem could be.

"It's a red alert George," Chain said. His tone had not lost its inflection. "Can't talk about it over the phone." There was silence on the other end of the line. "Sorry to call you back but I had to do it. There's no one else," he said simply.

Bakari did not hesitate. "I'm on my way," he said brusquely. "I'll be there in about ten or fifteen minutes."

Chain put down the phone after hearing a 'click' on the line. He gazed thoughtfully at the instrument and then turned to Susan. Without a word he turned everything off and then motioned to her leave the room. They went back to the bedroom. Chain sat down on the bed.

"Chain?" queried Susan.

"We have got to think about this," Chain said. "Something doesn't fit." He ran a hand distractedly through his hair. "Let's try to put ourselves in the mind of the killer for a while. Say it's Mordred the hit-man. It's probably him because he had sent someone to kill Otieno and the person messed up. He would want to finish the job himself."

Susan nodded. "That makes sense," she said.

"Somehow Mordred learns that Otieno isn't dead. How he finds out doesn't matter right now, not much anyway." Chain paused to think. "He follows Otieno straight to the B.I.O. headquarters, notices Otieno hasn't made any stops on the way, assumes Otieno is intelligent enough not to talk to every Tom, Dick, and Harry on the way up, but will demand to see a specific person."

Susan nodded again. "Otieno knew that many people at B.I.O. have been bought," she said. "Presumably Mordred would have known that Otieno knew and therefore couldn't talk to anyone unless he had complete trust in him; maybe a senior official who hadn't been bought."

"Right," Chain said. "What doesn't make sense is how Mordred was so sure that the people he killed in the room, were the only ones who had heard Otieno's story."

Susan frowned. "We can't be sure that Mordred was sure of that," she said.

"You can be ninety per cent certain," Chain said firmly. "If Mordred wasn't sure, you, for one, would probably be dead by now. So would the receptionist downstairs and everyone else who happened to be in the building at that time."

Susan thought about that for a while. "You know about our floor," she said, "the eleventh floor elevator thing. You can't get there or away from there unless you sign in or out. The elevator only opens on eleventh or ground floor and there's always a guard in it. Presumably Mordred has done his home work. All he really had to do was check the receptionist's book to ascertain that everyone except Mwatata and Anne had left the eleventh floor. The elevator book would confirm it. And that no-one except Otieno had gone up again since the last entry was made.

"That makes sense," Chain agreed. "I had forgotten about the tight security on eleventh floor. What doesn't make sense though, is the fact that Mordred didn't find out that you had been back in the building while Otieno was there and had left again. All the telephone lines had been logged of course. All he had to do was check."

"Easy," Susan said smiling, almost triumphantly. "I used the back entrance."

"Susan," Chain said quietly. "There is no back entrance at B.I.O."

Susan grinned widely. "There is now. It's almost ingenious really. Very simple. You know how the fence is rather harmless looking but heavily charged with electricity?" she asked. Chain nodded. "Well B.I.O. is a big compound with three main gates, heavily guarded of course, and one guard at the back. If you come out of the building from the west wing through the fire escape, no one will see you at all; it's obstructed. That's the wing that is nearest the fence. Right at the fence immediately opposite the building, conveniently, there's a rather large gopher hole. I don't know who noticed it first, but I think less than ten people know of its existence now. It goes directly underneath the fence. Someone enlargened it considerably and covered the bottom with cardboard, making it easier and cleaner to scramble through to the other side. Both the entrance and exit are covered by a very big berry bush and once you have cleared the building you can't be seen from any of the windows on that side. I have checked. It is a privilege to be trusted enough to be told about the passage. It's used for sneaking out just for the heck of it; to be able to feel one up on the guards; the whole security system."

Chain smiled slowly. "You can't get the better of a good B.I.O. agent for long," he said, almost smugly.

"Nope, you definitely can't," Susan replied. "I left the normal way, at around five, remembered that I had left my umbrella and sneaked back in hoping to just get it and go. One thing led to another and I was still there when Otieno arrived. Then I left through the back again; not wanting to explain to the receptionist how I had gotten back in. When I came back, I used the front."

Chain nodded, but before he could make any kind of comment, the doorbell rang. He stood up and went out of the room, Susan following him slowly. As she reached the living room she heard him asking Bakari to come in. She entered the room as Chain closed the outer door. Bakari was very surprised to see her.

"Sit down George, we have something very interesting to tell you," Chain said. "You see, someone is trying to kill the Vice-President of Kenya." He kept quiet and waited for the shock to settle in.

Chapter Seven

It was dawn by the time Chain and Susan finished telling their story. Bakari, his face a sickly grey, had interrupted continuously. Disbelieving, he had listened to the tapes, and heard the testimony. He had no words to express his shock on learning of Mwatata's death. He simply had no words. He looked bemused but no longer incredulous. The facts had spoken for themselves.

Susan stood up after it was all over. No-one spoke but she was getting used to the silences. The stunned silence, the contemplative silence, the panicky silence . . . the list was endless. What good would ever come out of those tense, scared moments? The only thing one could gain from them was the knowledge that they weren't the only ones lost for words; they weren't alone in their shock.

"I'm going to make coffee," she said. She was beginning to function again and things were starting to settle down into their proper slots. No longer was the world a large kaleidoscope of colours being violently shaken every few minutes and not making any sense at all. No longer was life looking as if it was going to end abruptly round the next corner. She was in control again. All she had to do was take the corner cautiously.

Chain tried to speak to Bakari as Susan left the room. "George," he said, "try not to think about Mwatata. If we try to blank our minds of his death, we might be able to function a little better."

Bakari sighed. "Your reasoning is right of course," he said. "I just can't seem to take it in. Maybe because he put up such a show of being invincible. He certainly had me fooled into believing that he would live forever." Bakari stopped talking, gave a wry smile and turned to stare at the door.

"He had everyone fooled," Chain agreed. "But the time to mourn and add up all the 'I wish' and 'if only' is later, not now. We have got more important things to do now. That may sound callous and unfeeling but it's true."

"Who can these clowns be? Do you have any ideas?" Bakari seemed to ease into a different gear altogether. It seemed that he had decided to follow the advice.

"They're not clowns," Chain said. "It would make it so much easier if they were. No, these people are dead serious. They fully believe that their plan will work. If we don't get some kind of break, I believe their plan will work too."

"We do have a break," Susan said calmly as she entered the living room. carrying a tray laden with cups, milk, sugar and coffee. "The tape." She set the tray down and began to serve the coffee.

"What about the tape?" Chain asked anxiously.

"Nothing earth-shattering," Susan replied. "The sound is a bit muffled because the tape recorder was hidden but we still have one very important thing: voice prints. Perhaps that might not be of great significance in connection with most of the people in the room but it could be a clue in tracing the minister."

"How?" Bakari asked interestedly.

"Voice prints," Susan said again. "At B.I.O. we have sophisticated technology to identify a person by his voice prints. They are like finger prints; no two prints are alike. Even if we can't identify the man just by matching his voice to the voice on the tape, we can run it through the computer and get his voice prints. It's not as if we have got one thousand ministers in Kenya. We can get samples recorded and try to match the prints."

"Sure," Bakari said. "We shall walk up to them and say, 'please talk into this tape recorder so that I can have a sample of your voice.'" His voice was laced with sarcasm and Susan reacted at once.

Her voice was scathing, "obviously you are very tired from your excursions George, so I'll forgive your momentary lapse into stupidity. My idea was to attend public rallies or press conferences where the ministers are speaking and get a personal copy of their voices. Perhaps you have a better idea."

Bakari looked surprised at the sudden attack and turned to gaze helplessly at Chain. The latter also seemed slightly bemused.

"You have overlooked something, Susan," he said. "The 'minister' referred to in the tapes may not be a current minister at all. He may have been a minister in the past and the others were using the expression as a courtesy title. It happens a lot, you know."

"Yes, I know," Susan said, calming down a little. "I have thought about that and I have come to the conclusion that he is a current minister. There was once in the tape where he spoke about 'using his office'. That would seem to indicate that he is currently serving as a minister."

"You seem to have something there," Chain admitted. "It's worth a try, and it's the only lead we have at the moment. We could get a list of public appearances tomorrow. The sooner we start on this the better." He turned to Bakari. "But if there are any other angles then let's work on them too." Susan abruptly took the coffee pot and left the living room.

"What's up with her?" Bakari asked.

"She is going to replenish the coffee pot," Chain said dryly.

"That's not what I meant and you know it," Bakari said.

Chain sighed. "We're going to have to get used to her being a bit sensitive. At least for a while. You see, I told her about your lady love," Chain said in a flat and uncompromising voice.

Bakari's face looked blank, and then dismayed as realization sunk in. "Why?" he queried tightly.

"I had to," Chain said. "She tried to call you today to give you the tapes on Mwatata's orders. That's why she had left the building when they gunned Mwatata down. You weren't available and in her book; your credibility dropped to zero. Later on, when I decided that the only thing we could do was to call you she was against the idea completely. I need her on my side. We are going to have to work on this together. So I had to tell her where you were. She wasn't exactly thrilled but at least she understood why you were unavailable."

"I see," Bakari said. "Well, you win some, you lose some."

"According to her, straying from the family home makes you a total loser," Chain said wryly. "Don't get me wrong, she still has confidence in your brain-power even if she tends to make a few degrading remarks. But as a person you're a complete nobody; lower than the dust. You have lost every last vestige of her respect."

Susan came back in, carrying fresh coffee. She put the pot on the table and sat down.

"We have got to assume that if there is a Mordred and a Lancelot, then there are others," Chain said. "A King Arthur, for one, co-ordinating everything. The minister spoke about receiving his orders from someone, so there must be other 'knights'. May be one or two others. After all, Mordred mentioned 'the others' one or two times."

"There were other knights in the legend," Susan said thoughtfully; "Galahad, Balain and Bohert. I think there were one or two more but I can't remember their names off-head."

"We've got to conclude that the others, whoever they are, are also very important people; maybe they're millionaires. They might even all be minsters," Chain said.

"Well we know for sure that Mordred is not a minister," Susan said. "And I have the feeling that King Arthur isn't a minister either. He must hold a much higher position, and is very wealthy. He would have to be in a superior position in society in order to have the right to boss Lancelot around. As for Mordred, I don't think he needs to be rich or hold any position at all. He sounds like a very talented hit-man. They would need him on their table as a sort of trouble-shooter; as insurance, if you like."

'Okay,' Chain agreed. "That makes sense. Mordred and King Arthur are not ministers. Lancelot definitely is and the rest could be. What do you think, George?"

Bakari nodded. "I think in a nutshell, we are not sure who the others are or even if they exist at all. But at least we have got a firm beginning."

"One thing we can't do is bring any other agents in on our ideas," Susan said. She turned to Bakari. "That includes B.I.O. and C.I.D. agents. If B.I.O. has been infiltrated then the C.I.D. probably has been too. We can't just say, 'Oh Bob is all right, he has been on the job for forty years and there's no way he could have sold out'. It doesn't work that way. Everybody is a suspect until proven undisputedly innocent."

"I have got one or two people that I can rely on at B.I.O.," Chain said conversationally. "People, who in my mind, are undisputedly innocent."

"You?" Susan asked in disbelief. "I didn't know you had any links at B.I.O.!"

"You learn something new every day," Chain declared dryly. "I know common knowledge was that I had severed all links with B.I.O. but that wasn't true. Once an agent, always an agent I guess. But my friends are loyal to me and the information has never once leaked to anyone. I trust them to keep their mouths shut."

"But Mwatata said . . ." Susan started.

"Yes?" asked Chain interestedly.

"He said you wouldn't meet me because I was a B.I.O. agent," Susan said slowly. "He said that everything about B.I.O. was so painful to you that you couldn't even stand seeing a B.I.O. agent." She intercepted a swift look between Bakari and Chain. "It wasn't true, was it?" she accused hotly. "He was just trying to let me down gently. You had other reasons for refusing to see me so unconditionally all those years, didn't you?"

"That's hardly worth going over now," Chain said wearing a tired expression on his face. "But I promise you, it wasn't anything personal. Nothing to do with you really."

Susan ignored him. "You really do learn something every day. If you had asked me ten minutes ago who was the one person who had never lied to me in my life I would have said Mwatata with no hesitation at all. And to think I fell for it so easily. I guess he knew what I wanted to hear."

"It's not important," Chain said impatiently. "Not now. I guess he decided that there was no reason to hurt you and we both put him in a spot. You, by asking to see me and me, for refusing. I can't see any alternative, can you?"

"No," Susan said shortly, her face totally expressionless. I want your contacts to be put under a thorough test first, before you use them. The information we want could be gained by using the ministries or even getting in touch with the newspaper reporters. They always have a list of events taking place." Her voice was flat and totally devoid of any emotion.

"There are a few people over at C.I.D. who I can run through some sort of test as well," Bakari said. "We'll need some sort of reinforcement once we work something out. And it's not even important to tell them much. We only need to use them to find certain bits of information here and there. One thing is certain though. We're going to have to succeed. The future of this country depends on us now."

The thought was truly awesome; almost unbelievable, but it was true. Everything else paled into insignificance beside the fact that there was a group of people, somewhere in the night, who had the power to plunge the nation into total chaos. Perhaps the only thing more frightening than that was that only three others in entire country knew about it and they had very little information to guide them. The odds were heavily stacked against them.

"The only way we can succeed is by staying alive," Chain said trying to sound hopeful. "That's one thing we'll have to remember."

"It shouldn't be too hard if we keep our heads," Bakari said negligently as he stood up. "It's time I went home and got some sleep. Life is too short for constant worries. We'll get ourselves out of this somehow but we have to keep our heads."

Chain stood up and took Bakari to the door. As they said goodnight, Susan remained seated, thinking. She was trying to find another angle in her mind.

Chain came back into the room and sat down. For a few minutes they stared at the walls in silence. Then he cleared his throat.

"I want to explain," he said. She knew what he meant, and suddenly she didn't want to hear any more. She stood up hastily.

"There is no need," she said with a tight little smile. "It has been a long day so I think I'll take myself off to bed . . ." her voice trailed off.

"Sit down," he said. His voice was weary but there was a thread of steel running through it. Susan sat down.

"I never thought that women should be included at B.I.O. at all," Chain said. "I always thought that they were unstable and unreliable," sighing as he saw the stiff look on her face. "As I said before, don't take it personally."

She tried to erase the expression from her face and her voice was deliberately light as she said, "I have to, I'm the only one in the room."

Chain's look was enigmatic. "It really has nothing to do with you or any other woman. I concede that there are quite a few top level women agents at B.I.O. today, you being one of them. I guess it was a sort of prejudice I had which I tried to fight. It's not as if I went around shouting out to the world what I thought. I knew it was unreasonable and I really tried hard to be fair, but guess I always vaguely resented them and I never really trusted them," he paused, trying to get his thoughts together. "When I was at B.I.O., I had a partner named Sam. His full name was Samuel Kamau. We had been through a lot together and it was a relief when we were finally made partners."

Chain lapsed into silence, once more. Susan didn't know what to say or where the connection came in. She had heard of Samuel Kamau, of course, everyone at B.I.O. had. Chain's partner was a talented, active young man whose feats were only excelled by those of Chain. He had been killed in active duty just before Chain quit. Everyone had speculated as to whether the two events were linked, but Chain's disillusionment and disgust with B.I.O. seemed to run far too deep for it to be a simple mourning for a friend. No one had been able to persuade him to come back to the fold.

"I've heard of him," Susan said at last. "He was a real hero at B.I.O. He still is, in fact."

"Yeah, a hero," Chain said. "Anyway, he was in love with this girl. Her name was Carol. She was an agent at B.I.O. They had planned to get married and she would give up her work and raise the kids. I didn't know it but he was confiding in her about absolutely everything we were working on. Unknown to us, she was selling the information to the other side. Sam couldn't believe it when he found out. He confronted her and asked her about it. She shattered his dreams by telling him that she had never really loved him and that she was just using him. Then, she killed him."

Susan wasn't even capable of feeling shock anymore. She just nodded. "What happened to Carol?" she asked Chain curiously.

He looked her squarely in the eye and said, "I killed her."

Susan pulled the covers over her head, ten minutes later in bed. She knew she would be able to sleep now. Things would be better in the morning. She drifted off to sleep as Bakari's words echoed in her head: "All we have to do is keep our heads . . ." Talk about easier than done!

Chapter Eight

Susan rolled down the window of Chain's smooth metallic grey Honda Civic. It was nine o'clock the following morning. She had been right; sleeping hadn't been a problem for her. She had been able to sleep soundly for what remained of the night and had woken up early in the morning to prepare breakfast for Chain. The whole scene was becoming very domesticated she thought.

At breakfast they had decided that she would take immediate leave of absence from her work at B.I.O., making it clear to anyone who wanted to know, that she was very upset about Mwatata's death and needed time off to learn how to function without him. The leave was unconditional but if they demanded that she stayed to lead the investigation team she was to refuse. If they persisted she would resign. That would lure whoever was watching B.I.O. into an imaginary calm as he would assume that Susan wasn't investigating the case.

"It won't work, you know," Susan commented as they stopped for a traffic light. They were on their way to her apartment to pick up a suitcase and other essentials. They had decided that Susan would be better off staying in Chain's house.

"What won't work?" Chain asked as he revved up the engine and negotiated the car back into the traffic as the lights turned green.

"Saying that I'm too upset to continue working," Susan explained. "B.I.O.'s credibility relies on the fact that its agents don't get hysterical. People would expect me to be out for blood, looking for revenge and raring to go. They'll be shocked and immediately suspicious if I cry off the investigation."

"Hmmmn . . . you have a point there," Chain conceded. "Well, we'll just have to think of something to persuade them otherwise, won't we? Because no matter what, we've got to convince them that you cannot help conduct that investigation. That's vital to our plan." He turned the car into Susan's apartment block's driveway. "Where shall we leave this?"

"Just over here," Susan directed him to a secluded corner of the garage. They both got out of the car and locked the doors. As they went up the back staircase they discussed what Susan should tell the landlady.

"Not much I suppose," Chain suggested. "But it's possible that if someone is investigating you, he will question her too. Better explain that you have had a bereavement, and have gone to stay with a friend for a while. No need to make it look as if you're running away, or trying to hide something."

"You know, it's still hard to believe that he is actually dead," Susan said soberly. "That he's gone."

"I know, Susie, I know," Chain said gruffly.

They entered her apartment and started sorting out her stuff. She packed a few items for herself in a suitcase and picked up her valuables, her passport, credit cards and other necessary papers. As she looked around the place, it was suddenly hard to believe that she had left that room only the previous morning. It seemed like such a long time back. The items looked strangely unfamiliar and the atmosphere was alien. It was as if she was visiting a neighbour's apartment. The sensation was gone in a little while, but it had been quite unsettling while it occurred.

When she mentioned the feeling to Chain, he soothed her and explained that she still hadn't fully recovered from the shock. But that it was all going to be alright. Somehow though, she had the feeling that it was never going to be the same.

They descended the stairs and went to the landlady's little apartment on the ground floor. Chain was holding her luggage and coat. She had changed into a pair of grey woollen trousers and a long-sleeved white shirt and her long hair had been smoothed back into a serviceable pony-tail. Her face was settled into dull lines of grief and frustration. She was ready for her part.

The door opened and her land-lady, Mrs. Ondieki, smiled as she saw Susan.

"Susie," she said in delight. "How nice to see you. But why aren't you at work? Why are you here?" She switched a curious gaze over to Chain.

"You see, a good friend of mine has died, Mrs. Ondieki." The tears in her eyes were not fake, not at all.

"Oh, darling, I am sorry," Mrs. Ondieki said. "Anyone I know?"

"Yes," Susan said. "Mr. Mwatata my boss. We came to your place for tea once, remember?"

"Oh yes," said Mrs. Ondieki. "I remember your boss well. How terrible. This must be really hard for you, dear."

"It is, Mrs. Ondieki, it is," Susan said. "Oh this is my friend Christopher, by the way," she said as an afterthought, dragging him forward. "Christopher Mathenge. He is a work-mate. "

Mrs. Ondieki and Chain shook hands and murmured pleasantries; her curiosity momentarily satisfied. She expressed deep regret at the death of the 'boss' and offered to make tea for the two.

"Oh no thank you," said Susan. "We can't come in. In fact that's what I wanted to tell you. I'm going away. Upcountry for a little while, I think, at least until I get over the shock. I want to leave my key with you so that you can check on the place every once in a while? And please, while you're in there, could you put a little water in the plants for me? There are only two pots in the sitting room."

Mrs. Ondieki found it much easier to cope with these mundane matters and readily rose to the occasion.

"Don't worry about a thing dear," she said, taking the keys from Susan's slightly shaking hand. "You just go and have yourself a nice rest; it's the only way to cope with grief. You're taking a holiday from work, too, I suppose?" Susan nodded. "Good; you work far too hard as it is. Just take a break. I'll take care of everything here. Your plants will be fine."

"Thank-you, Mrs. Ondieki," Susan said. "You're very kind to me."

"Think nothing of it," said Mrs. Ondieki, looking pleased. "You would do the same for me, I know." Then she turned to Chain. "you . . . take good care of her, you hear? This girl is very, very special to me."

After a little more clucking and sympathising, she let Susan and Chain out of the front door.

"One down . . ." Susan murmured.

They walked round the building towards the garage in silence, each was lost in their own thoughts. As they got into the car Chain smiled faintly.

"What is it?" Susan asked.

"Nothing much," Chain said, starting the car. "I was just thinking how well you pulled that off."

They chatted lightly on the way to the office. The sleek car purred effortlessly through the traffic and Susan found herself envying Chain's skill. She could drive but since she didn't own a car and she didn't get many opportunities to do so. B.I.O. agents were not exactly paid a fortune. When on assignment, she usually used a government vehicle. She could operate a tractor, drive a bus, and fly a helicopter . . . being a B.I.O. agent was not smooth running all the way.

Chain manoeuvred the car into the gates at B.I.O. After Susan presented her identification card, they were let in. At the reception, the girl looked up sharply as she saw Chain and Susan.

"Susie!" she exclaimed. "My God, you're so late. We've been ringing your apartment to no avail. Where have you been?"

"It's a long story, Janet. Is his royal highness in? I've got to talk to him," Susan said.

"Yes, Mr. Kimani is in," Janet said.

"Please call upstairs and see if he can fit me in for a minute or two," Susan said.

"Both of you?" asked Janet, busily connecting the phones.

"Yes, both of us," Susan said. "This is Christopher Mathenge. The boss knows him."

Janet nodded abstractedly and turned to the phone. Then the name must have registered because her head flew back up and she took an involuntary step back. Her mouth opened in shock. "Chain?" Her voice was almost a whisper.

"That's right, Janet," Susan said conversationally. "It's Chain. If we could just tell Kimani . . ."

"Of course, Susie, right away." Janet was flustered and her face was filled with awe. She punched a few numbers and managed to get the head of B.I.O., J. F. Kimani on the line.

"Yes, Mr. Kimani, sir," said Janet, still shaking. "I have Susan Juma here, requesting to see you . . . Yes, Juma; Susan Juma. She has got someone with her sir, Christopher Mathenge . . . Yes sir, I said Mathenge . . . I think so sir . . . I'll send them up, right away."

She replaced the phone and turned to Chain and Susan. "He says that you should go up immediately," she told them.

She escorted them over to the elevator, her face still reflecting the awe she felt. Susan began to feel amused. One would think that Chain was some kind of god by the way Janet was staring at him. Next thing you knew, people might start bowing as he passed by. She thought of him as a very ordinary human being, now that she had met him. It seemed funny that people around them had decided to worship him.

"Leave all the talking to me," Chain said confidently as the lift steadily climbed upwards. "I know how to handle J. F. K. Just follow my lead. Oh, and be sure to put on that incredibly forlorn look, hmmn?"

Kimani's shock was written all over his face. The fact that his prize agent, Chain, was stepping into B.I.O. after all this time, had obviously surprised him.

"Chain!" he exclaimed, shaking Chain's hand. Susan was completely forgotten as the head of B.I.O. tried to digest the fact that this man, this legend, was standing in his office. "It has been a long time," he said at last.

"Yes it has, boss," Chain said genially. "Far too long."

"What can I do for you?" asked Kimani.

"Well it's really not what you can do for me, but what you can do for Susan," Chain said, smoothly.

"Ah, Susan." Kimani seemed surprised to see her in the room.

"Yes, we heard about Mwatata," sighed Chain. "Or rather, Susan came back to the office last night and saw him. She came and told me."

"Ah, yes," said Kimani, seemingly galvanised into action. "I heard you came back to the office at a bad time, dear," he said sympathetically. "It was very unfortunate that you had to see him like that."

"It was very upsetting," Susan said quietly, trying not to relive the moment when she had entered the room and found the bodies.

"That is what we wanted to talk to you about," interposed Chain. "I would like Susan to take immediate leave of absence. I don't think she will be able to cope with the stress."

"But . . ." Kimani started.

"Susan wants to stay, of course," Chain interrupted. "She . . . was hoping to be part of the team solving this case. But I disagree. She's too emotionally . . . er . . . involved in this case to be . . . allowed to take part in it. It will be too much of a vengeance trip." All this was said haltingly while Chain watched Susan.

"I'm sure Susan will be able to put her emotions aside and do a good . . . if not great, job," said Kimani, finally finding his voice.

"I'm sure under any other circumstances she would be all right and able to," Chain said, "but you have forgotten one very important thing; Mwatata was like a father to her. There is no way she can be objective about this, even if she thinks she can at first. I was very shocked when I heard about Jackson's death. But one thing I know for sure was that Susan was the daughter he never had. If he left me any responsibility at all, it's to take care of her the best I can. I don't want to feel that I have failed him. And I know he wouldn't want her on the investigation team."

Kimani sat down and nodded distractedly. He obviously agreed with Chain but was trying to find a way to counter his arguments.

"Putting Susan on the team would be a ticket to death for her, you know that," Chain said firmly, pressing home his advantage. "You know once an agent is emotionally involved he or she is no longer a hundred per cent reliable. It's just touch and go. We shouldn't do that to her." He turned around and looked at Susan and she understood that he expected her to do or say something. As she turned over the possibilities she came up with one which was totally uncharacteristic of her.

She promptly burst into tears which startled the two men, Chain took her into his arms and he . . . turned to an incredulous-looking Kimani and tried to explain.

"I'm sorry about this," he said. "You can see she is a wreck. She hasn't been the same since yesterday evening. I'm taking her away for a while, until she calms down and starts functioning again. You will arrange everything for me I hope."

He talked as if the leave was a foregone conclusion and Kimani could only nod bemusedly as the couple said their goodbyes and walked through the door. Then he turned to look out of the window.

Chain waited until they were cruising away from the building before making any remark.

"Those tears weren't fake," he said gently.

She laughed shakily. "I seem to be doing a lot of crying lately," she said. "I never thought I had that many tears to shed."

"How do you want to do this?" he asked. "Do you want to ring up the ministries or go to the reporters, or what?"

"I have a good friend who works with the *Nation* newspaper," Susan said, "a real news hound. I'll get together with her and I'm sure she can give me all the information I need."

"Can you trust her?" asked Chain.

"Oh, yes" Susan said almost laughing. "I can definitely trust Barbara."

"Barbara," Chain remarked.

"Barbara Kwanda; she is half Zairian. Babs in short," Susan said, still smiling.

"What's so funny?" Chain asked.

"The thought of Babs betraying me. It's hilarious," Susan said, her grin growing ever wider.

Chain dropped her off at a telephone booth and waited while she called and explained the situation to Barbara. Evidently they reached an agreement because Susan replaced the receiver and returned to the car, with a smile on her face.

"What did you tell her?" Chain asked.

"Not much," Susan answered. "I asked her to find out for me if possible where the ministers were yesterday, if they made any speeches and so on. We can eliminate some of them that way. Barbara will try and get me a schedule of their activities: where they will be appearing during the coming week, and that sort of thing."

"She didn't ask any questions?" Chain asked as he turned to look at Susan. "Didn't she want to know what is going on?"

Susan laughed this time. "Barbara stopped asking questions a long time ago," she said. "She will meet us for lunch at the Green Corner Restaurant."

At one o'clock, Susan and Chain were sitting at Green Corner when Barbara breezed in. It did not take Susan's whispered, "that's her" to identify her. She came over and kissed Susan then sat down. After the introductions she turned to her friend.

"I have got most of the information you wanted, Susie," she said. "I knew it would be easy to get. All the ministers were in Mombasa yesterday, attending a fund-raising meeting at which Mrs. Janet Musyoka was the guest of honour."

Chapter Nine

Both Chain and Susan starèd at Barbara in total silence. After a while she seemed to notice that something was wrong.

"Neat huh?" she questioned hopefully. "All at one place, just where you need them."

"That's impossible," Susan blurted out. "They couldn't all have been there!"

"Why not?" Barbara asked, surprised. "It has happened before. If it's an important enough function they all turn up."

"Er . . . what was the fund-raising for?" asked Chain quietly.

Barbara brought out a sheaf of notes. "Know what? I don't know. Let's see," she said. "Er . . . ah! It was to raise money for a new secondary school."

Chain and Susan looked at one another for a long moment, then. "What is so important about that?" asked Susan.

"You know all these small fund-raisings are important. More so especially when Mrs. Musyoka is the guest of honour. She has really pushed the 'giving-money-to-charity' thing. In order to appear pro-government, the ministers usually have to show up and contribute something when she is there."

"At what time did it end?" Chain asked.

Barbara consulted her notes again. "Er . . . Mrs. Musyoka left at 11.00 p.m. and a few people left with her but the main 'do' lasted until about 2.00 a.m. Most of the ministers left then."

"Who was the exception?" Susan asked.

"What exception?" Barbara asked wondering at Susan's question.

"The minister who didn't turn up. There is always one you know. The one whose sick mother had to be visited or whose wife was in hospital or something. Who was it?" Susan asked quietly.

Barbara turned back to her notes. "There were no exceptions this time," she said firmly.

"How can you be so sure?" Susan demanded.

"I have my sources," Barbara said, a bit flustered. "All the ministers were there. There was a full house."

"Are there tape recordings of the event?" Chain asked interupting the uneasy situation developing.

"I'm sure the Kenya Broadcasting Corporation covered the event," Barbara nodded. "They always record these functions and keep them."

Chain looked pleased. "I want that tape," he said earnestly.

Barbara sighed. "Susan can get it out for you," she said. "K.B.C. is usually quite willing to co-operate with the C.I.D. She would only need flash her card and ask for it."

"I'm not working for B.I.O.," Susan said. I'm on leave. In fact I'm in the country-side. You have not seen me or heard from me at all. And I definitely haven't been asking any questions."

Barbara sighed again. "Okay, so you can't," she said. "Ask someone at B.I.O. to get it for you; maybe Mwatata." She knew immediately that she had made a mistake, by the way Susan's face froze. "I take it that you can't ask Mwatata by the look on your face," she said.

"I can't," Susan said flatly. "Mwatata is dead. He was shot to death in his office yesterday."

"What?" Barbara's face was in total shock.

"Confidential," Susan added.

Barbara sank back into her chair. "You're on to something big, aren't you?" she asked. "And you're not working with B.I.O."

"Don't let it bother you," Susan said dryly. "But you must go back and dig deeper, Babs. There has to be an exception. When you find him, let me in on it. And get us that tape. I'm sure you have a few people inside K.B.C."

Chain watched Barbara staring listlessly at her notes for a while. Then she turned to him and studied him intently for a few minutes.

"You're Chain, aren't you?" she queried. "The legend, the one and little-less-than-superhuman Chain?"

"I already told you that," Susan said impatiently.

"No you didn't," Barbara interrupted. "You told me his name was Christopher Mathenge. I have only just made the connection. I'm pretty slow today. I had no idea that I was sitting with a legend."

Chain could see that Susan was getting exasperated. With a lot of amusement he noted that Barbara was probably needling her on purpose, just to get that reaction.

"Babs," he said gently, "may I call you Babs?" He lifted his eyebrows and she nodded. "There's something going on that we have to get to the bottom of; something that we cannot discuss and we need your help. No one should know that we're working on it, at least, not for now. We need to know if there were any exceptions from the group of ministers at yesterday's official fund raising. We know for sure that there was at least one. Please, find out who it was. If there was more than one, find out who the rest were and let us know. That tape and the schedule are just as important."

Barbara looked at him intently. "Has it got something to do with Jack?" she asked.

He hesitated only for a fraction of a minute. "Yes," he said.

Barbara nodded. "Then count me in," she said.

"Thanks," said Chain, a relieved grin spreading over his face. "This means a lot to us."

"There was never any doubt that she was going to help us anyway," Susan said scornfully. "She is just trying to get attention."

Barbara laughed a little shamefacedly. "You know me so well, Susie darling," she said. "I won't stay for lunch because I think I better get on this right away. I could probably find out something for you in about an hour or so. Where can I reach you?"

Chain gave her his apartment number, where they would be until she got all the information. After a goodbye rivalled in quickness only by her hello, she left. A swish of clothes, a waft of perfume, and she was gone.

Chain was silent as he looked thoughtfully after her. "You know your friend is pretty . . . interesting," he said.

Susan laughed, her good humour restored. "That's Babs, alright; interesting, if you want to be polite, that is."

They ordered lunch and proceeded to eat amid light-hearted laughter. Susan told Chain of all Barbara's outrageous exploits; half of which he did not believe. The life she seemed to have led did not belong to the real world; it belonged to a comedy thriller.

"How come she didn't join you at B.I.O. when you left school?" Chain asked Susan. "She certainly seems to have all the qualifications."

"Oh, Babs never wanted to be a detective," Susan said. "She kept saying that she was a 'writer, not a fighter.' Journalism seemed the best way to express her natural talent and she certainly has never had any regrets about not joining 'the brown ferrets' as she calls B.I.O. agents."

"I didn't know such people existed," Chain commented. "She has definately made a believer out of me. No one can accuse her of not living life to the full."

"No," Susan agreed. "You definitely couldn't accuse her of that."

Chain paid the bill and they walked out of the restaurant. The ride back to his apartment was made in companionable silence. Susan couldn't help having a faint smile on her face as she reminisced Babs' exploits of days gone by. It seemed strange to be in such good spirits especially if one paused to think of all that had happened in the recent past; but Susan did not want to think of the recent past. The present was difficult enough to deal with, as nothing seemed to be working normally. Everything was uncertain and one was never really sure what would happen next.

When they reached Chain's apartment, they sat in the living-room discussing the case and trying to find different angles to it. As they talked, they found that they tended to think alike; they were on the same wavelength, a discovery which was pleasant and strange to both of them.

After some time they stopped talking and sat back to think about the points they had agreed on. There were a few scattered facts which were obvious. But there was one very important one which couldn't be skirted any longer.

"There must be a top official at B.I.O. who is not on our side," Susan voiced the suspicion eventually. "Someone very high up."

"Not that there are a million officials who can have total access to the king of information Otieno was talking about," Chain said.

"Not a million," Susan said. "They are only six, J.F. Kimani at the very top and five senior officials who form his senate. We can rule one out, Jackson Mwatata."

"So that leaves us five people to work with," said Chain. "J. F. Kimani should also be put on the list although you must agree he is the most unlikely candidate. Who are the other four?"

"Tim Kuria, Patrick Ondieki, Isaac Peters and Matthew Mucheru," Susan replied promptly. "All are heads of departments at B.I.O. I'm not sure who is going to take Mwatata's place but he can't qualify for our list since up till now he hasn't had access to any of the crucial information."

"So one, possibly more than one of those five, is our Benedict Arnold," Chain said wryly. "It's all so unbelievable. A couple of years ago B.I.O. was the eighth wonder of the world. The idea that any official working there had been bought would have been unbelievable. That a top official had turned traitor was simply unthinkable. The very suggestion would have made you be laughed at from here to London.

"A couple of years ago?" Susan asked. "A couple of days ago B.I.O. was an impregnable fortress. A few strategically placed taps have rendered it a magnificent ruin.

Just then the phone rang. It was the red one in the study and Chain picked it up. The equipment had already been set up.

"Hello," Chain called out.

"Chain," came a female voice, "Babs here. I've got the information you wanted."

"Okay Babs, why don't you bring it over?" he suggested and gave her the address. Babs hung up.

"She is on her way here," Chain told Susan and they both went back to the living room to wait for her.

The silence was tense this time; anxious. They were willing Barbara to get there as soon as possible; to hear the good news. Most of all, they were willing her to be carrying news of a minister who, for dubious reasons, did not attend fund raising hosted by Mrs. Musyoka the night before. With a name they could start to work on the others, whoever they might be.

The ringing of the bell made them jump; so lost in thought were they. Chain quickly moved to let Babs in, while Susan stood up slowly; her palms suddenly sweaty. As soon as her friend came in, she pounced on her.

"Well?" Susan asked, "what have you got?"

Babs sank into a chair and passed a hand over her face. She looked tired and worried. "Well," she said, trying to sound bright and lively, "well, well, well. Haven't you got over your 'well' habit darling?" She held up her right hand for silence, as Susan would have erupted. "I don't think you'll like what I have got," she said. "You were right, there was an exception to that fund-raising. The only problem is that he was not the only one. There were five ministers absent last night."

Susan slowly sat down and exhaled painfully.

"Five, huh?" muttered Chain. "I'm beginning to hate that number. Tell me, who were they?"

Babs removed a sheet of paper from her purse. "The honourable Adam Kariuki, Minister for Land, the honourable Rogers Kitili, Minister for Water, the honourable Francis Nzau, Minister for Natural Resources, the honourable Abdul Sheik Hakim, Minister of Sports and the honourable John Mwangi, Minister for Soil Conservation. They were absent for various reasons; sick mothers in hospital included. They had sent people with their contributions to represent them. That is why it was assumed that all the ministers were there, at first. I got you the tape." A bit more rummaging and she produced a VHS video tape for Chain. "There you go," she said.

Chain sighed. "I don't suppose this will be of that much use now," he said. "We can go through it just the same but I doubt that it can help us. The people we are really after are the absentees."

"No use asking why?" Babs asked Susan hopefully.

"None at all," Susan replied.

"Well, that says it all," Babs sighed. "Is there anything else I can do for you?"

"Not at the moment. Thanks Babs." Susan turned to look at her friend. "We'll let you know if there's anything . . ."

"Okay," Babs shrugged philosophically as she stood up. "I'll have to settle for that." "I had better get back to the office, before they fire me in my absence. I'll see you sometime." She walked quickly to the door and Chain followed to show her out. She handed him the piece of paper where she had written down the names of the five ministers, then, without a backward glance, she was gone.

"So," Chain said as he closed the door. "What do you say?"

He looked at Susan who was leaning back in her chair with her eyes closed, seemingly at ease.

"We have got so much to do within very little time," she said. "That is; provided we know what it is we are going to do in the first place."

"Let's look at the facts again," Chain said. "We have definitely got a hit-man code named Mordred and a Minister code named Lancelot. The odds then are that there are some more 'knights'. Maybe even government people, ministers, permanent secretaries and so on. There is probably a 'King Arthur' co-ordinating the whole affair. He's probably very rich and is providing all the funds for the . . . uh project."

"That's right," Susan agreed.

"We also have the voice-prints of Lancelot which we can match up with one of these five names we have got. Once we do, we will know for sure who Lancelot is. We also have five top B.I.O. officials under suspicion. We have to get the rat from there and eliminate him."

"Easier said than done," Susan argued, her eyes still closed. "For all you know there may be more than one who is guilty; then what?"

"Then we eliminate both or all three or whatever," Chain said with a serious voice.

"How are we going to find out who is guilty and who is not?" Susan asked, reluctantly opening her eyes.

"We are going to think hard," Chain replied, his face very grim.

Chapter Ten

The man they called 'King Arthur' paused before his car, a gleaming white Rolls Corniche which had cost him one hundred and sixty five thousand dollars. He looked around him, at the vast expanse of land on which he had placed his 'work-shed'. Neat and precise, the buildings seemed bigger than usual and more imposing somehow. Well, that wasn't a problem for King Arthur because nothing was more imposing than he was.

The 'work-shed' as he called it, comprised several large buildings which housed his brain-child, a scientific research centre which carried out experiments and investigations on genetics. It was run by a very skilled and talented man, who also happened to be a member of the Round Table; Tristan the brain surgeon.

It was independently owned and had nothing at all to do with the government. Security was tighter that anywhere else possibly on the entire African continent. The people who worked there were all hand-picked for the job. They had to sign secrecy documents and undergo several investigations before they were cleared to work. The pay, was excellent, of course. Nobody ever breathed a word to anyone about what went on inside that compound; not even to their family members or best friends, because the price one was to pay if he opened his mouth was too high. Not only would he lose his life, but his family's too. Each member would be tortured and killed before his eyes. It had only happened once, but that once was enough to guarantee silence. King Arthur had no problem carrying out his threats. He knew exactly what to do to those who disobeyed him.

The work at the research centre was interesting and this made potential employees comply with the investigations and sign the secrecy pacts. The young aspiring scientists, subordinate staff and security men joined the others at the institution shrouded in mystery.

The 'others' were well-trained military men, recruited from all parts of the country, from the highest echelons of the military to the lowest ranks. Some had been persuaded to join the course, while others were lured, bribed, threatened or blackmailed into it. They were soldiers wearing a different uniform from the one sported by the government troops; but there was no doubt that they knew their work.

They also differed from government troops in that they were better paid, had more privileges and were highly skilled in whatever they had been trained to do. Their devotion bordered on fanatism; the alternative was unthinkable.

The whole compound consisted of one huge dome and several smaller ones which were scattered around the area. Most of them housed very expensive scientific equipment which Tristan and his legions used in research. The rest did not house any scientific equipment, expensive or otherwise. The scientists never ventured near them. They were heavily guarded and what was inside them remained a mystery.

However, they held no mystery for King Arthur. He smiled as he thought of the rows upon rows of fire-arms neatly stored away there. The cartons of ammunition piled on top of each other, the assault rifles most of them soviet AK-47 and the riot of Israel Uzi machine guns. Uzi had always been his favourite . . . but most of his men preferred the soviet rifles or the new VX, M16s.

They had not been able to secure any nuclear equipment but it didn't matter; it was not even necessary really. They had some tanks and other combat vehicles, explosives, rocket-launchers, aircraft . . . a whole lot which they would use at the opportune time.

They had not been easy to come by. But now King Arthur's stock was complete. Gawain had kept his part of the bargain, easily shelling out million after million for the purchasing to be done. The plan was running very smoothly. Soon, he would really be the master of all he surveyed.

For as long as long as he could remember, King Arthur had craved power. He had wanted to be the biggest and the best. As a child, he loved playing war games. He was always the leader, of course. Who was better suited? Details of the war were unimportant; as long as there was a war, and he was the leader, he was happy. As he grew older, the desire to be better became a burning ambition. Whether it was in small things like answering all the questions in class or telling the most jokes at the campfire, or important things like being elected class president by a landslide victory, he had to win. If there was anyone who could sing better, talk better, run faster, dress smarter or reach higher than anyone else, it had to be him.

Later, the desire to win became an obsession. It stopped mattering how he got to the top, as long as he got there. Winning became his one reason to live. He made more money than he could ever hope to spend in one lifetime and spent it lavishly. His desire to be at the top had got him where he was now and it would take him to the presidency, of a country. To rule a country, especially one full of such unexplored potential like Kenya was really the pinnacle of success. From there, who knew where he would go? With a little work, he might even be able to become a supreme being.

He got into the beautiful Corniche and inserted the ignition key. The powerful engine came to life with a gentle purr. There could be nothing less for King Arthur. Why, the very idea was completely absurd; nothing but the best for the best he thought smiling to himself. No matter what people said about him nobody could take that away from him.

As he drove up to the huge iron gates; his car-phone rang. Picking it up, he slowed down and said, "Yes?"

"Mordred here," came a sharp voice. "I have just come from B.I.O. I need to talk to you about a few things there."

"Trouble?" King Arthur asked sharply.

"Nothing big," Mordred said. "In fact, nothing I can't handle. But I wanted your advice."

"Alright," King Arthur said. "I'm meeting Gawain for lunch at the Intercontinental Hotel. The usual table. Why don't you join us there?"

"I have got a few things to do here first," Mordred replied, "but I'll meet you there later, if that's alright with you."

"Fine, see you then." Mordred replaced his end of the phone.

King Arthur replaced his end rather more slowly, his eyes narrowing slightly. There could be no snags in their little operation now. They had come too far for anything to stop them, or get in their way. That unfortunate, in his opinion, totally unnecessary massacre which had occurred the night before would have to be 'cleaned up'. Anyone connected with it on B.I.O.'s side had to be eliminated. There could be no leaks; he would talk to Mordred about it.

Of course one had to make sure, that there was nothing the dead B.I.O. agents could have possibly known. The Otieno brothers did not have a chance to see Mordred and Lancelot or hear them. It was unlikely that they had known anything significant. However, there had been no sense in leaving them alive and running a risk of them knowing something, however small. He had agreed with Mordred's suggestion that they be eliminated, especially after they decide to back out of the deal. Simple lack of imagination had resulted in the massacre since the hit-man should have made sure that both of them were dead before leaving. He didn't, and the brothers went to B.I.O., meaning they must have had something to say. Whatever it was, they couldn't be allowed to spread it, so Mordred's decision was justified. With that he had to agree, although reluctantly. Now Mordred had to tie up loose ends it had created make sure that everything was still alright. Nothing would be allowed to get out of controi.

* * * * *

Half an hour later was talking about the same incident with Gawain at the Intercontinental Hotel.

"Oh he did the right thing alright," Gawain was saying stoutly. "Same as I would have done if I was in his place. Same as you would have too, I reckon."

"Yes, I realise that it was the only thing to do and I'm grateful that he acted so fast where I might have dithered . . .," King Arthur said.

"Then stop worrying," Gawain said. "Ain't no use crying' over spilt milk as my mama says and my mama is always right."

"I don't doubt it," King Arthur said smoothly. "I don't mean to criticise him but I just have a bad feeling about it. Killing several B.I.O. agents like that . . . . especially a man like Jackson Mwatata. B.I.O. won't let it go easily I promise you. You don't know them like I do."

76

"Reckon I don't, but we've got our share of those over in the States," Gawain said calmly. "Some say that the C.I.A. and the F.B.I. are the sharpest people in the world. But the way we've got our little set-up here, I don't think even they, would be able to cotton on to it; simple yet complex. I shouldn't worry about B.I.O. if I were you. Mordred will take care of them."

"We'll know one way or the other in a few days," King Arthur said with a sigh. "They never take very long to act or react, if you prefer. They will be out for blood to avenge one of their own. They will tear this town apart looking for us."

"And they won't find us because we don't exist," Gawain said firmly. "We don't exactly publicise our activities, now do we? No one has heard of us. Not even your little B.I.O. friends. They won't know what to look for so they won't find it. No problem there."

"Yes, but it will be a nuisance having them sniffing about," King Arthur said. "We definitely don't need them going around asking questions. Not now when plans are going so well for us that we cannot put them on hold until things cool down.

"No, we've got to strike while the iron is hot," Gawain agree.

"So with B.I.O. agents on the rampage in all parts of the country it will be very difficult," King Arthur said "but we've got to take the risk."

"Life is one big risk buddy," Gawain said. "No matter what you do, you can't avoid risks. The trick is to take them as they come."

"Yes, there's no other way, is there?" King Arthur asked morosely. "I guess I just like things to be cut and dried, neat and precise, predictable. B.I.O. is concerned you can't predict anything. It makes me nervous."

"It's alright to be nervous" Gawain said amiably. "It's good for the old heart. Gets the adrenaline going real fast."

"Either that or it kills you," King Arthur said dryly. "Ah, here comes Mordred now."

Mordred strode up to the table and sat down. His smile was quite friendly, and his manner was relaxed, as he greeted King Arthur and Gawain. They both sat in silence as he ordered a drink for himself and a fresh round for them. They were used to him enough to know that there couldn't be anything all that wrong. When something went wrong it immediately showed in Mordred's manner. He was usually tense and edgy in those cases. However, whatever it was that he had to say to them at that moment couldn't be all that important, if his attitude was anything to go by.

"So," King Arthur said after a while. "What did you find out?"

"Our people at B.I.O. tell me that their boss; J. F. Kimani, is in a justifiable fit — with most of the top shots siding with him. They are screaming for revenge and are determined to get it. The team investigating the incident is to be finalised today. From what I have seen of the names so far, we have got nothing to worry about. Talented small fry. They won't be a problem."

"How many people have been assigned so far, and who is heading them?" King Arthur asked quickly.

"Tim Kuria is leading them," Mordred replied. "He has got about twenty good agents attached to him and several more attached to each agent. But I don't see a problem there. Most of the man power they are using is loyal to us."

"So where is the catch?" King Arthur asked wearily.

"Not a catch really," Mordred's eyes grew thoughtful. "Just something that doesn't add up."

"What is it?" Gawain asked interestedly.

"An agent called Juma," Mordred said. "Susan Juma. She is the new toast of B.I.O. at the moment. People say she is so good that they may even make her the head of B.I.O. one day."

"The head of B.I.O., a woman!" King Arthur said incredulously. "That would never happen. Never."

"Probably not," Mordred agreed. "But they do talk about her a lot. And from what I've heard — when the going gets tough, she is the one to watch out for."

"How good could she be?" Gawain asked with disdain. "A woman! I'll bet it's no problem watching her."

"The problem is that she's not on the team," Mordred said. "She is not included anywhere and this baffles everybody. After all, she is the best they got at the moment; so her name should have been automatically there."

"So why isn't it?" demanded King Arthur.

"She is not at B.I.O.," Mordred said. "She is on vacation, indefinitely, and that is very strange. She took the vacation this morning. It seems she just turned up at the office and informed them that she was going on leave and that she did not want to be included in the investigation team. It also seems that Jackson Mwatata was her best friend; her father figure if you like. They were very close. Yesterday she came back to the office just after I had wasted him, to look for him. I don't know why, maybe they had a date or something. Anyway, they say she went pretty hysterical when she found out that he was dead. She left and they didn't see her until this morning."

"Nothing strange there, really," King Arthur shrugged. "I never understood why B.I.O. had allowed such a crazy thing as women agents; very unreliable. They're always letting emotion get in the way. She probably can't cope with the fact that her beloved mentor is dead and so doesn't want anything to do with B.I.O. for a while."

"Yes nothing strange there," Mordred agreed. "However, she did turn up with someone today. She came to the office with one Christopher Mathenge."

"Chain!" King Arthur whispered hoarsely. It was no secret to him who the legendary Chain was.

"Yes; Chain," Mordred said deliberately, his face grim. "Coincidence? Or was she looking for reinforcement? We don't need Chain sniffing around right now especially with B.I.O. already on our tails. I think I'll run a check on Susan Juma,; just to be sure."

Chapter Eleven

It was 7.30 pm that Friday night, another King was pacing restlessly about his room. But in this case, 'King' happened to be his real name. He was King Musyoka, the younger son of Kenya's Vice-President, Janet Musyoka.

He always felt that the name was rather silly, but that was what his mother called him and that was the name he was known by. People always tended to keep themselves aloof when first meeting him because they believed that he deliberately called himself that as a result of some strange superiority complex. He had to work extra hard to prove himself free and friendly; that he was worthy of real friends. If he had any complex, it was over friendliness. He wanted everyone in the world to love him and couldn't bear to think that he wasn't liked.

King was pacing the room waiting for a phone call from a girl; a very, special girl. Her name was Alice Karauri, a fellow student at the University of Nairobi. King was studying law and Alice was taking a degree in education. She was driving him crazy because she had refused to acknowledge his existence for several weeks while he had pursued her relentlessly.

When she finally started going out with him, she refused to commit herself and insisted on going out with other guys. He was not used to having a girl refuse him anything; no other girl ever had. With his suave good looks, outgoing personality, limitless reserves of money and most of all; his name (or at least his mother's name), he had never had to do the running, until now. Alice did not like casanovas (was he really a casanova?); did not like people with limitless reserves of money, did not trust good looking guys, and in general, was frightened to death of him. She had accused him of being a user, and a shallow, insincere introvert. That last one really rankled. The last person who could be called an introvert was King. His major problem was that he talked too much!

Nevertheless he had persisted and today he was supposed to be taking her to a party. She had called earlier in the day and cancelled the date. He called her back and demanded to know why. After a long and heated argument she promised to call him at seven to let him know whether or not she could make it. Seven o'clock had come and gone. She was determined to make him suffer.

He wandered through the house until he found himself outside his mother's study. After a moment's hesitation, he knocked on the door.

"Come in," a female voice called out and King turned the handle and entered the room.

Janet Musyoka was a beautiful woman. Very small, very well-shaped, especially her face; exquisite. She had perfect features and a perfectly proportioned body. Her height was barely 5 foot 3 inches and everything about her was understated; tiny hands and feet. She resembled a perfectly groomed doll and was no threat to anybody.

Her husband had died ten years earlier and people had thought she would fall apart. She didn't look as if she could take care of herself, let alone support two growing boys: King and his older brother Martin. When she had given up her job as a magazine editor and entered politics, everyone thought she had gone stark, raving mad. When she couldn't cope with the advice, the incredulity and the recriminations any longer, she packed, took her sons and moved away.

Ten years later, at the age of forty-eight, she was Kenya's first woman Vice-President. She had got there through hard work, brains and sheer guts. The pretty little doll-woman had nerves of steel.

"Hi mom," King said, coming into the room.

"Hello darling," Janet said, pushing herself away from her desk. She stretched delicately and put down the pen she had been writing with. Then she looked at him in surprise. "What are you doing at home on a Friday night?"

He flung himself onto the couch next to her desk. "My date bounced me."

"Sorry?" she asked.

"Bounced," he said impatiently. "You know, decided she didn't want to go out after all, and didn't even have the decency to call me and tell me so in person." He sighed disgustedly.

Janet hid a smile. "A girl who has said 'no' to you?" she mocked gently. "Is this possible? When do I get to meet this 'Superwoman'?"

"Cut it out mom," King said.

"Why don't you just call her and find out what's going on?" his mom suggested.

"No way!" he exploded. "I've done enough chasing. She has to initiate the next move or it's all over. King Musyoka is not treated like this by any woman."

Janet's smile grew wider. "Poor baby," she soothed. "Never mind. There are lots of little fishes in the sea." He glowered and she laughed. "Where is Martin? I thought he said he would be home early tonight."

"Oh you know Martin," King said. "When he says early, he means anytime before midnight. What a workaholic! He is just like you."

Martin Musyoka worked for one of the firms in the city 'gaining practical experience' as he put it before going to Harvard University in the United States of America to get his Masters degree in business administration. He really enjoyed his work and usually stayed at the office until quite late at night. Nobody worked as hard as Martin; maybe his mother.

"You, on the other hand, never work at all," Janet retorted, not able to keep a stern face. "How you ever manage to pass your exams I'll never know."

"I'm a natural genius," her son said with a grin.

"You are a natural clown, that's what you are," she retorted again, not managing to break his bubble.

"Mom," King called, "do you think I'm an introvert?"

"Darling, if you are an introvert then Hilter was a Saint!" Janet said as she laughed. She sobered up as she saw his serious face. "Seriously though, I think you're a bit of both; a hardcore introvert followed by layers and layers of determined extrovertism." She looked at his mutinious face and added, "That doesn't make you any less likeable, darling. You are a very nice person and I'm sure anybody with half a brain will notice that."

"She has got more than half a brain." King said heatedly.

Janet laughed. "Of course she does," she said soothingly. The phone suddenly shrilled through the house. "See? There she is now."

King tossed an agonised look at his mother before running out of the room to answer the phone in the hall.

As Janet was settling down to her work again there was another knock on the door; Martin this time.

"Hello Martin," she said. "Very early today, aren't you? It's not even eight yet."

Both her sons were always estatic when the weekend came. Martin, because he had two whole days alone in the office which he could work solidly through and King because it meant sleeping all day and partying all night.

"I couldn't stand the sight of another business document," Martin said with uncharacteristic emotion. He flung himself on the couch his brother and just vacated with equal aplomb though perhaps not with as much enthusiasm.

Janet looked surprised at his disclosure because Martin was married to business documents. They were his one passion. Since when did he start hating them? Her face cleared in rueful understanding.

"Burn-out," she said with some satisfaction. "It was bound to happen sooner or later. You have been working too hard. You need a break. Tell you what, it's still early. Why don't we both put away our briefcases for the night and go and watch a movie? It's been ages since I last went to the cinema. What do you say to that?"

"Sounds good to me," Martin said with a big sigh. "But what they will say when they see the Vice-President entering the cinema-hall, I'll never know. Still, it might be rather interesting." he added brightening up considerably. "Just let me run up and change out of these clothes."

"Fine," Janet said as she started putting away her files. King came running back into the room. "Hey mom, Martin is home," he called out, "and you were right. It really was Alice on the phone. She couldn't call earlier because of a few problems at home. I'm going to pick her up now."

"That's nice," his mother said. "And yes, I know Martin is home, we are going to watch a movie together."

"Martin is going to watch a movie?" asked King incredulously.

"Wonders never cease," Janet agreed dryly. "I thought we would just take the Jaguar and pop in informally, hoping we won't be recognised."

"No way," King said firmly. "You take the limousine and some security men; this is a crazy city. I don't want anything to happen to you."

"Nothing will happen . . ." Janet began.

"Well let's just make sure okay?" King countered. "I'm taking my Alpha Romeo and I probably won't be home till late, or early if you want to look at it from a different point of view. See you later, have fun!" And with that he was gone.

Janet leaned back in her chair and contemplated the ceiling. She had come a long way from the shy, frightened eighteen-year-old who had married Kenya Airways pilot Gibson Musyoka some thirty years ago.

* * * * *

She was born in one of the filthy shanty villages on the outskirts of Nairobi. Her mother had no idea who her father was; it could have been one of several men who were her customers. Janet's mother was a prostitute.

Being a call-girl, however, did not mean that she didn't possess any brains at all. She had cornered one of the wealthiest of her regular customers and convinced him that the child was his. He was a political figure of some importance at the time and couldn't afford the risk of scandal. As docile as a lamp, he had paid out huge amounts of money as child support year after year. Janet went to the best of schools and her mother managed to rent a hair-dresser and set about planning her daughter's future. Janet dressed like the daughters of the very rich women who frequented the salon. She talked like them and acted like them. Her mother sheltered her fiercely from any outside influence and as a result, Janet grew up with no real confidence in herself; no independence. She was a shy, retiring, introverted person who was unable to talk openly with anybody, until she met Gibson.

Captain Gibson Musyoka had come into her life the day she had gone to get her 'A' level results from the school. She had done well but not well enough to get into the university. She had gone into the park near the city centre, sat down on a bench and started crying. She knew that her mother would not be pleased that she had failed to get into university and was scared to go home and face her. Captain Musyoka had been sitting on another bench watching the beautiful girl with the wide, innocent eyes, crying her heart out until he could not stand it any longer. Her ethereal beauty haunted him, and her racking sobs tore at his heart. Almost of their own accord, his legs carried him to her bench.

At first she ignored him and resisted all his attempts to know her and to find out what the matter was. But he doggedly continued until she softened and told him everything. He persuaded her to go to lunch with him, then to a movie, then for coffee and finally, dancing. He swept her world completely upside down and she didn't know how to say no. By the time he took her home to meet her mother she was deliriously happy; in a dream.

Her mother was predictably furious but her recriminations and sarcasm had no effect on Janet. She was in a dream-world where no one could reach her and after a while; her mother stopped trying. But Gibson was never very far from their door and after a whirling romance, he asked her to marry him. Janet did not need much convincing to say yes.

There had been so much laughter after that. Nothing was ever too hard as long as they were together. Gibson had made life seem so good; so necessary. He had a gift for living so rare to find in most people.

Four years after their marriage, their happiness was complete in the birth of their first born son, Martin Rogers Musyoka. This new being that they had helped to bring into the world was so beautiful, so clever, so marvellous. And Martin was an unusually clever boy. He always strove to do better much faster than anyone else. From the moment he took his first tiny step (or rather his first five steps then a little stumble, he was walking confidently and had never looked back since then), it was obvious that he had ambition.

Kingsley Simon Musyoka was born five years after his older brother. Janet had gone to college in the United States and had got a degree in literature. She had started a small women's magazine on her return home. Gibson had left Kenya Airways and started a highly successful charter business. From being comfortably well-off, they had become very rich. But this hadn't changed their view of life.

Janet had given King his name because she wanted a baby to love. Martin had never had much use for hugs and kisses. He was too busy trying to change the world. King was a very amiable child. The more love lavished on him the more he seemed to blossom. Janet had been in her element – delighting in her new role of mother as opposed to her former one of female encyclopaedia. Her happiness, which she had thought to be overflowing already, increased by another drop.

Of course it was too good to last. It was bound to end sooner or later, probably sooner. The only thing Janet could be grateful for was that she had had two decades with him. Twenty great years of sunshine and love and unparalleled happiness. And then, one rainy night, it had all ended with a violent plane crash over Lake Victoria on the western border when Gibson was on his way back from neighbouring Uganda. They had said that it was quick; that he never felt a thing and Janet was grateful for that.

After that she had wanted to emerse herself completely in something, in order to leave a mark; something worthwhile. She had chosen politics as it was very interesting, and she genuinely felt that she might be able to make Kenya a better place to live in. Martin's plans to change the world were infectious. With more drive in her than she had ever believed possible, she had succeeded beyond her wildest dreams. She had shut her critics up once and for all and had justified the faith of those who believed in her. Most of all, she had made her mother proud.

Martin came back into the room and touched her shoulders gently.

"Mother," he said anxiously. "Are you alright?"

She snapped back to the present. "Martin," she said, "whoever said 'what is in a name, a rose by any other name would smell as sweet' was wrong, you know. Margaret Thatcher would not have been Prime Minister if her name was Jane Smith. Let's go, darling."

Chapter Twelve

Susan looked at Chain over her coffee cup. He had not said anything for the last ten minutes or so and he didn't look like he was going to say anything in the near future. They had just finished listening to the tapes again at his request, but didn't seem satisfied with what he had heard. They had listened to the tapes three times in the past two hours but he still hadn't got what he was looking for.

It was 8.00 am Saturday morning; and Susan had barely had two hours of sleep the previous night; Chain had had none at all. They had gone through the videotape of the fund-raising time and time again, and had gone on to reading schedules obtained for them by Babs and a colleague of hers at the Kenya Broadcasting Corporation. Susan had fallen asleep at 4.00 am only to be awakened at 6.00 am by Chain who wanted to listen to the tapes again. So they listened again, and again, and again. Susan didn't even know what it was they were supposed to be looking for.

"Do you have any brothers or sisters?" Chain asked unexpectedly.

"No," she said, startled. "I'm and only child." She wanted to ask him what that had to do with it but decided not to. She had no idea how his mind worked and she was often left wondering what tack his mind was taking. Now was one of those times.

"Any boy friend, fiance?" he continued absently.

"No," she said, mystified.

"Why not?" he asked sharply. "Are you afraid of men? Or are you waiting for Mr. Right? He doesn't exist, you know, he is a figment of every young woman's imagination. Or maybe that's not it either. Maybe you were so involved with Jack that having a boy friend would have seemed unfaithful. Let me tell you lad Jack didn't need that kind of ego trip."

"What are you talking about?" Susan cried totally bewildered. He was making even less sense now.

"Sorry," Chain said, looking down. "I'm being stupid," then he looked back up at her again. "But you didn't answer my question.

"There has never been anyone that special," she said. "But what did you mean, 'Jackson didn't need an ego trip'? What ego trip?"

"Why hasn't there ever been anyone all that special?" Chain parried. "Are your standards that high?"

"No," Susan protested. "They aren't that high. There hasn't been anyone special because I'm looking for 'that something extra'. What ego trip?"

"What 'something extra'?" Chain asked.

"What ego trip?" Susan insisted.

"Leave it, Susie," Chain muttered.

Susan looked at him pensively; too afraid to go on. She debated whether or not to pursue the subject for a while. "That 'something extra' is whatever will attract me to someone against my better judgement. That will make me feel happy; delirious; safe. Do you understand?" She sighed and continued quietly.

"What ego trip, Chain?"

"I'm sorry, that wasn't meant to come out. It shouldn't have," Chain sighed in turn. "I guess maybe there is something you should know. Another reason I didn't want to meet you was plain, old-fashioned jealousy."

"Jealousy?" echoed Susan. The whole conversation was getting more bizarre by the minute.

"Yes, stupid isn't it?" Chain asked. "I used to sit and listen to Jack extolling your virtues all night, almost every time we met. I have very few friends and I am very possessive about those few. I tend to want them all to myself. I was supposed to be Jack's golden boy; the best agent there ever was or that ever walked the halls of B.I.O. Actually I was, until you came on the scene. Then it was Susan this, Susan that."

"He used to talk about me that much?" Susan queried, her face glowing with pleasure.

Chain looked at her. "Constantly," he said. "At least, at the beginning. He wouldn't stop going on about you all the time. He kept telling me how clever you were; how dedicated. I thought, at the time, that it was a small dig at me and I was angry. One thing I didn't want to hear was how well B.I.O. was functioning without me; how they had easily found a replacement, another super-agent. What galled me most was the fact that this super-agent was a woman. I kept waiting for you to slip up, but you never did and that just annoyed me more. I refused to meet you although I knew that Jack was very disappointed but I didn't care. I was feeling very spiteful. I told myself that Jack was blind where you were concerned; that he ignored your faults because you're a woman. In fact there was a time when I was convinced that he had fallen in love with you and that you were probably using him to further your career."

Susan took in a deep breath but continued her silent perusal of Chain's features.

"Not very pretty, is it?" Chain asked grimly. "It gets worse. I got upset one evening and challenged him with my accusations. I told him that he was an old fool to let a young girl fool him like that and that he was bound to get hurt," Chain sighed. "He was blazingly angry. He said that not only was I doing him a terrible injustice, but that I was insulting someone I had never met; someone whom I didn't know. He said that he couldn't believe I was talking to him as if he was senile, but the thing that annoyed him most was that I had dared make a character slur on the formidable Susan Juma," he said and smiled humourlessly. "We never talked about you again."

"How strange," Susan commented.

"Isn't it?" returned Chain rather dryly.

"No, not your story," Susan explained, "but the coincidence. You see, I was insanely jealous of you. Crazy, isn't it? You are such an impossible act to follow. If ever there was anyone who ran further, thought faster, investigated better, laughed louder or simply was much cleverer than anyone else, it was the one and only Chain; the legend. Did Jackson tell you that I inherited your office? People always commented on how different I was from you, 'Chain never used to . . ., Chain always . . ., why don't you do it like Chain?" It used to drive me mad. And Jackson never made it any better you know. Every time I came back from an assignment he would criticise all my efforts extensively and give me a blow by blow account of how you would have handled the same situation."

Chain grinned. "I suppose that must have rankled," he said.

"Oh, it did," she agreed. "It did indeed."

"What did you do?" he asked curiously.

"What did I say, you mean," she chuckled. "Or rather, what didn't I say? I said a lot. I screamed a lot and upset him. We upset each other as a matter of fact." She stood up as he started laughing and moved over to the living room.

"I'm glad you think it's funny," she muttered.

"What did you do then?" Chain asked, a huge grin still on his face.

"We agreed, by mutual consent, never to mention your name unless in extreme circumstances," Susan replied.

He started laughing again and she turned around to glare at him in mock anger just before she reached the couch in the living room.

"So you got upset, eh?" he asked. "Why? Didn't you think the great Chain was better than even you?" She shook her head.

"No?" he growled. "You shall regret this!" His hands shot out to her waist where his long, slim fingers started tickling her.

"Stop!" she shrieked, convulsed in laughter. She collapsed onto the couch behind her wriggling uncontrollably and shaking in a convulsion of giggles. Tears of mirth streamed from her eyes as she weakly begged for mercy. Chain stopped tickling and sat down on the couch next to her.

"I didn't know you were ticklish," he said.

"I'm not ticklish," she gasped. "I promise you I'm not. Don't," she groaned as his hands, went back to her waist.

"Don't what?" he asked, his voice sounding very close. Reluctantly she opened her eyes and met his quizzical gaze, only inches from her. She drew a shuddering breath and closed her eyes again.

"Don't tickle," she whispered.

"I won't," he assured her. Her eyes flew open again at the sound of his voice. His eyes were gleaming, his hands exploring the curve of her waist. As she made a small protesting noise, he lowered his mouth to hers and captured her lips in a stunning kiss.

His kiss was unexpectedly gentle as his lips moved on hers softly at first, exploring the outline of her mouth with an intimate tenderness. He slackened his hand which was still exploring the curve of her waist and pulled her fully into his arms. His hold on her then became more possessive; more passionate, as his kiss deepened and tried to force her lips to part for him. She stiffened and moved protestingly beneath him. His lips slanted across hers and he murmured incoherent words of encouragement which made her mind swim and her lips part helplessly. The sensation was incredible. She felt as if she was falling, slowly into a deep, dark, bottomless abyss from which there was no escape.

After a few seconds it was over. Chain raised his head and focused his dream-drugged eyes on her uncomprehending ones. He seemed to be as bemused as she was. Her lips still throbbing from his kiss, she pushed at him half-heartedly. Reluctantly he moved away, allowing her to sit up but his eyes never moved from her face. As if mesmerised, she raised her fingers to her lips. His eyes followed the motion hungrily, and then sighed and looked away.

"Sorry," he muttered.

"What for?" she said lightly, trying to appear amused and casual. "It was just a kiss."

"Yeah, well," he cleared his throat gruffly. "It won't happen again."

She echoed his sigh; trying to get her thoughts in order. "Why were we listening to the tapes again? You never did tell me."

"I was trying to determine whether or not we could tell whose voice it was on the tape simply by listening," he explained. "But we can't. It could be anybody's voice on that tape. The accent doesn't help either."

"I could have told you that," Susan sighed.

"Yeah, you probably could have," Chain acknowledged. "But I still wanted to confirm it for myself. Now I'm sure."

"Okay, now what?" Susan asked. "Where do we go from here?"

She immediately wished that she had kept her mouth shut as the import of what she had said sunk in. It was filled with innuendo. Chain regarded her thoughtfully for a while.

"While you were catching up your beauty sleep, I was doing a little thinking," he said.

"Oh, you do?" she asked, quirking a smile.

"Do what?" he asked, puzzled.

"Think," she said innocently.

After a moment of reflection he decided to ignore the comment. "Very funny," was all he said. "As I was saying; I came up with a solution to our small problem."

"Then I would very much like to hear it," Susan said, "if you would care to share it."

The look he gave her was hard. "We can start a few rumours," he said.

"How will that help?" asked Susan curiously.

"Well, what do we have?" Chain asked. "We have five top-most B.I.O. officials suspect. One of them is definitely guilty. How do we separate them? That is the question." He paused for a minute. "Suppose we let it be known that someone is threatening ministers in the country and we know who it is? We tell each of the five privately, and make sure he doesn't tell the others."

"How will we do that?" Susan asked.

"Simple," Chain said and smiled. "We tell them that one of the others is in on the plot and we don't know which one. We'll make it convincing so that they will be scared to go to talk to each other. It should get them thinking, and we shall know by their reactions who the culprit is."

"I must be very slow today," Susan said as she shook her head. "Or maybe we're not speaking the same language. Please tell me how we are going to know their reactions?"

Chain sighed. "Okay, I'll spell it out," he said. "How is this for a scenario? You call Mr. X and tell him that you know who is killing all the ministers but to keep his mouth shut and not to tell the others that you know because one of them is in on it. Unknown to you, Mr. X just

92

happens to be the man you are looking for. He panics thinking that it is just a matter time before the whole game is up. Naturally, he won't discuss it with his colleagues because he considers them a threat. Thanking his lucky stars that you came to him instead of one of them, he rushes to the telephone to set up a meeting with his Arthurian friends. Once there he tells all, especially the fact that you had refused to give him any more information over the phone and instead set up a meeting in a mildly populated area of town. What do our friends do? They tell him to go of course. And send their own hit-men there to cover him. Their intention is to kill you as soon as you turn up. But on the other hand our own people are on the spot. They see the hit-men getting into position and relay the information back to us. The rest is up to us." Chain came to the end of his monologue, and turned triumphantly to look at Susan.

She whistled through her teeth in amazement. "That's pretty impressive," she said in awe. He nodded; pleased.

"Of course, it still has some rough edges," he added, quickly.

"Yeah, I know," she agreed.

"But we don't have the time to polish them off. We have to start right away," he said.

"Let's get it right first," said Susan. "We'll telephone each of the five, right?" Chain nodded. "Give them each the same story I presume, and different places, of course. I think we should also give them different times." Chain nodded again. "Well then, there is no time like the present. Let's start right away." She stood up, and walked towards the phone.

"Hold it," Chain said. "We don't know how long it will take whoever it is to act. We are going to have our own people already in place before we call."

"Oh yeah," Susan said, crestfallen. "Do we have enough people to go around?"

"Around two people, strategically positioned, with long range rifles should be enough," Chain said. "Two for each spot; that's ten. I have enough loyal people to do the job with no questions asked. You had better start picking the spots while I get on the phone and rally up some support."

They both turned towards the phone; Chain to dial numbers and Susan to use the note-pad to write down the places she was deciding on.

"This is a plan that cannot fail," Chain said, rolling his eyes comically. "Trust me."

Chapter Thirteen

Timothy Kamau Kuria tried gulping down the cup of coffee on the kitchen table. It burnt his tongue, his mouth and his throat on its way down. He was late, but that was not unusual. He was usually late for everything. A bad habit; but a habit nevertheless and therefore hard to break.

He was supposed to be meeting a friend at the Nairobi Club for a game of squash at 9.30 that morning. It was already a few minutes past nine. He had been meeting the same friend at the same time at the same place for the same purpose every Saturday morning for the last ten years, and he had been late always. However, that didn't stop him from trying. It didn't stop his friend from coming on time for the past ten years either.

His wife, Martha, came down into the kitchen. She hadn't properly woken up yet and was still in her dressing gown.

"You're late again," she yawned, looking at the kitchen clock. She stood on tip-toe and gave him a perfunctory kiss on the cheek.

"As always," he admitted wryly. Martha yawned again and picked up the coffee-pot. She poured herself a cup and sat down. She gulped the coffee easily although it was scaldingly hot.

"How come you never manage to be on time?" she queried. "You wake up early enough."

"I don't know. Something always comes up," he said. "Like this morning, I was finishing some briefs so that I don't have to do them when I get back. I guess I just lost track of the time."

"You do that a lot," his wife agreed.

"What are you planning to do today, Martha? Anything special?" he asked.

"Nothing special, really. Just a little shopping, then I'm taking Connie to the dentist," she said. Six-year-old Connie was their last-born, the only daughter in a family of three. Their first-born Eric, was seventeen and their second-born, Mark, was twelve. Timothy believed in planning his family.

"I was thinking that maybe we could buy lunch out today," he suggested. "We could go to a restaurant or have a picnic in the park or something. It will be a good change for all of us. We can then catch an afternoon show for the kids after lunch. What do you think of that?"

"Sounds good to me," Martha said happily. A family outing was a very rare occurrence. "I'll tell the kids."

Tim set his cup in the sink and picked up his sports bag. He said goodbye and kissed Martha's forehead on his way out. As he passed the hallway, the telephone rang. With an exasperated sigh, he picked it up.

"Yes," he said impatiently.

"Timothy," came a voice, "it's Susan Juma".

Five minutes later Timothy put the phone back down. For the first time in ten years, he was going to miss his squash game.

* * * * *

Patrick James Ondieki lay back on his bed and sighed. Where had all the years gone? It seemed like only yesterday when he was washing cars and dreaming of a better life. Where had the teenager with dreams and ideals disappeared to?

He turned his head to look at his wife. Lindsay Ondieki had class. She was over forty, and still the most beautiful woman he had ever known. She was from a rich, privileged family and it showed. But she left him cold and dissatisfied.

He sighed again and turned to look at the ceiling. What was the use of thinking such morbid thoughts especially on a bright and lovely Saturday morning when one did not need to make an appearance at that nut-house they called B.I.O.? B.I.O. was another thing that had not lived up to his expectations.

Being the illegitimate son of a shoeshiner was definitely nothing to brag about, but Patrick had had plans; big plans. Of course none of them included B.I.O. at the time. He had had no idea that such an organisation even existed. He had more or less forced himself through school, getting an education against all odds. When the offer to work for the Criminal Investigation Department had come, he had been hesitant to take it. But then he reasoned that the work would probably be interesting and the pay good. Then he found himself working for B.I.O.

He had been a good agent, if he said so himself. Maybe not as good as some of the others but good nevertheless. He had a reputation of being a good detective with an uncanny ability of feretting out secrets from the most stubborn and most unsuspecting of souls. It was no surprise therefore that he had risen in the ranks to the highest echelons of the organisation. He was convinced that he had a good chance of taking over from J. F. Kimani once the old man retired. Not that Kimani showed any signs of retiring or anything like that in the near future, Patrick acknowledged grimly.

He had had a good life and although most of it had been spent climbing and clawing it had been worth it. In fact the reason for his present dissatisfaction was probably that there were no more mountains to climb, no more bridges to cross or obstacles to conquer. For the first time in his life he had everything he wanted: a beautiful house, a beautiful wife, a beautiful rose garden to look at in the bark yard . . . He bought a farm in the countryside, and had sent his two sons to the most expensive schools in the country. He had more money that he would need in his lifetime yet there was nothing else left to do.

With a frustrated sigh he hit his pillow. Just one more challenge; 'would that be too much to ask?' One more then he would lie back and enjoy life. Just then his telephone rang and reached over to pick it up.

* * * * *

Isaac Aaron Peters reached the end of his olympic-size pool, touched the wall, did a perfect tumble and knifed through the water in the opposite direction. It was his seventh lap that morning, almost halfway through his daily fifteen laps. He cut through the water easily with his powerful stroke, his muscles rippling and his face occasionally turning upwards for air.

He was the picture of health. His skin glowed in the morning sun, long since tanned to a deep bronze colour by days of relentless physical fitness under the scorching heat of the African sun. His blue eyes were sharp, alert. His blond hair, streaked with silver at the temples, clung wetly to his head. There was no sign of weariness or fatigue as he turned again and continued the long journey back.

Kenya had been good to him, he acknowledged. In fact, there was no other place in the world he could consider home, even though he was not a native by birth. His birth place was London, a whole different world away; one that he had never regretted leaving. He had come to Kenya at the age of eighteen, running away from poverty, misery and the instability of life in the slums of the suburbs of London. He had heard of B.I.O. through his room-mate, who had been asked to join and had refused. Isaac resolutely dug out a B.I.O. recruiter and more or less invited himself to join. He had never looked back since.

Isaac Peters had a flair for solving mysteries. It was an ingrained talent that could never be learnt or acquired. It was simply born in some people and he was one of them. Apart from that he was also a fitness freak. Apart from the olympic-size swimming pool, his large estate had tennis courts, squash courts and badminton courts. All these were fully utilised. Isaac did not believe in letting things go to waste. They wouldn't have been put there if they weren't essential.

He finished his tenth lap and started on his eleventh. Swimming was by far one of his favourite recreations. After his fifteen laps he planned to go on an incredible five-mile jog, something he could easily indulge in on weekends. As he completed his eleventh lap, he saw his wife Betty coming from the house, her long hair blowing gently in the morning breeze. She was a native, a gentle Kikuyu girl he had met shortly after his arrival in the country. He had married her on impulse and had never regretted it. Sixteen years down the line he still thanked his lucky stars that he had her.

"Darling," she called from the edge of the pool. "There is a phone call for you. Someone called Susan Juma. She says it's urgent."

Isaac never did complete his fifteen laps.

* * * * *

Jason Francis Kimani sat at the head of the dining table and surveyed his family. His eldest daughter Janet, was twenty-three. She was at home that morning because she was on a one month leave from work. Janet worked as an air-hostess for Pan-Am: she was exceptionally beautiful. Kimani was proud of her and in his opinion she was almost as beautiful as her mom.

"Pass the sugar please, darling," he said, turning to his wife, Maureen. She passed on the sugar dish with a tender smile on her face. Maureen Kimani, after twenty-five years of marriage, was still besotted with her husband and didn't bother hiding, that fact.

He turned to study his three sons, who were attacking their food as if it was going out of fashion and he smiled indulgently. If there was one difference between boys and girls it was in their eating habits. Girls had to be forced to eat and boys had to be forcibly restrained from eating one out of home.

"How is school coming along, Ken?" Kimani asked his eldest son. Ken and Rick were twins, but Ken was the elder by two minutes. Kimani watched impassively while they both described animatedly how well school was going and how much they were enjoying it. They were both sitting for their 'O' level exams at the end of the year, and had decided that they wanted to study architecture at the university. They were both very clever boys and excellent students.

When they finally finished recounting their adventures, Kimani turned to Ian his last-born, and asked him the same question. Ian was thirteen and in his first year at high school, but everyone knew that he was destined for greatness. A quiet, even-tempered, self-composed boy he tended to talk little and gave away very little of himself. Kimani fondly liked to imagine that Ian took after him.

"What about you, princess?" he asked his other daughter, Stella. "Managing to get any reading done?" Stella pulled a face at him. At fifteen she was already showing signs of being as beautiful as her mother and her sister. She was very good at creative art and fashion design. Her father was already making tentative plans to get her into a good college in the United States where she would be able to exploit her talent to the maximum. He was convinced that she would be a world-famous fashion designer one day.

He turned back to his breakfast, idly pushing his scrambled eggs back and forth on his plate as Stella talked. He was wondering about Susan Juma. She had come to B.I.O. with a very impressive work-sheet and high recommendations from all her superiors. She had been Mwatata's protege and he had been very proud of her. Everyone was convinced that she was going to be another Chain. But, after her first real crisis, she had fallen to pieces. Puzzling, but then, not really unexpected of a woman.

His head came up as the phone rang.

* * * * *

It's tough but it's life. Matthew Mucheru sighed contentedly and leaned back in his rocking chair on his front porch. He was one who was very aware exactly how tough life was. Mucheru had brought new meaning to the words, 'When the going gets tough the tough get going'. The going had been really tough for Mucheru several times, but he was still going.

He sighed again as he thought back to the toughest time of his life. It was when he had been a first class negotiator for B.I.O., in what he considered his 'younger days'. He had had a clean track record with absolutely no failures whatsoever. Whenever there was a tough case to crack; B.I.O. called Mucheru; he was the best. The case he remembered most vividly was that of a young girl called Rose. At sixteen, Rose was the most promising young gymnast in the country and was poised for stardom. She had been kidnapped just before leaving for a big gymnastics meeting in Japan. Mucheru had been called in to negotiate terms for her release.

Everything had been going on quite well. The terms had been agreed upon and Mucheru had been persuaded to accompany the girl's parents when they delivered the ransom. Normally, in cases like Rose's, the ransom was dropped, the victim collected and then the kidnappers were hunted down and eliminated by B.I.O. agents. It was all very routine. Mucheru had been through it many times before and he spent quite a lot of time talking to the girl's parents and reassuring them that everything was going to be alright.

100

This time however, things went a little differently. Mucheru and the girl's parents arrived at the designated clearing with the bag of money. As agreed, he advanced to the centre of the clearing and left the money there. Then he moved back slowly until he came to the edge again. Then one of the men came out, leading Rose by the hand. He took her to the centre of the clearing and made her wait while he counted the money. After this he nodded to her and told her to walk towards her parents while he backed away with the money.

Nobody except Mucheru saw the kidnapper swing a hand grenade and release it towards Rose. All eyes were trained on her as she stumbled happily towards her parents.

Mucheru vividly remembered screaming in horror and running towards her, but he was too far off to reach her in time. Terrified he watched the grenade sail through the air and then land right at the girl's feet, exploding immediately. She was thrown into the air, dying instantly before the disbelieving gaze of her parents.

Mucheru had resigned from B.I.O. and it had taken them two years to convince him to go back. Two long years for the wounds to heal and the nightmares to end.

He was married now and he led a good, quiet life. He had two children, a son and a daughter whom he adored. He lived in a big house in the suburbs. As Mucheru sat immersed in deep thought, his son came running out of the house, "Daddy," he shouted, "You have a phone call, from someone called Susan Juma. She says it's urgent."

Chapter Fourteen

Walking down the city streets on a Saturday morning may convince an outsider that the world was coming to an end the following day. The atmosphere is frantic, and the rows and rows of people walk quickly and endlessly, scurrying here and there desperately searching. The question is, what are they searching for? A general cross-section of the masses, can easily put them into three groups; the shoppers, the workers and the pleasure seekers.

The shoppers are those people who do their weekly shopping from supermarkets in town on Saturdays. They consist of middle-aged housewives who have planned the organisation of their homes down to the last spare second; working mothers who are desperately trying to hold onto two careers, their jobs and their homes, and have no other time that they can possibly use for shopping, and boarding-school children, who come home every weekend to do some major shopping and then return to school. These people cram the shops in town, seriously testing to the limits the number of people the shops can hold.

If one was to follow one of the shoppers on her Saturday morning rounds it might finally be realised that women are no longer the weaker sex. One Saturday morning of serious shopping would be equivalent to running a marathon. Not to mention that after this, most of them go home to cook and care for their husbands and families. That frantic desperate search is a way of life for them. Never mind that all they're looking for is a particular brand of soap flakes for their washing and if that particular brand is not found, the world may very well come to an end.

The cashiers pound away at the cash registers, their faces feeling and growing more sullen and aloof as each customer pays thousands of shillings and walks away with a large shopping bag.

Kenya wasn't a very bad place to live despite the rapid inflation and the threat of imminent war in the Middle East. Perhaps the standard of living wasn't as high as it could have been and perhaps commodities were getting rather expensive, but Kenya had one great advantage over all other African countries of the time; it had peace. The government was stable to the point of being rather monotonous. The president was strong and quietly reassuring. The few petty squabbles that broke out among the ministers from time to time were never taken seriously and made interesting reading in the morning newspaper over breakfast. The country was tranquil and placidly calm despite the mad Saturday morning shoppers. Small and big businesses thrived and flourished, and the economy was stable. Kenya was a calm, welcome oasis of peace which was never touched by the nightmares surrounding it.

However, Lancelot planned to change that. Being good and righteous never paid off in this world. Only the strong survived, and Lancelot was strong.

Perhaps 'Lancelot' wasn't the correct name for him. After all, if the Arthurian legend was anything to go by, Sir Lancelot had been a gentleman and a gallant knight. The honourable minister was neither. He believed in himself alone, and he would never dirty a good coat by putting it on the ground for some idiot female to step on it. Not even if it was his mother! Lancelot was described as 'handsome,' something which the minister was definitely not. Nobody with bulgy, bull frog-like eyes and an incredibly fat nose sitting slightly off-centre on his face could possibly be called handsome. His head was big and bore a striking resemblance to the drawings of the '*Homo habilis*' man of old. He was short and nothing was in correct proportion. His feet were too big, his arms were too short, his hands gigantic, his torso unbelievably thick and his legs were incongruously thin. No; by no fantastic stretch of the imagination could one think of the minister as handsome. Not even if you compared him with a gorilla. The animal would come out the clear winner even if it had a bucket over its face.

No, God had not graced him with good looks, but Lancelot believed that his intelligence more than made up for this rather sad fact. He consoled himself with the thought that it was brains that got a person anywhere in the world, and in this department, he had been greatly over-compensated, perhaps to make up for his uninspiring looks. He had a very sharp mind which grasped details surprisingly easily for a person who had looks like he had. People who talked to him for the first time were always surprised by his intelligence and depth of understanding. He was also very shrewd and cunning and seemingly a step or two ahead of everyone else.

One thing Lancelot and his friends craved more than anything else in the world was power. In order to feel at peace with himself, it was necessary for him to order and to have his orders followed. 'The more people he had under his command, the more at peace he felt'. Power was like a drug in his blood; the more he tasted it, the more he wanted. If that power was obtained through acquisition of money and property, he would get it legally or illegally. If power could be obtained only through politics, then he would be a politician, whether or not the people liked him. But to have a whole country to oneself was the ultimate thrill, the ultimate power. That was what Lancelot wanted.

He started shuffling the papers on his desk. He was in his office in a modern high-rise building that housed his ministry. He always went to work on Saturday because there always seemed to be so much to do. He stood up and stared out of the window. Around fifteen storeys down, he could see people pounding the pavements, their movements quick and anxious.

Then his secretary knocked on the door. "Come in," he said without turning around.

"I have brought some letters for you to sign, sir," she began nervously. Her small voice petered off as Lancelot turned around and looked at her grimly. She lay the sheaf of papers on his desk.

Lancelot regarded the young woman standing before him critically. She was very young and beautiful. Beauty was a prerequisite when it came to being a high-ranking government secretary. That and a definite willingness to sleep with the boss.

"Where were you last night?" he asked quietly. She had not shown up for their weekly assignation at the usual place.

"Sorry sir," she said, "my sister was very sick when I got home last night. I had to rush her to the hospital and we stayed there for half the night. In fact, she was admitted. It's the truth," she added defiantly.

Lancelot raised his eyebrows. "Of course it is," he agreed calmly. "You wouldn't dare lie to me, would you? The consequences would be severe."

"Er . . . yes . . . I mean, no," babbled the poor girl helplessly.

"No what?" queried the Minister.

"I mean no, I wouldn't lie to you and yes, the consequences would be severe," she said firmly, getting herself together.

"Calm down, Jane," the Minister said with an amused smile. "I know you are not lying. I had you followed last night." He watched the expression of relief cross her face and then the small spurt of anger. Finally, she faced him impassively. "There will be other nights," he said dismissively. "Which letters are those that you want signed?"

"This stack over here," she said efficiently. She walked over to the desk and leafed through the papers one by one explaining to the Minister what exactly was to be done where. The Minister stood behind her and regarded her intently as she went through the process. As a secretary she was invaluable.

She had come to work at the ministry three years earlier, very young and full of ideals. Like every other young and naive person expects, she had thought that hard work and devotion were the only things necessary to ensure success where her career was concerned. Her friends learnt much faster than she did, and soon got promotions and higher salaries in return for their favours. She was passed over time and time again because of her unforthcoming attitude.

When she finally realised that the only way to get anywhere was to 'go with the flow' she had planned a strategy and set out to get the Minister. After all, why settle for anything less when one could reach the pinnacle? It wasn't long before Jane was the Minister's personal secretary; the highest-paid in the ministry.

"Will that be all, sir?" Jane had come to the end of her monologue.

Lancelot nodded thoughtfully. "For now, that will be enough," he said. Jane nodded and started to leave the room. As she reached the door, Lancelot called out to her and she turned back.

"Yes?" she asked politely.

"I'm sorry to hear about your sister," he said. "Tell her I wish her a very speedy recovery."

"Thank you, sir," Jane said, brightening up considerably. The Minister wasn't such a bad person when one got to know him better. One could even get over the fact that his head was shaped like an ape's.

As Jane left the room, Lancelot turned back to the window. The frantic, Saturday morning human traffic was still going strong. The gaily dressed people moved in confusing disarray amongst each other. Some carried huge parcels, making it hard for them to see others and so they were continually slamming and crashing into other people. They were obviously experts at it, though, because the perpetual stopping and starting again did not seem to bother them in the least bit.

* * * * *

Lancelot thought back to his childhood. His father had been some kind of a 'big noise' in the little village where he was born, and the family had been very well-off by village standards. Lancelot was his mother's only child, and his father's only son. His father had another wife who had bore him six daughters. Village custom decreed that girls could not inherit anything; therefore all of his father's wealth would go to him. This made his half-sisters extremely embittered, and as some might say justifiably embittered. They set out to make his life as miserable as possible and from the time he started walking, they managed to do just that. Even at that tender age, it was obvious that he was no thing of beauty and his sisters' taunts rang through his ears all through his life; the echoes never quite dying away.

Lancelot had never had any friends because he was withdrawn and constantly felt insecure. He had grown up believing that everybody in the world hated him, but that was something he could live with. His unfriendly attitude annoyed the village children who then declared him a snob who thought that his father's riches made him better than anybody else. They set out to show him differently, and his schooldays were filled with vicious fights and abuses. He stopped crying at a very early age because he found out that tears did not help him in the least. It was fists which did the talking. He learnt to use his fists to defend himself.

In the classroom, he soon found out that he was better than anyone else. Everything the teacher taught sounded very simple to him. When he found out that his classmates resented the fact that he was so clever, he redoubled his efforts and worked even harder. Soon he was the self-proclaimed genius of his class. His teacher was delighted with him and he was a joy to teach. His father was proud of him, and he even boasted about him. His mother was pleased with him because there was at last a good trait that could be attributed to him.

As the learning progressed he was made the class monitor. It was his first taste of power. He had never looked back since that time. He was in a position of authority then — and he let everyone know it. The children lived in mortal fear of him a fear that helped him control them. He learnt that the more frightened they were, the quicker and more willingly they would do things for him. The taunts ceased, and not even the bravest would allow himself to incur Lancelot's wrath. His presence was greeted with silence and for the first time in his life, he found peace. The feeling was so pleasurable that he never wanted to give it up. He worked harder than ever before to keep his place as the head of the class. Nothing and no one was allowed to stand in his way.

Lancelot had met King Arthur a few years previously. Together, piece by piece, they had set up the plan. Both of them wanted the same thing; power. They both agreed that there was really only one way to obtain that power.

Mordred had been, and still was, a major asset to the group. King Arthur had said that nothing would be possible without Mordred's brilliant and extraordinary skills. He had been right. Mordred was essential in all their plans and his greatest asset was his ability to kill cold-bloodedly. He derived no pleasure and felt absolutely no pain from taking a human life.

The others had drifted in one by one. They liked the idea, each for his own reasons, none of which bothered Lancelot in the least bit. The main thing was that they had all agreed to do it and it was proceeding well. All of the knights of the Round Table had a specific task, and as long as each one kept to his particular task the plan would continue as outlined and agreed upon by all the members.

'What could possibly go wrong now?'

The telephone in his office rang. It was his direct line; the confidential direct line. It was there in cases of extreme emergency and only one person had the number. His mouth went dry as he picked up the phone.

"Lancelot," he said.

"Come in at once," said King Arthur. "Something has gone wrong."

Chapter Fifteen

The Saturday morning workers were the second group of people cluttering up the Nairobi streets. People who came to work on Saturday were usually businessmen who were out to earn an extra shilling during the weekend. Therefore, those who worked for private businesses were unfortunately forced to go to work on Saturday as well.

Most of them were young men, in their mid-twenties. They had a feeling of self-importance, as they walked from this point to that and then back again. They sported charcoal-grey, navy-blue or russet-brown suits, and their ties were short and pencil-thin. They usually came in three shades: the dark conservative ones, the cheerful, pastel colours and the outrageously screaming ones. The ones in the last category ranged from luminous pink to bright orange with purple polka dots. They were supposedly making some kind of statement.

Bright coloured socks were also in vogue. Gone were the days of grey, blue, black or brown socks. Bright pink, bright green, bright purple, bright red . . . bright was right. And since these defiant colours were meant to be seen, the trousers were made shorter. Several trousers abruptly ended a few inches short of the ankles to afford the onlooker a better view of the magnificent socks underneath. Shoes came in all styles, but the most revered was the flat mocassin. There were many variations of it and it came in all sizes and colours. But it showed off the socks to the best advantage.

Apart from the cool, young executives, there were the messengers. These were in a hurry for a very good reason. After delivering their messages or doing whatever it was that they were sent to do, their time was their own. If they were allocated an hour in order to complete a specific task and they completed it in half that time; they had thirty minutes to spend in whichever way they considered best. This was an incentive to hurry.

The final group of Saturday morning workers was the door-to-door salesmen and advertisers. These people probably clocked a mileage of a hundred kilometres every twenty-four hours. They were seemingly tireless, walking from building to building, launching into scintillating accounts of their wonderful products. Brilliant smiles fixed firmly in place, they set out to conquer the masses. Determinedly they gave their speeches over and over. Slammed doors did not deter them; nor did turned-away faces discourage them in the slightest. They marched confidently from here to there, rarely having anything to show for it; rarely having a good day. They did it because they had no option, and they did it well because they had to do it well or starve. Hunger or the thought of hunger kept them going day after day. Saturday morning was their last working day of the week, so their smiles were slightly brighter, their step slightly lighter.

* * * * *

"Get your backside off that chair, man." The sleepy-eyed university student who was being thus addressed reluctantly stood up and moved away from the chair. He promptly fell onto a freshly-made bed in the room and regarded hi companion in temporary awe.

Galahad, as he was known to the Round Table, was busy clearing up the room and putting things away; no mean feat, considering the clutter involved. His room-mate was watching him in fascination due to the fact that both of them had been partying all night and had fallen exhausted into bed, only two hours before. The bemused student, whose name was Ken, was unable to comprehend exactly where his friend had got the energy to wake up at that hour and start digging into the mess that was their room.

"Hey bro," started Ken hesitatingly.

"Yeah?" said Galahad.

"What are you doing? No, let me rephrase that," Ken shook his head as if to clear it of cobwebs. "Why are you doing that?"

Galahad smiled and turned to his friend. "We have got to keep going, friend," he said, "laziness . . . inactivity . . . these are social evils. They invade a society corrupt. and corrode it. Drip, drip, drip like a leaking faucet. And then what happens? We live in filth and pestilence and get plagued by all that is bad in life. That is why we have to keep one step ahead of them always; running as fast as possible. Wake up friend and take hold of your life before it's too late!"

Ken looked even more astonished than ever. "You must have had more beers than I thought you did," he said. "You are not making much sense to me; not that you usually do, but today you sound as if talking Greek or Russian. And you are speaking still haven't answered my question. What's up?"

Galahad sighed. "Shiko is coming over in the afternoon." Shiko was his girl friend, the latest in a long line of many.

"That explains it," Ken said, relieved. "I honestly thought that you were losing your mind. Not that you have not already lost it. What time is she coming?"

"Oh, around two, I think. Maybe later. She is not good at keeping time," Galahad admitted wryly.

"What is with you and Shiko anyway?" Ken asked inquisitively. "She is not your type." Galahad's girls were usually tall, thin and dark. He usually looked for good legs, and prided himself as being a 'leg man'. His girls were usually hard and demanding and more after his pocket-book than anything else. But, as Galahad put it, they knew how to give a man a good time. They expected to be taken to the best discos, movie theatres and restaurants but they understood that they were expected to pay for it.

Shiko was the complete antithesis. She was short and very curvy, small hands, small legs, small everything. She was shy and rather innocent and to get her to do anything at all took some convincing. She was the type of girl that Galahad, or indeed most university students, wouldn't bother with at all. She didn't 'know the score' as it was so delicately put.

"Shiko has something I want," Galahad said, "and I'm going to get it."

"If it's what I think it is then you are not going to get it," Ken said. "She would rather die first than 'engage in premarital relations' as she so nicely puts it. She won't give it to you."

"That's where you are wrong bro," Galahad said. "She is going to sleep with me eventually. In the meantime, there's the thrill of the chase."

"And you are not going to catch anything," Ken declared. "Empty-handed. That's how you're going to be; empty-handed."

"You are wrong," Galahad insisted.

"Aw come on," Ken said, "you know the girl as well as I do; better even. You know she is not going to give it up. Not unless you marry her."

"Marry her!" snorted Galahad. "You must be crazy. I'm not about to marry her, or anyone. Why on earth would I tie myself down to one woman when there's a whole world of them out there just waiting to be conquered? Come off it, man."

"Well then, there is your answer," Ken said lazily.

"Listen pal, I'm going to have her," Galahad said. "I have never yet met a girl who could say no to me for long."

"You have met one now," Ken stated.

"Why should Shiko be any different?" Galahad asked. "With looks like that I will bet you anything that won't be the first. That innocent look is probably just a put on. I know girls like her. All women are out of attract attention. Girls like Shiko just use a different approach. She is just like the others."

"Alright," Ken said, "but what if she isn't 'just like the others'? Suppose all that innocence isn't just an act but it's all real? What then, casanova?"

"Highly unlikely, you know," Galahad stated. "But if that is true it shouldn't be too much of a hindrance. If she really is sweet and shy then that means that she has never really met her kind of guy. She needs someone to make up her mind for her. Someone who won't take no for an answer."

Ken looked at him sharply. "Hey bro, you wouldn't force her, would you?" he asked in a concerned tone.

"No way," Galahad said firmly. "No girl is worth that trouble." Ken let out a relieved sigh. "But I don't see why you are so worried. In a little while, you will see, she will be begging for it."

112

Ken lay back and grinned confidently.

"Alright, let us bet on it," Galahad said. "I'm willing to bet you money that within a month, that girl will be mine in every sense of the word."

"Serious?" Ken asked.

"I'm willing to put my money where my mouth is," Galahad said.

"Okay," said Ken. "I will give you up to the end of next month - the last day. If you do it by then I will give you cash, when I get some kind of evidence one way or another. If you don't manage to do it by then, you will have to give me cash. How much?"

"Two reds, five reds," Galahad said carelessly. "Whatever you want."

"Five hundred?" Ken asked with raised eyebrows. "No way. Let's really make it bite. Make it a significant sum of money. After all, you are betting on a sure thing, aren't you?" He grinned again. "I have the utmost faith in Shiko. Let's make it two grand," Ken said.

"Two thousand shillings?" Galahad asked sceptically.

"Real Kenya money," Ken affirmed.

"You realise you'll actually be paying me to perform a very enjoyable act? An act I perform on an average of twice a week?" Galahad asked.

"Yes, I realise that," Ken said. "But then I don't believe I'll have to pay you anything."

"It's a deal," Galahad said confidently.

"You will regret it, bro," Ken grinned again. He stood and stretched. "Let me get myself under the shower. We have got company coming." He picked up a towel and left the room singing something that sounded like, "Oh virtuous, virtuous Shiko'.

Galahad gritted his teeth and continued with his task. Like it or not, Shiko was going to have to capitulate now. There was his honour and two thousand shillings at stake; not just some task he had set himself. But Galahad was convinced that she would eventually say yes. After all, she was the sweet innocent type; the type that was very easily seduced.

* * * * *

Galahad's mother had been the sweet innocent type. His father had convinced her that he loved her; convinced her to run away from a comfortable home and a well-off family to live with him; convinced her to have five children, one after the other in quick succession, and then left her. He had found another sweet innocent young woman to seduce. He wasn't interested in Galahad's mother or 'her children' any more.

The shock of finding herself homeless, destitute and having to support five children on her own was just too much for her. She had always believed that one day she would get married to the charming man she had lived with and that he would take care of her forever. She just couldn't believe that he had been lying to her all that time; using her and cheating on her. All her illusions were shattered and she no other choice. She found a length of rope and hanged herself while the children slept. Galahad would never forget waking up one morning to find his mother swinging from a rope in the living room. Nobody had needed to tell him that she was dead.

The children were distributed among members of their mother's family. Galahad had wound up with an embittered aunt who was a spinster and had no idea how to bring up a child. She never stopped complaining about being dumped with a 'snotty-nosed' child whom she had no use for. and she never stopped telling Galahad that his mother had been a useless fool who didn't know any better than to fall in love with an equally useless, unfaithful, irresponsible, liar like his father. She had made it clear that Galahad's mother had been extremely stupid to listen to his father, and his father was solely responsible for killing her. She had also made it clear that with a stupid fool for a mother and a murderer for a father, Galahad was never going to amount to anything.

However one thing Galahad's aunt provided was a good education. She put him through the best schools and encouraged him to do the best he could. She had wanted him to become a lawyer or a doctor but Galahad had other ideas. In the last year of his secondary education, he had met King Arthur.

King Arthur's plan to take over the country appealed to Galahad. Kenya was a country that had seemingly infinite potential. The most

114

exciting of all were undiscovered oil reserves in the country needing a geologist. Galahad decided to take up engineering in the university and then take a masters course in geology in the state of Texas in America. All this would be arranged by King Arthur. After his masters, he would be in charge of excavation and drilling in the country. He was going to be somebody at last, after so many years of being a nobody.

Discovering new oil wells during the days when so many were drying up and there was genuine fear of finishing up all the oil in the world, was truly a stroke of luck. In a couple of years, Kenya might be controlling the world economy. It was imperative that whoever wanted to enjoy the benefits should manoeuvre himself into position now, while there was still time.

There was a faint beeping sound coming from under a pile of clothes. Galahad scrambled around and found the beeper. He switched it off and left the room; he was worried. Only one person beeped him and very rarely. It could only mean something had gone wrong.

He quickly strode towards the phone booth in the corner and picking up the hand-set he punched in a series of memorised numbers. When he heard the ringing tone he dropped in some coins.

"Galahad," he said tersely as the phone was picked up on the second ring.

"Come in at once," King Arthur said. "We have got a problem."

Chapter Sixteen

Tristan as he was known by members of the Round Table sat in his office and twiddled his thumbs. It was a very bad habit, one that he had grown up with and could not easily get rid of.

No one could deny that he was a brilliant man. In fact, the intricacies of the brain had always delighted and fascinated him. As long as he remembered he had always longed to become a surgeon; to open people up and see how they work. Later, as he was studying surgery, he decided that the best part of the body to study was the brain.

It had always amazed him that the human brain was so large and capable of so many things and yet the average man only used a tiny fraction of it. He had wondered exactly what man was capable of doing if only he could use more of his brain-power. At the moment, he could think, reason, grasp concepts and ideas and, most important of all, create. In a few hundred years he had completely changed the face of the earth with his creations. Men had become mini-gods; God's helpers. The only difference was that God created matter out of nothing. Man could create also but he had to have something to start with in order to make something out of it. He could not make something out of nothing. But if he could use more of his brain, who knows? One day man may actually become like God, as the serpent had promised Eve so many years ago. Man may be able to create things from nothing and bring things into existence simply by the power of his will.

Tristan was determined to find a way to persuade more of his brain to work for him so that he could control the world. He has set up a laboratory to study human behaviour and was particularly interested in the phenomenon of mental telepathy. He was astounded by the ability of some people to be able to communicate with each other simply by flicking a glance in the right direction, or were able to communicate with animals simply by looking at them.

In the lab at the moment he had a very extraordinary pair of twins, a boy and a girl. No matter what the distance, they always seemed to be able to catch thought waves from each other. Tristan thought back to the last experiment they had done a few days before.

He had taken the girl, Fridah, and booked a flight to the coastal town of Mombasa. They had left her brother, Peter, in Nairobi. They had booked into a hotel from where Tristan could communicate with one of his assistants by phone. He had left Fridah downstairs at the reception in the company of one of the clerks, then he hurried upstairs and called his assistant. He asked him to take Peter into one of the rooms at the lab where neither of the twins had ever been before. Then he had gone back downstairs to get Fridah. The clerk confirmed that the girl had not left the reception area or moved from her seat the entire time.

Tristan took Fridah upstairs to the suite. He closed the doors and asked her to sit down.

"Fridah I would like you to ask Peter where he is now," he had said. Under his steady gaze Fridah had closed her eyes and communicated with her brother.

"Peter says he's in a room inside the laboratory compound," Fridah had said. "He says that the room is white, and it has a white carpet on the floor and white curtains on the windows." She had opened her eyes and looked at him.

Tristan was amazed. Even though, he knew that the twins were extraordinary, it was turning out even better than he had anticipated.

"Ask Peter if there is a table in the room," he said.

Fridah had closed her eyes. "Yes," she had said almost immediately. "There is a table on the left-hand side of the room."

"What colour is it?" Tristan had asked.

"White," she had said.

"What is on the table, Fridah?" Tristan asked.

Fridah shut her eyes again and concentrated. "Peter says there is a telephone on the table," she had said. "Next to it is a telephone directory; a 1985 Kenyan directory. On top of the directory there are two pieces of white chalk and a new unused black board eraser. Next to these is a small radio, and next to the radio is a pair of pink and white roller skates." There had been a slight pause as Fridah frowned and then smiled. "Peter says that they must be girls' skates because they are very small and dainty," she had said indignantly.

"There is a pile of exercise books" she had continued, "six in all, a tube of lipstick and a bottle of bright-pink nail polish. There is also a little black box which he thinks may be a compact set. That's all," Fridah had ended.

Tristan could hardly contain his excitement. It had been a major breakthrough on his part. For a long time he had been waiting and studying, and now this; it was almost beyond belief. The twins were everything he had hoped for and more. It was obvious that they were both highly intelligent and were able to engage in extra-sensory communication. In fact, it was certain as time went by that they were able to communicate with a variety of animals.

The most successful in this area were the dolphins — whether in the wild or in captivity. The twins succeed in summoning the dolphins from almost everywhere and asking them to do anything. They were easily able to distinguish the dolphins and soon named all the ones in the wild that they knew. They knew which one was which on sight and insisted that every dolphin was different and was as distinguishable as a human being. They could sense when the dolphins were in trouble or when they were simply happy and 'having a party' as Peter put it. It was simply astounding and definitely a break through.

Something which was even more interesting, however, was the sleep-walker's story. He had been working on it for months. The separation of the mental body from the physical body; nothing could possible be more complex than that. It seemed that for certain people, once they were asleep, managed to have their spiritual boy, so to speak, actually awaken from their physical body and walk away. The surprising thing was that they did not know that they were doing it.

A woman had reported a very strange occurrence to the lab. One night she had dreamt that she had gone to visit her sister who lived in another town. The sister, on that particular night (in the woman's dream) was having a fight with her husband and the woman could see and hear very vividly, what was going on, but she couldn't make herself be seen or heard by either of the two. At one point, her sister had thrown a bright pink vase at her husband, and the vase had shattered. The following day, the woman had decided to write to her sister, detailing the dream of the fight and the actions that had taken place. She had vividly described the setting, the words used, and finally, the shattered vase. She wound up the letter by amusedly remarking, 'Isn't that funny. You and John have never fought the whole of your married life?'

Her badly shaken sister had immediately taken a bus to the woman's house as soon as she received the letter. She had demanded to know how the woman could possibly have known about the fight. The woman said that she didn't know of any fight but that she had just dreamt of one. She insisted that if a fight had taken place at all, it was just a coincidence.

Her sister refused to accept that it was a coincidence and she said that the words in the letter were the very same ones she and her husband had used. The way the woman had described the whole incident was exactly the way it had happened. Finally, as irrefutable proof she had produced several pieces of the shattered pink vase, which she had not yet thrown away.

The two sisters were confused. They didn't know if what seemed to have happened was really possible and they decided to put the whole bizarre thing to the test.

The out-of-town sister had decided to stay for the night. They had talked about it and she asked the woman to go back, if possible to her home and find out what John and the children were doing that afternoon. The woman duly went to sleep in the sitting room while her sister watched her. She dreamt that her brother-in-law, John, and the children, had gone to a nearby swimming pool. Once again she could clearly see and hear them but could not make herself seen or heard. She stayed until they went back home and then woke up. Her sister listened avidly as she described what had taken place. Then they went to a telephone and called the sister's home. They got a full account of what had happened during the day from each of the children and finally, from John himself. Each account was exactly as the woman had described it.

Tristan had not believed what was said about the woman. He had heard of no similar cases and had never encountered this phenomenon before. He decided to take the woman into the lab and run a few tests on her.

Tristan wanted to run the same test several times to determine whether it was really successful or not. The first test was quite simple. The woman, whose name was Dora, would sleep in a secure room where there were television monitors and video cameras. In the next room, also secure, there were two sheets of paper. On one paper was a short, hand-written message which had been written by Tristan himself and seen by no one else. Tristan's papers were sitting on a small table in the middle of the room. The security matched that in Dora's room; no one could enter it undetected.

Tristan was not prepared for what had happened next. Apparently what Dora had claimed was true. She managed to leave her physical body when asleep and slip like a ghost through the walls and into the other room. There, she successfully managed to read what was on the paper after which she simply slipped back into her body, and then woke up. Then she reported to Tristan what she had read. Every single word was correct. It was incredible.

The whole experiment had been repeated twice, just to prove that things like that really happen and are not just a figment of a few people's imagination.

The experiment was successful time and time again. Physical tests showed that Dora was completely normal. Psychiatrists had ascertained that she had a normal brain, but that she could do what she did was unexplainable.

Tristan had kept her with him for a long time, studying and analysing her. When he had been unable to come to any conclusion, he had allowed her to go home but still called her to the lab from time to time. That wasn't the end of it; it was just the beginning.

Perhaps the most bizarre case of all was that of Sandra, a beautiful 18 year-old girl who was able to speak to the dead. Not through seances or witchcraft or any other accepted form but by simply sitting down, looking around and calling the name of the dead person. It seems that the person then came into view, her view, after which she started talking to him or her as if she was talking to any ordinary person.

When she was brought to Tristan's office and her case explained, Tristan did not believe a word of it. She quietly asked him to name anybody close to him who had died. Playing along, he had named his friend who had died when they had just finished high school.

Sandra had quietly sat down and said, "Derek. Derek Samuels, please come." Tristan had looked at her amusedly as she hurriedly searched the room. Then she had looked him straight in the eye and told him that Derek was standing right next to him and asked him what he wanted to say to him.

Still smiling, Tristan had said, "Ask him who won the football trophy in the schools' league in our first year at high school?"

Sandra had looked at a point beyond his shoulder. "Well, Derek?" she had asked. After a minute of silent contemplation, she had turned back to Tristan. "Derek says that there was no winner that year. There was a big fight during the final game and every player was suspended. Derek says you broke your leg during that fight."

Tristan became interested. "Ask Derek what I said to him the night he died," Tristan said curiously.

After a few minutes Sandra said, "Derek says you told him that the life he was leading was stupid and the way he rode his motor-cycle, suicidal. He didn't listen. He says you told him that it was time he sat back and considered his priorities in life, otherwise he might just find that he no longer had a life to lead. Ten minutes later he was involved in an accident and he died."

Tristan was stunned. Sandra had definitely made a believer out of him. He spent a long time communicating with Derek. After all, how could anyone repeat word-for-word a conversation that had taken place between him and Derek and had not been overheard by anyone else?

Sandra was still coming for tests. So far, no one had been able to prove her a fake. Tristan was a man with a mission.

The phone, the very special private line rang, interrupting his thoughts. He stopped twiddling his thumbs.

"Tristan," he said.

"Come in at once," King Arthur said, "something has happened."

Chapter Seventeen

Gawain smoked his cigar and gazed out of the window. He had just finished his breakfast and was feeling replete and content. Food was one thing that was still able to content him; money was the other. But the one thing that Gawain really craved and could never have, was Misty.

Misty was five-foot-three, blue-eyed and red-haired, with a temper to match. She was breathtakingly beautiful. At first glance she looked like an exquisitely fabricated porcelain doll, fragile and delicate. It was only after a while that one discovered the back-bone of steel that was part of her make-up.

Gawain had met her years ago at a party. She had been seventeen at the time. It had been her first party and she had come with brother, who happened to be Gawain's friend. Her brother had noticed a girl whom he liked, handed Misty over to Gawain, and shot off to his own pursuit. Misty had quietly seethed at this all evening and she had rebuffed all his efforts at communication, had refused to dance with him, and had generally frozen him out. Towards the end of the party he had lost his patience, hauled her over his shoulder, and left the place.

He dumped her unceremoniously into the front seat of his car and climbed in beside her before she could catch her breath. Swiftly, he turned the ignition key while she spluttered with rage. The car was speeding along the highway before she retrieved her voice, and then she turned it on full blast. She hurled insults and screams at him at an alarming rate. He would never have believed that such a small person could possess such a loud shriek. After five minutes he had pulled off the road and brought the car to a halt. Her voice had slowly died away.

"Have you quite finished?" he asked.

Her voice escaped in an astonished hiss.

"You know, I have never met a more selfish, more conceited, more egoistical girl than you in my entire life," he said conversationally.

"How can a girl who like the Madonna herself, beautiful and pure, and who moves like a queen, fluid and graceful be so rotten inside?" "What a disappointment!" he exclaimed. "You're so lovely to look at and yet have absolutely nothing more to offer. One sees you and expects so much more when he sees you. But as the time passes I guess he would have to come to the conclusion that he is not going to get anything else apart from what's on the surface; no charming smile, no humourous joke, no stimulating conversation, no wit, no intelligence, nothing. No encouragement at all."

"What do you mean?" Misty gasped, her face as white as a sheet and her mouth agape in amazement.

"I mean no matter what I tried to do tonight, I just couldn't get through to you," Gawain said. "I was met with rudeness that I have never encountered before. Frankly, I was shocked because I had done nothing at all to provoke you and I didn't deserve what I had to put up with tonight. You made it so clear that you were angry with your brother, it hurt. I didn't do anything to you, and the least you could have done was show me some courtesy. But oh no! Not Miss high-and-mighty. It never occurred to you that I might be just as peeved as you were by being lumped with my best friend's spoilt brat of a sister to cart along for the whole evening? That I might be sticking around for the sake of good manners? It wouldn't occur to someone who doesn't think would it? Well think about it, Misty, being beautiful ain't enough baby. You would need much more than beauty to have me panting at your feet in breathless anticipation."

With a thoroughly disgusted jerk of the ignition key, he started the car. Swiftly and silently, he drove a shocked and dazed Misty back to the party; courteously escorted her inside, and then calmly took off, leaving her by herself.

Two days later a subdued Misty had called him.

"Yes," he said curtly after picking up the phone.

"I'm calling to say I'm sorry," Misty said. "About the other night," she paused and then continued in a rush, "you were right. I acted like a jerk. I had no right to treat you the way I did. My only excuse is that I've got a terrible temper. When I'm angry I tend not to think. Will you let me make it up to you? I would like to take you out to dinner tonight if you are free.”

Gawain was silent as he turned the request over in his mind. He decided that it must have taken great courage for her to call him, at the risk of possible rejection, and she sounded sincere enough.

“Please,” Misty said into the silence, “I would like to prove that I can provide stimulating conversation.” She gave a nervous laugh. “And that I’m not a spoilt brat; not really.” Gawain had agreed and they arranged to meet in town for dinner.

True to her word, Misty could really provide stimulating conversation. She was very well informed on politics, sports, world economy, business matters, ecology and a very wide range of other subjects. She was not afraid of stating her opinion on any of them and she did not mind engaging in heated debates where her opinions differed. She was also ready to listen to other theories and to accept them if they happened to make sense. Misty was charming, intelligent and possessed a lively sense of humour that could keep people laughing the whole evening. In all, she was all Gawain had accused her of not being and more; she made him feel alive.

After this first night out, Gawain was captivated. He had invited her out for coffee, the theatre, drinks, movies, operas . . . everything. He wanted to be with her all the time. He took her swimming, dancing, skiing . . . she excelled in everything. He learned about her great passion for classical music and how she was able to sit for hours next to a piano, playing melodies that one could not help but be stirred by. She played with an amazing skill that rivalled any that Gawain had ever heard, but she refused to play professionally. Music was private, according to Misty and she played only for herself. After a while, she was, however, persuaded to play for Gawain.

Neither Misty nor Gawain ever needed to work. Both their fathers were first-generation Texas oil-millionaires. Gawain had decided that in order to satisfy his own self-respect he had to do it his own way. With absolutely no financial assistance from his father, he had branched off on his own and succeeded in building a small empire through grit and determination. After he had made his first million, he asked Misty to marry him and she agreed.

It was during their engagement that Misty had shown the first signs of a deep possessive streak. It was nearing the wedding and Gawain had started growing restless about the idea of tying the knot. He had decided that there was no harm in having 'one last fling' before settling down to a staid respectable life. After looking around, he had decided on a stacked blonde typist who worked in his office; extremely empty-headed, but she suited him fine. After all, he wasn't looking for a meaningful relationship; he had that with Misty. Just a brief affair to prove to himself that he hadn't lost his touch.

He took the typist out once or twice, not realising that rumours would circulate so furiously. He was out with the girl one night when Misty descended on him from nowhere, while they were having dinner in an out-of-town restaurant.

"Well, well, well! Ain't we cozy?" Misty's voice interrupted Gawain from the task he had set himself on of kissing each and every finger of the blonde's left hand. He jumped, and whirled around to face a very angry Misty.

"Working overtime or so, we said, didn't we?" Misty purred as she wove a hand through her hair. "Exactly what kind of work is it we are doing? Does it involve checking out her typing technique? See if her hands taste as good as they look?"

"Now Misty, I can explain," Gawain said miserable at being caught.

"Can you?" Misty asked. "Why, you two-timing, self-centred little bastard, what kind of fool do you take me for? What do you need to explain? That you want a main course but wouldn't mind sampling a little dish on the side as well? Let me tell you my fine little friend, you are not going to treat me as some peasant girl, married and kept properly in the background while you have your fun. Nothing doing. Want to get married? Find yourself a nice hooker. I'm sure you would make a charming couple." So saying she had moved away from him.

"Misty, please . . ." he said desperately.

Misty wasn't finished yet. She moved across to the blonde. "You look hungry sugar, want some soup?" she asked casually before dumping the soup bowl upside down on the shrieking and utterly humiliated girl's head. Then, just as casually, she had wiped her hands

126

on a nearby napkin and gracefully undulated out of the deathly-silent restaurant.

It had taken Gawain the better part of two years to win Misty back. Two long years while she bedded every man in sight; every man within her radius. Two long years of slammed doors, shredded post-cards, unopened letters, replaced phones and public confrontations. Misty treated Gawain like a leper, and Gawain could not believe that he had lost her. He completely lost interest in women and constantly berated himself for having betrayed Misty once. He couldn't imagine life without her; it stretched out cold and bleak before him and he was determined to have her back, at all costs. The stakes here were very high. Losing meant losing his life. He finally succeeded in convincing Misty of that.

By the time Misty and Gawain got married Misty had settled down and had complete trust in him. The thought of straying never occurred to Gawain again. The very idea of losing Misty again, made him shudder. It was too much for him to bear, so for a while they lived an idyllic life.

A few years later, it happened; Gawain couldn't be expected to be a saint forever, could he? There was a new girl in town, a model. She was the first to attract Gawain in a long time, and he hadn't felt inclined to resist. Not after some years of being the perfect and faithful husband.

This time he planned it carefully. They didn't meet often and when they did it was always out of town. Gawain took the trouble to cover his tracks carefully, although the longer the affair lasted, the more difficult and dangerous it become. Gawain could not honestly say why he kept it up because he had a happy marriage, stability in his home and a wonderful wife. He honestly loved Misty and couldn't envision life without her. He knew that if she found out about the model she would leave. She would just turn and walk away. The fact that they had two little sons, and a wonderful home would not mean anything to her. Misty would understand and forgive a lot of crimes that many other people wouldn't. One thing she would never forgive was unfaithfulness. She could never forgive it again.

Then one day a tragedy occurred; Gawain had recently inherited his father's fortune and was one of the richest men in Texas. Because of this he was under constant threat of terrorism and attacks by other criminals. On that particular day he had gone rendezvousing with his mistress. An attack had occurred which had left the guards and all the workers in the house dead. The thugs had then taken great pleasure in beating both of his sons to death. An enraged Misty had succeeded in plunging a pair of garden shears into one of the men's chests before she herself was shot in the chest. She had been rushed to the intensive care unit two hours later when the police had found her lying in a pool of blood on the family estate - still miraculously breathing. Nobody could explain how.

Gawain had been looked for high and low while the top surgeons in the country fought to save Misty's life. Police investigators finally tracked him down in the arms of his mistress and brought him to the hospital just as Misty recovered from her anaesthetic. The story of where Gawain had been while his family was being killed one by one was too juicy to suppress. It had spread like wildfire all over. Misty was not the last to hear it.

"Just tell me this," she had said flatly the second time he came to visit her. "Were the lives of two innocent boys really worth what you shared with her?" Gawain had no response. "Was she really that good?" Misty's voice did not alter as she continued, "you killed my children as surely as if you were the one slowly clubbing the life out of them. Why weren't you there to hear their cries for mercy? To feel their terror and pain as they were made to pay for a sin their father had committed? A sin they knew nothing about?"

"Misty . . ." Gawain pleaded as the tears coursed down his face. He knew he had lost it all - the home, the life, the family. All in one go. The police had taken him down to identify his sons' bodies at the mortuary. Their faces had been beaten into pulp. To the day he died he would never forget those masses of crumpled flesh and bone. Never.

After her accusation at the hospital, Misty had simply refused to talk to him again. Her eyes were flat and lifeless as she regarded some point on the ceiling when he was in the room. She didn't appear to hear any of his excuses or remarks and she never spoke to him again. It was as if a part of her had also died that day.

He had spent weeks trying, months pleading and years begging all to no avail. Misty had simply ceased to exist for him. He had nightmares where he could actually see the men beating up his sons. Nightmares where Misty was running around everywhere trying to find him while he beat against a glass wall trying to get her attention but always failed. The nightmares prevented him from sleeping well at night.

Misty had gone back to live with her parents. She spent the days in the spacious grounds gazing at the green hills in the horizon. She had nothing much to say to anybody; nothing much to live for. Gawain was eventually banned from going anywhere near the estate.

He had dedicated his life, or what was left of it, to amassing money to add to his incredible fortune. Getting rich was the one pleasure he still had left in life. He lived for the day when he would be declared the richest man in the world.

He had met King Arthur a few years earlier and had got to know of the Master Plan. It appealed to him immensely and it gave him more pleasure and anticipation than he had felt for anything in years. He spent hours plotting, planning and gloating; feeling good. Once again he was living — to a certain degree. Not merely existing.

But he never stopped thinking about his beautiful Misty. She was still his wife because they didn't divorce. But she was a complete and utter stranger. And destined to remain one forever. Yet Gawain could never stop hoping that one day he might be able to persuade her to love him again. To make him whole again.

The phone rang, interrupting his thoughts.

"Yes?" he said.

"Gawain? It's King Arthur," came a voice. "Come in at once. We have got a problem."

Chapter Eighteen

Rioting! That's what makes the world go round. School riots, university riots, general riots . . . you name it. The most interesting thing in the world is starting a good, fast moving riot and watch it snowball.

Perceval sighed heavily. Being a high court judge had severely cramped his style. His days of rioting were most definitely over. He was a public figure who commanded respect and oozed with dignity and righteousness. He could make a man shake in his shoes just by looking at him, quelling his protests with a hard glance. The black robe and long horse hair wig brought with them a kind of power that was definitely a turn on for Perceval.

It hadn't always been that way. He had spent most of his years playing fool. His parents had been rich, and he a happy carefree little fool. He spent a good deal of time doing terrible irresponsible acts and jumping from one country to another. He swung wildly from being arrested in Rio to being beaten up in Baghdad. He even climbed the Alps to get a better view of Europe! He then proceeded to climb the Rockies in North America, the Atlas in Northern Africa, and the Himalayas in South-East Asia just so that he could make an intelligent comparison. He went swimming in the Dead Sea, scuba diving in the Indian Ocean, surfing in Sydney, skiing in Switzerland, joy-riding in Japan, racing in Rome and fishing in France.

The world had been a tiny, oyster in which he could dash about, wreaking havoc from one end to the other in a feverish attempt to extract as much fun from it as was humanly possible.

He had definitely been the black sheep of his family. In a family of staid bankers, lawyers, doctors and stockbrokers, what could one expect? Education had never been important to him. Blessed with more than his fair share of brains, he just breezed past his class-mates in school, always managing to secure the top position in class no matter what horrific episode in his life he had just managed to extricate himself from.

One of his obsessions was trying to get himself thrown out of school. He was as incorrigible as possible, waiting anxiously for the principal's patience to wear thin. It was harder than it might have been because his family was wealthy enough to offer the principal huge bribes to keep Perceval on. Most principals patience had their fortified by the knowledge that there would be money every month, in their bank accounts. So no matter what Perceval did, they usually just gritted their teeth firmly and persevered.

There always came a time, however, when not even the money in the bank could atone for Perceval's misdeeds and he was asked to leave. The shortest it had taken him was four days, a new all-time record for the shortest time ever spent in a school. He had been expelled more times than he could possibly remember and his average duration at a school was a measly one and a half years!

However, he had good brains and had managed to muddle along. He passed both his 'O' levels and 'A' levels with flying colours, surprising all those who knew him. Nobody believed that he had it in him. Then Perceval went to Harvard to study law. It was something which had always fascinated him and he had taken for granted from a very early age the fact that he would one day study law, and be extremely good at it.

That didn't stop him from playing the fool though. There were almost no limits to the outrageous things he did. He was almost always at the centre of controversy. Whenever things were happening, Perceval was somehow involved, he had to have a piece of every action. He was not made to be an observer, or one waiting for things to happen. Instead he went out and made things happen. After all 'life is short' he argued, 'and one should try to squeeze out every drop of fun from life before it is too late. Who could be certain that the future would be any good?'

'Live for today' was Perceval's menu for life; do what feels good. That was until some students got hurt in a fireworks display caper and he was told to shape up or ship out. He was given a last chance to prove that he could settle down but if he blew it; that was the end.

Thereafter he made up his mind that his youthful, carefree days were over. He disentangled himself from the wild bunch in school and settled down to study law. He realised there was no use of getting kicked out of Harvard without his degree.

Unfortunately for Perceval, things got out of hand once again; an explosion in the chemistry lab this time. A young and budding science student had been trying to impress his girl friend and her friends by mixing together some rather volatile chemicals. The explosion rocked the area, killing one of the girls in the lab and injuring several other people.

Perceval had been nearby and he was the first to arrive there. He had found the dazed student trying to revive his girl friend and looking shattered. Perceval thought it was all a huge joke and decided to take the heat. When the administration officials arrived he proudly 'confessed' his misdeed.

There was an investigation and charges of manslaughter. The science student and the other girls tried in vain to persuade him to change his mind, but he was enjoying playing the villain too much to stop. The others had to give their oath not to tell the truth about what happened that day. The charges were dropped, but he was kicked out of school. He played the martyred hero to the fullest, leaving behind thoughts of courage and bravery in the minds of his former class-mates. His departure sparked off a spate of riots which only justified the administration's decision to expel him.

Back home Perceval's father refused to receive himor even to listen to his side of the story. Instead, he kicked him out of the house and cut off his allowance, leaving him penniless and homeless. But none of that hurt as much as the thought of being uneducated.

He got himself another pair of trousers, a back pack and took off to neighbouring Uganda. There was war going on there, and he felt like doing a little fighting at that time. He joined a resistance movement, was given a machine gun, and set off to release his frustrations.

Perceval didn't last a week before he became sick of it. The soldiers performed horrible acts on their victims. It was not the killing that bothered him as such, but the way it was done the kind of torture inflicted before one was allowed to die. The mangled, bleeding or burnt bodies rarely looked like or even resembled anything that could be mistaken for a human being. He saw people being skinned alive, burnt alive, buried alive, eaten alive, and dismembered alive. He watched in horror as everyone around him turned into a sadistic animal whose only pleasure was derived from seeing their fellow human beings suffer the most inhuman of torture.

But he gritted his teeth and stayed for a year. A year in which he learnt finally not to take life as a big joke. He learnt to treasure life more than anything in the world. Then, he managed to get his priorities right and he was changed irrevocably. His light, carefree days were truly over and he quietened down considerably and learnt to accept responsibility. Then he moved back home.

Surprisingly, this time around he was received with a lot of warmth from all sides. It turned out that the science student had been plagued by so much guilt that he had finally confessed to the whole affair. Harvard had written a letter of apology, cancelling the expulsion and asking him to return to campus. The whole case had received a lot of publicity world wide, most of it negative on the University's part. 'Poor student from third world country gets thrown out of Harvard', and that sort of thing. They were anxious for him to return so that they could restore good public relations. Perceval was surprised that things seemed to be going his way for a change. His father received him with a warm embrace and tears in his eyes but Perceval nearly snorted in disgust. He remembered telling his father in no uncertain terms that they could never be friends.

"Why not?" his father asked, startled. "Now that I know that you weren't responsible for the accident which killed a student, I'm willing to accept you back as my son."

"Oh are you?" Perceval asked. "Only when things go right?" he asked and gave his father a flinty-eyed stare. "I'll never forget that during the one time in my life that I truly needed a friend you turned your back on me. Don't expect me to fall prostrate at your feet in joyous thanks just because you have decided you want a son again. I don't need you. Not now, not ever."

His former teachers at Harvard found him equally intractable. He had agreed to go back to college on condition that no charges were pressed against the science student and no punishment exerted. He also insisted on joining the class he had left, doing make-up work in the evenings and on week ends for the year he had missed; he had completely changed. He was now immersed in his books and was not concerned about anything else. His happy, carefree days were over and he no longer used his sharp mind to think up tricks and jokes to play on the staff; he had a different use for it now. His reputation as a troublemaker changed. Suddenly, he had become the most hardworking student Harvard ever had. He graduated from his class with honours and set out to make something of his life.

But something was missing; gone was the sparkle in his eye, the careless shrug in his shoulder and the light spring in his step. Gone was the brilliance of his smile and the startling beauty of his laughter. Somewhere along the transitional road from childhood to adulthood he had lost the ability to truly enjoy life. He had forgotten the good things in life and he could no longer see any beauty, laughter or love. He had lost the ability to entrust another person with his heart or with any part of himself and so he was entirely alone; surrounded by a cloak of darkness and of silence which nobody could penetrate.

Only one thing was still able to stir him; riots. He still got excited by the thought of a large, rampaging mob. University students and group leaders brought to him for inciting members of the public to riot got a receptive audience; he understood them. That was why King Arthur's plan appealed so much to him; Kenya would be one big riot soon. He could hardly wait.

Then the red phone on his desk rang interupting his thoughts.

"Perceval," he said.

"Come in at once," came King Arthur's voice. "We have a problem."

Chapter Nineteen

Imbeciles! He was surrounded by imbeciles! The man they called Bohert stood by his window and impatiently twirled his blonde moustache. Being the president of an international company, a successful one at that, hadn't turned out to be a bed of roses.

He had started out with a few hundred French francs in his pocket and a big idea. Several years later, he was a millionaire and it never ceased to amaze him that his dream was now reality and that nothing had changed. The same nagging sense of unfulfilment remained intact and he was not in the least bit different in any way other than the fact that he now possessed a bank account. He lived in mortal fear of bankruptcy, even though the possibilities of that happening were remote.

Bohert felt that his staff was incompetent and that he might have to fire the whole lot of them. Take that morning for instance. They were supposed to have a staff meeting but half the staff had not shown up on time and so the meeting could not start. He was thoroughly exasperated considering that he had a million and one things to do and now nothing would be on schedule. He knew very well that each of them would have a perfect, excuse as to why they were late; the car broke down, the bus had an accident, the baby got sick and had to be taken to the hospital . . . the list was endless. Bohert let out another exasperated sigh and he turned impatiently to the others.

"When the rest of my staff deign to grace us with their presence, will one of you please come and inform me?" Bohert asked dryly. "I will be in my office."

He left the room and went down the corridor to his office. It never ceased to amaze him that he had actually managed to build a successful company. On days like this and with a staff like the one he had it seemed like a minor miracle; no, not a minor one, a major one.

He had not really been born desperately poor or anything like that. His family was a comfortable, middle-class one. His father had been a career civil servant and his mother, a secretary with a large company. He had a younger sister who was now married to a military personnel officer. They had lived in a four-bedroomed house and had two cars, a cat and a dog. They had lived very much like other middle-class families in France, worked in the capital, had taken one vacation every year in the country, in the south or on an exotic tropical island somewhere. The only difference was that Bohert's parents had insisted that he went to very expensive schools. A small legacy from an uncle had taken care of his education.

It was at school where Bohert first came across the rich and their lifestyle; a whole different world from his. A world of weekend shopping trips to Milan, lunches or cocktails in London, dashing off to the theatre in New York, going to San Francisco for a film premiere of just taking a week off to go to the Bahamas for a well-earned rest.

It was a world which Bohert just couldn't understand. Everybody liked luxury, of course, but caviar sandwiches for a snack at break-time? Wasn't that going a bit too far?

It got worse when they went to high school. Rich people it seemed, did not suffer from acne. They made special trips to doctors in Moscow and Tokyo to ensure that they never broke out in pimples. Their skin was as smooth as a baby's and destined to stay that way for as long as modern technology held out. For the not-so-rich like Bohert, life was painful and miserable. His face was covered in acne which pursued him relentlessly. To make things worse he was extremely tall and thin and very uncomfortable with this. He looked like a joke and was often the target of very cruel taunts and insults. He had often felt that he would rather face a room full of rabid rottweilers than go through those high-school years again.

It really looked as though it couldn't get worse but it did. It got worse with the 'car-craze'. As soon as the kids got old enough to drive there was suddenly a boom of Alpha Romeos, Ferraris, Jaguars, Porsches, Aston Martins, a sensational whole new range, of exciting vehicles. How on earth was someone supposed to compete with that? The dating game was no longer just difficult; it was impossible. No girl in her right senses would want to go anywhere with a guy who looked like a bean pole, had a face full of the dreaded pimples, slouched, had no self-confidence whatsoever, and worst of all, did not have a car.

Life was a misery, but one day, everything changed. In every school there is a class bully, and in Bohert's class there was one named Jean Pierre. He was big, almost Bohert's height with corded muscular forearms. The teases and taunts of his class-mates could be fielded or ignored; they were more or less bearable. But the regular beatings Bohert received from Jean Pierre depressed him beyond belief. It was too much.

One day Bohert just couldn't stand it any longer. Jean Pierre's paw landed heavily on his shoulder and he exploded with fury. He whipped around angrily and grabbed the bigger boy with his left hand. His right fist connected solidly with a large jaw and with his class-mates looking on in disbelief, he had beat up the class bully. Fists working furiously, he vent out all his frustrations and all his pent-up fury on the other boy. To him, he was hitting out at all those people who had teased him and insulted him while he sat passively and absorbed it; all those who had told him that he was nothing, and that he would always be nothing.

He had been put on detention and his parents were informed of his efforts. His father had shrugged and intoned that 'boys will be boys', while his mother had shaken her head at him disapprovingly. There was no general condemnation from them. From his class-mates Bohert had received respect and the taunts had ceased. In fact, one or two of the boys had become quite friendly and slowly but surely, he had become part of the elite group.

To make matters even better, the boxing coach had heard a graphic description of the one-sided fight and called Bohert to the gymnasium. He quickly managed to convince him to try out boxing. Finally, there was something Bohert excelled in. He learnt very quickly the techniques of a first-class boxer and he became the best in the school. Soon, he became the champion in the area. He managed to find a new confidence in himself and he no longer slouched or bent but walked proudly upright. Wherever he went people couldn't fail to notice his presence. Words of praise from his coach, his class-mates and the school administration were like music in his ears, wine in his blood, especially the coach's favourite phrase, "Walk like a champion!"

The acne quickly cleared up leaving his face smooth and clear. Hours of working out in the gym had given him muscles and new breadth to his shoulders. His physique was suddenly that of a well-toned athlete and his blond look resembled that of a movie star. His new confidence in himself made him relax and be friendly with those around him. He had a quick wit and a sense of humour that made him very popular among the boys and the girls. He had compassion and a talent for listening and understanding which were rare in the elite upper class. Best of all, he was not a show-off; he didn't throw his weight around or set out to prove that he was better than anyone else. The days of "bean pole" and "pizza face" were long gone. He had a new nick-name now; "Champ."

To make sure that his cup really ran over, he got the one thing he had craved most of all; a shiny red BMW which was a present from another well-heeled uncle. Suddenly, he didn't have to ask for dates any more. Girls were literally beating a path to his door, trying their desperate best to get him to take them out.

His popularity had preceded him to university where he was planning to study business administration. He found life very easy there and he had no objection to living like a king. No party was a party unless he was there "to grace it with his presence." No event was complete if it didn't have his approval.

It was at one of these parties that Bohert had first met Annette. She was the daughter of one of the richest men in France but she didn't have any airs. She was extremely beautiful, and had silver-blonde hair and smokey-grey eyes; she was captivating.

Annette was extremely aggressive. She knew what she wanted and was not above going after it with everything she had. Bohert found this out at one party when he was talking to a girl from his class, one he had dated often and he had brought to the party. Annette descended upon the two of them and practically thrust herself between them.

"Want to dance?" she asked him in a low sultry voice. Bohert had been surprised. He was used to women throwing themselves at him but never so blatantly or so obviously. He had learnt that the female sex did things much more subtly.

"Maybe later," he'd said lightly. "I'm busy right now."

138

"Busy doing what?" she asked challengingly.

He raised an eyebrow. She was certainly being very rude. All for a dance? Wasn't that going a bit too far? "I'm busy talking to Christine," he said firmly, reaching around her and grabbing Christine's hand. Christine's face had turned bright red and she was glowering.

"Oh, her!" Annette exclaimed with a little laugh. "She won't mind, will you darling?" she said with a bright smile. "After all, she has had you all evening. She has to share."

Christine was furious but Bohert was beginning to get amused by the sultry beauty standing in front of him. He put his arm around Christine and drew her to him. "Christine might not mind but I most certainly do," he said. "If I leave her alone for a minute she might get snapped up by some other guy. I can't afford that for a moment, can I?" he smiled down at Christine and watched some of the fury drain from her face. She smiled gratefully back at him.

"Don't be ridiculous," snapped an annoyed Annette. "You know very well she will be right here waiting for you when you get back, she won't go anywhere. Not as long as she believes you will throw her a few crumbs here and there. It makes us all sick watching her follow you around on campus with that stupid moonstruck expression on her face. What you need is a real woman."

Bohert had looked at her in amazement "What I don't need is a woman like you," he said. "I can't stand aggressive women who don't ever stop to consider other people's feelings. I prefer my women soft, loyal, and thoughtful. I would rather have a single Christine to one hundred of you. Have I made myself clear?" Without waiting for an answer, he had turned to Christine. "You know, come to think of it, I do feel like dancing," he said with a smile. "Will you dance with me?" He took her arm and led her away – leaving Annette watching them broodingly from a distance.

Half an hour later she changed tactics. Waiting until Christine was on the dance floor, she cornered Bohert who was trying to get a couple of drinks. Sighing, he turned to her.

"What do you want?" he asked her.

"You," she said.

His eyes widened as he regarded her. He was convinced that she was crazy. That had to be the only explanation for it, otherwise why else would she be coming on to him so strong? "Am I supposed to be flattered?" he asked dryly.

"I like you," she announced, totally ignoring his comment. "I like a guy who isn't afraid to stand up to a girl. Who isn't afraid to stand up to anyone. Most guys play along with me, you know, for who I am. They can't afford to put me down flat. It's rare to come across someone who isn't afraid to."

"Did it ever occur to you that I might not like you?" Bohert asked, a bit impatiently, "that I might not be in the least bit interested in you?" He shook his head and wondered if perhaps the girl was drunk, even though she didn't look drunk.

"No," she said with a grin. "It never occurred to me at all." She moved closer to him and stared at him out of those smokey-grey eyes. "Dance with me," she whispered. "Please."

Mesmerised, he let her lead him out onto the dance floor. The music had turned soft, slow. The lights were dimmed and the couples were all swaying to the music. He felt bewitched, bewildered. He had no idea what it was she was doing to him but he didn't want it to stop. She was a good dancer. In fact, she was just plain beautiful and for the first time that evening, he let himself acknowledge that fact and it stirred him. When the music ended and she slipped away, he was desolate.

Dancing that one dance with Annette had cost him both Christine and his sanity. He desperately tried to convince the former that it was nothing but just a way to get Annette off his back, but Christine refused to listen. As for the latter, he had no idea what he could do about it. He only knew that he couldn't stop thinking about Annette. The way she had looked at him out of those smokey-grey eyes; the was she had felt in his arms; the way she had danced with him, he knew that he had to see her again.

As a matter of fact, he did see her again. Running true to form, she had called him and in a coaxing, wheedling tone, she had managed to convince him to go out with her. Thinking briefly of Christine, Bohert had decided that he might as well be hang for a sheep just as well as a lamb. He went out with Annette, his conscience relatively clear.

It was the beginning of a long and very satisfying affair. He was with her almost everyday. She had woven her own special kind of magic around him, chaining him to her. He couldn't bear to be away from her and he couldn't bear the thought of losing her.

But lose her he did in his senior year in college. He had always assumed that once he finished college and went into business, she would marry him. He had never asked her to but he assumed that that was how it would be. Annette had other ideas, however, and announced her engagement to an extremely rich baron out of the blues. Bohert, who couldn't believe it, went to confront her. She met him with scorn and amusement.

"Don't make me laugh, darling," she had said. "Why on earth would I want to marry you? Your father is a nobody, and you my dear, are a nobody too. You are too much beneath my station for me to even consider the idea. You are okay to spend time with but let's face facts: you're penniless. I could never marry you."

Stunned, Bohert had set out to show the world once and for all that he was somebody. Within a few years, he had become a multi-millionaire and he had taken his revenge on Annette by marrying Christine. He had proved that he was better than anyone and he was now looking for new fields to conquer. King Arthur's offer of a piece of Kenya was too good to resist. He could hardly wait for the day he became master of all he surveyed.

Just then, the telephone rang and he picked it up carefully. It was his special phone and only certain people had the number.

"Bohert," he said.

"King Arthur," came the reply. "Come in at once. Something has gone wrong."

Chapter Twenty

Was Sunday the Sabbath? Or rather was the Sabbath meant to be on Sunday? The man they called Balain lay in bed pondering an issue which had always mesmerised and fascinated him. Very few people still believed that the Sabbath was supposed to be observed on Saturday. In fact it was only a section of people, who called themselves the Seventh Day Adventists, who believed that man was meant to worship God on Saturday and not on Sunday, as the majority of Christians now did. Their argument was very sound and convincing. Balain had heard them all his life and the more he thought about it, the more confused, and frustrated he became. It was a case of follow the masses or re-read and re-interpret the Bible. If one really put one's mind to it, one could convince people they ought to pray on Monday or Tuesday or any day of the week they chose.

But Balain couldn't afford the luxury of such thoughts. He was a Catholic Bishop, after all. It wasn't easy to get to the rank of Bishop in the Roman Catholic hierarchy. One had to read a lot, study and do all sorts of things before one became ordained a Bishop. There was just too much work put into it to even think of opting out. Suggesting that mass should be held on Saturday instead of Sunday may be enough to get one thrown out of the Roman Catholic Church permanently and branded a heretic. Balain had absolutely no wish whatsoever to be branded a heretic; not yet anyway.

He thought back to the days when he was a deacon. He had thought the most wonderful thing in the world was to become a fully-fledged priest. To be able to conduct mass to have so many people and looking up to him for guidance and help. It was the ultimate trip . . . the Bishops and Archbishops and Cardinals had all seemed so far away, and unreal; so saintly and pure and untouchable, much closer to the angels than to the common man.

For years Balain had known that he was going to be one of them; one of the bishops and other saint-like officials. He really deserved to be one of them because he was utterly devoted to the church. No one deserved it like he did. But the real reason Balain wanted to be a bishop so much was so that he would spend less time in purgatory.

Purgatory; the name struck fear in Balain's heart. Yet he knew he must go there before he was fit to enter Heaven. How else would he purge himself of all his sins? But he had always been afraid of the thought going there. It was almost too much to bear.

He had dedicated his life to doing good deeds for the church, trying to buy as much time as possible out of purgatory. He had practically lived the life of a saint. As a matter of fact, he saw no reason why he shouldn't become a saint eventually. He believed that no one strived to do good more than he did. No one was as religious and as dedicated or as hopeful as he was. After all, the saints had all started off as human beings too, but because of their courage and devotion, they had been canonised and their souls lived on, on earth and in Heaven. He honestly deserved to be one of them. He had a plan, you see, a great wild, plan to help bring God's Kingdom here on earth, with the help of the angels, of course.

Balain's favourite saint was Agnes; Agnes of God, they called her. She was one of the most celebrated Roman Catholic martyrs. Born in Rome, around the year 304 A.D., she was the virgin and patron saint for girls. Her story was a very sad one.

After so many years the story had become distorted and unclear. One version told of how very young she was, only 13, when she had declared herself married to Christ and would accept no other suitor. Being an extremely beautiful girl, there were several young men who wanted to marry her but all were spurned. After being rejected, the suitors revealed her Christianity (being a Christian was illegal in those days) and she was captured and taken to a brothel. In the brothel, her clothes were thrown off to expose her. Awed by her ethereal presence the youths did not dare to touch her. One of them, however, attempted to violate her and he was immediately struck blind. Agnes herself healed him with prayer. The emperor at the time, whose name was Diocletian, was enraged by the stories that circulated after this incident and condemned Agnes to death. She was therefore murdered on his request.

Another version told of her unearthly beauty and grace. The emperor's son saw her and fell in love with her. He asked her to marry him but she declined, since she had promised her life to Christ. The emperor's son pleaded with her, begged her, but she held firm. Then he became enraged and threw her in a room where he ordered all her clothes taken off as punishment. This version claims that a searing, blinding white light had immediately come and surrounded her, making it impossible for anyone to see her. Other attempts at punishment also failed miserable. Finally, the emperor ordered her death. They say that the emperor's soldiers lit a large fire around, hoping to burn her at the stake. The fire refused to burn inwards, towards Agnes, but burnt outwards, towards the soldiers. It engulfed them and killed them all - leaving Agnes untouched. Other attempts ended in the same way, until finally, she was beheaded. They had destroyed her body but Agnes of God lived on. People still saw her, heard her, and believed in her. Soon, she was canonised and became a saint. Her feast was kept on January 21st; and she was proclaimed the patron saint for girls. Her story is still told.

There were other saints as well, among them Saint Anne and Saint Joachim. Their story ran remarkably parallel to that of Samuel's birth. Anne and Joachim were a childless couple who longed for a child. Anne then prayed to God, lamenting her barren state and asking for a child. She promised that if she conceived a child, she would give that child in service to God. True to form she conceived and gave birth to a little girl. When the child was old enough to leave her mother, Anne took her to the church and gave her over to the service of God. It was the story of Samuel all over again.

Balain was already putting a phase of his plan into action. He had formed a movement called the 'Spiritual Awareness League', aimed at the youth. It was like a school or institution, designed to bring the youth closer to God. It gave lessons in religious studies as well as skills like typing, accounts, public relations and others. It was full boarding and once one had entered, one could not leave the place for a year. Balain used this time to put the real plan into action.

144

Together with a former psychiatrist, Balain was attempting to take over the minds of his young recruits. The psychiatrist had been banished from the medical community and stripped of his right to practise because of his bizarre attempts to achieve mind control. That he had driven most of his patients to insanity before being discovered only made it worse. However, by the time they had found him out, he had perfected what it was he wanted to achieve. Balain found him very useful.

Through a system of drugs administered in the food, the 'students' were made receptive and passive and the first phase was complete. Then came a series of lessons where they were fed with a lot of information which they absorbed and stored for further use. They then had therapy sessions where the psychiatrist managed to achieve mind control, making the students believe everything they were told, all under the guise of religion.

Balain thought back to a video tape he had been watching the other day on one of the latest recruits, a nineteen-year-old girl called Victoria. She had just finished her secondary school education and decided to join the league. On her arrival, she had been interviewed by the psychiatrist, Dr. Wamae.

"Why did you decide to join us, Victoria?" Dr. Wamae asked.

"I heard about the league from a friend," Victoria answered. "She told me about the classes here and the religious studies and it sounded like just the place I wanted to live in for a while."

"Are you a Christian?" he asked.

"Yes," she replied, "a Catholic. Both my parents are Catholics and I was brought up in a Catholic environment."

"Do you believe in God, Victoria?" he asked.

"Yes I believe in God," she answered.

"Would you like to help God build his kingdom here on earth?" he asked, watching her intently.

"Yes, I would do anything to help God," Victoria said.

"So you are a true follower of God's word?" Dr. Wamae asked.

"Yes, I am," Victoria ascertained.

"I think you will find it very pleasant here," the doctor said. "We have several courses which you can choose from. If your talents are in skills or languages or other studies, we will soon find out and help you exploit them. In the meantime, you will have a chance to grow closer to God, and to help Him bring His Kingdom to earth."

The next scene was enacted three months later, after Victoria had settled in and was in the process of 'beginning her conversion'.

"I hear that your studies are getting on well." remarked Dr. Wamae. "Have you been able to read the books we have in the library about spiritual revelation?"

"Yes, Dr. Wamae," Victoria said.

"Did you understand the concepts?" he asked.

"Yes, Dr. Wamae," she said. "I believe that it is possible to have a divine world without any sin or disobedience if we work hard enough at spreading the good word of the Lord."

"Do you believe in our Bishop's divinity, Victoria?" Dr. Wamae asked.

"Yes," she replied. "I believe the Bishop is God's chosen one who will lead us to God's Kingdom here on earth."

"Do you believe in God and the Bishop?" he asked.

"Yes I believe in God and the Bishop," she said. "I believe the Bishop does God's work."

"Do you believe that the Bishop will help build God's Kingdom here on earth?" he asked.

"Yes," she replied.

"Would you like to help God and His Bishop bring their Kingdom here on earth?" he asked.

"Oh yes," she replied.

"I can see that you are a true follower of God and of the Bishop's work," remarked Dr. Wamae. "You will be a great asset to our institution in the future. Just continue with your studies and concentrate of your therapy sessions. With your help, we shall bring God's and the Bishop's Kingdom to earth."

The next scene took place three months later. Victoria had shown great talent and intelligence and the Bishop had wanted her to start

146

rising up the ladder of importance in the institution. On the first rung were the Bishop's holies. A holy had the importance of a church deacon. After that came the divinity who was the equivalent of a priest. The third rung was an angel, which was of slightly less importance than an archangel, who was the closest of the Bishop's helpers. But before achieving any of this, Dr. Wamae had to interview her to make sure that her conversion was complete.

"Your name has been recommended to me, as a nominee for the post of Bishop's holy, Victoria. We are very proud of you," Dr. Wamae said, beaming across at her.

"I would be happy to serve," she replied.

"Do you believe in the Bishop?" he asked.

"I believe in the Bishop. He is the supreme power, the incarnate of God on earth, the true revelation," she answered.

"Do you believe in the Bishop's plan?" he queried.

"I believe in the supremacy of the Bishop's plan and power and I fully support his plan to build his kingdom on earth," she said.

"Would you like to help the Bishop bring his kingdom here on earth?" Dr. Wamae asked.

"I would do anything to help the Bishop build his kingdom here on earth," Victoria answered.

"Would you commit a sin for him?" he asked.

"A sin, committed with the blessing of the Supreme Power is never considered a sin at all," she said looking at him calmly.

"I will submit your name as a nominee for post of Bishop's holy to the Council, Victoria," Dr. Wamae said. "As soon as I get the results of the vote I will inform you. I am sure, that the results will be positive."

"I am honoured to serve," she said.

The tape ended and the Bishop was satisfied that Victoria's conversion was complete. He had given his okay for her to become a holy and was confident that soon Victoria would raise to the post of an archangel. His plan to covert the world was already in progress.

Balain was convinced that this was the only way to buy time out of purgatory; to be able to convert as many people as possible his way of thinking. The more people he succeeded in converting, the less time he would be forced to spend in the dreaded purgatory. No one in their right mind would want to spend time in a place where one's worst nightmares came true. Therefore the less time spent in purgatory, the better. Balain had always been terrified of suffering and the mere mention of pain scared him out of his mind.

At the same time however, his plan meant that the clever Bishop could indulge in life. He was able to pursue earthly pleasures that were otherwise forbidden. On the top of his list were adultery and fornication. Balain knew they were wrong, but what could he do when he was constantly seduced by the young, attractive women in his congregation? It was hard to resist. Now that his plan was working he could partake of as many earthly delights as he wanted and still escape a long, hard time in purgatory. It was a brilliant set-up.

The only thing that was still bothering him was the question of the Sabbath; was it Sunday or Saturday? Which was the true day? The Roman Catholic church stated that it was Sunday, and the Roman Catholic church was always right, or wasn't it? One couldn't be sure.

King Arthur's plan fitted into Balain's very well. Balain had readily taken the offer of being a member of the Round Table. He was ready to fulfil that for which he had been ordained to do; he was sure that the time had come at last.

Just then, his special bedside phone rang. Only a certain group of people had the number. Quickly, he reached out and picked it up.

"Balain," he said.

"King Arthur," came the reply. "Come in at once. Something has gone wrong."

Chapter Twenty-One

"I don't understand it. I just don't. How could something like this happen especially now, that we're so close?" Balain said as he stood up angrily and started pacing the room, visibly agitated.

It was not supposed to be happening. That particular meeting of the Round Table was not scheduled to take place. The Round Table had already congregated at 9.00 am, that very morning. Matters had been discussed and issues resolved and reports had been given round, handed in and accepted. Everything had been going smoothly and according to plan.

An hour later all the knights had left to go and pursue their own businesses and get on with their lives. They had never met twice on the same day before; it was too risky. But then, they had never been in such a situation before. There was a first time for everything.

It was twelve o'clock on Saturday afternoon, just half an hour or so since a series of phone calls had disrupted the lives of seven of the Knights of the Round Table. They had lost no time in getting to King Arthur's house.

They were all upset and didn't understand the story that Mordred was telling them. What on earth could be the matter now? How could anyone know what was happening? Who had betrayed them and why? Balain was simply voicing the question that was running through every member's mind.

"Calm down Balain," King Arthur said. "Getting upset is not going to get us anywhere."

"Yes, but I just don't understand how something like this could have happened," he said, running his fingers through his hair, distractedly.

"We don't know for sure that something has happened," Mordred said.

"What do you mean?" Bohert asked, looking startled. "It's obvious that . . ."

"What is obvious is the Susan Juma knows more than we thought she did," Mordred interrupted, "and that we were right to suspect her connection with Chain. But we have no idea what she knows or where she got the information from," he said.

"That was a rather cryptic message she gave our man at B.I.O.," Lancelot said.

"What exactly did she say?" Galahad asked. "I mean, we have the general gist of it but what exactly did she tell him over the phone?" They turned to Mordred.

"Not much," Mordred replied. "It seems that she phoned our man and told him that she knew who was killing all the ministers in the country and that it was linked to Mwatata's death.. Then she told him not to discuss it with any of the other top officials at B.I.O. because she suspected that one of them was in on the whole thing. Not very clever, our Susan. She didn't suspect hard enough and wound up telling the wrong person. Anyway, she said that she couldn't talk to him over the phone and asked him to meet her in town this afternoon," he said.

"Lucky for us she told our man," Tristan said, "we would really have been in a fix if she had gone to another top official."

"Yeah, I always knew it was a good idea to have a top official at B.I.O. on our side," agreed Perceval.

"Exactly how many top officials are there at B.I.O.?" King Arthur asked.

"Well, including our man there are five at the moment," Mordred answered. "They are supposed to be six but with Mwatata out of action that leaves only five. J. F. Kimani, the head of B.I.O., Tim Kuria, who is in charge of Mwatata's case, Matthew Mucheru, Isaac Peters and Patrick Ondieki."

"So out of those five she trusted our man most?" Gawain asked.

"Looks like it," Mordred replied. "Or at least she suspected him the least."

"Stupid girl," Gawain commented dryly.

"You can't blame her; she is a woman," King Arthur said rather sharply. "Let's just thank our lucky stars that she is a woman and decide what we are going to do with her."

"She will have to be eliminated," Mordred said. "It won't be hard. I will have two or three good hit-men take care of it."

"Alright, that is no problem then," King Arthur said. "Any objections from anyone?"

The Knights of the Round Table had a silent conference where they all looked around at each other and turned over the possibilities in their minds. Slowly each of them acknowledged that there was only one course of action that could possibly be taken.

"But what I want to know is how she found out," Balain said, making it sound more like a question than a statement.

"I guess that is a question that will never be answered, Balain," King Arthur replied. "And I guess we shall never know exactly how much she knew."

"It can't be that much," Lancelot said. "After all she hasn't even been able to work out which of the top officials at B.I.O. is our's."

"The fact remains that she did know for sure that one of B.I.O.'s top officials is not loyal to B.I.O.," Galahad said. "From all I have heard about B.I.O., with its dedication and adherence to the constitution, it must be shocking for any of their agents to turn against them let alone one of their top officials. I don't think that it's a concept which one can just pluck from thin air. Something must have led her to believe that one of those top five was disloyal. She was sure of it. She gambled with the idea of who it might be or rather, who it might not be, and lost. That's not her fault. She had to have some kind of help for whatever line of investigation she was pursuing and decided to contact the person she trusts most in the upper echelons of the organisation. It was just unfortunate for her that that person . . . happened to be the very person she fears most. Well, life is like that sometimes."

"I hope you realise that we are still overlooking one very important thing in this whole mess," King Arthur said. "We are all overlooking one Christopher Mathenge, the man they call 'Chain'. Where does he fit in all of this?" he sighed and sat back.

"Chain?" Galahad asked. "I have heard of him. One of B.I.O.'s best wasn't he?"

"Yes, he is very well known," Perceval agreed. "You might say that he is a legend."

"What exactly is so wonderful and legendary about him?" Gawain asked. "Why is he such a threat?"

"Not so much of a threat as a cog in the wheels," Mordred offered. "He might succeed in temporarily setting back our plans if he is involved. He was an agent at B.I.O. few years back. Now he is thirty-four years old, a millionaire and he lives on a large estate in Kitale. He was undoubtedly B.I.O.'s best agent ever, always at the right place at the right time and he could out-manoeuvre and out-think almost anybody. Four years ago he retired and has not gone near the place since then."

"Why on earth did he retire if he was doing so well?" queried Bohert.

"Personal problems," Mordred replied. "He had a partner called Samuel Kamau. The story goes that they were like brothers. The regulations when working on a case are that an agent is not allowed to arrest, search or interrogate unless he is in the company of another agent, so most of the agents have official partners whom they work with all the time. Samuel Kamau became Christopher Mathenge's partner."

'I guess the fact that Chain is so successful is no accident. He became what he is by sticking to the rule of not trusting and so got no surprises. He doesn't have many friends and has no confidants. Kamau was different because he learnt to trust and so opened himself to incredible weakness; it was the old Samson and Delilah story. A stunningly beautiful woman was thrown his way and he was so mesmerised that he babbled away all his secrets to her. The fact that she was also an agent at B.I.O. helped relax his guard somewhat as well. Anyway, it turns out that Kamau found out that his sweetheart had been using him to get secrets and then selling them to the enemy. He behaved rather stupidly once more by going to confront her, unarmed at that, with his revelations. The woman had no choice but to kill him. However, Kamau had had the sense to tell Chain the whole sordid story, so when he was killed, Chain then knew exactly who had killed him.

'They say Chain spent seven days solving the case on his own. Against regulations, I might add, he set out to track her down. The girl had disappeared but he stalked her patiently until he found her. I would hate to imagine exactly how she died, but Chain killed her. That was when he decided to retire from B.I.O., and went to live on his farm. He severed all contacts with B.I.O. except one, Jackson Mwatata, was one of his closest friends. The other is George Bakari, the head of the C.I.D. in Kenya," Mordred concluded.

"Are we overlooking him?" Tristan asked.

"No," Mordred replied.

"Yet the fact remains that after a four-year absence he has suddenly come back into circulation," King Arthur said. "Four years of self-imposed solitude during which he absolutely refused any contact with B.I.O. and its agents. All of a sudden he is back in town, accompanied by Miss Susan Juma. The same Susan Juma who claims to know who had been killing the ministers in this country. For the first time in four long years, B.I.O. had the honour of seeing its legend walk through its halls one more time. Those are all facts."

"It could mean something and it could mean nothing at all," Mordred suggested. "Perhaps you're forgetting that Mwatata was a mentor and father figure to both Juma and Chain. It stands to reason that the two had met and probably come to like each other over the years. We all know that there are certain things women can't handle alone. Susan probably convinced Chain to take her back to B.I.O. when she went to ask for leave. After all, it was not some trivial thing: the death of one of their best friends. But the evidence points to the fact that she hasn't told Chain whatever it is she knows."

"What evidence?" Tristan, suddenly asked.

"Today's little scenario, for instance," Mordred said. "It has none of Chain's genius in it. If there's one thing I'm sure of, Chain wouldn't trust any B.I.O. agent top, bottom or otherwise. He has had too many raw deals in that direction. If she was to tell him that she suspected one of the top officials there but that she didn't know which one, he would distrust her even more. That would be more than enough to convince him to keep as far away from the place as he possibly could."

"That makes sense", agreed King Arthur.

"It certainly does," Gawain said. "He doesn't seem the sort of person to pursue any line of investigation based on a complete gamble. That would be rather stupid and from what I have heard of the man, he's not stupid."

"For reasons best known to herself, Juma did not tell Chain about what she was going to do today," Mordred said. "So far he is not involved. Maybe she knew that he would disapprove of her plan; that he would either try to dissuade her or forbid her to carry it out altogether. She may have felt certain that she could trust that one particular official and at the same time felt that she has to warn him about some threat at her much beloved B.I.O. She might think that it's only B.I.O. that would lead her to the solution to this case and so she needs some inside help. She didn't want to join the official B.I.O. investigation because she can't be sure of all the agents who are involved. You can see that she is in a dilemma at the moment."

Perceval nodded. "I would have probably done the same thing in her situation."

"I don't know if I would have done the same thing but I think I can understand why she did it," Tristan said. "It all makes sense."

"Since she came to our man then we really don't have anything to worry about," Balain said, relieved. "All we have to do now is get rid of her once and for all."

"I'm afraid that's necessary," sighed King Arthur. "Mordred; you will have to do something about her. It's too bad really because she has a promising future ahead of her."

"How will you do it?" Galahad asked.

"It won't be difficult," Mordred answered confidently. "She has chosen to meet our man in a rather mildly populated area of town, this afternoon. We shall put two good hit-men somewhere in the vicinity before the designated time. As soon as she reaches the area, she will be hit, nice and clean. She won't even know what hit her."

154

"Isn't there some way we can let her talk to the man first so that we can find out exactly how much she knows or how she found out and whether she has told Chain anything?" Bohert asked.

"I'm afraid not," Mordred said. "You see, she probably won't want to talk to him while standing at that particular spot. She would either want to whisk him away somewhere in her car or a cab, or simply talk while walking around. From long-range, a moving target is almost impossible to hit accurately. We can't take that chance. We are going to have to hit her as soon as she arrives."

"What about Chain?" King Arthur asked. "What are you going to do about him?"

"We are going to have to prepare something extra special for our friend Chain," Mordred said. "It would be too much of a risk to let him go free; and we have already taken enough risks. I'm going to have to take care of him myself; today if possible. The sooner the better, anyway. I will have to think of something water tight. Chain won't fall for some simple trap. He is too clever for that."

"There is one other person," King Arthur said.

"Who?" Bohert asked.

"George Bakari, the immediate head of the C.I.D. in Kenya," King Arthur answered. "If Chain knows anything you can be sure that Bakari knows it too. Bakari would have heard about Mwatata's death, by now, and would want to know what was happening. Chain wouldn't keep it from him. He would tell him everything he knew and then probably ask him for advice."

"You're right," acknowledged Mordred. "We are going to have to take care of him as well."

"Be very careful," King Arthur advised. "Killing the head of the C.I.D. needs a lot of thinking."

The meeting adjourned, and the Knights of the Round Table left King Arthur's house one after another, at the usual 20 minutes interval. None of them noticed the boy in the opposite house watching, intrigued because they had met twice that Saturday.

Chapter Twenty-Two

Susan pulled her coat more snugly around her, as the wind blew forcefully around her. Nairobi's weather was unpredictable; one never knew exactly what would happen next.

Many pleasure seekers filled the streets of Nairobi on Saturdays, craving pleasure like a drug addict craves a fix. From her vantage point, Susan watched them scurrying hither and thither, some with tense worried expressions on their faces.

'But what were they tense and worried about?' One did not have to look deep to discover the delights and pleasures of Nairobi. There was an abundance of theatres, cinemas, bars, restaurants, shows, discos and a little of everything designed to make life bearable. There was always a sufficient number of people around ready and willing to join in any hunt for fun. One could spend the whole day and night in one big party often at minimum cost. It seemed like a terrific bargain.

Cinema halls were frequented more for the sake of being seen there than for any real inclination to watch that particular film. After all it was a well known fact that the films at the cinemas were usually repeats, or films which had been produced quite a long while back. They had already been watched, taken apart and scrutinised by those who flocked to watch them.

For all their frantic search for fun, most of the pleasure seekers weren't truly content or just plain happy. They worried so much about the thought of life passing them by that life in fact did pass them by. Those desperate searching faces whose sole goal was to pursue happiness with an intensity which they were unable to apply anywhere else were invariably the losers in the end. They had no direction, no existence besides that of their own closed-in, selfish world where nothing apart from themselves, thrived. There, happiness was a commodity that had to be obtained at all costs. There, peace and tranquility were completely alien concepts; unknown, untried and uncared for. This was Nairobi, the city in the sun.

Susan was completely oblivious of the manoeuvres of the crowds. She was in town to catch a traitor. She had a Colt semi-automatic .45 calibre pistol in one pocket and a long-range walkie talkie in the other. Her job was to track and identify the traitor and to gun him down in cold-blood if both of the two hidden gunmen equipped with long-range telescopic rifles were unable to do so. She felt no remorse, no twinge of guilt. One of the top 5 officials at B.I.O. was a traitor and there was no other choice. All through history the law made it clear that traitors had to be shot. No mercy was ever shown at a time like this.

They had already eliminated one of the five suspects. Timothy Kuria had walked up to the designated area and waited impatiently for half an hour before leaving. There had been no one with him; no hidden snipers, no gun men. It was not Tim Kuria and Susan was glad. She had always liked the man and had been waiting impatiently for news from Chain who had been staking him out. The moment he was pronounced clean, Susan had let out a sigh of relief.

Chain had left Kuria's area and gone on to stake out Isaac Peters. Susan was waiting carefully for Patrick Ondieki. The man in question had already arrived some ten minutes earlier. His every move was under careful scrutiny from several directions, but he didn't know it. He had been placed in a very open spot, where he could easily be seen. Susan herself was carefully concealed and could not be detected either from the ground or from above.

Ondieki fiddled with his tie and kept on glancing at his watch. Susan watched him keenly, silently. She had never really got along well with him but she couldn't actively dislike him. She usually avoided him when possible and didn't seek him out unless it was absolutely necessary.

"Radio three, can you hear me?" Chain's voice crackled through her walkie-talkie. She pressed a button and talked in a low voice.

"I hear you, radio one," she replied. "It's all extremely quiet around here. No action at all. Anything on your end?"

"Not much," he said. "Peters has just arrived. He looks harmless enough. I highly doubt it's him. Peters and I worked together once. He's a good man. Not really the type. But then you can't tell, can you?"

"No, not by looking anyway," Susan replied quickly.

"Well anyhow, keep your eyes open," Chain advised. "If there is a traitor at B.I.O., today he's finished. Over and out." His voice died out.

Susan pressed another button. "Radio five, come in," she said, "this is radio three."

Her walkie-talkie crackled to life again. "I hear you, radio three," said the young man on the other end. "Go ahead."

"See anything up there?" she asked.

"Not a thing," replied the man on radio five. "It's very quiet around and there is no sign of anyone else. I have had my scope trained on the subject for the last fifteen minutes or so. He hasn't moved a muscle."

"How about you, radio two?" Susan queried.

"I haven't noticed anything unusual either," replied radio two. "Watch out, he is leaving."

Susan switched off her walkie-talkie and turned to watch Ondieki. He was indeed leaving. He had apparently decided not to wait any longer and was rudely pushing people out of the way before him. She slowly switched her walkie-talkie on. Nobody had moved off when Ondieki did. He had been alone.

"Notice anything radio five?" she asked.

"No movement whatsoever," said radio five. "He was alone. I'm sure of it."

"What about you, radio two?" she asked.

"I agree there was nobody with our target. He came alone and he left alone in my opinion," came the reply.

"Alright, you guys stick around for a while," she said. She punched the first button, to change frequency. "Come in, radio one," she said.

"Go ahead Susan," said Chain.

"Ondieki is clear. I am leaving this area," she said. "I am already late for my appointment with J. F. K. How are things at your end? Any luck?"

"Depends on what you call luck," said Chain. "It's dead quiet here: no reactions at all. I'm sure that Peters is not our man either but I'll stick around just in case. See you later then, over and out."

Susan switched off her walkie-talkie again and set out into the human traffic patrolling the street. She swung aggressively into it, expertly weaving her way and adroitly avoiding getting pushed or shoved out of the way. Nairobi's pavement traffic was something she was used to. It no longer had the power to upset or terrify her as it once had.

She stationed herself in a sheltered corner at a pre-arranged spot close to where she was supposed to be meeting Kimani. They had already determined that that particular spot was not visible from the ground or the air. She made herself as comfortable as she possibly could and awaited Kimani's arrival.

He arrived a few minutes later, as Chain was calling her to inform her that Isaac Peters was in the clear; that he had left the area where she was supposed to have met him. Susan was beginning to get convinced that there was a flaw in their plan somewhere. Three of the candidates had already been eliminated, and of the two remaining, neither Matthew Mucheru nor J. F. Kimani seemed to be capable of doing the deed. Chain was on his way to Mucheru's designated spot but Susan had suddenly lost confidence in the whole set-up. Idly she watched Kimani play with his watch, turning it this way and that so that it caught the sun. There was no harm in staying around and seeing the whole thing to the end. After all, there was only Kimani and Mucheru left. It couldn't really harm and while standing around, she might be able to dredge up some idea from somewhere. She and Chain were going to have to rethink their strategy. Not that they had that much to go by in the first place. Susan glanced impatiently in Kimani's direction. The sun's rays were being reflected off the watch; making it glint in the sunlight. It was hurting her eyes.

A sudden thought stopped her in her tracks. The way Kimani's watch glinted in the light was mesmerising; but the movements seemed to appear synchronised in some sort of pattern, although the man himself appeared to be very casual. Horrified, Susan stared at the glinting watch in fascination. It was some sort of signal! 'Oh dear God!' she thought, 'it was Kimani. Kimani was the traitor!'

Her walkie-talkie crackled to life.

"Radio three, do you hear me?" asked a voice. "This is radio six."

"I hear you, radio six," she responded.

"I have spotted two gunmen," he said. "One on the ground, about five metres away from our target, and one on a neighbouring building."

"I see the one on the ground," Susan said. "Radio seven, can you spot them?"

"I see them both," answered another voice.

"Okay, radio six; you take Kimani and then try for the gunman on the ground," Susan instructed. "Radio seven, you take the one on the building then try for the one on the ground if you can."

"Roger," said both radios simultaneously.

Susan shut off her head set and started moving towards where Kimani was standing. Her head was reeling from the impact of the latest revelation. Kimani was the traitor! It was almost impossible to believe. Despite the trauma she had already experienced, the shock she had already received, she still found it impossible to believe.

She didn't hear the shot. She very much doubted that anyone had. But she saw Kimani clutch at his chest in horror as she came into full view. For a split second, his eyes met hers in dawning realisation before he crumpled to the ground, the bright red patch on his shirt growing and spreading as he fell on the cold, hard, unforgiving pavement.

The people around him started screaming and running around in panic. In a matter of seconds, pandemonium struck, scattering people all over the place and hiding Kimani from view. Struggling through the crowd Susan managed to catch a glimpse of him. There was a man crouched over him, undoing his shirt and calling for an ambulance in a strong competent voice. She turned away, highly doubting that Kimani had survived that bullet.

Eyes rapidly scanning the crowd, she saw the second gunman, who had openly removed his gun and was beginning to move rapidly away from the scene. Desperately, she clawed her way through the crowd towards him. Finally, she managed to find a break which she pushed through. Running towards him, she shouted for him to stop. Turning around sharply, he levelled his gun and started to fire. The screams and shouts intensified as Susan dived behind a car which was parked on the curb.

"Get down!" she shouted; trying to make herself heard above the noise. "Everybody drop to the ground! Now!"

Some instinctive part of the mass of people reacted to the commanding note in her voice and most of them immediately dropped to the ground, pulling and pushing others with them.

The enraged gunman continued shooting; shattering the glass windows of the car, bursting its tyres and denting the doors. Susan waited until he had stopped shooting, guessing that he must be reloading and then sprung to her feet, bringing her hands which clutched at her gun over the top of the car. As soon as she had him in her sight, she squeezed the trigger.

She continued shooting as he quickly turned and sprinted away by then had to stop when he was surrounded by a group of panic-stricken people. She couldn't risk shooting at him again as she might accidentally hit an innocent bystander. She vaulted over the top of the car and sprinted furiously after him.

He dashed into a nearby building and made for the elevator. Susan caught a glimpse of him as he roughly pushed people aside in a bid to get into it. His menacing gun and terrible expression threw fresh waves of people into panic. Susan stopped by the doorman as she attempted to dash after the elevator.

She whipped out her B.I.O. card and held it up at him. "Special agent," she said breathlessly. "That man is a killer!"

The doorman let her go bemusedly, urging her along and then staring after her in fascination. Those split seconds had cost her any chance of catching the elevator and so she sprinted for the stairs, praying that she had enough time to complete the long flight of steps.

She came up to the first floor pantingly as the elevator opened. She raised her gun but couldn't fire a shot since the gunman was at the back of the elevator which was full of people. She turned back to the staircase as the elevator doors closed again. Adrenalin pumped through her, helping her scale the stairs which loomed before her like immovable mountains. The elevators didn't stop on the second, third and fourth floors. On the fifth floor; as she heard it opening; she crouched down on the stairs, concealing herself from sight. The gunman came out quickly, glancing around, but seeing no sign of her, he started walking away fast as she sprang to her feet again.

"Stop," she shouted again as she brought her gun up over the banisters and trained it on him. She watched dazedly as he brought up his gun and started to turn around.

She started shooting before he could bring it up fully to focus on her. Her first shot caught him in the stomach, and the second on the chest, sending him reeling backwards. As she ran towards him to look at his staring eyes and feel for his by then non-existent pulse, she pressed a button on her walkie-talkie.

"Chain," she said, "it was Kimani. We have got him. Over and out."

Chapter Twenty-Three

Barbara Kwanda ran a tired hand through her hair as she left the library. Working on a Saturday was not exactly her idea of fun. Unfortunately, she didn't find it unusual either. More often than not, she found herself working away her entire Saturday and on occasions, half of Sunday as well. In her world, weekends were almost non-existent.

She had spent almost the whole day running around trying to find out what the five absentee ministers were doing last Thursday when they were supposed to be attending a social function in Mombasa. It seemed that when ministers wanted to disappear from the public eye, it was very easy.

Barbara couldn't imagine being anything other than an investigative reporter. It was one thing that she had always dreamed of; the one thing that made her life fulfilled. It was rare, however, that she found herself investigating anything for Susan Juma who was so good at investigating, herself. But the impression Babs had got was that for once Susan's hands were tied, firmly and securely. It was strange and very unusual and Babs wished fervently that she knew what it was all about.

She hadn't always known Susie. They had met in college. It turned out that they were room-mates as a matter of fact and it wasn't long before they discovered that they were kindred spirits. They more or less liked the same things, enjoyed the same past-time activities listened to the same type of music and ate the same foods most of the time. Susan had been there to help her through Rick.

Rick was just a nick name; short for Patrick. He had been their class-mate in college. It was strange, but when Babs thought of the 'good old days', college always came to mind. The young carefree days when the most traumatic thing that could happen was to break a fingernail. But when she was asked to dredge up all her bitter memories, bad times or days of misery and excruciating pain, Patrick immediately came to mind.

He had been the carefree type; the life and soul of a party. The very epitome of fun and games. Babs was attracted to him by his devil-may-care attitude, his unpredictability and his love for pleasure.

She had come from a family where there was no laughter and laughing was treated as a cardinal sin. She had strict Catholic parents who had ceased to love each other a long time before and saw no reason why they should love her. They took it upon themselves to bring her up to be a model child; perfect and pious: a veritable little saint. There was nothing funny in that. How could one laugh when inflation was steadily on the rise and prices of commodities bordered on the incredible? How could one laugh when millions of people were dying every day? How could one laugh when crime, immorality, unemployment, epidemics, drought, starvation, economic depression, nuclear warfare and mental retardation were on the increase? The earth was no place for laughter. One should wait to laugh in heaven.

They taught her that everything was to be endured even when it brought suffering. Nothing on earth was good; everything was evil. If it felt good then it had to be evil and it had to be avoided at all costs. Babs was a depressed child.

When she was thirteen she discovered her father in bed with the maid. After many days of soul-searching she had decided to tell her mother. She needn't have bothered because her mother called her a liar and gave her a slap on the face for her efforts. She had told her never to think such thoughts or even; say them out loud again. So Babs had kept her mouth securely shut.

One day, when Babs and her mother came home rather unexpectedly from a shopping trip to catch her father with the maid once again, Babs had had her first laughing fit. The look of horror on her mother's face and the look of guilt on her father's were suddenly too hilarious for her to resist. She laughed long and loud while her father and the maid both tried to scramble into their clothes. Enraged, her mother turned around and hit her across the cheek. Calmly, Babs reached out and slapped her mother back. Her stunned look was well worth it.

164

"It's all a lie isn't it?" Babs asked, still grinning. "All that crap about heaven and virtues and denying yourself all the earthly pleasures!"

"Barbara . . ." her father said, reaching out.

"Don't touch me," Babs said sharply. "I'm going to have my say now. If this is the way you get to heaven then you'll have to count me out. You preach against immorality and adultery and then indulge as soon as you feel your back is turned. If your adultery and lies are your ticket to a better place then I would rather stay right here. It is not a perfect world, but then it has never claimed to be. I would rather go to hell my own way. Now if you'll excuse me," she said with exaggerated politeness before leaving the room.

From that day on life was one big laugh for Babs. It was not as if she found anything particularly amusing; it was just that she felt that if she did not laugh she would probably go insane. Or worse, if that was possible.

The thing that fascinated her most about Patrick, was the fact that his laughter was real. He really did think that life was one funny thing after another; a series of laughs. Susan had warned her not to get involved with Rick. A man who couldn't take life seriously couldn't take any relationship seriously either; or so Susie said. Rick was the original heartbreaker. He flirted aimlessly from girl to girl, taking his pleasure and then leaving. He seemed calmly oblivious of all the tears and self-recrimination he left behind. But for all that, Babs was unable to resist. When Rick claimed her, she went willingly, floating above the surface on cloud nine. She resolutely blocked out all thoughts of tomorrow and concentrated on the present; on attaining happiness.

Their relationship had been fraught with ups and downs from the word 'go'. Rick had discovered a deeply possessive streak somewhere within him which threatened to make life absolutely unbearable from the beginning. To make matters worse, he didn't see why he shouldn't also have his fun on the side. He flirted shamelessly with every female within a ten mile radius but completely blew his stack when a man so much as opened the door for Babs.

Some of their worst fights were as a result of his attitude which he just couldn't see as selfish and unfair. But their fights were by no means restricted entirely to this subject. They fought about his carefree attitude to life, which Babs had finally come to understand as irresponsible and immature. They fought about his choice of friends who ranged from merely irritating to hopeless, drunken bums. The more they fought the more miserable she became.

Everything came to a head one day when she walked into his room to find one of her friends on his lap and the room littered with an assortment of drugs. After a small pause which assessingly took in the whole situation, she had simply turned around again and walked out. She vividly remembered going to her room and sitting down frozen on her bed, not saying a word to Susan, who was trying as best as she possibly could to find out what was happening.

"It's Rick, isn't it?" Susan asked after a while.

Babs had burst into tears and blurted out everything. She screamed, ranted and raved, and nearly went hysterical. All through this, she kept expecting Susan to say, 'I told you so' but Susan never did. She managed to calm Babs down and then provided her with a stiff drink. After this she put her to bed where she slept deeply until the following morning.

Babs remembered the depression she had sunk into after this. For days she did not respond to anything and did not communicate with anyone. She left the handling of Rick entirely up to Susan, who informed him, point blank that Babs never wanted to see him again. Susan screened Babs' visitors, filtered her phone calls and scanned her mail for her. And then, after about a month, she took her out for a night on the town.

It was incredible, that was the only way Babs could describe Susan's idea of a night on the town. Susan knew the best spots and how to make the most of them. She knew a great assortment of people who had carefully honed having fun into a fine art. It was impossible not to enjoy oneself. Babs suddenly felt alive again and learnt how to laugh once more.

She agreed to meet Rick somewhere, told him what she really thought about him and steadfastly refused to renew their relationship. He begged and pleaded, trying to convince her that he had changed but she had had heard that line too many times to listen to it any more.

Strangely enough however, Rick really did seem to have changed. The laughter had gone out of him and all the light had been switched off, leaving him dull and lifeless; an empty shell of his former self.

When she heard that he was in the hospital, Babs was very surprised. She had been thinking that his lifelessness had been a result of depression from the break-up of their affair or a deliberate ploy to convince her to go back to him. She had never thought he might have been sick. But even then she had no idea how serious his illness was. She couldn't believe it when Susan told her that Rick had an incurable cancer and was calling for her; Rick was dying.

Of course she had gone to him; rushed to the hospital as soon as she could, hoping that it was all some strange joke. Unfortunately it was not. Rick confessed to her that he had known about the cancer for quite some time but hadn't wanted anyone else to know. He felt that by making it known then it would have meant acknowledging the fact that he was going to die. Babs understood so much after that; his frantic search for pleasure, his off-hand attitude and his whole outlook was simply based on a desperate bid to live. But he also made Babs understand that he loved her, and that he never wanted to cause her pain.

She stayed close to him for the last few weeks of his life. She was sure that God wouldn't be so cruel as to snatch Rick away from her just as she had found someone whom she could truly love. She had nursed him, fed him, sat with him, prayed for him and most importantly she had laughed for him, since it was something which he could no longer do for himself. Then one day, he had called her to him kissed her, closed his eyes and then just . . . died. It was almost too much for Babs to bear.

Once again it had been Susan who had brought her back to the land of the living. It was Susan who had kept her sane when she thought she would go mad with grief. She would never forget the words Susan had spoken to her immediately after the funeral.

"This is probably not the best time to say this to you," Susan had said, "but you have got to keep on living. That's the only thing you can do for Rick now. He gave laughter and love, don't lock them up inside. Go and spread the value of true laughter and the power of real love to all those who come near you for his sake. Go and make people happy, and think that Rick was set free forever; that he is soaring above the clouds, watching you and approving. Remember that, Babs. Go and cry. It will wash out the bitterness, and cleanse your soul. After that, you have got to live Babs. It's all you have been asked to do."

Babs had been touched. She had never forgotten those words. But then, she had never forgotten Rick either. She still felt his loss everyday, and she was incapable of having any kind of relationship with a man.

The fact that Susan had decided to conduct an independent investigation shunning any help from B.I.O. was very unsettling. That she did not want any one from B.I.O. to know made it even worse. Babs could draw a million conclusions from those two facts but she was too scared to try it. It was impossible for her to contemplate. She decided to pass by the Kenya Broadcasting Corporation headquarters and pick up a few papers which she would need at home. She was surprised to find pandemonium inside the building. Life at K.B.C. was usually hectic but not like this. Babs stopped one of her colleagues.

"What's going on, Tom?" she asked.

"Some crazy shooting incident in town," he replied. "Kind of like cowboys and Indians. It seems that there were some criminals running loose and some B.I.O. agents were running after them. We have two dead and one critically injured.

"B.I.O. agents?" asked Babs in horror.

"Yes," replied Tom. "And you'll never guess who our critically injured person is," he said, eyes twinkling in anticipation. At the negative shake of her head he decided to put her out of her misery. "J. F. Kimani himself. The brains, the driving force behind B.I.O. I didn't know he still took part in active duty."

Babs was stunned and breathless. There was definitely something wrong at B.I.O. First Mwatata's death, then Susan's defection and now this. She couldn't make out what was going on but she was convinced it was not anything good.

"How did it happen?" she whispered.

"Oh, we are not too sure yet," Tom said. "We have so many witnesses and they all tell a different story. It seems that Kimani was

168

chasing one of the criminals who turned and shot him. After that, another agent, a woman this time, followed the criminal into a nearby building and killed him. As this incredible chase was going on, there was another agent outside who managed to get the second criminal. Kimani was shot through the ribs and, it's a wonder he is still alive. However, nobody expects him to survive until tomorrow. Excuse me I've got to rush." And he sped off.

Babs stood there in stunned silence for sometime before dashing off to the phone. She repeatedly called Susan's apartment number but there was nobody picking up the phone. She waited and waited then suddenly remembered that Susan was probably at Chain's apartment. She dialled the number desperately hoping that it was the correct one. Still, nobody answered. Making a quick decision, she picked up her purse and ran outside. Once there, she hailed a cab.

She was at Chain's apartment twenty minutes later, pushing at the bell. She vaguely realised that she was probably growing hysterical but didn't know what to do about it. All she could think of was that Susan could be hurt or worse.

The apartment door was flung open by Chain with Susan close at his heels. "Babs, what's the matter?" Susan asked anxiously.

"You're all right," Babs said a little breathlessly as she was ushered in and the door closed. "I thought they had shot you too. I tried to call but nobody answered the phone in your apartment."

"We have only just got in," Susan said.

"Oh," said Babs inadequately. "They have shot Kimani. Did you know?"

"Yes I know," Susan said, a funny look on her face. "I had him killed myself."

"Oh," Babs said again. She was totally disorientated now. Then what Susan said filtered through. "You didn't kill him," she said. "He is alive but in critical condition at the Nairobi Hospital," she said.

Chain and Susan looked at each other and then moved to pick up their coats. Babs followed them anxiously. "Does this have anything to do with your five ministers?" she asked.

"Yes," said Susan.

"Well I know where one was on Thursday," Babs said. "Adam Kariuki was the Guest of Honour at a beauty contest in Thika."

Chapter Twenty-Four

Chain drove his Honda Civic expertly through the congested traffic on the way to Nairobi Hospital. He had no idea what it was that he was supposed to do to Kimani once he got there. If there was some chance of interrogating him, he would definitely try. But after that, he didn't know what would follow. There was no point of killing him. King Arthur and company would know by now that Chain and Susan knew something was going on. They would soon come after them. So what would he do if he allowed Kimani to live? They obviously couldn't allow him to return as head of B.I.O., could they? Susan and Babs sat in nervous silence in the car. Nobody really had anything to say.

"Do we try again? Do we let him live, or what?" Susan voiced his thoughts aloud.

"I don't know," Chain sighed. "He really isn't in any position to do any harm at the moment but you never know. Let's try and talk to him if we can but then leave him alone for a while; until we figure out what to do next."

"Could someone please explain," Babs began carefully, "the reason for this strange behaviour?"

"Kimani wasn't loyal to B.I.O. Babs," Susan said. "He had been bought by a certain group who are members of some kind of organised crime. These characters are hoping to commit a rather outrageous felony in the near future and had paid Kimani to work for them. It seems that this same group congregated and decided to buy several B.I.O. agents, a feat which may sound incredible but which apparently succeeded. In fact, the story goes that they now own almost half of B.I.O. When we suspected that a top official was involved, we set out to trap him. Kimani was caught in the trap."

Barbara's breathing was shallow and strangled. "You're joking, of course," she said.

"I wish I was," Susan replied. "I really wish I was. Maybe if it wasn't for the fact that Mwatata is dead then I might not believe any of it myself. So many people have died, and one way or another, many more are destined to die before long."

"Does this have anything to do with the ministers?" Babs asked.

"Yes," said Susan. "It seems that one of our five, sorry four, ministers is a member of this group. Believe it or not, a cabinet minister is involved. We don't know his name as yet. All we know is that he didn't attend Mrs. Musyoka's fund-raising and that his whereabouts on Thursday are unaccounted for. Tell me about Adam Kariuki, by the way."

"I have been digging up the dirt on him," Babs said, "trying to find out exactly where he was on Thursday. I don't blame him for preferring to attend a beauty contest rather than a boring fund-raising but it wasn't publicised because he was definitely not supposed to be there. It was just a small affair organised by his sister-in-law so I suppose he felt obliged to be there and safe that he wouldn't be found out. There are five or six people who will vouch for his presence there on Thursday."

"Okay, that effectively takes care of Adam Kariuki," Chain said. "But it still leaves us four others to deal with. What wouldn't I give to know where those particular ministers were on Thursday afternoon! The tape doesn't help much. It could be any one of them. Our best bet is the voice prints."

"Babs, is there any way you could get us individual copies of each of those four remaining ministers?" Susan asked. "It should be as recent as possible. Then we can run them through the machine as well as the sample we have. Whoever matches it is our man. Sounds simple, doesn't it? Now all we have to do is get hold of the machine."

"I can easily do it," Babs replied. "If any of them opened his mouths in public in the last 24 hours then we have got them on tape. The machine shouldn't pose any problems. You have got one at B.I.O. haven't you?"

"We have got one at B.I.O. alright," Susan said dryly. "Unfortunately, B.I.O. is a death trap; or hadn't I told you? There is no way you can convince me that all I have to do is walk in and ask to use their facilities. I would probably be shot on sight, at the gate even before I entered the premises."

"Well, why don't you get someone on the inside to do it for you?" Babs suggested.

"That would be a solution," Susan admitted. "Unfortunately, assuming we were absolutely sure whom to trust, anybody we asked would probably be placed in mortal danger as well. He or she would not be able trust a soul. As soon as there was a little slip-up, the penalty would be death. Still it does seem to be the only way. If we could get hold of someone with a good head on his shoulders, we could give it a try."

The car turned into the expensive Nairobi Hospital car-park. Chain smoothly parked it near the entrance of the building and they all got out. Striding swiftly, he led the way to the reception.

"We would like to see J. F. Kimani," he said firmly to the receptionist. She blinked at his tone and looked at him more intently.

"I'm afraid Mr. Kimani cannot have any visitors," she said.

Susan stepped forward and produced her B.I.O. card. "We are from the C.I.D.," she said smoothly, flashing her card in front of the girl's face. "We work with Mr. Kimani. He would most definitely want us there with him in case there is any important information he wants to give us." She returned her card into her pocket.

Without any further hesitation, the young receptionist gave them Kimani's room number and directions on how to get there. She pressed a buzzer and called Kimani's floor, to let the security guard there know that Kimani was being visited by three C.I.D. officers. She got an affirmative answer and nodded to the little group, bestowing a special little smile on Chain. Her eyes followed them until they disappeared from view. Susan threw an almost impatient glance at Chain, wondering if the receptionist had recognised him from somewhere or if she had just been attracted to him by his good looks. She was finding it increasingly difficult to accept that other women may find Chain as attractive as she did.

She flashed her card again, this time to the police officers at the door. They glanced at it, recognised the B.I.O. insignia and ushered them into the room. It was a small private room and Kimani was its sole occupant.

Susan glanced at Chain and silently asked to be allowed to handle the situation. Chain nodded his consent. Kimani was breathing shallowly and was connected to many tubes which must been painful and exceedingly uncomfortable. She reached out and touched his hand. His eyes slowly opened.

"Hey chief," she nodded down at him, "they got you, didn't they?" His eyes grew wide and uncomprehending. "I caught one of the guys you were with," she said. "He told me that he was with you as a hit-man and he was supposed to kill me as soon as I appeared. That was when I knew that you were on the other side. You must have had a good laugh at my expense when I called you and confided in you that there was a rogue agent among the top officials at B.I.O. when all the time it was you."

"I don't know what you're talking about," Kimani replied weakly, his eyes wary and hooded as he met her gaze.

"Come off it chief," Susan said, "the game is over. You don't understand, do you? You came with two hit-men, didn't you? One was supposed to kill me and one was supposed to kill you."

Kimani's eyes grew wider with shock and his breathing became more ragged.

"Think, old man," Susan said. "You were no longer needed. You were expendable. They wanted you out of the way as much as they did me. I was lucky my assailant didn't hit me. Yours hit you. It was as simple as that. But don't worry I took care of the would-be killers. However, I must tell you that going to King Arthur, Lancelot and Mordred was a pretty stupid idea if I may say so myself."

Kimani slumped back in his bed, clearly believing that everything was over.

"Co-operate, chief," Susan urged. "It might help, you to know it could mean being saved from the electric chair or the gallows. Just tell me who the others are."

Kimani was silent for a few minutes, then he sighed. "There are nine of them," he whispered. "I have never met any other apart from Mordred. King Arthur, Mordred, Lancelot, Balain, Bohert, Gawain,

174

Galahad, Tristan, and Perceval," his breathing was becoming more laboured and his face turned ashen grey and haggard. "I have never heard them being called by their real names ever."

"Is there anything else," she asked again. "Anything more, that might be of use?"

"Balain is . . . a Bishop," Kimani's breathing was getting even shallower, "a Kenyan Bishop. Gawain is an oil baron from Texas and I can recognise the accent. Tristan is a brain surgeon. They keep referring to a big lab they have, operated by Tristan. He carries out his experiments there."

"Where?" Susan asked eagerly. "Where is the lab?" she leaned closer to him.

"Near Wilson Airport," Kimani said. The pain was evident now. It racked through his body and made him grimace sharply.

"Anything else?" asked Susan.

"No," Kimani said, tiredly.

"I will personally arrange all the formalities," Susan said. "I will have to tell them what was going on and to what extent you were involved but I will stress that you helped me a lot with my investigations. Try and get a little rest now. We shall come back and see you later."

The three exited, leaving the head of B.I.O. lying on his bed, looking more dead than alive. Kimani did not watch them go. His eyelids had already dropped back down over his eyes and he was desperately trying to control his breathing. He felt more dead than alive.

Chain arranged for a doctor to go to Kimani's room and make sure that everything was still okay with him. The doctor quickly examined him and confirmed that everything was alright and there was a big chance of his complete recovery. Susan was unsure of whether she wanted Kimani to live or die.

The receptionist smiled openly at Chain again, hardly noticing that Susan and Babs were there. As they passed by her, she slipped a small piece of paper to him and then turned back to her work.

Susan's glances in Chain's direction were red hot daggers of anger as they walked towards the car park. He appeared unconcerned as he unfolded the piece of paper and glanced at it then he turned his amused eyes on her.

"Yes Susan," he said with a smile. "It is her phone number. Some people are so pushy, aren't they?" And he casually crumpled up the paper and threw it into a nearby waste bin.

"You didn't have to do that," Susan said stiffly. "It really isn't any of my business whether you call her or not."

"Isn't it?" Chain asked ruefully.

Babs turned from Chain to Susan, wondering what the exchange was all about. She was amazed by Susan's startling display of emotion. Susan never let her feelings show, but in this case she was being painfully transparent. However, Chain didn't seem to mind at all. A look of dawning comprehension spread on Bab's face.

They got back into the car and Chain gunned it to life. He backed out of the car-park swiftly, and back out onto the street. Susan seemed at last to realise Babs' presence and turned in her seat to glance furtively at her friend. Babs gave her a mischievous grin. Susan's face flushed and she turned apprehensively back towards Chain. Then her anxious eyes flickered back to Babs whom she gave a warning glare. Babs grinned at her, undaunted.

Susan sighed and turned back again to Chain. "What do you think we should do now?" she asked him, gazing at his profile.

"We shall have to try and find Tristan, Balain and Gawain," Chain said. "At least we have got some kind of lead on them."

"A Kenyan Bishop?" Susan asked in disbelief. "How many Bishops have we got in the country? A Texas oil baron? What kind of lead is that? Maybe we can get hold of Tristan. After all, a big lab near Wilson Airport shouldn't be hard to find if it exists. For all we know; Kimani could have been feeding us a lie, all this time."

"I agree he could have," Chain said. "It might be a wild goose chase, but we have got to try. It's all we have got. One thing we won't have to worry about," he gave a twisted smile, "Mordred. We won't have to find him; he will definitely find us."

176

Susan thought of Mwatata's office and the horrible scene she had witnessed there. She felt a sudden shiver as she remembered the bullet-ridden bodies and the lifeless flesh. The unknown Mordred was a distant menace; a terrifying spectre.

Chain took his eyes off the road for a moment to face her. "Don't worry; I won't let him get you," he assured her with a smile.

Strangely, just those few words seemed to comfort and reassure her. All her life she had looked out for herself and couldn't bear the thought of putting her life indeed, her safety, in someone else's hands. Now, it seemed like the logical thing to do. With those words Chain had made her a promise; one which she was surprisingly ready to accept. His calm and quiet confidence made her feel safer. Suddenly she knew that one way or the other, Chain would get her out of the whole mess alive. The spectre that was Mordred gradually receded from her mind. 'Who was Mordred when she had Chain?'

"I think we'll have to get in touch with Bakari," she said. "We'll have to tell him to send some C.I.D. personnel whom he trusts to guard Kimani's room. Mordred and his gang may decide to return and get rid of him; after all he might talk. Personally, I don't care whether they kill him or not but he would be a great help if it all comes to trial."

"I don't think it will come to trial," Chain said. "I don't think something as big as this would be made public; it may cause chaos. If they surrendered, I suppose they would be detained for treason. However, I don't think they will surrender, so they will just have to be killed.

"I wonder if they have set a date for Janet Musyoka's demise," Susan pondered aloud.

"They might have by now," Chain conceded. "If we get any of them, we should try and find out."

"Why aren't there any B.I.O. agents guarding Kimani's room?" Babs queried.

"B.I.O. agents aren't authorised to be used as protection," Susan explained. "That is for the C.I.D. and the secret service-men. We can investigate, make arrests and are licensed to kill, but we cannot act as bodyguards or any other form of protection."

"Sounds like fun," Babs suggested, excitement evident in her voice.

Chapter Twenty-Five

Stupid! That's what he was; stupid, stupid, stupid! All it had taken was a young, insignificant woman and a washed-out ex-B.I.O. agent, Chain, to prove it.

Mordred was furious with himself. His anger spread around the room and one could almost touch it. He had received the report of what had happened that afternoon but he still couldn't believe it. He had never misjudged anyone so badly in his life. Chain and his little friend Susan Juma, had showed him up for a fool. Mordred did not like being made to look like a fool. It was the one thing he couldn't bear.

His name was Nicholas Tanui; that was the name King Arthur had given him after adopting him so many years before. He had no idea who his mother was, and his mother had no idea who his father was. His mother had been a hooker, so there was no way of knowing which one of her customers had made her pregnant. She had given birth to him and dumped him in a dustbin in the city streets. He had been found and taken to a children's home where he had spent the first few years of his life.

His earliest memories were centred around fighting for food, attention, blankets at night and other things. Life had seemed like one long fight those days; there was never enough of anything. Not food, beds, clothes, playthings nothing. If one wanted something; he had to fight for it. It was "Survival of the fittest." Only the strong survived.

He was ten years old when he first killed somebody, a youth seven years older than him, who had stolen his money. Ruthlessly, he had tracked the youth down and strangled him to death. The youth had been one of King Arthur's henchman — one of the tougher ones. King Arthur had heard rumours of the killing and had asked to see Mordred. When Mordred came he was defiant and fearless. King Arthur had taken one look at him and decided to adopt him. He thought that here was someone he could use.

For years he had been King Arthur's right-hand man. He was an expert in several forms of martial arts and considered himself a bit of a connoisseur in various methods of killing and in the field of firearms and torture. He had a razor-sharp brain.

Modred had never been so wrong about a situation before. The whole thing stunned him. He hadn't even contacted King Arthur yet because there were still some things he had to do. He intended to go to Nairobi Hospital and take care of Kimani. It was much too dangerous to let him live any longer. Mordred was sure that Chain and Susan had already heard that Kimani was still alive and had rushed off to interrogate him. He was not going to underestimate Chain again.

Mordred was sure the whole thing had been done under Chain's directions. Perhaps if he had known that Chain was behind all this he would have been more suspicious. But he had assumed that the move, which had looked silly in the extreme, had been initiated by Susan; and so had simply passed it off as a simple mistake committed by a woman. Women were prone to mistakes, he thought with disdain.

But Chain wasn't. With hindsight Mordred could see exactly what had happened. Susan had suspected one of the top B.I.O. officials of being a traitor. She had told Chain who had come up with a brilliant idea to suck him out. Since they had no way of knowing who it might be, they had probably telephoned or sent messages to all five candidates. The messages were all to the effect that Susan knew what was happening; "Please meet her so that she could explain; and not to tell any of the other top four because she believed that one of them was a spy but she didn't know which." Of course whichever one was the traitor would automatically assume that he was very lucky Susan had gone to him instead of to any of the others. He would think it was because she trusted him more than she did the others.

The traitor would at once scurry off to tell the people he was loyal to about the whole thing. They would be shocked to hear that there might be a slight threat somewhere. Then they would be relieved to think that their secret was still safe as the silly woman had delivered herself to "the jaws of the lion" so to speak. But Susan Juma was not as stupid as everyone might like to believe. She had gone to Chain, which was after all a smart move.

180

Therefore, while the Round Table was celebrating for escaping a close shave, Chain and Susan were busy plotting its downfall. No one could even be sure how much those two knew. For all they knew, there might be a battalion of cops sitting outside just waiting for them to make a move. Mordred had done his best not to make the true identity of the members of the Round Table known. He was sure that if Chain had any idea of the true identify of even one of the knights, he would have acted a long time ago. He would either have had the knight killed or hauled in for interrogation. He wouldn't let them go free, perhaps waiting to catch the whole lot. It would be too much to risk. But then Mordred could not be sure about that either. He certainly did not want to try guessing about Chain or figuring out exactly what Chain had in mind. He would just have to kill him.

It definitely wasn't as easy as it sounded. Chain wasn't an easy man to kill. The lady, Susan Juma, might be an easier nut to crack but one never knew with these temperamental women. She seemed very emotional and high-strung at the moment but one had to remember that she had been Jackson Mwatata's protege. Mwatata never bothered with anything less than the best. She must have something stored up her sleeve, and she had also accumulated a sizeable following in her years at B.I.O. That was definitely another point in her favour. B.I.O. prided itself on being the best. To be an outstanding agent there meant that one was the best. On Chain, this label was justified. 'Was it also justified on Susan Juma?'

Although killing them off was not going to be simple, in the world Mordred hailed from, nothing was impossible. As King Arthur said, the impossible simply required a little more effort.

Mordred had tried to get through to Chain before; a few years back when Chain was still at B.I.O. He felt that everyone had a weakness, even super-heroes. In the case of mortal men, a small, rather shapely invention called woman was usually his downfall. History had proven time and time again that the quickest way to convince an intelligent, well-balanced man to start acting like a babbling fool was to introduce a woman into the picture. Take Adam, for instance. The man had been quite content to live in Paradise, quietly naming animals and minding his own business. Okay, maybe he was a bit lonely but he would have survived. Come Eve the only and most beautiful in the world at the time, into the picture, and there was chaos! The world is still paying for it.

Then there was Samson; a man with a mission. Enter Delilah, and he didn't know whether he was coming or going. He was suddenly doing flips to please her. He must have known that she was trying to deceive him but the silly man simply did not care. He more or less sold his soul in order to be with her, and then paid for it heavily. But he didn't go down alone. Oh no. He dragged his people with him; didn't he?

Samson wasn't the only one though. Several hundred years later came Helen of Troy who so entranced a young man named Paris. That she belonged to someone else seemed to pass him by completely; all he knew was that he wanted her. He went and took her forcefully, and thereby starting the Trojan War. Many suffered and numerous died. And for what? Another pretty face? Granted she was the most beautiful woman in the world (again at the time). But was she really worth it?

And was the sultry Cleopatra really worth throwing a whole empire away for, the way Mark Anthony had done? He had been one of the greatest warriors in Caesar's legionaries and the rightful heir to Julius Caesar's throne. But to Mark Anthony, the Roman empire was nothing if it meant losing Cleopatra the Egyptian queen.

That kind of story could only be really understood by someone like Leander who fell in love with a pretty face, Hero. Night after night the stupid man used to plunge himself into the long stretch of water known as the Dardanelles which separated them so as to be with her. Night after night without fail, he turned up. And the stretch of water involved was not an easy, smooth crossing. It was suicidal. But Leander reasoned that his Hero was worth the risk. One night, there was great storm, which made the stretch impassable. The thought of not seeing Hero was too much for the poor besotted man and once again he threw himself into the water. He did not survive the storm; he died.

Mordred had therefore concluded that if all it took was a woman to bring the greatest of men to his knees then that was exactly what Chain needed. He shopped around his recruits at B.I.O. and came up with a reasonably good-looking girl. Her guts and sense of adventure looked like they might appeal to Chain. Mordred asked her to go after Chain and try to get as many secrets out of him as possible. It was the oldest trick in the book but it had never really failed to work before, if history could be trusted. It was definitely worth a try.

Unfortunately, Chain was impervious to Jenny's charms. In fact, he seemed rather impervious to any woman's charms and Mordred started wondering if his nemesis was normal. Jenny tried hard to get close but Chain always treated her with amused tolerance and kept her at arm's length. He kept everyone at arm's length. There was no one who could manage to get close enough to him to be the recipient of confidences apart from Bakari and Mwatata. Chain was a recluse, but nevertheless a popular one.

Fortunately for Mordred the whole plan wasn't a complete loss. Chain's partner, the irrepressible Sam Kamau had fallen head over heels for Jenny. Mordred told her to encourage him and forget about Chain. They needed a different type of stone to crack. Kamau was willing to supply all kinds of information to his darling Jenny, which she in turn, relayed to Mordred. It was a perfect arrangement.

However, all good things must come to an end. Kamau had found out about Jenny's treachery and Jenny was forced to kill him. Of course, Chain couldn't allow her to live after that. It was a pity she had to die; a big waste of a perfect body.

But it had shown Mordred a rather cynical side of Chain. If nothing else, one knew that he couldn't get to Chain using traditional means. So if one wanted to get to him, one had to think of completely new ways of doing so. It was rather hard when the man didn't seem to indulge in any activity that involved coming into contact with other human beings in a social setting. He seemed to totally shun human contact in any capacity. Nobody really knew how to approach him or how to gain his trust. Mordred would find a way. He would have to find a way to kill him.

A friend of his had once told Mordred that life was a thin tight thread which easily snapped. One couldn't expect to live forever.

"None of us is inexpendable. When you die, you leave as much of a dent in society as you would leave if you withdraw your finger from a bucket of water." Mordred had grinned. "The water particles rush in to fill the space almost before your finger has moved."

Killing Chain would be a shame because the country would be robbed of a great mind which was capable of doing great things if given the chance. But Chain would never agree to become a Knight of the Round Table and keeping him around otherwise was too dangerous. Mordred was enough to acknowledge that Chain was one of the best. He also acknowledged that Chain would never be as good as he was. Chain had a deep moral streak which just wouldn't allow this. Too bad for Chain, that meant he was history.

But before all this, Mordred had to take care of Kimani first. Mordred had no doubt that Susan Juma and Chain had already "persuaded" Kimani to tell them everything he knew. It wasn't much but still Kimani knew about the Round Table. The only one he could positively identify was Mordred. But they could not afford to take any chances. Kimani was a man who was definitely expendable.

Mordred made up his mind not to inform the Round Table of what was happening until he had successfully taken care of Kimani. He moved around the place, collecting items he would need to carry out his plan which he hoped to do before the end of the afternoon.

Twenty minutes later he was on his way to Nairobi Hospital. As he drove he went through what he was about to do once again in his mind. When he reached the reception area he produced a B.I.O. card; they weren't so hard to get hold of. Mordred announced that he was in charge of security in Kimani's room and he was allowed to go up.

Once in the elevator, he removed a white doctor's coat from his bag; and a pair of glasses which he quickly put on. He didn't want to be stopped in the hallway. Quickly and confidently, he strode towards Kimani's room.

Five minutes later, the deed was done. Mordred walked away from the crime scene quickly after he had ascertained that Kimani was dead. As he waited for the elevator, he removed his glasses.

The elevator door opened and a woman came running out. She bumped into him and apologised profusely before rushing on. Mordred pressed a button in the elevator and thoughtfully removed his coat. Stuffing it back into his bag, he decided to use the back entrance and get out fast. He had no doubt that the woman in the elevator was Susan Juma.

Chapter Twenty-Six

King Musyoka groaned and rolled over in bed. It was five o'clock on Saturday afternoon and he couldn't convince himself to wake up. Not that he had had that much sleep anyway. He had gone to an 'all-night party' and danced until seven o'clock that morning. He knew that it was definitely time to leave only when someone started making breakfast.

Alice had lived up to all of his expectations, and more. She was a truly fascinating person once one got to know her. She found it hard to relax but once she did, she was nothing but fun. He had the feeling that it was the beginning of a beautiful friendship, but one which wouldn't last.

They say that opposites attract but King and Alice were on two ends of the scale altogether. There was almost no common ground. Alice was basically quiet and liked to keep to herself; she preferred her own company. King, on the other hand, couldn't survive and liked to make his presence felt. Alice didn't drink, didn't smoke and didn't go crazy over the normal things young people considered fun. King was willing to try out anything for the sake of fun. Alice liked jazz music, while King liked rock or rhythm and blues. Alice stayed at home most of the time and studied hard to get her good grades. King was the original party animal who stayed up all night dancing and accepted his good grades as a personal right. In short, Alice was a slow mover and King was a fast mover; the hare and the turtle. They were probably going to drive each other crazy.

But King smiled thoughtfully and looked forward with pleasure, to the thought of Alice driving him crazy. It would be an interesting experience; after all, everything about Alice was interesting. King had persuaded her to go swimming with him at eight o'clock that morning instead of going back home. After that, he had taken her for breakfast at

Lilian Towers in town and then to an ice-cream parlour for a treat. It was almost lunch-time by the time he took her back home.

"What are you smiling at?" he had asked, looking sideways at her as he drove the car slowly along the Nairobi streets.

"I'm wondering why I'm here with you instead of being at home studying for the test on Monday," she had answered. "How did you ever manage to convince me to do this?"

"Let's face it, I'm irrestible," King said with a grin. "Don't worry. You can study this afternoon."

"No way," Alice replied. "I'm so sleepy my eyes are almost dropping out. It is definitely bed for me. You, on the other hand - look fresh enough to address a delegates' meeting."

"Are you kidding?" King asked. "It's definitely bed for me too. I'm just as sleepy as you are, only I'm better at hiding it than you are." He turned his face and leered at her.

She laughed at his silly expression and then yawned loudly, making King laugh at her.

Laughing with Alice was an enjoyable experience. King had trained himself to laugh and could produce almost automatically, a laugh that sounded amused and uncontrived whenever he was required to, regardless of whether or not he wanted to. But with Alice it was different. The laughter was real and spontaneous. It felt good.

King had left her at her home with a promise to go over and study with her the following day, although he hated studying. It was something he avoided like the plague. He figured that since Alice had given him so much pleasure the night before, he should also show some support. Relationships were about giving and taking, after all, and he acknowledged that she had done her best to please him. She had agreed with his every wish readily and enthusisastically. Now it was his turn to oblige her.

However, he had other obligations to fulfil in the meantime. He was meeting his friend Peter, at around half-past six for a beer. He had noticed that Peter was very withdrawn and thoughtful for some time and had decided to talk to him about it. Peter had agreed to meet him that evening so he had to go.

186

Groaning again, he pulled himself out of bed and stumbled to the shower. The ice-cold water managed to liven him up and he gasped as the needle-sharp spray hit him. He had never enjoyed cold showers. Martin and his mum thought that that was the only way to live but he only took them when it was absolutely necessary.

Ten to fifteen minutes later, King was striding out of his room, fully dressed and ready to go. He ran down the stairs quickly, in search of his mother. He knew where to find her — Janet Musyoka rarely moved from her study. He came to a halt outside her door and knocked carefully.

"Come in," she called.

King opened the door and went in. As usual he felt a warmth and softness inside as he looked at her. People may call him 'Mamma's boy' but he didn't really care. He couldn't spend a day without seeing her. The truth was that he loved his mother very much. He would probably go to pieces if anything ever happened to her. With another warm rush of love, he bent down and planted a kiss on her smooth, cool cheek.

"So you have finally surfaced, have you?" she asked him with twinkling eyes. "How was the party? Did you have a nice time?"

"I had a wonderful time," King said, as he perched himself on her table. "Alice is a great girl. You would like her. Is it okay if I bring her around to visit you tomorrow?"

"It's fine," Janet answered smiling. "I would like to meet her."

"You won't show her any baby pictures, will you?" he asked suspiciously. "Promise me you won't show her any of my baby pictures."

"I promise," Janet said solemnly.

"Well, that's a relief," said King. "How was your evening? Did you watch the movie?"

"Yes we did," Janet said. "It was some strange Ninja movie in which everybody died in the end. Very stimulating. There's something rather relaxing watching other people solve their problems by blowing each other to pieces. Martin laughed so much you'd have thought that it was a comedy or a cartoon show."

There was another knock on the door and Martin walked in. "Hello Martin," Janet said. "I was just telling King about the movie last night."

"Martin is home and the sun is still shining?" King asked increduously. "He who leaves the house before daybreak and does not return until the sun has set in the West? What on earth happened? Did they kick you out?"

"I should be so lucky," Martin said dryly. "I never went to work today. I'm forcing myself to stay at home this weekend; you should try it too, sometime, bro."

"Plenty of time for that," King said easily. "I might just stay at home permanently when I become Vice-President. I'm going to contest against you at the next election mom," he said.

"Speaking of Vice-Presidents, you should have been at the movie last night," Martin said enthusiastically. "We arrived with full escort but Mom insitsted on going to buy the ticket herself. The ticket-sales man gave her a whole handful of complimentary tickets and insisted on having her autograph. Wherever we went, people were just staring at us in awe. It was amazing. However, no one really bothered us or anything and the movie was a blast. I don't think anyone really believes in ancient Japanese art forms but there's a great deal of enjoyment to be derived from people dressed in black from head to toe hacking at each other with glittering swords." He chuckled as he remembered the scenes.

"I'm glad you took some security mom," King said. "You can never tell which madman is going to go for you next."

"I believe Kenya is a safe country, King," Janet said gently.

"The best in the world," agreed King, quickly. "But there is no sense in taking chances, is there? Granted this isn't New York, but we have got our share of madmen too."

"That's right," Martin said. "It was over the radio today that B.I.O.'s top-man, J. F. Kimani was shot this afternoon. He's in critical condition at the Nairobi Hospital."

"Really?" Janet asked with a frown. "Poor man. But then, when did B.I.O. start advertising itself?"

"They didn't," said Martin. "The radio identified him as a senior C.I.D. official. But we all know who Kimani is."

188

"How on earth did they manage to get J. F. K. himself?" King asked.

"Every man has his day," Martin answered. "The point is, there's no need to hasten yours. If you take all the necessary precautions at least you can say you did everything you could. There is no need of taking chances. If someone can shoot a well-trained senior B.I.O. officer enough to critically injure him, what chance have you got if you wander around alone? You weren't built for self-defence, you know."

Janet was silent for a moment. "I see what you mean," she said at last. "Okay, I'll take your advice. I'll have as much security around me as possible when I leave the house."

"Good," King said approvingly. "I always knew I had a smart woman for a mother. Now you've proved it."

"Silly child," Janet said with a laugh. "Where do you think you got all your brains from?"

"From the stork who dropped me here, of course," King answered with feigned surprise. "Who else?"

"No wonder you're such a bird-brain," Martin commented. "Now we all know why."

"Mom," said an affronted King to his laughing mother. "Are you going to let him insult your favourite son in this way?"

"What makes you think you're my favourite son?" Janet teased.

"Who else could it be?" King asked in mock innocence. "Martin doesn't have a brain in his otherwise delightful head. He can't possibly be your son; stork or otherwise."

Janet roared with laughter as Martin promptly started chasing King around the room. Sometimes she thought that they would never grow up. The scene taking place in her study at the moment was a very familiar one; one which she had seen time and time again for so many years. For as long as she could remember, King had been teasing Martin and Martin had been chasing his 'baby' brother around the room in consequence. Their father had once asked Martin what he would do if he caught King.

"Beat him to a pulp of course," Martin had answered ferociously.

Both Gibson and Janet had laughed at that for they knew that Martin couldn't hurt a fly. He couldn't bear to kill a cockroach or a mosquito. Whenever anyone or anything was in pain, Martin felt the pain too. The idea that Martin might beat anything 'to a pulp' was truly hilarious. Janet felt a rush of longing for Gibson to witness this scene one more time. She wished that there was some way she could let Gibson know that Martin was still chasing King around the room, and still not catching him.

"Mom, are you okay?" She looked up to see King's anxious face peering down at her. Martin was bending over his shoulder wearing a similar expression. "If it's about the security thing, we didn't mean to upset you," King said. "We wouldn't want you to go around looking over your shoulder all the time. We would feel better if we knew you were safe."

Tears sprang to Janet's eyes. Gibson would have been so proud of both of his sons. He had always known that they would grow up right.

King and Martin looked at each other worriedly as her expression was alarmed, bordering on frantic.

"Mom?" asked Martin.

"It's not that," Janet hurriedly assured them. "I'm not really worried about security. It's just that the other day my little King was in diapers and here he is, all grown up. Ready to hold my hand when we cross the street."

Both King and Martin looked at each other again and relaxed. "Mom," King protested, "will you get the thought of me in diapers off your mind?" he sighed. "You know I hate to be reminded that I was less than I am now."

"And that is?" queried Martin with a raised eyebrow.

"One hundred per cent self-sufficient," King replied confidently. Janet laughed again as she saw Martin roll his eyes heaven-wards.

"I preferred you in diapers," Martin said.

"I ought to ask you to step outside for that," King said, "but due to the nature of my sweet and loyal disposition, I'm going to forgive you."

"And the fact that he just might win has nothing whatsoever to do with your decision, right?" Janet asked with a mocking smile.

190

"Nothing whatsoever," King said firmly. "I wish I could stay and make small-talk but I have to go. I'm meeting a friend of mine for a drink. You remember Peter, don't you mom?"

Janet nodded. "One of your never-ending fellow university students," she said.

"That's the one," agreed King. "I'll see you two later."

"Much later," Martin said. "In fact, I wanted to talk to mom about something, but I got side-tracked. Beat-it, bro," he advised, "and drive carefully."

King made a face at him and left the library after kissing his mother goodbye. He quickly made his way to the front door and let himself out. He reversed the porsche carefully out of the gates and speeded down the streets in pursuit of another of his goals.

Peter had been acting completely out of character of late. He was uneasy and withdrawn and rarely turned up for lectures. He didn't like joining the rest of the crowd in any of their activities. It was definately not like him at all and King was determined to pull him out of this ridiculous state of apathy. King couldn't bear having cheerless people around him. Everybody who formed part of his crowd knew how to enjoy himself. Peter just had to be brought back in line.

As he stopped at some traffic lights, he spotted a lecturer of the university walking down the street. Professor Wambua was his favourite lecturer and they got on well. King hooted and waved frantically to get his attention. The professor saw him and came towards him.

"How are you, Professor?" King asked. "Need a lift?"

"I was just going home," the professor said, "on the outskirts of town. I wouldn't want to take you out of your way."

"I don't mind," King said. "Come on, get in. It's the least I can do for you."

Professor Wambua got into the car and gave King some instructions. They chatted amicably as the sleek car speeded smoothly along the streets towards the professor's house. King had many questions to ask his lecturer who was only too willing to answer them.

All too soon, King drove up to Professor Wambua's gate. He let the professor out of the car and declined an offer to go in for coffee.

"I have to meet a friend," he explained. "But this is strange coincidence; my girl friend's house is just opposite yours." He pointed out Alice's house with a grin. "So I'll probably be seeing more of you than I bargained for."

They parted on that note and King went flat out to get to his appointment as soon as possible. He broke every speed limit, overlooking the fact that he was already late. With a sigh he concluded that Peter would just have to understand, and wait.

He was a 'King', after all.

Chapter Twenty-Seven

Susan Juma rushed up the stairs, her heart pounding. It was only a short flight of stairs which needed to be scaled before she reached Kimani's room but they seemed to take forever. She had just come out of the elevator, bumping violently into a doctor going into it, and feeling extremely foolish. She still felt foolish.

Yet there was something strange about that doctor. Worried as she was, she still felt that there had been a slightly jarring note; something out of place. He was a very ordinary-looking person; someone one wouldn't look at twice if one met him on the street. Young and quietly good-looking, he resembled thousands of other men on the street, there was nothing outstanding about his looks. Perhaps it had been his eyes. He had soft, large brown eyes that seemed to invite you to melt in them, their long dark lashes making them seem almost feminine. They were quite extraordinary eyes; such as which she had never encountered before in her life. Yes, she decided. It must have been his eyes, so clearly visible after he removed his glasses.

She had come back to the hospital to make sure that nothing happened to Kimani until the C.I.D. arrived to protect him. Chain had phoned Bakari and asked him to check out a few agents thoroughly and then send them out. Bakari had agreed to but then said that it might take a little time. Susan had accepted to drive out to the hospital and guard Kimani herself for a while. Both she and Chain had concluded that Kimani was important if they managed to bring the Arthurian crowd to trial. He was their one solid witness.

Downstairs she had found a different receptionist on duty who had informed her that there was an agent from B.I.O. already upstairs, guarding Kimani's room and that the police officers had all left an hour before. Her heart suddenly thudding in her ears, Susan's own words came back to haunt her. B.I.O. agents weren't authorised to be used as protection. That job belonged to the C.I.D. or the secret servicemen.

She had shouted for the receptionist to call hospital security at once and rushed for the elevator.

During the elevator ride up, she had hoped and prayed desperately that she was wrong. Above all things, Kimani had to be kept alive now. He was much too important to lose grip on.

As she sped around the corner towards Kimani's room; she saw a security guard running towards it from the other end of the hall. She reached the room first and threw open the door. The sight that met her eyes was expected and yet not any less nauseating for it. She felt as if she might faint.

Kimani's body lay on his bed, the white hospital sheets stained a grotesque crimson with the blood which still spurted out of the veins and arteries in his neck. His head had been savagely ripped from the rest of his body by severing his throat with what looked like a very sharp wire dangling next to his face. The blood was running over the bed; gushing out over his head which dangled uselessly to one side; and spilling over onto the floor to form a thick, red pool on the cold, sterilised floor. Kimani was definitely dead.

Belatedly, Susan realised what had been wrong with the doctor she had seen walking into the elevator. He shouldn't have been entering that particular elevator at all. All the medical staff had keys to the two reserve elevators in the building which were much more reliable and quicker to use than those of the general public. They never used the ordinary elevators. That man with the really extraordinary brown eyes hadn't been a doctor at all. Suddenly Susan knew who he was. She knew beyond doubt that that was Mordred.

"Oh Lord in Heaven," moaned a voice behind her. She whipped around to see a rather grey-looking security guard clutch the doorway for support. His presence galvanized her into action.

"Call the police," she instructed sharply as she pushed him out of the room. "Seal off this area. I want the entire floor cut off from everybody, and that goes for medical personnel as well. On no account should you let anyone into this room. Nothing is to be touched until the police get here. Is that clear?"

She didn't wait for an answer to her authoritative question but sprinted for the elevator. Luckily, it opened almost as soon as she pressed the button and she hurriedly entered it and then depressed the button for the ground floor and sweated while it went slowly down. The doors were hardly open when she came running out, making for the front entrance as fast as she could. The bewildered receptionist watched her remove her gun as she ran towards the door and looked at her in horrified fascination.

"Have you called the police?" Susan shouted as she released the safely catch on her gun and raced towards the door.

"Yes, they're on their way," the frightened girl answered.

Susan frantically searched the parking lot, knowing even as she did that Mordred was probably long gone. She raced from car to car, trying to keep a look-out for him but he wasn't there. It was obvious that Mordred was not hanging around for a show-down. Not this time anyway; he simply wasn't there.

She pulled back the safety catch on her gun and carefully returned it. Then she trudged towards a pay-phone at one corner of the parking lot and ineffectually swiped at the beads of sweat gathering on her forehead. She then inserted some coins and dialled Chain's number. With any luck he would have already dropped Babs home and was at his place now. She cut the connection after the required number of rings and dialled again.

Chain picked it up on the third ring. "Hello," he said.

"Chain, it's Susan," she said. "I'm at the Nairobi Hospital now. Kimani is dead. I think Mordred did it."

"How long ago?" asked Chain.

"Can't be much more than five minutes," she replied. "I met him running into the elevator as I went upstairs. After checking on Kimani, I ran down into the parking area but I couldn't see any sign of him. The police should be here any minute now. Mordred may still be inside the building, hiding out. I can go back in there and check it out."

"No!" Chain said sharply. "He may still be in there and if so I don't want you finding him. Not alone. It would be like feeling around in the long grass at night for a snake. You would find him alright, but it wouldn't help you much. Wait until the police get there and then take two heavily armed officers with you. I'll be there just as soon as I can." He hung up without another word to Susan.

She replaced her end of the phone and quickly walked back towards the hospital building. What Chain had said made sense but she didn't know whether she would be able to wait until the police arrived. Fortunately though, she didn't have to wait at all. As she reached the hospital entrance, she heard the shrill sounds of the police sirens loudly approaching the parking lot.

She waited until the cars had been parked and officers were streaming towards the doors of the hospital's main entrance. She searched quickly for a badge that would identify the inspector then walked up to him; removing her B.I.O. card in the meantime.

"Agent Susan Juma, B.I.O.," she said briskly holding out the card. He studied it, nodded and returned it to her.

" Inspector Richard Wali," he said. "What's going on here, Juma?"

"There has been a murder, Inspector," she said as they walked towards the entrance. "J. F. Kimani the head of B.I.O. He was brought in here this afternoon."

"I heard of it," the inspector said as he nodded.

"The man was probably being pursued by a gang. We don't know why. Someone entered his room ten minutes ago and killed him. Cut his neck through with a sharp wire. It's not a pretty sight." She grimaced, then continued, "I have reason to believe that I actually saw the assailant. I was coming out of the elevator when he was entering. I went to Kimani's room; found him dead and rushed back downstairs. But there was no one in the parking area when I got there. He may still be in the building."

"Right," said the inspector as they stopped at the entrance. He raised his voice. "I want the parking lot sealed. No car is to get out of here without my authorisation. And I want the building sealed as well. Officers on every single floor. Nobody leaves unless I say so. Kariuki," he said to a young officer standing nearby. "You come with me. Come along Juma, if he is in this building then we'll find him. But we had better have a look at the victim first." He strode into the building and reassured the now distraught receptionist. An officer had moved over to take her statement.

There was a crowd which had now gathered near the entrance made up mostly of medical staff most of whom were anxious and bewildered. The police officers moved among them and tried to calm them down. Inspector Wali led the way towards the elevator radiating confidence and authority as Susan moved hurriedly behind him, followed closely by officer Kariuki. In the elevator, Susan once again went through the events of the last ten minutes. She described coming to the hospital and being informed that there was a B.I.O. agent upstairs, guarding the room. She told him that this had made her suspicious at once and she had hurried upstairs to make sure that Kimani was alright. She recalled bumping into the 'doctor' in the elevator and feeling sure that something was wrong. Then she told him about entering Kimani's room and finding him dead.

The trio reached Kimani's floor and strode through the halls in total silence. Throughout Susan's recitation, officer Kariuki had been taking notes. There were several security guards outside the room now. Inspector Wali opened the door and looked in.

Both the inspector and the officer visibly recoiled when they saw Kimani. Susan felt a small spurt of satisfaction to know that they were not immune to all feeling, after all. Several other officers poured into the room, also showing shock. In a slightly toned-down voice, the inspector gave terse instructions for the area to be dusted for fingerprints and for the corpse to be photographed.

After this, Susan, Inspector Wali and Kariuki searched the entire building from top to bottom. They looked in every nook and cranny in the hospital. They examined every single place he could possibly have hidden and came up with nothing. Mordred had disappeared. Susan carefully looked at all the people they met in the building, trying desperately to recognise something. But it was hopeless; Mordred was gone.

Half an hour later, she went downstairs to sit at the reception and watched people being interviewed for any information they might have. Surprisingly, everybody had some kind of information to offer and lots of advice to give. Unfortunately, not all of it was useful. If eye-witnesses were to be believed, there were short fat men carrying razor blades who had been running undetected around the building. Then there was an assortment of tall, dark, sinister-looking men wearing sun-glasses, and sporting fake beards. There were men with machine guns and big, amazon-like women with axes and electric saws.

There were foreigners, Swedes, Germans, Americans, Chinese, Filipinos and so on running around causing havoc. All this had been witnessed and duly reported by a variety of people. It was almost amusing.

When Chain walked through the entrance, Susan suddenly realised just how much she had missed him. She got up and ran towards him as he scanned the crowd, a worried expression marring his countenance. His face relaxed into a very relieved smile as she flung herself into his arms. He gathered her into his embrace and hugged her tightly to him. Then, regardless of the people around them, he bent down and kissed her full on the mouth.

"Everything is okay," he said as she shivered. "Don't worry, we shall work this thing out." Reluctantly, she disengaged herself from his embrace.

"Do you want to see him?" she asked.

He nodded slowly. She declined to go with him, another shiver running through her as a picture of Kimani's broken, bleeding body passed through her mind.

"It's okay," said Chain. "I understand. I'll be right back and then we shall go on home. Don't worry."

Chain left her to hurry upstairs. She sat back down on a chair in the reception area and thought about Kimani as she had first seen him. He had been so full of life in those days and genuinely happy. She shuddered as she thought of his cruel death.

Susan did not notice the police officer who was walking towards the entrance of the hospital building, pulling on a pair of very dark sun-glasses. Nobody noticed him because the whole building was full of policemen in uniform coming in and then going out. She would have been shocked to know that that particular one wasn't a police officer at all; that was Mordred.

He had decided that there wasn't enough time to escape from the building without notice. In a few minutes, Susan would have been in the parking area before he could make any kind of move. He couldn't have got away without her seeing him and he had no wish to start playing 'Cowboys and Indians' in a hospital parking lot with Susan Juma.

He had changed into an orderly's clothes and started pushing a huge hamper of dirty linen around. Susan herself had passed him, three times without glancing in his direction. He had mingled with everybody else until he saw that things were beginning to settle down. Then he had taken a policeman, hit him over the head and then dragged him into a nearby closet. He had undressed him and donned his clothes in a hurry. Then he set off confidently towards the door. He had passed right next to Susan Juma and she had looked right through him. He opened the door and left.

Ten minutes later, Chain came back downstairs; visibly shaken. Susan had finished making a statement and was more than ready to leave. He took her by the arm and steered her out of the building which was beginning to feel very claustrophobic. Susan was getting paranoid.

"Where do you think he could have gone?" Susan asked once they were outside.

"Mordred?" queried Chain. Susan nodded. "Well, he could be anywhere," Chain conceded. "For all we know he may still be in the hospital."

Susan sighed frustratedly. "I would feel like such a fool if he was," she said. "We searched every nook and cranny in that building. I don't understand where he could have hidden. And yet, at the same time, I don't think he left earlier on. I would have seen a car leaving the parking lot or him running towards the gate, or something."

Chain shrugged. "He might possibly still be in the hospital even now," he said. "There's not much we can do about it. We do know one thing about Mordred though. The man is ruthless and very thorough. I'll have to take care of him."

Chapter Twenty-Eight

Chain lay back on the sofa, his eyes staring sightlessly ahead against the glare of the overhead light. Susan's head was on his lap and her eyes were tightly closed. His right hand was slowly and rhythmically stroking through the wild, tangled hair towards the sensitive base of her neck. Neither of them spoke. They were both lost in thought. The room remained silent.

It was Saturday night and Susan thought fleeting things were supposed to really swing on Saturday night. If someone had told her a week earlier that she would be spending her weekend in Chain's apartment wondering whether she would live to see daylight again, she would have booked the person a one way ticket to a good mental hospital. She didn't feel as if what was happening was actually happening to her. She felt distanced from the events; as if they were somehow happening to someone else and she was being forced to watch from the sideline.

They had left the hospital and gone straight back to the shelter that Chain's city apartment offered. On reaching there, they had eaten a quick meal and cleared up the dishes before going to sit in the sitting room. There, they had lapsed into another companionable silence.

Susan thought of a Saturday night she particularly remembered. It had been a few years previously, while she was still in her teens. She had been going steady with a guy called Mike, at the time. He had faithfully promised that he would come and pick her up on that Saturday so that they could go to the Carnivore. She had accepted his invitation and then spent the whole evening waiting for him to show up. At around eight o'clock her friend Anna had called and enquired whether she was going to the Carnivore that night.

"Yes," Susan had replied. "Mike is picking me up, soon. Did you want a lift?"

"So you haven't heard," Anna said.

"Heard what?" Susan asked.

"Maria is back in town," Anna said.

"Who is Maria?" Susan asked, perplexed.

"You mean you don't know?" Anna asked in astonishment. "Maria is Mike's old flame. She is back in town for her birthday. They always give a big party for her at the Carnivore on her birthday and Mike always takes her. There is no way he is coming to pick you up tonight, sister. He has bigger fish to fry. We were wondering if you wanted a lift into Carnivore to watch the fun."

"Don't be silly" Susan snapped. "Of course he is coming. He promised to."

"Really?" Anna queried dubiously. "He must have forgotten that it's Maria's birthday when he made that promise. I'm telling you, there is no way he is coming to pick you up tonight."

"He is coming," Susan insisted.

"Suit yourself," sighed Anna. "If you happen to change your mind then give me a call and we'll arrange to pick you up. It's just the usual crowd of girls going. One of us can bring you back if things get too hot for you."

"Thanks but it won't be necessary," Susan said.

"You never know," Anna said. "We won't be leaving until nine. You have my number." And with that she had replaced the phone.

Susan had sat back and wondered if Anna was simply being malicious and trying to break her relationship with Mike or whether there was any truth in what she was saying. Ten minutes later she got her answer.

Mike called to cancel the date. Susan had sat very still and clutched the phone in a death grip, as she listened to Mike explain that he was meeting a long-lost uncle at the airport and could not make it. She had calmly assured him that it was quite alright and that she would find her own way to the Carnivore. She held her breath while waiting for his answer.

"Sweetheart, I would prefer it if you would stay at home," he had said hesitantly. "I might get a free hour or two when I can sneak away and come to see you. It would be better if I knew you were at home where I can easily find you."

That was all the confirmation she had needed. She assured him that she would stay and wait for him at home and then endured a further five minutes during which he had tried to explain how much she meant to him.

By the time she replaced the telephone, Susan was seething with anger. She couldn't understand why it was happening to her and she just couldn't believe that Mike had lied to her. She had paced up and down in the living room wondering. Susan had really been eager to go to the Carnivore. She was in a short, red, sequined mini-dress which she had bought the previous day and fabulous make-up to match. She knew that she was looking good.

In the end she decided to go, partly because she didn't want to be all dressed up with nowhere to go and partly because she felt that she had to know for sure whether Mike was cheating on her or not. She knew that if she did not find out the truth herself, he would be able to persuade her that it had all been a lie.

She had called Anna who arranged to pick her up half an hour later. She was extremely quiet and tense during the ride but there was something Anna had said which she had never forgotten.

The girls had been talking about a couple who had crashed their car when coming from the Carnivore recently. It seemed that the man in question had been very drunk but that he wasn't the one driving. The woman was driving and she had been cold sober. One of the girls commented that maybe it would have been better to let the man drive, drunk as he was. It might have averted what had turned out to be a terrible tragedy.

"That road to Carnivore has killed very many people," Anna commented, sadly.

"What road?" Susan asked. After all, there was more than one.

"It doesn't matter what road it is," Anna said. "You may be driving from Cairo, Egypt. Just as long as you're on your way to or coming from Carnivore, the road is definitely a killer."

Susan had never forgotten that statement and subconsciously, had always equated going to the Carnivore with making a death-wish. It hadn't sounded funny then and it didn't sound funny any of the other times she had thought about it since then.

Susan had walked into the Carnivore expecting to see Mike there in the company of another woman. She was not disappointed. Mike was there with the infamous Maria by his side. He was obviously drunk and was all over her, touching, kissing, panting and generally making a fool of himself. But nobody seemed to mind, least of all Maria. She didn't mind at all.

Susan walked up to their table slowly, followed by a group of her friends. There was a general silence that descended around the area she was approaching as people turned and recognised her and expected trouble. Mike and Maria went right on with their activity not realising that a tense silence had fallen over the people around them. Susan stopped next to Mike's chair. He turned around at last and saw her and almost fell off the chair in surprise and genuine astonishment. Total silence reigned at last, and Susan's voice carried clear across the area as she started speaking.

"Hello Mike," she said. "Still waiting for your uncle at the airport?"

"Susan . . ." he said.

"You know I hear the airport can be pretty chilly at this time of the night," she continued conversationally. "You should have had the sense to bring a thicker jacket." She arched an eyebrow upwards. "But how silly of me!" she exclaimed, "you don't need a jacket at all, do you? You have got someone to keep you quite warm don't you?"

Maria turned to Mike, "Darling who is this person?" she demanded.

Susan turned brightly to her. "How amiss of me. We haven't been introduced," she said with fake politeness. "My name is Susan. I am Mike's new girlfriend. Pardon me. I meant Mike's new ex-girl friend. There seems to be quite a lot of us around. Maybe we should form a club . . ." she smiled archly. "I can just see it now. 'Association of Mike's ex-girlfriends'."

There was a ripple of laughter from the crowd.

"You must be Maria," Susan then continued smoothly. "I seriously doubt that you are the long-lost uncle he went to meet at the airport. You are not that old, really."

The ripple of laughter became even louder. Susan smiled around at her little audience and then turned back to Mike.

"You can do whatever you want with your life baby," she said in a suddenly hard tone. "But don't lie to me. That is really living dangerously. I'm not the kind of girl who is pushed around Mike. I'm not a child and I'm tired of being treated like a half-wit simply because I'm female."

There came a spontaneous applause from the girls standing behind her. Then she turned back to Maria.

"As for you," she said, her eyes narrowing, "you look thirsty. Have a drink." Susan lifted a Bloody Mary from the table and poured it over Maria's permed hair. "Happy Birthday, Maria," she said. Then she turned on her heel and walked out.

She could still remember the intense anger she had felt and it was Mike's biggest mistake to run after her, out into the parking-lot. She turned around to face him angrily as she felt his hand on her shoulder.

"What do you want?" she demanded.

"I want an apology," said Mike. "For what you did in there. You had no right to come in there and embarrass me like that."

"I had no right?" Her eyebrows went up again as she gazed at him in astonishment.

"There is nothing between me and Maria," he said. "We broke it up a very long time ago."

"Then why did you lie to me, Mike?" she asked. "Why the elaborate story about long-lost uncles and airports? Why did you ask me to stay at home twiddling my thumbs, hoping you would be coming to see me when all the time you knew you were going to be here with her?"

"Okay, I made a mistake. I'm sorry," he said. "But that still doesn't give you the right to do what you have just done. Maria will never forgive me. How am I going to explain it to her?"

"You are crazy Mike," Susan said. "Why should I care if Maria forgives you or not? You must be drunk!"

"I am not drunk!" he shouted.

"Oh! I am not interested," she hissed at him. "Why don't you just crawl back to your lady-friend, oops pardon me, I mean ex-lady-friend and try hard to get her back into your life?"

"You're a jealous bitch, Susan," he said.

Her left hook caught him completely by surprise. As her fist connected with his jaw, his head snapped upwards and he whirled violently around and reeled backwards from the force of her blow. He staggered a bit and then went crashing to the ground. Susan didn't spare him a backward glance as she flounced off to her friend's car. Anna had driven her home.

Since then, Susan couldn't bear to stay at home a Saturday night. She always felt uneasy staying at home feeling like she was Cinderella, depriving herself of some kind of excitement or other. So unless it was imperative that she stay at home, or circumstances made it impossible for her to leave, Saturday night was usually her night on the town.

But strangely the need to go out on Saturday night was absent on this particular night. She supposed it was because of the events of the past few days. She had never really considered herself a patriot but she honestly believed, at that moment, that she was ready to die for the sake of her country. If it meant stability for the lives of the people of Kenya, then she was willing to give up her life. The only regret she would have was leaving Chain.

It was truly amazing how close she felt to him. She rarely felt close to people and truly believed herself to be the 'last of the rugged individualists'. However, she felt as if she had known Chain all her life; that she understood him the way she had rarely bothered to understand anyone before and that she couldn't live without him. She had no idea whether or not he felt the same way about her but that didn't stop her from feeling the way she did.

"We'll have to leave," Chain said at last. "It's just not safe to stay here any longer." He paused and looked down at her, briefly. "I have a few other houses scattered around the city that we could use. We can rotate in them at least for a while."

Susan stared up at him. "Do you think we'll make it?" she asked. "Do you really think we can come out of this whole mess alive?" Her voice was almost beseeching.

"Yes," Chain said. "We have to." He didn't elaborate and Susan didn't ask him to.

"So, what are we going to do now?" she asked.

"Well, we've got a few leads," Chain said. "We will have to see whether they can get us anywhere. I'll get in touch with one of my people at B.I.O. and ask him to run voice tests on our ministers and match the prints with Lancelot's. That probably won't be easy. We shall have to get hold of very recent recordings of their voices first."

"I'll get in touch with Babs," Susan answered. "We can get to work on it, first thing tomorrow morning."

"Fine," said Chain. "In the meantime, let's pack and get going."

They both stood up and went to pack whatever light clothes they might need along with a few essentials into overnight bags. Fifteen minutes later they were heading towards the front door. Chain stopped Susan and turned her towards him.

"Susie," he said. "We are going to make it. I know we shall. Please trust me."

With that, he opened the door and walked out. Susan knew that she would always trust him.

Chapter Twenty-Nine

It was Sunday morning, nine o'clock. Susan was at the Jomo Kenyatta International Airport, accompanied by a sleepy-eyed Babs. They were waiting for Abdul Hakim, a minister in the Kenyan Government, to arrive from Mombasa, where he normally resided. The flight had already been delayed by two hours. Babs and Susan had been there since seven that morning. Not that there was any surprise in this lengthy delay. Kenya Airways was about as reliable as the Nairobi weather. They observed African timing which emphatically stated that one must never be on time and that it was never too late. In other words, they might have a set timetable, but they would come and go as they pleased. Some airline!

Susan had called Babs at five and gone over to her place, leaving Chain going to bed. He had been pacing up and down all night and had finally decided to go to bed at five in the morning. Once at Babs' place, Susan had told her the whole story, from beginning to end. And what a story it was! Babs didn't believe a word of it. Susan had assured her that there were two dead bodies to prove it; Kimani's and Mwatata's. Babs had simply yawned.

They had gone to the K.B.C. archives at six, to search for tape recordings of the remaining four. They had only come up with one which could be used as it was only a week old. It belonged to Rogers Kitili. Susan had told Babs that somehow, they needed to get recordings of the three remaining ministers fast. Babs had thought for a while and immediately come up with the idea of going to meet Hakim from the airport that morning. He was coming in for a special meeting at State House.

"We'll blend right in," Babs said enthusiastically. "There is always a horde of photographers and journalists waiting to meet these people wherever they go. It's as if they were kings. Personally; I hate the early morning jobs. But since we're already awake, we might as well go."

They had taken a tape recorder and gone. They had reached the airport by seven and had been waiting ever since. A sleepy voice over the intercom kept on apologising for the delay.

"I wish she would stop saying that," Susan said, testily. "You would think she was the one solely responsible for the plane's delay."

"Maybe she is," Babs commented dryly. They were sitting on a bench two or three feet away from some sleepy-eyed journalists. In fact, most of the journalists had arrived around thirty minutes before. Babs had remarked that those must be the pros; the ones who knew when to come after being given a specific time. Some of them were drinking coffee while others were just clattering up the waiting lounge - their bodies sprawled all over the area.

"So, what is up between you and our one and only Chain?" Babs asked suddenly.

"What do you mean?" Susan asked.

"Exactly what I say," Babs retorted. "I want to know exactly how far things have progressed between you and the legend."

"Things haven't progressed at all," Susan said. She could now feel her cheeks and ears growing warm and knew that they must be turning pink under Babs' steady gaze. Susan hated to be scrutinised.

"Why not?" Babs asked.

"Barbara!" Susan said in exasperation. "You might find it hard to believe but we're in the middle of a war. Neither of us is sure whether or not we shall live out the next hour. There's absolutely no time for romance at all!"

"No time?" Babs asked. "What exactly do you mean by that?" You have never had time for the opposite sex. It was always exams or practice for basketball, or training or too much pressure at work. You have never had the time. Why should it suddenly and miraculously come now? You will never find the time, my girl. You will just have to make time. Otherwise that elusive special something is just going to pass you by."

"I can't make the time," Susan said. "Not right now. It just wouldn't be right. You know that, don't you?" Susan answered pleadingly.

"Alright kid," Babs said. "So you can't make the time right now, is that not so? Well, what happens if you don't ever get another chance; what then, sweetface?"

"What do you mean?" demanded Susan.

"I mean what if something happens to either one of you, especially him?" asked Babs. "You are in this together, aren't you? Could you really forgive yourself for not making a move while you still had the chance?"

Susan silently stared at Babs in shock, not knowing what to say.

"Maybe it's a mean thing to say," Babs acknowledged calmly. "It does sound a bit macabre. Do you understand, Susie? Life is mean. Life is macabre. You have to make the time now. Not tomorrow, not next week; not when this whole thing is over whenever that may be. You have to get even with the situation now. If you don't; it means that you don't really care either way."

"Maybe I don't" Susan said crossly.

"The hell you don't," Babs retorted sharply. "All you ever talk or think about is Chain. A fool could see that you love him. And I know that Chain loves you too. What do you say to that, Juma?"

"I say, stop swearing," Susan said. "You're crazy, you know. How can you possibly tell whether Chain loves me or not?" She looked at Babs with fresh interest.

"Take it from me, the man is in love," Babs said with a nostalgic smile. "I can read all the signs. But he is going to fight it. I know he is. He is going to tell himself that there is no way he can get involved with you, because you're a B.I.O. agent and you're very young. There are a thousand different reasons why not, and Chain is going to think of all of them. It's up to you to convince him otherwise. Nobody else can do it for you. But if you don't start now, you will find that it's too late if you know what I mean."

"Yes, I know what you mean," Susan said with a heavy sigh. She thought back to the night before, when she and Chain had gone to his safe house on the outskirts of town. They had settled in and decided what it was they were going to do about the whole situation and then decided to have some coffee before going to sleep.

Susan had gone into the bedroom to put on her night-shirt, a huge T-shirt with Mickey Mouse all over the front. It reached about mid-thigh and was quite comfortable and decent. And anyway, she reasoned, she didn't have anything to hide. Her legs were really quite good.

She had gone to the kitchen after that to start preparing the coffee. She heard the shower in Chain's room running and assumed he was taking a light shower before going to bed. She then became engrossed in the task before her.

Susan knew Chain was with her the minute he entered the room. It was a strange tingling of the senses that warned her. She had got used to those tingling sensations whenever he was near her. An old phrase 'shivers down my spine' came back to haunt her. Finally she was learning that the phrase was entirely feasible.

"Got enough for me?" he asked huskily. He stood directly behind her, sending a fresh wave of sensation coursing through her body.

"It should be enough," she said lightly. "I have made enough for two and I can't see anyone else in the room; can you?" She turned around to face him and her eyes widened slightly.

He was wearing an old track suit bottom and nothing else. He was still damp from the shower and there were little droplets of water still clinging to his hair. The small whorls or dark hair on his broad chest were also wet; and sticking to each other. He smiled at her as she started trembling, and reached out behind her to turn the coffee percolator off.

She watched his muscles flex and unflex as he performed this simple task. The bronze flesh glistened and rippled in a fascinating way. Slowly, she extended her hand and touched. She let her fingers trail lightly down, going softly over the tendrils of hair she encountered there. Her face was filled with wonder as she felt the taut skin, covering the hard muscle and sinew there. She sighed with pleasure and ran both hands back up his torso, firmly and tenderly.

He groaned and pulled her closer to him. Bending, he lowered his mouth to place gentle kisses all over her neck and shoulders as he tugged at her T-shirt, pulling it up to gain access to her skin. His mouth burnt her, everywhere he touched and she moaned softly as his lips met hers.

She shifted under the weight of his kiss, protesting softly. He took no heed, but continued to pull her closer to him, his mouth slanted over her's questioning, and demanding. She refused to give him entry and drew her head back, her breath coming in short gasps. He stared at her for a breathless moment and then bent again to continue planting small, sweet kisses all over her face. He dropped them on her nose and eyes and cheeks and forehead. He kissed her while she writhed in ecstasy, begging for more. Then he lifted his head again and he smiled with satisfaction at her obvious surrender and moved to claim her waiting, parted lips with his own. His mouth played on hers, improvising the symphonies of taste and sensation. Then he crushed her to him — moulding their bodies into one as she dug her nails into his back.

He made a triumphant sound deep in his throat and deepened the kiss. He could feel the tremors running through her body and it made him feel heady with excitement, knowing that he was capable of affecting her in that way. He ran his hands urgently over her body, probing, seeking, exploring. His hands dipped and curved according to her shape - eliciting more trembling and pliance from her. But when he urged one hand underneath her T-shirt she gave a gasp and wrenched herself away from him.

They both started at each other, trying to get their breath back and waiting for the slowing of their heart beats. Susan lowered her eyes away from his face and clenched her still trembling hands into fists.

"I'm not ready for this yet," she said in a small voice. When there was no answer her eyes flew back to his face. He smiled at her and grimaced wryly.

"I can see that," he said. "That's okay really, I understand." He reached past her and switched the coffee percolator back on.

"I hope you're not upset," she said in a husky voice. She cleared her throat.

"Upset?" Chain asked. "Who me? Never." He dropped a kiss on her nose and then headed for the sitting room. "I won't rush you," he said.

Susan remembered all this now and knew that Chain wouldn't wait forever. Suddenly, she also knew that she didn't want him to. If she waited until she was 'ready' forever may become a distinct possibility.

Babs was right. It was better to throw caution to the winds and just let nature take its course. She loved Chain and she was going to let him know one way or another. She would convince him that they would be good together. After all, the most important things in life were those worth fighting for. Susan made up her mind. She would fight for Chain as well as for her country. She knew that she could do both.

"Susan!" came an exasperated voice which abruptly broke into her thoughts. She turned to Babs and saw her looking annoyed.

"Hmmmn?" she asked sleepily.

"Where were you?" snapped Babs. "I've been calling you for the past minute!"

"Right here with you," said Susan.

"Oh really?" queried Babs. "Did you hear the sick lady on the intercom say that the plane will be landing in two minutes?" Susan looked blank. "I thought not," Babs commented dryly. "Do you think you can keep awake and alert until we get the recording we came for?"

"I was thinking about Chain," Susan said apologetically.

"Of course you were," said Babs caustically. "I didn't think that you were thinking about the Pope. Not with that look on your face, anyway!"

Susan felt her cheeks grow warm again. Being around Babs could really embarrass a person. Susan didn't know why she ever put up with Babs' silly comments and strange behaviour. No, that wasn't true. Susan knew exactly why she put up with Babs. It was because Babs was her best friend; as simple as that.

"Why don't you stay here with your day dreams, and let me go and interview the minister?" Babs asked.

"Oh but . . ." Susan protested.

"Need you tag along?" queried Babs. "I am very good at my job, you know. I'm sure I can perform the task to your satisfaction."

"Okay," said Susan, defeated. She watched Babs pick up the tape recorder and walk off. She was going down to the tarmac, to meet the plane as the other journalists were doing. Susan sat back and drifted off into her daydreams again.

A pleasant-faced young man came and sat down beside her. She gave him a small smile and continued staring off into space. Then she became aware of an elderly man with lovely brown eyes clutching a cane in one hand and a gold travelling bag in the other. He was looking worried and upset. Glancing in her direction he hurried over.

"My daughter," he began distractedly. "Can you help me? My grandson has disappeared and I can't go looking for him while carrying this bag. It is too heavy. Please, could I leave it here with you while I search for him?"

She nodded her head with a smile of consent.

"Thank you," he said. His eyes were really extraordinary. They reminded her of someone but she couldn't think who. "May the Lord bless you, my daughter. Thank you." He put the bag down next to her. "Please don't leave it; my life savings are in there," he said worriedly; and then he went in search of the missing child.

All at once, her eye started smarting painfully. She tried to blink the tears out but the pain just got worse. She felt like screaming. Thrusting the gold bag at the nice-looking youth at her side — she ran for the staircase; intending to go to the bathroom.

It was after taking two stairs that she realised why the old man's eyes were so familiar. They were Mordred's eyes.

She turned back in time to see the gold bag and the whole lounge, explode.

She was thrown back against the wall by the force of the explosion and momentarily blacked out.

Chapter Thirty

Susan looked back in horror. What had been an airport waiting lounge a mere two seconds ago was now a sickening mass of charred and bleeding bodies. All Susan could think of was the terrible mess it was all making. They would need an awful lot of money to clean this place up.

She realised dimly, that she must be in shock. She walked slowly through the rubble, barely registering the screams and the mass hysteria the bomb blast had invoked. Her feet slid on a sticky patch and she looked down to see that she had absently walked over a small river of blood. Her eyes followed the blood to its origin, which appeared to be a human heart, hanging limply out of its body; among crushed ribs and burnt flesh. She stared at the whole thing for a moment and then continued picking her way through the debris towards the place where the bag had been. Small pieces of bright gold material heralded the spot and she moved towards it like one possessed.

The friendly man whom she had left holding the bag was most definitely dead. It was just as well. She had no idea how she would have explained to him why she had given him a travel bag containing a live bomb. Now Susan knew where the phrase "Never trust a stranger" had come from. Undoubtedly it had first been uttered by a bomb blast victim who had been stupid enough to accept an innocent-looking travel bag from a complete stranger but had somehow, miraculously, survived the bomb.

Still thinking inane thoughts, Susan crouched down over her designated spot. She picked up a sliver of gold material and tried to wind it through her fingers. The man had been blown to bits — there was no part of him that was still recognisable. Or if there was then it had been buried under the slimy gore which seemed to constitute the remains of human bodies.

She started shaking uncontrollably when she imagined that it might have been her. The itch in her eye had long gone but she wouldn't have felt it anyway if it had still been around. She was beyond feeling anything. A strange hanging numbness had descended over her.

She became aware of several different smells, most of which were nauseating. She smelt the fresh blood that reminded her of a butcher's shop. The smell of putrid flesh and burnt meat should have made her throw up. In fact, a great number of people who had rushed to view the scene were busily and indiscriminately vomiting all over the area, adding to the smells. But the most permeating smell of all was that of fear. Susan knew that smell because she had experienced it many times before. There was an overall atmosphere of great fear. Things like this did not happen in Kenya. It was a quiet, calm, peace-loving country which disturbed no one and expected to be left alone in return. Unfortunately, something seemed to be going seriously wrong with a policy that had worked for years. Kenyans were not used to violence. It was a totally alien occurrence and they had no idea how to deal with it.

She was still crouched down when she become aware of Babs' voice, calling her name. She thought of Babs with a rush of warm feeling. Susan had never encountered a person quite like Babs before and probably never would. At least, not in the near future. Then her mind registered, rather vaguely the fact that Babs was actually calling her in a strained, panic-stricken voice quite unlike her own.

She stood up slowly, regretfully. Scanning the area, she saw Babs at the edge of the crowd, desperately calling out.

"Babs!" she called, "Babs, I'm here!"

Babs' eyes searched even more frantically, until they finally saw Susan. With a stunned look on her face, Babs made her way roughly through the crowd of milling people towards where Susan was waving her arms.

"Susan, what the bloody hell is going on?" she wailed as she finally reached her friend's side. "What is happening?"

"There's no need to swear," Susan said mildly, remembering that Babs always swore colourfully and enthusiastically when she was scared. 'Old habits die hard.'

"Susan!" Babs called, nearly screaming.

"A bomb went off," Susan said calmly. "They are dead, Babs. Look around you. All these people are dead!"

Through the haze of fear that had enveloped her, Babs noted that Susan was much too calm to be normal. She suddenly shuddered and grabbed Susan's arm which was extremely cold and clammy to the touch. She pulled her through the debris and away from the crowd and activity. Susan passively allowed herself to be led downstairs to the lobby of the airport. She still showed no signs of life.

"Susan, are you okay?" Babs asked her anxiously as she pushed her into a nearby chair, not knowing what to do next.

"I'm fine," said Susan showing a hint of surprise. "Why shouldn't I be?"

"But . . . ," spluttered Babs. "Do you realise that you have just survived a bomb blast?"

"I certainly have," agreed Susan. "And you know what makes it even better? That bomb was meant for me. I was the one who was supposed to be blown to bits all over the waiting-lounge. Did you see the sea of blood out there? Well, that was supposed to be my blood. So explain to me how come I'm still alive and talking to you and so many innocent people are dead?"

"What are you talking about?" asked Babs.

"Mordred," Susan said. "I saw Mordred here, but I wasn't quick enough to recognise him. I'm just lucky, I guess. Instead of killing me he ended up killing a room full of innocent people. What a price to pay for waiting around for a delayed flight. There is truly no justice in the world."

"I still don't understand what you're talking about," said Babs.

"No, you wouldn't," agreed Susan. "Mordred disguised himself as a harmless old man," she said. "He gave me a gold-coloured travelling bag to hold for him for five minutes, making me believe that there was definitely something valuable inside. He said I was not to let it out of my sight. Unfortunately, I got a speck in my eye and tears started streaming down only a minute after he left. I asked a man sitting next to me to watch the bag and raced for the stairs so that I could go to the bathroom and wash it out. When I reached the stairs I realised why the old man's eyes had looked so familiar; they were Mordred's. As soon

216

as I realised this and turned around, the gold bag exploded. It was just a sea of red after that."

Babs breathed deeply trying to come to terms with what Susan was saying to her. Susan seemed okay but Babs still couldn't understand how she could be so calm and composed in the face of such a crisis. Especially if what she had said actually was true.

"Are you sure?" asked Babs.

Susan nodded. "Absolutely," she said. "I would recognise those eyes anytime, anywhere. It was Mordred alright."

"What do we do now?" asked Babs.

"Well, the first thing I have to do is call Chain," said Susan. "And then we have to get out of here. The faster the better." She got up and headed towards a phone booth.

With Babs trailing anxiously after her — she rang the number at the safe house where she and Chain had spent the night. She unconsciously crossed her fingers as she waited for the customary number of rings. She replaced it and called again. It was picked up on the third ring. Susan breathed a sigh of relief.

"Chain," he said tersely.

"Chain' it's Susan," she said.

"Are you okay?" he asked. She could now detect a distinct note of relief in his voice. It made her feel better. "Did you get the recording?"

"The recording? Yes, I think so," she turned distractedly towards Babs, who nodded. "Yes, we did. But Chain, Mordred is here. Or at least he was here a few moments, ago."

"What?" Chain exploded. "What do you mean?"

"Chain the entire lounge at the airport is a mess," she said. "Mordred blew it up with some kind of bomb."

There was silence at the other end of the line as she once again told the story of the old man and the golden bag. She told him about leaving the bag, running to the stairs and then realising just who the old man was. Her voice went bleak as she described the explosion and the way everybody around that area had died. The whole thing had really affected her.

"Chain, we've got to leave this place, now. I don't know if Mordred is still around here but I'm not going to stick around to find out," Susan said. "I don't know how he knew we were here but somehow he found out. He might have followed me from the house so he knows where you are. Chain if he knows then he'll be after you next. I want you to leave that place right now."

"Don't worry, I'm leaving," Chain said. "I don't think that he could have followed you from here but I won't take any chances. Go on, get out of there, I don't want you to take chances either. Get Babs and move out of the airport. Keep a sharp look out for anyone who may be following you and if there is anyone try and shake him off. When you get to town, park your car somewhere then take a bus. Take as many buses as you can to wherever you want to go and make sure you do it without any set pattern. Just do it until you are sure that nobody is following you. Then come and meet me in town. I'll be at the New Stanley Hotel from eleven. Don't reach there before then."

"Okay," Susan said. "That's fine. We'll see you there then."

"Susan," Chain continued.

"Yes, Chain?" she asked.

"Be careful," he said before replacing his end of the line. There was a whole world of concern packed into those two words and Susan felt gratified and reassured that Chain really seemed to care. Her eyes misted for a moment as she thought of him and what he had come to mean to her. She started as a hand gently touched her shoulder. It was Babs.

"Susan, are you alright?" asked Babs. "You've got to pull yourself together, you know."

"I'm okay," Susan insisted, wiping her eyes. "I have never felt better."

"Sure," Babs said sceptically. "She slanted a sly sideways glance at her friend." Now tell me he doesn't mean a thing to you," she taunted softly. "If you dare."

"Oh, I can say it alright," Susan retorted, her head coming up. "But I definitely wouldn't mean it," she added sheepishly.

"You bet you wouldn't mean it." It was Babs' turn to retort. "Come on, we've got to go. Let's get out of here now."

218

"What about Hakim?" queried Susan.

"He is probably long gone," said Babs. "But that's okay. We've got him on tape. Probably not much but enough. Don't worry about it."

"Okay then, let's go," said Susan.

They walked rapidly through the crowd towards the front entrance of the airport. Several policemen were rushing in towards the staircase holding their guns in front of them. Their expressions were frantic and disbelieving. Susan knew exactly how they felt. The same feeling had invaded her senses a few days ago; on Thursday to be precise, and had not had the grace to leave her since then. Her face was perpetually screwed up in one big frantic and disbelieving expression.

They stood to one side, to allow the policemen to pass. Neither Susan nor Babs was willing to chance being knocked to the floor and trampled to death. Not yet, anyway.

As soon as there was a break in the rush of oncoming policemen, Susan and Babs made a wild sprint for Babs's car; which was parked outside. They jumped into it and gunned the engine to life. Slowly and carefully, Babs pulled out of the parking area which was now filled with people either scrambling to get away or scrambling to get in. One could easily separate the sadists from the cowards at a time like this.

"So where are we going?" Babs asked.

"We are going into town," Susan Replied. "We shall find a convenient spot to park your car. Then, we shall get onto the first bus we see and go wherever the bus will take us. After this we shall jump onto another then another then another — until we are absolutely sure that we are not being followed. Then we shall go to New Stanley Hotel to meet Chain, at eleven o'clock. Chain's orders. Got it?"

"Got it," Babs said. "We'll spend the entire morning jumping from bus to bus. Because of orders from above, huh? Okay; wherever you go I'll follow, even if it sounds nutty."

"Nutty or not," Susan said, it should work. If it doesn't work and someone is still following us then we'll have to split. He can't follow us both. "Whoever he doesn't follow will go and meet Chain."

"Yes, sir!" Babs replied.

"Very funny Babs," Susan muttered. "Listen, I'm really sorry I got you into this Babs," she said. "Honestly, I didn't think you would get involved to this extent. It's one thing to get myself in trouble but I don't want anything to happen to you. I mean that."

"Have you gotten that off your chest?" asked Babs, dryly. "It's really sweet of you to feel sorry and all that but unnecessary."

"But . . ." began Susan.

"But nothing," Babs interrupted. "You didn't get me into anything. Nobody twisted my arm. You were in a fix and you asked for my help. I am honoured to serve. I mean that. Too many times it has been the other way round, with you trying your best to bail me out of trouble. Asking me for help made me feel good, Susie. It made me feel needed and I realised that you believe in me. Don't take that away from me. I've always had a choice and if there was too much heat I could have said no at any time. Trust me."

"The old 'what-are-friends-for' maxim, is it?" queried, Susan lightly. "What you're doing is above and beyond the call of duty."

"That's your opinion," Babs shot back. "I believe that anything that is important to you is important to me too. Anything that you feel is big enough to risk your neck for is big enough for me as well. Your war is my war."

They both lapsed into silence; each thinking of the same person.

Mordred.

Chapter Thirty-One

"**B**alaine, Bohert, Tristan, Perceval, Lancelot, Galahad, Gawain, Mordred and King Arthur. If Kimani is to be believed, these are the nine members of the Round Table in Nairobi," said Chain.

"Knights," Susan said.

"What?" Chain asked.

"Knights," Susan repeated obligingly. "They are called Knights; the Knights of the Round Table."

Susan, Chain, Babs and George Bakari were all sitting at a table at the New Stanley Hotel in town. It was lunchtime. Susan and Babs had just arrived and found Bakari and Chain already there. They were discussing the case.

"There is no way we can let them live," Bakari said firmly. "We are talking about treason of the highest degree. We'll have to think about terminating it with extreme prejudice."

"You mean killing them," said Babs flatly.

"Yes, that's exactly what I mean," Bakari agreed testily. "What did you think I meant? Throwing them all birthday parties? They can't be allowed to live."

"I'll be the judge of that," Babs said sharply. Everyone turned to her. "You're right, they can't be allowed to live," she said. "However, we have no right to make that decision. It is not for us to decide who lives and dies."

"Really?" drawled Bakari.

"Hold it, you two," Chain interjected. "This isn't getting us anywhere. Babs, you've got to understand these people forfeited the right to a fair trial when they started indiscriminately killing off people like they were cockroaches. If they do get killed it will only be in self defence."

"All this talk about killing them is fine," said Susan. "But you forget — first we've got to find them. That isn't going to be as easy as killing them."

"Yes, Susan," Bakari conceded. "However, how we're going to find all of them, I'll never know. Do you think that if we got one of them out of action the whole Round Table thing would be dissolved or something?"

"Not a chance," Chain said. "They've gone too far now to stop because one of them has died. For some reason or other; their aim is to take over the country. We have to stop them."

"True, but how?" Babs asked. "If we don't even know where to find them then we are already defeated. We don't even know who they are."

"We know that Lancelot is a minister," Chain replied . "One of four — in fact. We know that Gawain is an American oil dealer, probably very rich. We know that Tristan is a brain-surgeon who owns a lab near Wilson Airport. We know that Balain is a bishop. Not much to go on, I must admit, but at a glance, at least it's something."

"We can start moving on it right away," Susan said. "Take Balain for instance," she continued. "I know that we've got quite a number of bishops in the country but we can still narrow it down. Let us try and figure out where the bishops were on Saturday morning. We know for certain that there was a Round Table meeting held. Whoever was missing without any explanation is the one we are looking for."

"I think I can help you there," Babs said, sitting up and looking excited. "There were two bishops who were shall we say upgraded to arch bishops on Saturday. The ceremony ran from nine in the morning to three in the afternoon, I think. I can verify that for you."

"That's wonderful," Bakari said. "Any bishop worth his salt would have to have been there attending it and any who did not had a good reason for his absence."

"Yeah, if a bishop misses an event like that one, many people start talking," said Babs. "If he doesn't go then the others start saying that he was jealous of the success of his colleagues."

222

"I can see how that would be a problem," Susan commented. "He probably wouldn't have any chance of being elevated to the level of arch-bishop for quite some time."

"Only a bishop who feels certain of inheriting the entire country some day soon would take a risk like that," said Bakari.

"I can't argue about that," Babs said. "I think I'll go on down to the office and try to dig up an attendance sheet for the ceremony. Let's pray there's only one name missing from the list."

"It's never that easy," Susan said dryly. "Well, what do you think?" she enquired of the other two. "Is it a good idea? Babs and I can go and check this and see what it leads us to."

"That's fine," Chain agreed. "You two can go and dig up whatever you can. In the meantime, George and I can start researching into which relatively rich Texas oil barons live in the country. They shouldn't be too many. Do you think we can do that George? We might be able to find Gawain that way," he concluded.

"That might just work," Bakari said and nodded.

"Okay, but supposing we do find Balain?" Babs asked. "What happens then?"

"We eliminate him," Bakari said promptly. He sighed when he saw the mutinous look on Babs's face. "Okay; suppose we give the choice to him."

"What do you mean?" Susan asked.

"I mean we give him the gun," Bakari said. "When we're sure that he's the one we want. We make it very clear that we know everything. We leave it up to him. If he wants to die, he shoots himself. If not, we have him formally arrested and charged with treason."

"That's not feasible either way," Chain said. "If you give him the gun he's quite liable to shoot one of us. If you have him formally charged, the remaining 'knights' will have him out of there in no time. It can't work either way."

"So what do you suggest we do?" Babs asked.

"That we shoot him," Chain said forcefully. He saw her wince. "Look Babs; you don't seem to understand. We're all playing for keeps. It's them or us. The stakes we're playing for are much too high to start getting squeamish because of a few human lives. We are talking about people who will stop at nothing to get what they want. They will kill anyone; trample over anything. And they want to turn this country into a blood-bath, Babs. Innocent men, women and children whose only crime is that of existing, will be killed; slaughtered by the hundreds. It may offend your senses to kill a person but there's no other way. We have to get rid of them because they are criminals. All we shall be doing is acting in self-defence."

Babs looked down at the table for a long time. Then she looked up to find three pairs of eyes watching her intently. "Okay," she said at last. "I don't agree with you entirely on that one but if you say that it's the only way then there is nothing I can do."

"Fine then. That is settled," Susan said, as she stood up. "Well, there is a job to be done. Let's get on with it."

"We shall be in George's office if you need us," Chain said. "When you do find something then let us know, as soon as possible."

Everyone stood up and the two girls made their way to the door. Bakari and Chain stayed behind to settle the bill. But before Susan had taken more than two steps, Chain called out to her, then strode rapidly towards her.

"Yes?" she answered.

He placed his hands on her shoulders and kissed her roughly. "Take care," he said.

* * * * *

Babs and Susan were knee-deep in papers at the former's office. They had rescued her car from its place of abandonment and driven out on their mission. They had found all the details about the ceremony and were trying to verify the record of attendance.

"Babs, I hate to say it, but your office is messy," Susan muttered.

"Don't say it then," Babs retorted.

"I already have," Susan countered.

"I'm a very busy woman, and I just don't have the time to clean out the mess," Babs said as she smiled smugly.

224

"How the hell do you ever manage to find anything in this disaster?" Susan asked.

"I have got a radar," Babs answered mischievously. "Developed after years of stretching and straining and trying to dig under piles of paper and junk." She pulled out another paper from the heap on her desk. "Well, that looks like it," she said. "Only those two Bishops; Bishop Dave Mwita and Bishop James Masana. All we have to do now is find out whether or not one of them has an alibi."

"That's easy enough," Susan said, walking towards the telephone. "I hope your phone works; at least." She flipped through the directory that was next to the phone, and then rang a number. "Hello" she said, into the receiver. "This is Barbara Kwanda of the Kenya Broadcasting Corporation. "I'd like some information on why Bishop Mwita was not at the Archbishop's ceremony yesterday morning." She paused "What?" she asked. "I see. Can I quote you on that?" She paused again. "I understand completely. Thank you," Another pause. "No, there's nothing else. Thanks again. Goodbye." She hung up the phone and turned to grin at Babs.

"Very ingenious," Babs said.

"We B.I.O. agents are known for our ingenuity," Susan said, smoothly.

"So, what did you get?" Babs asked impatiently. "Tell me,"

"Bishop Mwita is off," said Susan. "He had a bona fide excuse not to be there. He's in the hospital with a ruptured spleen. Beautiful, isn't it? Now let's try the other one. If he also checks out, then we have a bit of a problem."

"How come it's sounding so simple all of a sudden?" Babs asked. "I'll phone Bishop Masana's place."

She picked up the phone and leafed through the directory. When she had found her number she punched the keys in at the telephone and then posed her question after identifying herself. The answer she got in return was short, rude and to the point.

"It seems that it's none of my business why he didn't turn up," said Babs ruefully, hanging up the phone. "It's not as simple as it seems, it?"

"That's the man we want," Susan said confidently. "They're just getting uptight because they can't explain his absence. It's certain that if they could, they would be too willing to tell the press and absolve the Bishop from any blame."

"That makes sense," said Babs.

"Do you have any information on Bishop Masana?" Susan asked. "Anything off-head?"

"Well," said Babs, "we know that he runs a youth centre called the 'Spiritual Awareness League' or something like that. He runs it with a famous psychiatrist called Wamae."

"Wamae!" Susan exploded. "Dr. Peter Wamae? That guy is a sadist. You wouldn't believe the kind of things he does to people. A youth centre? More like a torture chamber, I'll bet. Yeah, he's our man alright. Do you have the address for this 'Spirits and Awareness' thing?" Susan was clearly excited.

Babs dived back into her stacks of papers and began to search in earnest. A few minutes later she re-surfaced with the information on a piece of paper.

"Here, it is," she called out. "The 'Spiritual Awareness League."

"Okay," Susan said. "Now we call Chain and Bakari and give them the address. They can meet us there."

She went back to the phone and dialled Bakari's number at the office. She explained the situation to Bakari who promised to bring special C.I.D. agents and a warrant to search the premises.

"Come on, let's get out of here," Susan said, pulling Babs out of the room.

"But what happens if he's not the right one?" Babs asked. "How can we be sure?"

"We'll make sure as soon as we see him," Susan said. "I know a way. Now come on!"

They ran to Babs's car and roared off. Susan was driving. They drove for forty minutes, out of the city, with Babs calling out the directions. She felt like a navigator in the Safari Rally. Susan was certainly driving as if she were in an important race. The phrase 'life and death situation' took on an entirely new meaning.

226

As they screeched to a halt, Susan explained that they would have to bluff their way in as they didn't have a warrant to enter and Bakari hadn't turned up with his yet. Babs agreed to the plan and Susan suggested the old 'press' act.

"What do you mean?" Babs queried. "I don't have to pretend at all. I am a press-man."

"Okay, keep your feathers on," Susan said soothingly. "You handle getting us in. Demand for an interview with the Bishop. Once we are in, leave the talking to me."

Babs agreed and they headed for the gate. Convincing the guard to let her enter wasn't very difficult. She was used to that kind of thing. The Bishop was supposedly in one of the back gardens, talking with a group of students. A guard took them there.

They approached the group from behind. The Bishop was clearly discernible in his multi-coloured robes. Susan took a deep breath.

"Balain," she called, making sure to keep her voice normal and quiet. The Bishop's response was all that she needed. He turned around violently, his face a mask of fear. Susan did not take her eyes off him. "I have a message for you from Mordred. Can you take us somewhere private?"

Relief and wariness marred the Bishop's expression as he calmly agreed and excused himself from the group. Susan glanced at Babs and saw that she was also convinced. Bishop Masana was Balain. Nobody else had turned when Susan had called out. The Bishop had easily recognised the name.

Susan saw Chain and Bakari heading a large group of C.I.D. men just before they entered Balain's office. "There's no need to go any further," she said, as she withdrew her gun and levelled it at him. "You've come to the end of the line, Balain."

The look on his face was that of a trapped animal. He frantically looked around but seemed to be surrounded by C.I.D. wherever he looked. Finally, he made a desperate lunge for Susan, just as Chain and Bakari reached them. Her gun went off; pumping lead into his stomach and killing him instantly.

Chain caught him as he started to fall and dragged him into his office. Bakari directed some agents into restoring some kind of order outside as mayhem erupted.

"What next?" Babs queried as they all went into Balain's office.

"Now we open the safe," Chain said, already fiddling with it.

"The safe?" Babs asked.

"It may contain some important documents," he said. "Don't worry. I'm an expert with safes."

He got it open and withdraw a sheaf of papers which he passed out to the rest.

"George, you had better get some men to look for Dr. Wamae," Susan said. "We don't want him getting loose."

"We have sealed all the exists," Bakari said. "But we'll get onto it right away." He left the room.

Susan turned to the papers in her hand. They showed clearly that the Bishop was or had been Balain. The plot to take over the country was discussed and the names of all the knights mentioned. They were all Arthurian names.

"Guess what?" Chain said, "Mrs. Janet Musyoka's assassination day is next Tuesday. "

"Next Tuesday?" Susan asked. "Great. That is just great. How are we supposed to stop them before then?"

"Especially with Mordred trying to blow us up at every turn," Babs sighed.

"What is it?" Bakari enquired as he re-entered the room. "What is wrong?"

"We have just had the pleasure of finding out Mrs. Musyoka's assassination date," Chain said sarcastically. "It's this Tuesday."

"Why Tuesday?" Bakari asked. "What's so special about that particular day?"

"It will be budget day," Babs said flatly.

"That's right," Chain said, leafing through the papers. "They're planning to get her as she arrives for the budget speech. Neat, huh?"

"Very neat," Susan said wearily. "Have you found the good doctor, Bakari?"

"Yeah, we've got him," Bakari answered. "I don't see how he has been allowed to run an organisation like this at all. That man is definitely dangerous."

"Well, the next thing to do is to search the premises," Chain said. "They must have some kind of archive or something where they store their information. We may be able to find something really incriminating here."

"These guys are really sick," Susan said. "They are actually planning to split up the country and divide it among themselves," she said as she scanned her sheaf of papers. "Turn them into states, The United States of Kenya. That's just what we need. Why are people so selfish?"

"We can't all be as clever or as gifted as you my dear lady," Chain said mockingly.

They spent the next half hour going through the building, turning everything upside down. Sure enough, there was an archive building on the premises where they had stored all the important information, and it took several C.I.D. men to cut through the doors and break in. The tapes, logs and letters found there were more than incriminating; they were dynamite.

While Bakari and his agents gathered all the students into their hall to let them know what was going on, Chain, Susan and Babs went through the information in the archives.

"Here's something interesting," Babs said, and the other two turned to her. "A taped conversation between Balain and Perceval."

The other two hurried over and rewound the tape. It wasn't very long and it wasn't very informative either.

"Why don't these guys ever call each other by their real names?" Susan asked frustratedly.

"Because they don't want to be found out," Chain reasoned. "Anyway it shouldn't be too hard to find Perceval. He is obviously a powerful high court judge, and if this rather strange conversation is to be believed, he recently managed to get a murderer off the hook. An American called Greg or Craig Farrell who apparently stabbed his girlfriend to death for reasons best known to himself. Perceval was asked to try and get him off and he apparently succeeded. It shouldn't be too hard to find him."

"We can go through the records at the High Court and find out; see which judge presided over the Farell case," Babs said. "And bingo, we have got our man."

"Too good to be true," Susan murmured.

"But first, we have got to get hold of Gawain," Chain said firmly. "Bakari and I managed to get three names which we now have to check out," he said.

"If we can get hold of Perceval and Gawain, then we'll be getting somewhere," said Susan. "We also know how to get to Tristan's lab — if it really is near Wilson Airport."

Bakari joined them and they explained the situation to him. He decided to remain at the Institute while the other three went to check out Gawain. Babs refused to go with them.

"If you're going after Gawain, I'd rather not be with you," she said. "I think I'll stay here and hitch a ride back with Bakari. You can take my car, Susie."

"No that's okay," Chain said. "She is coming with me. You two have a nice time, with all the kiddies. See you later."

As Chain and Susan left, Chain was striding rapidly towards the door. Susan trailed after him, sensing that he was upset about something or other. With a smile she realised that she was beginning to read his moods better. She wondered what it was that she had done to bring about his formidable wrath upon her, but she didn't have to wait long to find out. As soon as they reached the car, Chain turned savagely around.

"What did you think you were doing?" he asked, trying to rein in his temper. "What gave you the right to come storming in here to take Balain by yourself? What exactly do you think you could have done if Mordred was here?"

"Mordred wasn't here," Susan said.

"That's no excuse," Chain raged. "We know very well that these people are dangerous and that they wouldn't think twice about killing you. Why did you have to take such a stupid risk?"

"Chain," Susan said, blinking in utter astonishment. "I am a trained B.I.O. agent, not a novice. I knew what I was doing. It is what I was trained to do. Maybe you could have handled it with a little more finesse . . ."

"That's not what this is about and you know it!" he exploded. "How well you handled it is not the issue. I know you're trained but it's not enough. You got by with plain good luck out there today. You should have waited for me to come."

"Don't you think you're over-reacting just a little bit?" Susan asked.

Chain forced himself to calm down. He drew in several deep breaths and turned away while he brought himself grimly back under control. "Yeah, maybe I was over-reacting. I just don't want to see you get hurt," he sighed. "I know that there's no way I can convince you to get out of the whole mess and leave it to me. I'd love to wrap you up in cotton wool and keep you safe somewhere, because . . . you mean . . ." He cleared his throat, loudly. "You mean a lot to me, and I don't want to lose you. I just don't want you taking unnecessary chances. First Mordred with the bomb this morning and now this. Hey how much is a guy supposed to take? Just slow it down a bit, okay?" He sighed again. "Now please get into the car."

He slid into his seat and waited until she got into hers and closed the door. Then he pulled her to him and kissed her deeply but roughly. Not giving her a chance to react. He immediately turned the key in the ignition and started the car.

They drove swiftly back to Bakari's office in silence, Susan still glowing from Chain's kiss and Chain still worried about what he viewed as Susan's folly. Susan sighed contentedly and thought that if that is what was meant by being swept off one's feet, then she was all for it.

At Bakari's office, Chain made her sit down while he searched through the sheaf of papers that he and Bakari had amassed. Quickly, he verified the information and then turned to Susan. He explained to her that those three names he had, seemed to be the only ones available, and he was convinced that they were the only ones around that could actually be Gawain.

Then he picked up the telephone receiver and proceeded to flip open the telephone directory and use Susan's method of elimination. He called the oil-men one by one, and identified himself as a reporter. He then asked why the oil-man involved hadn't turned up for the conference on small-scale oil prospecting in the country (contrived, of course) on Saturday morning.

The first one's assistant appeared very flustered and hastened to explain that they hadn't received an invitation to attend the conference and then added that her boss had attended a session of golf with the Minister for Sports in the country.

The second one's assistant was very brusque and rude and could not explain where his boss had been.

The third one's assistant apologised profusely for her boss, explaining that there must have been a mix-up in the schedule, and the conference must have been overlooked. She told Chain that her boss had been in a meeting with the Minister for Natural Resources for the entire morning.

"Well, there we are," Chain said, swiveling in his chair to face Susan. "What do you think?"

"Do you want an educated guess on that one or a simple opinion?" Susan asked.

"Both," Chain said with a smile.

"I think oil-man number two is our bet; Frederick Travis. What do you think?" she asked him.

"I think it's definitely worth a try," said Chain. "It looks like a very easy hit."

"What are we waiting for?" Susan asked, as she stood up. "Let us try and get him at home. It's the best place to start. Or do you have any qualms about killing a man in his own house?"

"On a Sunday, to boot," Chain said lightly. "Anyway, he is not at home. He is at his office. His otherwise unhelpful assistant did tell me that."

232

"Then let's get moving," Susan said. "The sooner we get going, the quicker we can get him and maybe one or two others before the others find out and call a security meeting.

Chain looked at her broodingly. "I don't suppose that there is any way I can convince you to wait for me here, is there? The look on her face told him what he wanted to know. "Come on then," he said. "But I want you to promise that you'll do exactly as I say, as soon as I say it without asking any questions."

"I know how to take orders, Chain," she said with a small smile.

They left Bakari's office and the C.I.D. headquarters. Getting into Chain's car, they discussed the different methods they could use to confirm Gawain's identity. Finally they settled on the same one they had used with Balain. They decided to more or less, arrest him and take him back, if they could, to Bakari's office.

They got to Travis' office in twenty minutes. It was heavily guarded from all sides and Chain had to stop for a minute in order to confer with Susan on which was the best approach to use in order to get in. They decided to continue with the press disguise; it was the safest cover up.

Sure enough, the guards at the gate let them in quickly when they identified themselves as journalists. They drove up to the main block and parked. They were shown into a waiting room while one of the guards went to check if his boss was busy. He returned in a few minutes and asked them to go with him.

He took them into a room where a middle-aged American was sitting at a desk and sifting through some papers.

"Sit down please," he said genially, without looking up from his task.

"Thank you Gawain," Chain said smoothly.

Frederick Travis' head came snapping upwards with an astonished expression on his face. There was no mistaking it; this man was definitely Gawain.

"Sir Mordred sent us," Susan said confidently. "He does not trust your usual lines of direct communication and he asked us to come and pick you up. It seems like King Arthur wants to hold another meeting because things seem to be going wrong."

"There's a new meeting place," Chain added. "Since you already held one emergency meeting yesterday, Mordred thought it better that you all meet elsewhere."

Travis obviously believed them. He had no choice but to believe them. His expression of shock was replaced by one of relief. He seemed to take it for granted that Susan and Chain were two of Mordred's people; maybe it wasn't the first time that this had happened. He stacked his papers neatly together, and stood up, indicating that they should leave right away. Susan and Chain were only too happy to accommodate him.

They led the way to the car and all three of them got in. Chain gunned the engine to life and all were silent as he carefully drove away from the buildings and out of the gates. Only after they were cruising along the highway did Chain activate the automatic door and window locks. Susan turned with a gun in her hand.

"You are more or less under arrest, Mr. Travis," Susan said calmly. "I'd read you your rights but they don't really apply in your case."

"Who are you?" Travis whispered.

"My name is Susan Juma," she said. "I believe you have heard of me and of my associate Chain."

"Chain," Travis whispered again; enlightenment dawning on his face. He slumped back in his seat and did not say another word for the rest of the journey.

They took him back to Bakari's office and silently escorted him inside. His face was chalk-white and he looked unhealthy and disturbed. Susan feared that he might have a heart-attack and she told Chain so.

"Let him," Chain said without any compassion. "It would take him off our hands."

They went into another room to discuss what they should do next. Chain decided that they would have to get Perceval as soon as possible. It was going to three o'clock in the afternoon but Chain was quite sure that he would be able to get into the law courts's record room and dig up the old case. They agreed that Gawain would most probably not tell them anything useful but decided to try and get him to talk just for the sake of it.

234

However, as soon as Chain unlocked and opened the door to Bakari's office, Gawain hit him full in the body, knocking him to the floor and took off in a dead run.

Susan immediately sprinted after him down the corridors and round the corner. He run down the hall with Susan only a few metres behind him. Behind her, she could hear Chain gaining ground on them as well.

As Gawain got to the front entrance, Susan called out to him.

"Stop, or I'll shoot!" she shouted, dropping to her knees and taking a careful aim with her gun. Gawain took no notice and he started pulling at the doors frantically.

Susan fired a shot which caught him in the back of the head, spinning him violently around. She fired another shot which caught him full in the chest as he fell. There was no need for a third shot.

Chain ran up to Gawain and turned him around. Then he shook his head.

"This is one knight who is not going to inherit a portion of the earth," he said. "Come and help me take him back to Bakari's office."

Susan reloaded her gun and put it away, as she walked towards Chain. It was two gone, seven to go.

Chapter Thirty-Two

Chain managed to have Bakari paged at the Spiritual Awareness League compound where he still was. When Bakari called him back, he explained the situation to him. Bakari caustically grimaced and promised to send some agents there to have Gawain taken to the mortuary, where Balain already was. There was still a lot to do at the League, so Bakari and Babs were still there.

After the agents arrived, Chain and Susan got back into Chain's Honda and headed for the law courts.

"What are you thinking about?" Chain asked after a few minutes of silence.

"You," Susan said. "You are an enigma; a total enigma."

"Oh?" he asked with an amused smile. "In what way?"

"In every way," she said, throwing her hands upwards. "Chain; that anti-social super-star! I can understand why you felt you had to cut off all connections with B.I.O. and have nothing more to do with it. But you seem to be so much of a recluse."

"Not all the time," he protested. "I do socialise, you know." "Rarely," she insisted. "You don't talk about yourself much either."

"Well, neither do you," Chain said. "You've never really told me about your childhood; your dreams and ambitions; your likes and dislikes and your fears. I want to know everything there is to know about you. You talk a lot but you rarely say anything about yourself."

"That is because there's nothing to say," Susan said with a sigh. "My mother is an Irish housewife who lives in Ireland with her husband and three children. She was in Kenya around two decades ago on a holiday, when she met my father who was based in Mombasa those days. I was the result of a holiday romance. They were married for three months and when my mother gave birth to me, she handed me

236

over to my father, got a divorce and went back to Ireland to put the past firmly behind her. Neither I nor my father saw her ever again."

"And?" Chain prompted.

"I had an okay childhood," she said. "I more or less had anything I wanted. My father was a rather rich, extremely busy man whose business took him away from home a lot. So I grew up alone. I don't have very many close friends but the ones I really have say I'm insecure. In a way, I guess I am, but I like to think of myself as well-balanced."

"Oh you're balanced, alright," Chain said. "And too self-sufficient."

"So that's the story of my life," Susan said. "I fear drinking most of all because it makes you lose control. I dislike men who cheat on their wives and people who don't have any loyalty except to money and power. My dream is to find happiness and my ambition is to achieve my dream. I like peanut-butter sandwiches, listening to classical music, and you," she ended her recital with a small smile in his direction.

"Ah," Chain said lightly. "You fell for the great hero as well did you? You are not as immune as you would have us think."

"But my hero is not Christopher Mathenge," Susan said. "My hero is a small, doll-like woman called Janet Musyoka. If ever there was a brave, intelligent and really perfect human being, it is her and I mean that."

"That is probably the loveliest thing anyone ever said about her," Chain said softly.

"It's probably not," Susan retorted. "Anyway that is more than enough about me. How about you? Are you going to tell me about yourself?"

"Susan, I would really love to," Chain said. "But we have reached our destination and we have, shall we say, more important things to do?" He negotiated the car into the parking lot at the law courts. "But I promise you, the first opportunity I get, I'm going to bare my soul to you."

Susan looked sceptical but then decided to give the man the benefit of the doubt. Chain fished around in the glove compartment of his car and got out an identification card.

"My B.I.O. card," he explained. "I was too attached to it to throw it away."

They went to the building where Chain showed his card and explained that some more research had to be done for a very important case which they were working on. A guard escorted them to the records' room where all the files of past cases were kept.

They went over the murder cases of the past year looking for an American called Farell. It wasn't easy but they persisted, knowing that it was there. They paid special attention to the acquittals and hoped and prayed for success. And they found it.

The man's full name was Greg Farell. He was twenty-four years old, and came from the State of Colorado. He had allegedly stabbed his girlfriend to death after a quarrel in a bar. For some reason the Round Table had some sort of interest in him if the conversation between Perceval and Balain was to be believed. Perceval had managed to get him acquitted and extradited back to the States. Perceval was the Arthurian name of the judge presiding over Farell's case.

His name was Simeon Wankio and he was one of the most brilliant, most admired and most talked about men in Kenya. Even though Chain and Susan had been expecting anything, they were both shocked when they found that out. Wankio's name was totally unexpected. He was rich, famous, powerful and possessed all the right ingredients to make him an invaluable member of the Round Table but it still came as a shock to learn that he was the one. He just did not seem the type.

"I don't know exactly who I was suspecting," Susan said. "But it certainly wasn't Wankio; anybody but him."

Chain agreed entirely. There were very few people who could be trusted. 'Who would be exposed next? If people like J. F. Kimani and Simeon Wankio were working for the other side then exactly who was on the side of truth and justice? Who was protecting the common man if high court judges and top government officials and the religious clergy were all involved in a power struggle?'

They left the law courts and headed for Wankio's residence, which was situated in one of the posh areas in town. On the way they discussed ways through which they could get Wankio out of the house

238

without rousing his suspicion. They finally thought of something and decided to try it out.

Parking around the corner, they got hold of a box and some brown wrapping paper. They set it out to look like a special delivery parcel and even stamped it with date and time. Then they walked over to Wankio's gate and explained that they were from the post office with a special delivery parcel which could only be signed for by him. They were let through and went to the main house.

They waited on the verandah while Wankio was called outside. He came after five minutes, beaming genially and asking where he was supposed to sign.

"Right this way, sir," said Chain leading him over to a piece of paper where the judge was to sign. Susan positioned herself behind them.

"Make sure to sign your full name, Perceval," she said softly as he picked up the pen, and began to write.

His head snapped sharply up and he turned to look at Susan in horror. He was definitely a Knight of the Round Table, although Susan wished that they had been wrong.

She walked up to him, her hand in her overcoat. He stared at her as she quite casually took his arm and turned him back towards Chain. Then she let him feel the muzzle of the gun on his back.

"I would feel much better if I didn't have to use this," she said softly. "We're going to leave now, carrying the parcel; and you are going to act as if nothing is wrong. Is that quite clear?"

Perceval nodded quickly. His forehead was damp, as perspiration formed along his hairline. As Susan and Chain escorted him out of the compound, Chain told the guards that they were going to solve a small problem back at the post office. Perceval confirmed it and the trio were let through the large gates. The gates were closed, leaving the guards out of sight.

They led him to the car and stood him next to it as they questioned him.

"Who are the others?" asked Chain as he idly fitted a silencer to his gun. Wankio maintained his silence.

"The game is over, you know," said Susan. "We are going to get them with or without your help."

"You'll have to do it without my help then," said Wankio, tight-lipped.

"We were thinking more of you," Chain said smoothly. "If you co-operated you just might get a reduced sentence. You could certainly use a little help. Treason is a serious charge."

Wankio smiled thinly. "Who are you trying to tell about the law?" he demanded. "I know very well that there will be no reduced sentence for me. I will be executed whether or not I co-operate with you."

"We might be able to get you off," Susan said, suggestively. "You never know."

"I do know," Wankio said dryly. "You won't." Without any warning, he pushed violently between them and started running hard towards the corner that led to his house.

Chain raised his gun and fired thrice in quick succession. All three bullets struck Perceval's fleeing back. He was arrested in mid-flight and arched in agony for a moment. Then he crumpled to the ground.

Susan and Chain ran over to him and Susan checked his pulse. Perceval was dead. They dragged him back to the car and pushed him inside. Chain drove off as Susan searched Wankio for any clues at all. She hit pay-dirt in his little pocket diary.

It seemed that Perceval dealt most with Balain and Bohert. Balain, they already knew about but there was quite a bit of useful information about Bohert. Susan quickly flipped through the book, trying to fit the pieces together while watching Chain weaved through the traffic in the city. Susan tapped her fingers against the dashboard of the car thoughtfully.

"There is an entry here for Bohert, which says that Bohert was to fly 'back home to Paris'. Bohert must be French," she said.

"He could be," agreed Chain.

"Then there are many entries which refer to meetings at Bohert's company. The way I see it, it must be an international company," Susan continued.

"So it would be safe to assume that Bohert is the owner of a French company based here," said Chain.

"Yes," agreed Susan. "And then there is another entry indicating that Bohert returned to the country last weekend. On Sunday last week, to be precise. At least it's a lead, even though it doesn't sound like much. We know he is French and the president of a company and that he returned to the country from France, last weekend. It's a start."

"That should help," Chain said. "I guess it's back to Bakari to look for the directors of French companies in Nairobi and to find out which one of them was returning to the country last Sunday. Am I right?"

"You are right," Susan said and then she began to laugh.

"What is so funny?" Chain asked with raised eyebrows. "Do you care to share the joke?"

"What a day," Susan said. "Here I am calmly travelling in a car with a dead body in the back seat and not butting an eye. We have killed three people today, and I feel absolutely no remorse. In fact I wish that we could have killed more. A killer named Mordred is on the prowl somewhere, planning our demise and yet I don't feel frightened. I just don't feel anything but amusement."

"It's probably just shock," Chain said soothingly. "Let's talk about something better."

"Alright," Susan readily agreed. "Tell me why you never got married."

"I never met the right person," Chain said.

"Oh sure," Susan scoffed.

"No it's true," Chain said. "I don't believe in marriage for the sake of marriage. A means of giving in to public pressure. What is the use of spending the rest of your life with someone you can't get along with? I would rather wait for that special someone who will make all my dreams come true."

"Love hurts," Susan sighed.

"It's worth it," Chain said.

"Is it?" Susan asked derisively. "When I was nineteen years old a friend of mine fell in love with a guy who was just finishing his degree course at Nairobi University. Sylvia and Eric used to go everywhere together — they were so much in love they just couldn't bear to be parted from each other. They planned to get married immediately after Eric's graduation. Babs and I were to be her bridesmaids." Susan sighed again.

"On the wedding day, in the church, as Sylvia waited patiently at the altar for Eric to come, a message came from his best man to say that he wasn't coming. It seems that somewhere along the line Eric had fallen out of love with Sylvia and in love with her younger sister Joyce. Eric and Joyce had eloped that morning. That was why Eric couldn't make it for the wedding."

"I shall never forget the look on Sylvia's face when she heard the news. Standing up there in her beautiful white wedding dress looking as though someone had just kicked her hard in the stomach. She never cried, never uttered a sound. Babs and I couldn't believe it. We felt so bad. We took her home and left her in her room because she asked to be left alone for a while. When we got back a few hours later, she was dead. She had slit her wrists and just let the life drain out of her. You should have seen her lying in a pool of bright red blood, looking ethereal in her white wedding dress."

"That's the saddest thing I ever heard," said Chain. "What did you do then?"

"A week after the funeral, I managed to track down Joyce and Eric. Babs and I followed him and beat him to a pulp. It didn't bring Sylvia back but it helped us get some of it out of our systems."

"I would have liked to see his face after you had worked him over," Chain chuckled.

"No you wouldn't," Susan assured him. "It was not a pretty sight."

They arrived at Bakari's office and took the body inside, hoping that Bakari was back. Susan still felt no emotion but she couldn't help thinking that three Knights were gone. The game was beginning to warm up.

Chapter Thirty-Three

Janet Musyoka pulled on her white gloves. She was getting ready to go to a late afternoon mass. She often went to mass on Sunday afternoons and made sure that she could spare the time. Martin sometimes accompanied her, when he wasn't too busy trying to change the world. King also came, but rarely. It was very unusual to find him at home during weekends.

However, on this Sunday he was. He had come home half an hour earlier and told her that he was going to mass with her and that she should wait for him. Martin too was home and was planning to go for mass. Janet was really astonished by his behaviour that weekend. He had not been anywhere near his office since Friday. Instead, he had lounged by the swimming-pool, watched cartoons on television and finished reading a 500 page novel by an up-coming author. Such were the things that dreams were made of. Janet had shrugged her shoulders and enjoyed this strange and almost unheard of period of inactivity while it lasted because they never lasted very long. Martin had already started talking about coming from mass as early as possible so that he could work on some reports for Monday.

"Mom, are you ready?" King's voice came floating down the stairs. "We're going to be late." He came running down the stairs, two steps at a time; King believed in running while other men walked.

"Take it easy, dear," she called out to him, "We'll make it on time. We have got to wait for Martin, anyway."

"No! Martin is actually taking time away from the stock market report?" King asked quite surprised.

"Don't be nasty, King," his mother said reprovingly. "Your brother hasn't been near the stock market all weekend long." She caught his sceptical look. "Tell me what you have been up to today?"

"I went over to see Alice," he said. "I had promised that I would help her study. I have never spent a day studying with a girl before. The things I do for her!"

"Then she can only be doing you good," Janet said firmly. "When exactly do I get to meet this paragon of virtue?"

"You can meet her next weekend," King decided. "I will bring her over to see you. I am sure you will get along very well."

"Or else?" Janet asked teasingly.

Martin came downstairs before King could answer and he eyed his brother in surprise. His gaze shifted to his mother and then back to King.

"Are you coming to mass?" he asked. "Even if they have closed all the day spots, surely there are the night spots to get ready for."

"Martin!" his mother reprimanded. "Honestly, I don't know why you boys are always at each other's throats. If that is what you mean by brotherly love, I certainly don't approve."

"Why not mother?" Martin asked. "Any kind of love is better than none at all."

"Not your kind of love," Janet said. "Now if you are ready, we can leave."

They went outside into the big, official Rolls Royce limousine. Janet usually went to mass heavily guarded for her own sake. Several secret servicemen accompanied her safely to church and then back home again.

Martin was telling his mother and brother about the novel he had been reading. The story line was really fantastic and it involved a lot of kidnapping, espionage and intrigue. And the reason why the story was so interesting was that the main character was a middle-aged mother of five. The whole adventure just seemed to be following her wherever she went until at last she just accepted it and did her best to solve the mystery behind the whole big mess. It was a very well told story, spiced with large doses of humour and sympathy for the poor housewife who had absolutely no wish for anything more exciting in her life than washing dishes.

244

Janet was very enthusiastic about the whole story and she said that it was high time someone made his heroine a middle-aged housewife instead of a beautiful, intelligent young woman or a handsome, brainy, well-muscled young man. Choosing a housewife was 'very satisfying' she said. A stroke of genius.

"But hardly realistic," King said. "You'd need beauty and intelligence in order to penetrate a spying ring, for instance. Then you'd need muscle and brains in order to break out of it again."

"You have an answer for everything, don't you, King?" Janet asked him.

"Yeah, I do," he said confidently. "Well no, I don't, he said a second later with a rather crestfallen expression."

"Really?" Martin asked with a smirk.

"Yes, really," replied King. "I met a friend of mine last night for a quiet drink and a talk. A guy named Peter, who is studying engineering at the main campus. He is going through a major bout of depression and he doesn't socialise any more. He has gone all quiet and thoughtful and is becoming a radical. He seems to be doing a lot of quiet, underground inciting lately which is not like him. I mean, it's quite fashionable for all university students to be anti-government for some reason or other but Peter seems to be becoming excessive. I tried to talk to him but he wouldn't tell me what was wrong. I found that I just could not help him."

The car came to a halt as Janet tried to console her son. "Don't worry dear," she said. "I'm sure it will blow over soon, whatever it is. Trust me."

* * * * *

Mordred was trying to get in touch with Balain and it was proving impossible. He wanted to ask the Bishop to provide some manpower to scour the city for Susan Juma who he seemed to have lost completely.

He had been waiting outside Barbara Kwanda's house all night knowing that the two girls would have to meet sooner or later and fully intending to follow Babs to the ends of the earth, until she met Susan.

He could hardly believe his luck when Susan herself had turned up at Barbara's place early in the morning.

He had followed them to the airport and waited for the right moment before handing over the bomb. That girl had the luck of a saint. Her eye had obviously started smarting and she had run to the stairs, most probably going to find the bathroom to wash it out. At the last minute she seemed to hesitate. However, it was too late and the bomb had gone off. That last minute's hesitation had convinced Mordred that Susan had recognised him and he had immediately left the airport. He hadn't been able to pick up her trail since then.

He had had to tell King Arthur about the back-firing of their plan and of Kimani's death. King Arthur was justifiably upset. Mordred withstood the tongue-lashing that had ensued and then asked what they should do next. King Arthur agreed that calling a meeting should wait until Susan Juma and Chain had been taken care of.

"Where is she now?" King Arthur asked entering the room. "Have you found her yet?"

"Not yet," Mordred replied grimly. Susan Juma was getting to be a real problem.

"Have you got Balain?" King Arthur asked.

"No," Mordred replied tersely. That was another surprising thing. The Round Table members were not usually that hard to find. Nothing was going right any more.

"Keep trying," King Arthur said. "He has got to be around somewhere. The problem with Balain is that he indulges too much. "How he ever became a Bishop, I'll never know."

"Good play-acting," Mordred said. "In this world that is all you need."

"And Balain needs it more than most," agreed King Arthur grimly.

Mordred was getting impatient. The assassination was planned for Tuesday and everybody was already quite jittery about that. He didn't need anything else to go wrong at a time like this. To have people like Chain and Susan Juma roaming the streets freely with a lot of condemning information about the Round Table was certainly not helping matters at all.

246

"Keep searching," King Arthur said. "We have got to get Chain and the girl tonight." He left the room.

Mordred sighed and picked up the phone again. Mentally, he consigned Chain to the devil. He wished he had never heard of the man.

* * * * *

The said Chain was at that very moment dragging Perceval's dead body into Bakari's office, helped by Susan Juma. Both Bakari and Babs were in the office.

"Oh no! Not another one," Bakari said when he saw Perceval's body.

"You have killed another one," Babs gasped.

"No we gave him sleeping pills," Susan said caustically. "The man ran and we had no choice but to shoot him."

"So you've got three now?" Bakari asked, helping them to deposit Perceval's body on a chair.

"Yes," Susan replied. "We have got Balain, Gawain and Perceval."

"How long before the others find out that you're picking them off, one by one?" Bakari asked. He picked up the phone and called some agents to take Perceval to the mortuary.

"You can never tell," Chain replied. "They may have already found out and could be looking for us right now but have got another lead, this time on Bohert. It seems that he is the owner of a French company based in Nairobi. We have to find out which one it could be."

"That's great," Babs said. "What about the others? Any luck?"

"We have got Perceval's diary here," Susan said. "We may get something more from it. I noticed a few entries on Galahad, then we already have Tristan where we want him. Of King Arthur and his trusty sidekick, Mordred, we have no clues whatsoever."

"But I'm hoping that something turns up," Chain said as Bakari answered the phone that was ringing.

"For you, Chain," he said.

Chain picked up the phone and spoke into it for a few seconds. "Well," he said after putting the receiver down. "We can take Rogers

Kitili off the list of ministers. I took the recordings to a friend of mine at B.I.O. this morning and he has been running some checks. He says that the voice prints do not correspond at all. Which reminds me, I managed to get a recent recording of John Mwangi's voice which I sent along with Kitili's and the recording of Hakim's which you gave me. But there is no recording of Francis Nzau. Is there some way we can get one today?"

"I can get on it right away," Babs said standing up.

"Good," Chain said. "He is working on the others now but he tells me that it takes time. When you have finished, bring the tape right back to Bakari's office."

"Alright," Babs said and left.

Susan had been looking carefully through Perceval's notebook "Look," she said, holding out the book for Chain to see. "It mentions Galahad here. On this date Perceval met Galahad and his fellow engineering students at the main campus. Another entry shows that they were to meet in room 304, Galahad's, to discuss an issue. So we have a room number. It could be one of two people, because a room is shared by two students."

"Alright," said Chain. "As soon as we figure out who Bohert is, we shall go after Galahad. We have got to hurry up, time is very important. Let's go and look up all those French companies."

They went to the C.I.D. file room to use the computers there. The computers held a complete data-bank and could help them with almost anything. They searched for French companies and came up with five possible candidates.

Susan did the telephoning this time. She called the homes of the five presidents and enquired whether or not the president was now ready for an interview at the Kenya Broadcasting Corporation. She explained that they had called the previous Sunday but that he hadn't been available then.

She received a variety of explanations of why the chairman could not have attended an interview last Sunday. The first one had been out of the country and still was; the second one had been negotiating a deal in Mombasa; the third one had been quite ill, and the fifth one had been attending an important conference in town.

The fourth had just returned from a month-long trip to Paris. His name was Francois Farges; Susan had struck pay dirt.

She informed the others who were ready for the alleged interview that some arrangements would be made during the week. She told Farges that a car would be sent to pick him up and take him to the studios at K.B.C. He agreed.

Susan and Chain both agreed that Farges must be Bohert; there was no other explanation for the coincidence. They had been lucky so far and sincerely hoped that their luck would hold out long enough for them to get hold of the rest of the knights of the Round Table.

They went back to Bakari's office to find out what he was doing, before they drove off to Farge's house. The phone rang as they were there and it turned out to be Babs. She had gotten hold of Nzau's voice on tape and was bringing it over. Chain arranged with Bakari to have the tape delivered to his friend at B.I.O.

"Do you really think that you'll be able to get all remaining six members?" Bakari asked. "You've been lucky so far but for how long do you expect your luck to hold?"

"As long as it takes," Chain said.

"Suppose you can't?" Bakari asked.

"You don't realise that it's them or us," Chain said. "We either get them or we die. There is not much of a choice is there?"

"We'll get them, George," Susan said. "I know we will. Trust me."

* * * * *

Susan and Chain got into Chain's car for what seemed like the hundredth time that day. Chain started the car and reversed out of parking lot a little wearily and smiled when Susan looked at him with concern. She fastened her seat-belt and relaxed back in the chair.

"You never did tell me why you never got married," Susan said.

"I thought I had," Chain answered.

"You thought wrong," Susan said.

"Okay, I suppose like you I also had a rather nasty experience which put me off marriage for a while," he said.

"Let's hear it then," Susan suggested eagerly.

"It's not pretty," Chain sighed. "One of my work-mates fell in love with this girl and they decided to get married. He was really in love with the girl and she was the most important thing in his life. Well, the wedding went off without a hitch and everything was great. They moved into a beautiful house in one of the estates. It had a white picket fence and a garden for the children to play in. Within a few months she was expecting a baby and his cup was just running over. He was so excited about the whole thing that we also got affected by it. Everybody at work could hardly wait to see the baby born.

'Then one day he came home from work to find his wife dead. Mutilated and spread across the kitchen floor. There was a tape recorder and a note. The tape recorder contained a cassette in which they had recorded his wife's screams and pleas for mercy as they raped her and then started cutting up various parts of her anatomy. The note contained a message telling him to give up a case he had been working on. Susan, you don't understand grief. He went crazy and had to be locked up. That was ten years ago."

Susan felt sick. "That's the most disgusting thing I ever heard in my life," she said, and her hands started trembling.

"I had nightmares about it for along time afterwards," Chain said. "I would dream about coming home from work to find my wife and child dead; brutally murdered for something they had absolutely no connection with. I went into severe depression for a while, and it wasn't even my wife who died. I was just imagining that it may have been and I decided that there was no way I would ever put myself in such a position. To love somebody so much and then have them die in such a violent way; I know I'd go crazy. It didn't seem worth it."

They continued in silence for a little while. "You would think that after working at B.I.O. for a while, one would get used to seeing and hearing about all sorts of tragic and horrible events. One becomes quite cynical about most things and tends to shrug and pass them off as 'that's life!' But every once in a while, you hear something that just floors you all over again. At least I understand now exactly why you didn't want to get married," Susan said sympathetically.

"I have never really told anyone how I felt," Chain said. "You are a good listener," he added with a smile.

"I'm flattered," Susan answered lightly.

"It has taken me a long time but I feel that I have managed to calm down since I left B.I.O.," Chain said. "Being able to appreciate the little things in life like fresh country air, taking a walk in the sunset, milking a cow, harvesting . . . I felt as if there are other things in life other than frantically running here and there trying to solve a problem, always having to look over your shoulder just in case your enemy is chasing you to kill you; never really sleeping at night for fear that you may never wake up again. It is not worth the hassle."

"I know what you mean," Susan said.

The sun had begun to set over the horizon. It lent its bright red and sparkling orange rays to the surrounding environment and looked like a true work of art. There was a legend that the sun was driven across the heavens by a god named Apollo. His sister Diana, was in charge of the moon. Everyday he climbed into his chariot and drove the sun across the sky from one end to the other. At dawn, a goddess named Aurora opened the gates for him to go away and at dusk, she would wait for him to return, and then she would close the gates again. Sometimes, watching the sun's descent into the horizon made this story appear true.

They reached Farge's residence ten minutes later and Chain parked the car outside. He walked to the gate and asked the guard to inform Mr. Farges that the car had come to collect him to go to the studio. The guard relayed the information and Farges was soon in Chain's car. Chain re-entered the car and drove off.

Farges talked freely and unsuspectingly as they drove along. He cracked quite a few jokes and seemed perfectly at ease with himself and the others.

"This will be my first interview on Kenyan television," he confessed to them.

"Do you like interviews, Bohert?" Susan asked softly, still looking at him.

He went very quiet and looked shocked. His eyes darted in panic, his hand going instinctively to the door. It was locked; so were the windows. There was no escape.

"How did you know that name?" he asked quietly, finally conceding defeat.

"We know all about the Round Table and its members." said Susan. "The whole game is up, Bohert. We're taking you to C.I.D. headquarters where we will expect a little co-operation from you. I'm afraid you won't get an interview on Kenyan television for quite some time yet."

Bohert was silent. "I would advise you to help us," Susan said. "It will only do you good. You are in big trouble."

"It's not as if the others haven't also talked," Susan added. "Mordred has told us all about you. He's a bright man."

They drove on in silence until they finally reached Bakari's office. Then, when Susan turned around to face Bohert, she found his head lolling limply on his chest. He was dead.

"How on earth?" Susan asked incredulously.

Chain reached over and checked Farges's pulse. He looked into the man's eyes and checked his clothing. Then he sighed and sat back with his eyes closed.

"What is it?" Susan asked anxiously.

"Cyanide capsule," Chain said. "Instant death." He opened his eyes.

"Well, at least Babs can't accuse us of killing him this time," Susan said lightly.

"Come on," Chain said. "Let's get him to Bakari's office."

They dragged the body out of the car and took it into Bakari's office. Bakari helped them put the body on a chair. "Can't you bring me anything other than dead bodies?" he asked grimly.

"We never touched him, George," Chain said. "This one took a cyanide capsule."

Bakari went over to the phone to call some agents to take Bohert to the mortuary while Babs emerged from a chair at the back of the room.

"Why don't you just leave them wherever it is they die?" she asked. "Why do you have to keep bringing them here?"

"Because we don't want anybody from the Round Table to find them," Chain said. "The other members would get to know and then they would be on their guard."

The phone rang then and Bakari picked it up. "Hello," he said. "It's for you," he told Chain.

It was Chain's specialist friend from B.I.O., calling to say that he had just received Babs' tape recording of Nzau's voice. However, he couldn't continue working because people would get suspicious about why he was working so late. He then told Chain that John Mwangi was off the hook; it definitely wasn't him.

Chain thanked him and turned to the others and told them the news. He suggested that they stop for the day.

"Mordred is bound to find out if he hasn't already," Chain said. "We can't afford to go running around at night with him at our heels. Besides, Susan and I have got to find a place to stay for the night."

Bakari and Babs agreed and Susan and Chain left. It was dark outside, and a little cold. Susan shivered as she thought that four Knights were dead and there were five left.

* * * * *

"What were they doing at the airport?" Tristan asked hysterically.

The remaining members of the Round Table had met again at King Arthur's house. They were angry and very apprehensive.

"I don't know," Mordred said calmly, smoking a cigarette. "I thought maybe they had gone to meet a friend or something."

"And where are Bohert, Balain, Perceval and Gawain?" Galahad asked.

"I told you," Mordred said. "Missing; presumed dead."

"Undoubtedly Chain and Juma must have got them," King Arthur said. "If I were them I would certainly not let people like Balain live. We shall have to accept that they are probably dead. Chain is not a fool."

"I thought we had everything under control," Lancelot said.

"So did I," King Arthur said. "Seems we were both wrong." He was not as calm as he looked. His entire empire had come crashing, around him and he was helpless.

"What do we do now?" asked Tristan.

"Nothing," Mordred replied. "We lie low tomorrow and avoid getting into a panic because people might be watching us. We shall just go about our business quietly and with minimum fuss. We have to believe that if Chain and Juma knew about you they would have most probably taken you, by now. They couldn't really tell exactly how many we are and so tracked down four and managed to get hold of them. Juma knows about me but I suppose that's all. They will probably spend their time trying to track me down but they won't think of looking for you. I suggest that you simply continue with your usual Monday morning agenda tomorrow, as if nothing was wrong."

"Yes," Tristan said. "That is all very well. But what if something goes wrong?"

"Then we have all got to cover ourselves as best as we can," King Arthur said.

"Are you absolutely sure that the others are missing?" Galahad asked.

"I'm very sure," Mordred replied. "None of them can be traced. They can't just disappear from the face of the earth without a trace. Besides, each of them has a way of being reached at all times in case of an emergency. None of them is responding."

"Are you sure that there's nothing else we can do?" Lancelot asked.

"There is nothing really left for us to do," Mordred said. "We were caught by surprise. Evidently Chain and Juma knew more than we gave them credit for. All we can ask you to do is sit and wait in silence. I'm going to take care of both Chain and Juma tomorrow."

"How is this going to affect our plans?" asked Galahad. "Any changes?"

"None," replied King Arthur.

"We'll go ahead with Musyoka's assassination on Tuesday as scheduled," Mordred replied. "Then we shall proceed from there as planned."

For some strange reason King Arthur just could not stop thinking about the old Arthurian legend. Some said it had happened, some said it was a fairy tale. But whichever it was, it was very interesting:

The story goes that Arthur was the son of Uther Pendragon, King of all England. He was taken to live with a knight called Sir Ector, who together with Merlin, a great magician, did not want him to know that he was a future king. He was to find out much later because of the sword in the stone.

A stone had appeared in a churchyard with a beautiful sword stuck firmly in it. On it was written, "Whosoever pulls out this sword from this stone is the trueborn king of England." Many men had tried but had failed until Arthur came along. He was trying to find a sword for Sir Kay who was Sir Ector's son and who had gone to participate in a New Year's day tournament but had forgotten his sword. Arthur pulled the sword out of the stone easily and took it to Sir Kay. When this was discovered Arthur was knighted and crowned King.

He had formed the Round Table, which could seat a hundred knights, in order to protect his empire. Sir Mordred was his nephew, as was another famous knight, Sir Agravaine. Sir Lancelot was the bravest and most loved of all Arthur's knights and Sir Galahad was his son and best friend. Sir Galahad, together with two other knights, Sir Bohert and Sir Perceval, were the only ones ever to see the Holy Grail. Sir Gawain was famous for banishing Sir Lancelot to France, after war broke out between Lancelot and Arthur over Arthur's wife, Guinevere. Sir Lucan and Sir Balain were responsible for carrying Arthur's dying body to a little chapel by the sea shore. At Arthur's command; Balain threw his beautiful sword, the Excalibur back into the water. A hand clothed in silk reached above the waters and reclaimed it.

It had been Sir Mordred who had killed King Arthur in an effort to take over the throne and Queen Guinevere, for his very own. King Arthur had pierced Mordred through, with his sword, but Mordred had struck King Arthur a mortal blow, before he died. By this time the Round Table was no more since most of the knights were dead, either from fighting for King Arthur against Mordred or against Lancelot. The others had gone in search of the Holy Grail, which was supposed to be the cup Jesus and His disciples had drank from during the Last Supper. Most never came back.

After his death King Arthur had been rowed across the water on a mysterious barge, for his wound to be cured by the three queens who took him to the Paradise of Avalon. After this he would return once more to be King.

The present Round Table was falling apart but the present King Arthur believed in immortality and was sure that he would get his empire; no mortal was ever going to stand in his way, not even Chain.

Chapter Thirty-Four

"C an you help me?" Susan asked the two guards outside the gate at
Tristan's lab near Wilson airport. It was seven o'clock on Monday
morning. Susan and Chain had been awake half the night trying to find
out who was the owner of the large research centre situated near
Wilson Airport. Neither of them had been in the least bit surprised to
learn that it was the world famous scientist and brain-surgeon, Dr.
Kenneth Mutuli. They were past being shocked.

Susan and Babs had been waiting outside Mutuli's house since five
that morning, hoping to catch a glimpse of him. Their orders were to
wait and then follow him wherever he went. Then they were to report
back to Chain who was with Bakari, checking out the security plan for
the Vice-President from her house to Parliament on Tuesday. They had
waited, and then followed Mutuli to the lab near the airport and parked
their car a few metres away.

After discussing the issue, Susan had managed to convince Babs
that they should go after Mutuli then, instead of calling Chain and
waiting for him to get there. Then Susan had launched her plan of
action. She had walked up to the guards to lure them away from the
gate so that she and Babs could enter.

She was wearing a bright red mini-skirt and a large white
sweat-shirt with sequins on it. She was aware of the impression she
gave. She forced herself to appear relaxed but slightly anxious as she
approached the guards and was praying that the old maxim 'anything
for a pretty girl' would work for her this time.

One of the guards asked her what the problem was while they both
eyed her appreciatively.

"My car has a puncture," she said. "My sister is just around the
corner, waiting. Neither of us knows how to change a wheel. But then
we have never had to. Could you please help us? This area is a bit

secluded and there's no one else nearby," she said. Then she held her breath.

A hasty conference ensued where it became obvious that far from refusing to help, both guards wanted to be the one to go. In the end they decided to go together as they came to the conclusion that it was only for two or three minutes anyway.

With a grateful smile, Susan led the way around the corner to where Babs was waiting by the car. She was bending over deep onto the boot of the car, looking for a spanner. She was wearing very brief yellow shorts and a gold-coloured tank-top; which visibly showed all her curves and other attributes. Susan stole a glance at the two guards and could see them almost licking their lips.

Babs withdrew from the car boot looking frustrated. "It's too far down," she said.

One of the guards eagerly offered to go in and look around for it. He ducked into the boot and did not see Susan walk around his colleague. Standing behind him, she lifted her sweat-shirt and withdrew her gun from the waist-band of her skirt. She gently placed the muzzle of the gun on the small of his back and felt him stiffen.

"Don't make a move, friend," Susan said in a low voice as Babs grinned and moved over to the other guard who was still bent over the boot, scrambling around. She carefully slipped her hand into his holster and retrieved his gun.

"Alright get out of there," Susan said to the shocked and disbelieving guard. He came up slowly to face Susan's smirk. "Didn't your mother ever tell you that you shouldn't speak to strangers?"

She asked Babs to get the rope from the boot of the car, which Babs did. Then she courteously invited one of the guards to tie the other one up. Babs inspected the whole procedure to make sure that the rope was secure. Then Babs tied the second guard up and rolled both of them behind the car and out of sight. The two girls then started off for the lab.

They entered through the gates easily and were soon in the main building. The receptionist asked if she could help them.

"You certainly can," Susan replied. "We need to see Mr. Mutuli on a very urgent personal matter. Could you arrange it?"

"And your names are?" asked the girl.

"Just tell him that Mordred sent us," said Susan smoothly. "I'm sure he'll see us then."

The receptionist gracefully complied and soon they were being invited to follow one of the security guards to Mutuli's office. It was not in the main building. They walked briskly and silently in the cool crisp morning air to a building behind the main one.

The guard left them inside Mutuli's office. He had knocked and then escorted them inside before leaving. Mutuli waited until the guard had left before turning to the girls.

"What does Mordred say?" he asked them immediately the guard had gone.

"Sorry doctor," Susan said as she removed her gun. "We don't work for Mordred. We don't even know what he looks like properly. But I can imagine what he would say if he was here. My name is Susan Juma. Does that ring a bell? Stand up, Tristan," Susan ordered a little sharply. "I don't want you getting any ideas about pushing any buttons."

Mutuli stood up again and smiled a little grimly. "Unfortunately for me; there is only one button," he said, moving away from his desk. "That one there," he said, pointing to the red button on his desk. "It's a self-destruct button. It will blow up the entire lab if pressed." He smiled again. "But don't worry," he added. "I'm not going to press it. It detonates five seconds after being pressed so that doesn't leave much time for escaping does it? And I'm not quite ready to die."

"Aren't you?" Babs enquired. She had been looking through some books and files on the cabinet. "Susan this man is hiding an entire arsenal of weapons. If what is in these books is true, then he has got a cache of weapons here large enough to start the Third World War. Do you have any idea how many people he could kill with all these?"

"Oh God," Susan said. "I knew right away that there must have been a place where they were hiding some fire-arms but I never thought that it could be here. I will have to get in touch with Chain right away."

"You can't use the phones here," Babs said. "They probably have all the phones tapped and you would probably have this place over-run

with guards. You will have to go to the car and call him from there."
Babs car had a car-phone.

"I can't leave you here alone," said Susan.

"I'll manage," Babs said. "I'll just lock the door and keep him right
here with me. You go ahead and phone Chain. If he tries to move, I'll
shoot him" She removed the gun which she had confiscated from the
guard from her pocket.

"I'm not going anywhere," Mutuli said dryly.

"How are we going to find a way to destroy this place without
pressing that button?" asked Susan. "As Mutuli says, five seconds is
not enough time to run to safety."

"Don't worry, we'll think of something," Babs said. "Nothing is
impossible. Now go." Susan went. She couldn't resist one backward
glance before leaving the door and Babs gave her a thumbs up sign and
a crooked grin. She still didn't feel convinced but she felt that they
didn't have a choice and so she left. She closed the door behind her and
walked briskly away from the building.

Babs heaved a great sigh after Susan had left. She had a plan and
Susan was not a part of it. But she couldn't have told her friend exactly
what her plan was. Susan would just not have understood. She wouldn't
have approved.

She motioned Mutuli over to another chair and made him sit down.
She then went to sit in the chair behind his desk and kept her gun
pointed straight at him while she gazed at him in silence.

"What do you do for a living," Mutuli asked finally.

"I'm a reporter," said Babs. "I work for the Kenya Broadcasting
Corporation."

"Ah, so I will get proper television coverage for my deeds and
misdeeds," said Mutuli.

"Sorry," Babs said. "We don't televise traitors, sadists and
murderers as a policy. You wouldn't attract the right audience."

"You don't think much of me, do you?" Mutuli asked with a faint
smile. Babs didn't bother to answer. "I am a doctor," he said. "I save
lives. I study people and do research on better ways to live. I need more
money in order to carry out my research."

"At the expense of human lives?" Babs asked.

"If it means killing a few thousand in order to achieve a better life for all mankind, then it's worth the sacrifice," said Mutuli.

"It's not your choice," Babs said passionately. "It's not your place to choose who is to be spared and who is to be sacrificed."

She stopped short. Isn't that what she was about to do? It was fifteen minutes since Susan had left. Babs reached over and pushed the button.

Susan walked briskly across the long courtyard; through the main building and out towards the main entrance. Her casual stance and unconcerned expression ensured that she was more or less ignored on her journey, much to her relief. She reached the wide, unguarded gates very quickly; and gratefully left the compound.

A few minutes later she arrived at the car; and started dialling Bakari's office number. She drummed her fingers impatiently on the dashboard while she waited for one of them to pick up the phone. Chain picked it up on the third ring.

"Chain, I know you're going to be very upset with me . . ." Susan started.

"You went after Tristan," Chain said flatly.

"Yes, we did," Susan admitted, a bit cautiously. "How did you know?"

"I've been trying to ring you at the car," Chain said. "To no avail. The only reason why neither of you would be in the car is that you decided to go after Tristan yourselves."

"You are upset," Susan concluded.

"I don't see why I should be," Chain said. "Expecting you to wait and go with me was just too much to ask; wasn't it? So I really can't blame you for this."

"Chain, it was so easy to get in," Susan said. "It was such an easy hit. And if we wanted to get Tristan just like that, we could. It's like feeding candy to a baby. You just can't keep on treating me like this; like a delicate porcelain doll. I can take care of myself. You have got to believe me."

"It doesn't look as if you're giving me much choice," Chain said. "Why didn't you?"

"Why didn't I what?" Susan asked thoroughly confused by the question.

"Why didn't you remove Tristan if it was such a piece of cake?" Chain asked. "Where is he now? And where is Babs?"

"Oh," Susan said. "They are both still inside the lab. Babs is guarding Tristan. We shall bring him out in a minute. It's just that we have got a bit of a problem."

"Ah," Chain said. "Does that mean that Miss Super-efficient is actually asking for my help for once?"

"Chain, please don't be sarcastic," Susan said, starting to feel uncomfortable. "I know I shouldn't have gone in there but I promised you that I wouldn't have gone if I thought there was any danger."

"I don't care if it was as safe as a convent!" Chain exploded. "That's not the main point. The point is that we had agreed that you were not to go rushing after these guys alone any more. And then what do you do as soon as you're out of my sight? The very thing we had agreed you wouldn't do. Just this morning you were promising me you wouldn't. Exactly what gives you the right to disregard my feelings and break your promises to me so easily and without any twinges of conscience? How do you expect me to trust you if you can't grant me a simple request? Do you expect me to be constantly worrying about you and chewing on my nails waiting for you to call me so that I can calm down? It won't work lady — I'm not that kind of guy."

"Chain, stop shouting," said Susan, anxiously chewing on her lower lip. She knew that he had every right to be upset because she had broken a promise to him and she had disobeyed his orders. And all this after asking him to trust her and assuring him that she knew how to take orders.

"I am not shouting," he said in a relatively calm voice. "I was simply getting it off my chest, as the saying goes."

"I know you have every right to get angry," said Susan. "I shouldn't have done what I did and I regret doing it now. It's just that for so long I haven't been really answerable to anybody. I do what I want, when I want because I know that the consequences will only

262

affect me. I'm not used to stopping and thinking how my actions may affect someone else. I'm really sorry Chain."

"You're forgiven," he said lightly.

"I really wasn't thinking about it from your point of view," said Susan. "I wasn't thinking at all. It won't happen again."

"I know," Chain said softly. Susan felt warmed by his show of confidence. "Now tell me what your little problem is and exactly why you have left Babs alone with a dangerous felon. You know they are bound to strangle each other to death before you get back again." He tried to inject some humour into the situation.

Susan had totally forgotten about Babs and Tristan. "You will never guess," she said. "This is where they have got all their weapons stored. Chain, they have got enough to arm an entire army out here. With the Bishop's crazy followers, they had an army. These guys mean business."

"Is there any way to destroy them?" Chain asked anxiously.

"Not one that I can see," Susan said. "There's a button in Tristan's office which detonates all the buildings in the area but we found out it explodes five seconds after it has been pressed; no one can escape alive. I wish that there was some way we could make him press that button after we have left the area. But he would never do that; he would rather beat himself to death than press the button. He is scared of dying."

"Okay," Chain said. "Go back in there and get Babs and Tristan out. Then take both of them to our safe house. I'll meet you there and we can discuss it. If there is another way of destroying that place; then we shall use it."

"Fine," Susan said. "I'll do it right away."

"Hurry up Susan," Chain said.

"Don't worry. . ." Susan said. She never finished her sentence. She heard a tremendous explosion and turned back in time to see the entire centre simply explode. It was exactly fifteen minutes since she had left Babs and Tristan.

* * * * *

Susan was flunged against the dashboard of the car by the force of the explosion. She hit her head with a sharp crack and then fell back helplessly, like a rag doll. She immediately sat up and looked back at Tristan's research centre in disbelief.

What had been a beautiful layout of white-and-chrome buildings was now a smoking holocaust. Waves upon waves of black clouds billowed upwards towards the clear blue sky from the giant inferno which was eating hungrily at the remaining structures. The bright orange tongues of fire scorched everything in their path as they gracefully and teasingly danced around. Everything was completely destroyed; devasted.

Susan screamed as she closed her eyes and turned away. When she opened them again and saw that the explosion had been real and not just a macabre trick of her slightly overworked imagination, she let out another scream. Hysterically, she got out of the car and ran towards the flames. The wind swept the billowing black smoke into her face and her hair and her eyes started smarting. She started choking but her only thought was of Babs. Babs had been in that explosion which was now an inferno raging wildly out of control now. Her closest friend was being roasted to death in a place that closely resembled Hell on Earth. The choking got worse as tears rolled down her cheeks and grey ashes clung to her already sooty hair. She was forced to stop her advance as the heat from the terrible fire enveloped her and started singe her hair and her eyebrows. She turned back abruptly and stumbled away again. Her next thoughts were of Chain.

The car seemed miles away as she stumbled towards it on extremely shaky legs. The tears blurred her vision and her heart felt as if it was being squeezed tighter and tighter in a vice-like grip. Her head throbbed painfully. She walked unsteadily on her feet as the ground seemed to shake and undulate under her feet. She could not focus properly on the car as it seemed to swim in and out of focus right before her eyes, alarmingly.

When she finally reached the car, she was coughing and choking so much she could hardly see. The phone was dangling off the hook where she had left it and Chain's voice was cackling loudly on the wire. She caught the tail-end of his sentence as she lifted the phone to her ear with seemingly super-human effort.

"... answer me, damnit!" Chain was shouting into the phone.

"Chain," she croaked, before collapsing into another fit of coughing.

"Susan, for God's sake, what is going on down there?" Chain asked. "What on earth is happening?"

"The research centre is gone, Chain," Susan answered. "Tristan's lab is no more. It exploded and Babs is dead." Susan groaned with both mental and physical pain. "She is dead! What am I going to do?" she asked.

"Are you alright?" he asked.

"No," she replied weakly.

"Alright," said Chain. "Stay where you are. No, you can't do that. Do you know the short cut across the plains into Nairobi South C?"

"Yes," Susan answered.

"I want you to take it," he told her. "Just drive until you hit the dirt road leading to that new primary school, the Educational Centre. Park there and wait for me. You can't stay where you are any longer. I want you to move out now. Do you understand me?"

"Babs is dead, Chain," said Susan.

Chain swore forcefully once again. "Susan get out of there now. Do you understand me?"

His shouting penetrated the mists swirling around in her head. "Yes," she said. "Yes, I understand. I'll be on the dirt road in a few minutes."

"Good," said Chain. "So will I." He handed the phone over to Bakari and then left the room. Susan heard Bakari's soothing voice on the phone next.

"Susie, get into the car and close the door," he said. "Have you done that?"

"Yes," said Susan, slamming the door shut. Her hands were trembling.

"Alright, put the key in the ignition and start the car," he said. "Start the car, Susie." He insisted quietly when he heard no evidence of the ignition.

Still trembling, she managed to thrust the key into the ignition on the third attempt. She started the car with a jerk and managed to persuade her trembling hands to grip the steering wheel tightly. Then she started off on the road stretching before her.

Gaining a little confidence, Susan accelerated the car steadily and drove a bit faster. Bakari never stopped his monologue over the phone. He steadily instructed her and she unquestioningly responded to what he was saying. She let her mind go blank and simply concentrated on her destination.

She never knew exactly how she got there but she managed to make it. It took her an entire excruciating twenty minutes but in the end she got there. Still following Bakari's instructions, she stopped the car and parked it in the correct spot. She wiped the sweat on her forehead and saw Chain's car coming up the dirt road. Susan told Bakari this over phone and he cheerfully hung up.

Chain jumped out of his car and came running towards her. She stumbled out of Bab's car and fell into his arms, sobbing incoherently. He held her tightly to him for a while and then pulled her into his car.

"Susie, stop it," he said. "Try and pull yourself together now."

"I can't," she said with tears streaming down her face. "I just can't. Babs is gone Chain, don't you understand? I killed her."

"Don't be stupid . . ." Chain began.

"I killed her!" Susan screamed again. "I should never have taken her there. She pushed that button. I know she did."

"Susan, you can't know that," Chain said. "You are becoming hysterical."

"It had to be her," Susan insisted. "It couldn't have been someone else. Mutuli would never have done it. I know his type."

"Come on," said Chain. "I'll take you home." He pulled her fully into the car then closed and locked her door.

He drove like a maniac all the way home, tyres screeching and horn blaring all the way. He took her to the house where they had spent the night before. She sat stone-faced during the entire journey, not uttering a sound. Chain was very worried.

266

Half an hour later she was in bed heavily sedated. Chain had called a doctor friend of his to sit in the house with her. The doctor had been shocked to see Susan looking so badly off. She was obviously in deep shock and he had to treat her for that. Chain refused to tell him what had happened; saying that he had no wish to put the doctor's life in danger.

"Is she going to be alright, Keith?" Chain asked anxiously.

"She should be," Keith answered guardedly. "I'll watch her and see."

"Good," said Chain. "You stay here. I've got business to take care of."

He rang Bakari and told him that he wanted a few C.I.D. agents to accompany him to the University of Nairobi. He was going after Galahad.

Bakari told him that the research centre had been burnt to the ground and there were no survivors. If Babs had been in the lab when it exploded then she was most certainly dead. There had been two guards who had been found bound and gagged nearby. They had spoken of a gang of bandits who had over-powered them and blown up the lab. They were obviously not telling the truth. Chain agreed with him that Babs and Susan had most probably taken care of them but they hadn't wanted to admit it. However, that was okay because the publicity wasn't really needed.

Bakari agreed to supply the agents and dispatched them to Chain's house. Chain waited impatiently for them to arrive. He wanted to get to Galahad's room before the student learnt about the explosion, at Tristan's lab. He paced the room for fifteen minutes until the agents arrived, in two cars.

Chain jumped into one of the cars which raced off towards the University of Nairobi's main campus. He had been there himself and knew exactly where room 304 was. There was no time to waste and he jumped out of the car before it had come to a complete stop outside the campus grounds.

He positioned a few guards outside and along the way to Galahad's room. He was thinking fast and trying to find the best way of exposing him. He knew that there were two students in Galahad's room; one was a knight of the rather dubious Round Table, the other was not. By the time he got to room 304, he had already formulated a plan. He hoped it would work.

He directed the two agents with him to remove their guns in readiness for any action. Then he knocked on the designated room's door and pocked his head inside.

"Hey, is one of you called Galahad?" he shouted casually. "A man called Mordred wants to speak to Galahad."

There were two young men in the room. One of them was still dressing and the other was busily putting his books together. They had both turned at the sound of Chain's voice but their reactions were very different. The one who was still dressing turned sleepy eyes in Chain's direction. He seemed quizzical and a bit uninterested in the whole thing.

"There's no one here by that . . ." he started, only to be rudely interrupted by his room-mate who pushed him aside.

The other young man had almost visibly jumped when he heard the name Galahad. There was the customary look of shocked surprise on his face which Chain was beginning to get used to.

He pushed his colleague out of the way and advanced towards Chain quickly. "Where is he?" he asked feverishly.

"Galahad?" Chain asked softly.

"Yes," confirmed the young man impatiently. "Where is Mordred? Is he outside?" The minute he had said the words, Galahad knew he had made a mistake. Chain looked at him steadily for a full minute and then invited the other two into the room.

The two C.I.D. agents entered at once. One of them started 'reading' Galahad his rights while the other one walked up to him and started searching him. "You have the right to remain silent . . .," the first agent droned without expression. "Anything you say can and will be held against you in the court of law. You have the right to an attorney; present during . . ." He never finished his monologue. Galahad saw to that.

The most youthful member of the Round Table leapt out of the doorway; jumping violently out of the second agent's hands. He took

Chain and the two C.I.D. agents by complete surprise and was already racing down the corridors when they emerged from the room.

"Stop!" Chain shouted. "Stop or I'll shoot!" she shouted again.

Galahad took absolutely no notice at all of the warning. He continued running frantically down the halls and towards the stairs. Several agents posted along the way, alerted by Chain's shouts, joined him in firing at the fleeing figure.

They gunned him down as he approached the entrance to the campus. Immediately, he was surrounded by a swarm of C.I.D. agents who checked and verified that he was still alive. Chain walked more slowly to the area. He couldn't care less whether Galahad was alive or not. Idly, he watched as they bundled him off to hospital.

The agents who stayed behind scouted around to get some information from the gathering crowd of university students. One of them came to report their findings to Chain, who was leaning against a tree.

"His name was Marera," the agent said. "They say that he was a close friend to Kingston Musyoka, Vice-President Janet Musyoka's son."

'A close friend? That was ironic. How close can one be if he was plotting to kill your mother,' Chain wondered idly as another C.I.D. car came to pick him up. Friendships sure had changed since he was a kid.

But Chain didn't have time to think about Peter Marera's relationship with King Musyoka. He was too busy worrying about Susan.

When he reached home forty minutes later, Susan was still sleeping. Chain telephoned Bakari, passed the news, and asked to be kept posted. Then he and Bakari went over an elaborate plan for Janet Musyoka's entry and exit from Parliament building the following day. Bakari would go over it with the secret servicemen. Chain decided that it was over since the last three knights were still unknown.

He stayed at home with Susan the rest of the day, not knowing what the remaining members of the Round Table were up to and not really caring. All he wanted was for Susan to get well again.

The phone interrupted his dark thoughts at around nine o'clock in the night. It was Bakari. There was good news and bad news. The good news was that Chain's friend matched up the two remaining voice prints; Francis Nzau was clear; Abdul Hakim was Lancelot. Chain was stunned.

He went back into Susan's bedroom thinking of all the shocking revelations the whole mess had brought about. Whenever he thought that nothing else could surprise him, something did. He looked down at Susan's still sleeping face. "I'll get them all for you," he vowed. "Every single one of them."

Chapter Thirty -Five

Chain and Susan decided that Lancelot had got to be taken care of the next morning. The fact that it had turned out to be Abdul Hakim had shocked Susan out of her lethargy. She was more or less back to normal again. However, she refused to talk about Babs and couldn't bear to hear her name mentioned. Chain knew that it wasn't healthy but there was nothing he could do about it until this whole mess was cleared.

They had spent the whole night in each other's arms — literally. They hadn't slept at all, but had sat in the living room. Sometimes they talked but at other times they were silent. The night had not been a revelation; it had been a conclusion. They had both realised that they just could not spend the rest of their lives without each other.

"He will have to turn up for the grand opening of Parliament today," Chain was telling Susan in the morning. "There is no way he can skip it. Which means that he is most probably at home right now, waiting and wondering. What do you say? Do we go and put him out of his misery?"

"Sounds good to me," Susan said. She was feverishly active that morning and she couldn't seem to find enough to do. Chain had allowed her to rush about the house with hardly any comment, thinking that it was probably a way of dealing with her grief. She couldn't go on like this forever. She most probably would collapse from severe exhaustion before several hours had passed.

They had finished breakfast and Susan was in the kitchen; clearing up the last of the dishes. Three C.I.D. agents had taken turns guarding the house that night and so they were also there. One was cleaning the car, one was sleeping and the last was reading a newspaper. Chain was shaving with an electric razor which he detested.

"Well, are you coming?" demanded Susan from the living room. She had already finished the dishes and was raring to go.

"Okay, okay, keep your shirt on," Chain grumbled good naturedly. "Why don't you go and get the car out of the garage while I finish up?"

"I need some cigarettes," Susan said. "But the shops are so far off . . ."

The second agent walked into the room yawning and rubbing his eyes. The third one looked up from his newspaper and told him that he had missed breakfast. The one who had been cleaning the car entered the room whistling. Susan picked on him.

"Please get me a pack of cigarettes from the shops," she said brightly. "I want to reverse the car from the garage."

The agent agreed good-naturedly and the two of them left together discussing which brand he should buy. Susan couldn't seem to make up her mind.

"Where are the keys, Chain?" Susan asked, popping her head back in the house.

"In the ignition," Chain replied.

The two voices became fainter as Susan and the agent went towards the large garage at the other end of the compound.

Chain continued to shave, wondering why he hadn't remembered to pack his good old-fashioned shaving cream. He hated using razors of any kind; including electric. He tried to hurry so that Susan would not start honking the horn impatiently.

That was when he heard the explosion. A very large, ground shaking explosion just shattered the early morning calm and made Chain stop abruptly in his tracks and simply stare into his mirror as if he might find the answer there.

He knew what it was even before running outside and seeing the big mess that was the garage and what was left of the car. What else could it possibly have been? He stared in disbelief at the burning wreckage through the smoke-filled air. Then he started screaming.

He screamed Susan's name in agony and despair and launched himself at the now blazing fire hoping to catch a glimpse of her; to extricate her somehow. He had to save her. He couldn't believe she was dead; there was no way she could die!

One of the C.I.D. agents hurled himself forcefully at Chain; bringing him bodily to the ground before he could throw himself into the flames. Chain struggled to get up as the other agent joined in the fray. It took all their combined energy to subdue him.

When at last he stopped struggling, they let him sit up slowly. All three of them viewed the horror in front of them. None of them could believe that it had happened under their very noses. They just couldn't believe it.

They dragged a completely passive Chain inside. He had clenched his hands into fists so tightly that he had drawn blood.

'So this was what it felt like, losing somebody', he thought. No wonder his friend had gone crazy. No wonder Susan couldn't bear to talk about it, had nothing to say. His heart puffed and pounded and he felt as though he was being suffocated. The pain was unbearable.

The agents were making phone calls and trying to decide what to do next. Chain heard the gate open and someone ran towards the door. He turned tear-filled eyes towards it and saw a vision; the vision of Susan Juma.

"Chain!" the vision cried as it ran up to him and threw itself into his arms. "Are you alright? What happened?" It pressed tiny fevered kisses all over his face.

But wait a minute, visions were not supposed to kiss like that! He pulled her roughly away from him and stared at her. "Susan?" He stared at her in wonderingly, daring to hope. "Is it really you?"

"Begging your pardon ma'am," said one of the two agents who were also staring at her in disbelief. "But who was driving the car?" It was a question that Chain had badly wanted to ask her himself.

"It was the other agent," said Susan, breathlessly. "Kamau. He is dead, isn't he?"

"But Susan when you left, you were going to reverse the car and Kamau was going to buy your cigarettes," said Chain.

"Yes, but when we reached the gate I couldn't make up my mind exactly which brand I wanted, so I decided to go myself and then choose when I got there. I asked Kamau to reverse the car for me," she explained. "It was Mordred, wasn't it?"

"It must have been," Chain agreed. "I thought you were dead," he sighed, enveloping her in his arms. "I wanted to die myself. Never put me through anything like that again."

"Mordred sure doesn't give up," Susan said. "I have escaped narrowly twice. People keep on dying in my place. Do you think he will be lucky the third time?" she asked idly.

"Are you trying to get my blood pressure up again?" demanded Chain. "There won't be a third time. I don't care what I have to do but I'm getting rid of him today. There is just no other way."

They sat in silence as the agents rang Bakari again and explained that Susan was alive but that Kamau was the one who was now dead. Susan was depressed by the latest death and Chain was elated that she was still alive but terrified that Mordred may take her from him. Chain got up and went to talk to Bakari over the phone. He confirmed that he was going after Hakim and he needed a few agents again. He hoped to be able to catch Lancelot and arrest him, but he knew that it wasn't going to be very easy. Bakari agreed that they should try and they replaced their respective ends of the phone.

Susan insisted that she was also going and she and Chain had a brief but tension-releasing argument over it.

"I don't want to let you out of my sight," she wailed. "Anything could happen."

Chain agreed. He had no wish to come home and find her chopped into little pieces and spread out over the kitchen floor. He also did not want her out of his sight.

"You have got to promise me that you will do exactly as I tell you without asking questions," Chain said. He grinned suddenly. "Now where have I heard those words before?" he wondered aloud.

A cloud passed over Susan's face but she gave a shaky smile. "I will, I promise," she said. "You know I will," she added fiercely as she looked up at him.

"Yes, sweetheart," he said into her hair. "I know you will." They clung to each other until the agents from C.I.D. arrived. Chain and Susan got into one of the cars and it sped off towards Lancelot's house. They had no plan and no idea of what they might encounter there.

However, Lancelot was not the problem, Mordred was. Lancelot was just a minor inconvenience.

"You are sure it is Hakim?" Susan asked Chain.

"Absolutely sure," Chain confirmed. "It all checks out. Everything has been confirmed. Let us just go and pick him up now."

"You make that sound so simple," she said dryly and subsided into silence.

They rode in silence until they reached Hakim's residence. Rumour had it that Abdul Hakim had a house in every single town in the country. He was certainly rich enough to afford it, and everyone had reasoned that if that was what turned him on; then he should be allowed to do it. Now, Chain and Susan were beginning to realise where all the money had come from.

As they reached his house, he was leaving in a white mercedes. One of the C.I.D. cars went quickly ahead and blocked him off. Several agents accompanied Chain and Susan out of the cars.

"Chain!" exclaimed Hakim his eyes bulging as he camo out of the car.

"Lancelot," Chain acknowledged easily. "It is Lancelot, isn't it?"

"So," said Hakim, "you know everything. Mordred underestimated you."

"Mordred is only human," Chain said. "We all make mistakes."

"Even the one and only Chain?" he asked bitterly.

"Even me," Chain said mockingly. "I'm going to offer you a chance to co-operate, Lancelot. What do you say to that?"

Lancelot gave his answer in a sudden flurry of activity. Without warning, he jumped back into the car and turned the ignition key. The car roared to life and with a loud screech of tyres he swerved dangerously around the C.I.D. car blocking his path and sped away.

Chain's reflexes were as fast as they could be in the circumstances. He pushed Susan into their car while the agent driving fired the engine and drove noisily after the fast disappearing white mercedes. The other car was slightly slower, following several seconds behind. The chase was definitely on.

Chain's arms went protectively around Susan as they negotiated hairpin curves and rushed desperately after the now frantic Lancelot. He was driving like a maniac through the virtually impossible Nairobi city traffic. Time after time he missed crashing into all sorts of objects; lamp posts, buildings and other helpless motorists. Cars swerved dangerously off the road to give him room as he rushed towards them. The C.I.D. agent was doing his best to keep up with him, and little by little; was gaining a few inches. It was a car-chase right out of a movie, the only difference being that this was real.

Susan buried her head in Chain's shoulder as their car scraped shrilly against another one. She couldn't bear to look as car after car flashed by in a never-ending process that seemed to lead to death: certain death. And yet she knew that there was absolutely no way they could let Hakim to go free now. He was not sane. Something just had to be done. She stifled a scream as the car narrowly missed a lamp-post; climbed over a round-about and landed with a thump on the other side.

They followed him for another five hair-raising minutes until they got to the top of a fly-over. By this time Chain's car had almost caught up with him. They were almost bumper to bumper when the incredible happened.

Hakim drove his car over the crash barrier and onto the street below; bursting immediately into flames. The C.I.D. agent jammed on the brakes and skidded to a halt next to the barrier. They all got out and walked to the edge.

Lancelot's car had unceremoniously fallen on top of another car; taking it with him. Two other cars which had been travelling at very high speed behind them had been unable to stop and had joined the inferno. Three car-loads of innocent people were dead. Hakim had been determined not to die alone.

There was nothing more that could be done there so Chain and Susan were taken to Bakari's office. Susan wept softly throughout the entire journey and Chain was helpless to console her. He ran his hand through her hair and murmured softly to her.

"It's going to be alright," he whispered. "It is all going to be over soon. I'll make everything alright; you'll see."

276

He wished fiercely for a world with no hardships for his lady; a world full of happy laughter, beautiful sounds and captivating colours. A world that held no thorns which could prick her; no tears, no terror, no evil. A dream world. He wished fiercely that he could take her there.

They arrived at Bakari's office in twenty minutes and the agents went off to file a report as Chain took Susan into the office. Bakari stood up when they entered.

"Susan," he said. "What on earth was going on this morning?" He seemed upset. "I got a lot of conflicting reports. That you were dead . . ."

Chain shuddered. "As you can see there was a bit of a mistake there," he said.

"Perhaps you could tell me what exactly happened," Bakari said.

They sat down and Chain explained what had transpired that morning. He told Bakari about Lancelot's death and despaired about ever bringing any of the Round Table members to trial. They all seemed to prefer death.

While they talked Susan studied Bakari. He had turned out to be a firm ally in spite of her earlier reservations. She thought back to when Chain had told her of Bakari's sordid little affair with a girl young enough to be his daughter. She had no right to judge him. All that now seemed very petty and insignificant. As Chain had said, they were only human, after all. Human beings were prone to making mistakes.

She sighed and sat back in the chair. She had been spared twice from certain death. She had been given a second and a third chance with Chain, and she meant to make use of the situation.

Chapter Thirty-Six

It was an hour before the opening of Parliament. Chain and Susan were at the Parliament building already. They had been there for some time, discussing the new security plans which Bakari and the secret servicemen had implemented. They were also looking out for Mordred, who they were sure would be there.

The place was surrounded by guards, security men and an assortment of B.I.O. and C.I.D. agents. Susan had asked Bakari what would happen to B.I.O. for she couldn't believe that they would continue as usual. He had told her that most of the loyal members would be taken back to help expand the C.I.D. A major clean-up operation had been planned to determine who was working for the government and who was not. The traitors would all be prosecuted. B.I.O. was to be shut down and very soon it would cease to exist. Bakari had assured her that it would die out as quietly as it had been formed; unknown and inconspicuous. It would be the death of a dream; the Bureau of Investigative Operations would be no more.

It was just as well for it was obvious that the country was not ready for an outfit like B.I.O. What had started out as a top-secret organisation for safeguarding the citizens and keeping crime to a minimum had ended up being a breeding ground for treason and murder. Somewhere along the way B.I.O. had run off its tracks. Finally, it had derailed. It needed to be consigned to the scrap heap and designed all over again. Maybe some day someone would be able to come up with a new, streamlined, fool-proof organisation which did the job that it was meant to do. Susan, however, would not be a part of it. She had already decided this.

Chain and Susan had travelled over the grounds several times, looking for a weak link in the chain they had strung around the area. They walked slowly from post to post making sure that the guards were in place and that the security would rival only that at Alcatraz Prison.

No unauthorised people were allowed to come in and even the authorised people had to go through a complete third degree check conducted by Chain, Susan, Bakari and the heads of the police and the Secret Service before they were allowed in or out of the place.

C.I.D. agents and police officers had passed over every inch of the building and surrounding grounds with a fine toothcomb. There were no bombs or explosives in the place. All the vehicles and machinery which had entered or left the place had been checked and rechecked. And yet both Chain and Susan were sure that Mordred was there somewhere. It was this that was a chill in the bones more than mere intuition or a strange telepathic sense. It was sure knowledge that Mordred was there somewhere, only they didn't know where.

Even though they had satisfied themselves that the security was as tight as was humanly possible, they still roamed the grounds in the hope that they might come across him somewhere although it was highly unlikely. He wasn't likely to be walking aimlessly about waiting to be captured. Mordred was planning something and Chain would have given almost anything to know exactly what it was.

Finally they sat down on some steps near the building. They decided to wait and see what materialised. They had already made a deal with the secret servicemen that if Mordred was not caught, then the whole opening of Parliament was to be postponed to another day altogether. The risk was just too great to even contemplate.

"I had a rotten childhood," Chain said suddenly. "Really rotten."

Susan turned to him encouragingly.

"My father was quite rich," he continued. "He had a lot of land and herds of cattle and that sort of thing. He was quite respected in his community. My mother died when I was a year old and he married again immediately. The same old story of the wicked step-mother comes in. She was young and beautiful and didn't want to be saddled with another woman's child."

"Not even if that child was you?" Susan asked softly, her eyes shining.

"Not even me," Chain laughed. "She reasoned that since I was the first-born, I would get the giant share of the riches while her own children would be forced to settle for smaller portions. She did not entertain that idea. She arranged for me to be stolen and sold to a childless couple who lived in the city. Unfortunately for me, after buying me, the couple decided that they didn't really want a child after all. That was the beginning of the nightmare."

He stopped and clenched his teeth as he recalled those early days. The memories were obviously very painful and Susan's hand crept up to cover his in sympathy.

"They never stopped telling me that I was not really their child at all but that I had merely been bought," he said. "My earliest memories were of my surrogate mother beating the hell out of me and screaming at me that she should have left me in the first convenient ditch instead of bringing me to her home. She used to bang my head against the wall, cut me with a sharp razor, burn me with the iron and all manner of things, all in the name of discipline. I guess she is what you would call a sadist, or simply a child-abuser. I became really adept at making up lovely stories to explain the bruises on my face, cuts on my arms and burns on legs. There was no way I was going to tell my friends that my mother did all those painful things to me. I guess my teachers suspected it but had no real way of proving anything since I completely refused to talk. It was my private battle which I just couldn't let anyone else into. It was up to me to fight it alone."

As I grew up I grew more withdrawn. I learnt to be by myself and to live alone. My mother stopped beating me when I grew taller than her, which happened at the age of eleven. I found odd jobs after school and at night to pay for my school fees and to buy my own food. My parents provided shelter and nothing more. We could go for days without catching a glimpse of one another and weeks without communicating. That was my childhood.

It stopped when I turned fifteen and was introduced to B.I.O. They paid me to infiltrate gangs and find out how drugs were being spread into schools. "For the first time in my life I really felt wanted. I knew that I wanted to stay with B.I.O. forever."

"What about your real father?" Susan asked quietly. "Did he ever get to know what had happened?"

"In the end, yes," Chain said. "To give her some credit, my step mother felt some twinges of guilt after doing what she did. It was made even worse by the fact that she never had any children and she began to think that it was because of what she had done to me. As the years went by she became obsessed with the idea. She was convinced that it was a curse and I think that she started going a bit crazy towards the end. I don't know what she had told my father at the beginning but in the end she told him the whole story."

"What did your father do to her?" Susan asked.

"Oh he chased her from home," Chain said. "You know what these macho African men are like."

"Oh yes, I do," Susan said fervently.

"Anyway, he managed to track me down before he died. I was nineteen at the time," Chain said, looking down at his shoes. "He told me the whole story in detail and then he died and left me all his riches." Chain smiled a bit bitterly. "I would have given all those riches to have him live instead. As soon as I had found someone who would love me, he was taken away from me. There's no justice." He threw a small stone down the steps.

"You have got me now," Susan said tentatively.

"Yeah," Chain smiled and gathered her to him. "I have got you."

They sat like that for a little while, holding each other close and talking softly. Chain did not want to stay there. Each second spent brought them closer to Mordred and he was afraid of what Mordred might do to Susan.

After a few minutes they stood up and walked slowly over the grounds, their eyes ever watchful. They still saw no sign of trouble and so decided to go into the building itself. They had entered one of the halls and were talking in hushed tones when one of the guards entered and told Chain that Bakari wanted to see him for a moment. Chain agreed reluctantly and insisted that Susan stay inside; out of the sun. He said that the guard would stay with her until he returned.

He left her sitting on one of the benches with the guard standing uneasily by the door. As he looked in every direction but hers she studied him covertly. He was extremely good-looking; not too dark and not too light. Very even features, long curly lashes, broad shoulders tapering to a narrow waist and strong hips and thighs; he was perfect.

Too bad he was so shy. There was no way he was going to get a female by nervously fluttering his eyelashes!

Those eyelashes where really fascinating. She stood idly up and walked towards the door in an effort to get a better look at his eyelashes. A twinge of guilt ran through her as she thought Chain would definitely not approve of her admiring some other guy's eyes. But she consoled herself by saying that she was not interested in the guard; as handsome as he was. She just felt compelled to look closer at his really incredible eyelashes; sinful on a man.

He looked up and gave her the full benefit of eyelashes. "Would you like to go out, madam?" he asked politely. But she wasn't listening to his smooth, low voice. It was his eyes which had commandeered her full, undivided attention. Those beautiful brown eyes – which one could drown in. Bottomless, fathomless, angelic, ethereal. The most fantastic eyes she had ever seen.

"Mordred," she whispered as he removed his gun from his holster and trained it on her. Nobody had eyes like that. Nobody.

The expression in them never changed. They still remained the same: innocent-looking, friendly and angelic. Talk about deceiving. They bore no resemblance to the look of intent on his face and the gun he held in his hand.

"Sorry you recognised me at the airport," Mordred said as he took the gun from the holster she was wearing. "I was really wondering about that. Tell me something; if you don't mind. How is it that you always manage to recognise me so easily? No false modestly intended but I have been told just how good an actor I am; I have always been able to fool people in the past. What makes it so different with you? Are you psychic?"

"You mean you don't know?" Susan asked in complete shock.

"If I knew I wouldn't be asking," he told her dryly.

"Your eyes, Mordred," she said. "Its your eyes! Haven't you ever noticed?"

"Noticed what?" he asked impatiently.

She started laughing but then changed her mind. "You have the most incredible eyes I have ever seen on a human being," she told him almost reverently. "They're beautiful. They are just the kind of eyes that one would expect an angel or some other supernatural being to have. You can't help noticing that."

"I've never noticed a thing," Mordred said, looking at her suspiciously.

"Well I have," Susan retorted. "No matter what else you happen to be, let me assure you right now that your eyes are captivating; enchanting. I'm not just saying that to butter you up, it's true. And they're framed by very long and unusual eyelashes. There is just no way you can escape unnoticed."

"Leave it to a woman to notice something like that," he said disgustedly. "You kept identifying me because of my eyes? What kind of strange story is that? Sure they're not bad-looking but they aren't angelic. That's all in your mind. Beautiful, incredible, captivating. You are sick, woman."

"No, you are," she retorted. "Not me. Sick because you can't notice the only good thing in you and sick because of what you're planning to do to the Vice-President. You will never get away with it, you know."

"Who is going to stop me?" he asked lazily. "Chain? You?"

"Too many people know," Susan said as she shook her head. "You can kill me and you can kill Chain, but how many more can you kill? When this thing started falling apart it fell all the way. It's all over, Mordred. Give it up."

"It's not over until I get rid of that woman," Mordred said fiercely. "I promised myself that I was going to kill Janet Musyoka and that is exactly what I'm going to do."

"You are crazy," she said flatly.

Before they could make a further comment; they heard Chain's voice outside the door.

"Open the door," Mordred ordered. "Get lover-boy in here or I swear I'll shoot both of you now. Do it!"

She moved swiftly to the door. Her mind was working overtime. She opened the door and called out to Chain.

"Come on out darling," he replied. "I've not yet finished with Bakari."

"Christopher, come in here please," she said in a level voice. "I've got something I want to tell you."

She got Chain's attention immediately. He remembered a recent conversation they had had, and Susan had asked him whether anyone ever called him Christopher.

"Only if you hate me," he had grimaced. "I really detest that name."

So why was she calling him Christopher now? He was immediately on guard and alerted.

Susan moved back into the room and was immediately caught by Mordred who flung his arm around her neck and shoulders, and then pointed the gun to her head.

Chain threw the door open, his arms outstretched, a gun held firmly in his hands and pointed at Mordred. The only problem was that Susan was in the direct line of fire. And Mordred knew it.

Suddenly Susan extended her right arm and brought her elbow viciously into Mordred's stomach. He released her in pain and she immediately dropped flat on her face on the ground. No sooner had she done this than Chain started firing. Mordred was fractions of seconds too late to return the fire as he had become totally disorientated by Susan's blow. His gun came up and he fired feebly; the shot heading towards the ceiling. His chest was splattered with blood and his face was filled with shock. Those magnificent brown eyes looked at Chain in horror and reproach. He started to say something but his mouth filled with blood. He coughed and crumpled slowly to the ground and his beautiful eyes closed. Mordred was dead.

Chapter Thirty-Seven

Chain gently lifted Susan from the floor. He cradled her in his arms, not looking at the assassin who now lay dead behind them. He felt elated at his major victory but the thought of how near he had come to losing Susan once again left him trembling with reaction, helpless with fear. He held her tighter.

"Three times is strike out, isn't it?" she asked; her voice muffled against his chest.

"What?" he asked her bemusedly.

"Three times," she repeated. "In baseball. When you don't hit the ball three consecutive times then you are struck out, right?"

He caught her drift. "Yes darling," he gently murmured. "Three times is a strike out."

He let go of her to go and crouch down next to Mordred's prone figure. Quickly, he started rifling through his pockets.

"So this is Mordred," he said. "The enigma; the unknown entity. Quite good-looking for a mad killer, wouldn't you say?"

"I hadn't noticed," Susan said with a smile.

"Well, I have got some identification here," Chain said, holding up a card. "It says Nicholas Tanui. We can't be sure whether or not that's a true name. But it seems to suit him somehow."

They went outside and called Bakari and the C.I.D. agents inside. There immediately started an enquiry into how Mordred could possibly have entered the building without being detected. Somehow Chain suspected that they probably would never find out and at that moment in time, he simply didn't care.

Bakari and his men managed to certify that the dead man's name really was Nicholas Tanui and that the reason he had managed to enter the Parliament grounds was that he had every right to. He had been an authentic guard who had been hired several weeks before. His identification card and papers were all authentic; nothing had been forged. The Round Table had left nothing to chance. In his bag several long-range telescopic rifles had been found and the conclusion reached was that Mordred had been planning to shoot Janet from the top of Parliament Building. A fellow guard verified that the roof was where Mordred usually was. A heavy club would have been used to hit his partner on the head from the behind, before doing the deed. It would have been easy enough to club his partner while wearing gloves, so as to leave no fingerprints and then remove the gloves and toss them into one of the drainage outlets on the roof. Then he would simply have fallen heavily onto the cement; striking his head on the ground and pretending that he had also been clubbed from behind. It would have required a lot of acting but Mordred was definitely one of the best actors around.

"What would he have done with the bag and all the rifles inside it?" Susan asked.

"He probably had a hiding place picked out already on the roof," Chain said. "He could stash the bag out of sight and then come and reclaim it later when there was no danger. Mordred had it worked out."

"And now?" Susan asked.

"Now it's all over," Chain said.

"How can it be all over?" queried Susan. "We haven't finished off the Round Table. What about King Arthur? Had you forgotten about him?"

"He is probably not even here today," Chain protested. "It was Mordred we were after."

"I know," said Susan. "But King Arthur has to go. He was the cause of all this. How are we to know that he won't go and build another Round Table; bigger and better than this one? The original Round Table had over one hundred knights. Are you prepared to deal with one hundred Mordreds in the future?"

Chain shivered at the thought. "No, of course not," he said. "But we have no idea who King Arthur is; we have no clue. How on earth do you expect us to find him? It's going to take weeks and months of investigation. You can't do it in a minute. To make things even worse, he has probably skipped the country by now. It's not going to be easy tracing him."

"But we'll do it," Susan insisted.

"Yes we'll do it," Chain sighed. "I don't suppose we have that much choice."

After he had said that, one of Bakari's men came over to discuss details and take down statements from both Chain and Susan. They discussed the whole incident at length before writing down a general run-down of things. It was several minutes before Chain and Susan were let off the hook and by that time Chain was literally chomping at the bit. He definitely had something on his mind and dragged Susan away the minute the C.I.D. man had finished speaking to them.

She didn't have time to protest as he pulled her into a nearby corner and started dropping small butterfly kisses all over her face, until she giggled. He smiled but continued his task with renewed vigour and intensity.

"Chain!" called out a hearty voice, making them both jump. "There you are; I've been looking all over for you two." It was Bakari, bearing down on them. Chain stifled a rude comment and turned politely to his friend.

They talked at length about the security system and whether or not everyone was in his proper place. The arrangement had been changed so that every guard was accompanied by a known and trusted C.I.D. agent or a secret serviceman. Bakari was concerned that the security might not have been adequate but Chain persuaded him that it was. There was simply nothing more they could do. The security was as tight as was humanly possible.

Before Chain and Susan could escape they were accosted by the Chief of Police and Officer-in-charge of the Secret Service. They also wanted reassurance that everyone and everything would be alright. Not being aware of the Round Table issue, they had rather less to be worried about and so were not as hard to convince as Bakari was. And yet they could also sense that something was wrong and that made them very uneasy.

After several more minutes had been spent placating the three men, Chain once more pulled Susan away, looking distinctly put out. He found another corner and hurriedly rushed her into it. He wrapped his arms around her waist.

"Now where were we?" he murmured before bending his head and picking up where he had left off. He dragged himself upright after a few intoxicating minutes.

"Susan I want to ask you . . ." he began. But the question was ill-fated. He never got a chance to ask it as Bakari came bearing down on them once more again.

"Chain!" he called out.

"George, do you mind?" Chain exploded. "I am trying to get something constructive done here. Do you think you could give us a few minutes in private? Or is that just too much to ask?"

Bakari looked blank and astonished for a second and then a look of dawning comprehension filled his face. Looking a bit sheepish, he muttered an apology which Chain merely grunted to and walked away.

Chain let out an exasperated breath, and turned back to Susan. Slowly he traced the outline of her lips with his fingertips. Gently he brushed the hair away from her forehead and then tenderly, cupped her cheek in his palm. He studied her features in fascination, as if trying to memorise each one. All this time he never uttered a word. Susan watched him curiously, wondering what was going on in his mind. She didn't interrupt him but waited patiently for him to speak.

When at last he did, it was to say something which shocked her.

"Marry me, Susie," he said.

"Before or after we get King Arthur?" she teased him, trying to regain control of her reeling senses. A deep sense of joy bubbled up inside her and threatened to spill over.

"Now; tonight; this minute," Chain murmured urgently as he held her face in both hands and tilted it upwards to meet his probing eyes.

Susan smiled radiantly, the joy inside her spilling over into her eyes, her face, her smile. She reached up and touched Chain's face reverently. "Yes," she said simply.

Her joy became his joy, and he bent down to bestow another kiss on her willing lips. Murmuring happily he began to tell her of his farm in Kitale and how much she would like it there. She could see that to

Chain, it was the most beautiful spot in the world. She began to drear
of the future and of creating a home and starting a family. She felt tha
her life was just about to begin. 'Babs,' she thought dreamily. 'I'll ca
my first daughter Babs.' And someday she might even be able to thin
of her friend without that familiar shaft of intense pain and los
shooting through her.

"Well, did she say yes?" Bakari's voice broke into the intimat
moment, making them jump hastily apart. Chain looked at his frien
ruefully. He shook his head as if to clear it.

"George," he said calmly. "Are you going to intrude on ever
private moment of my life or is this just a passing trend?" he asked. "A
this rate, I may not even invite you to the wedding, for fear that yo
may insist on joining us on our honeymoon."

Bakari laughed heartily. "Congratulations," he said to both c
them. "I wish we could stand here grinning all day but I want you t
meet King Musyoka, the Vice-President's younger son. I think you wi
find that he has got an interesting story to tell."

* * * * *

Both Chain and Susan were struck at once by the force of Kin
Musyoka's personality. He was the kind of person who would alway
draw crowds wherever he went. He looked calm and composed as h
shook Chain's hand.

"I have heard a lot about you," he said, his eyes lighting up i
respect. "You are an asset to this country."

He went on to explain that he and his brother Martin had arrive
some time ago to check out the security. It seemed that this was
routine whenever their mother appeared in public. Just a few minute
ago he had heard Bakari mention the assassin Nicholas Tanui a
Mordred and it had immediately struck him that something wa
happening. "My mom is in danger, isn't she?" he asked in
self-possessed voice.

Chain tried to reassure him that the danger was over but King wa
unconvinced.

"My girl friend Alice lives on the outskirts of town," he said. "The last time I was there, I had a chat with her 13-year-old brother, Joe. Now Joe goes swimming at the house opposite their's every afternoon at the request of their kind-hearted neighbour who insists that nobody uses the pool anyway. The reason why I recognised the name Mordred so easily was because Joe had told me that on his numerous trips to the house, he had heard the neighbour call his son Mordred. The son then referred to his father as King Arthur. But Joe knew quite well that the son was called Nick; Nicholas Tanui; to be precise."

They all stared at King's impassive face in stunned astonishment. Nobody had a single comment to make so he continued.

"Joe got very curious and so went and read up on the entire Arthurian legend," King said. "Still, it wouldn't have really interested him much if it wasn't for the assortment of cars bringing a wide range of people to the house every Saturday morning. Twenty minute intervals separated their arrivals and departures every Saturday. There were seven in all. Joe was convinced that they were plotting something; so am I. So you see even if you have got rid of Mordred, you have still got those seven to think about. Eight, if you count King Arthur."

"One," Susan whispered.

"What?" King asked, looking puzzled.

"Only one," she said. "We've got them all, except King Arthur."

At that moment, the Vice-President's motorcade entered the Parliament grounds. By this time there were plenty of cars there already, and the camera-men and crews had turned up in very large numbers, ready to record the event. Chain watched the cars approach the building before turning abruptly back to King.

"So you know the identity of this King Arthur?" he asked tersely.

"Of course," replied King, a little startled and bemused. "He is a lecturer at my university."

Chain and Susan both blinked at him. The cars came nearer and slowed down.

"Do you know where we can find him right now?" Chain asked urgently.

"Of course," King repeated, looking even more confused. "There he is over there, at the bottom of the steps," he said as he pointed at a middle-aged man standing in the Vice-President's welcoming line. "That's why I know that my mother's life is in danger," King explained.

The cars stopped and the door opened.

Both Chain and Susan gave an almost simultaneous groan of anguish and each of them sprinted off. Susan ran for Janet Musyoka's car and Chain ran towards King Arthur. They both saw the middle-aged man remove a gun fitted with a silencer from his coat pocket, as if in slow motion. The world went silent. In despair, they both noted that everyone was busy cheering the Vice-President, who was now emerging from her car and did not notice the gun. Time stood still as they raced with pounding hearts towards their respective goals. They could neither see nor hear anything else.

Susan appeared from the blues, and launched herself at the Vice-President, toppling them both to the ground. Immediately; a bullet smashed into the car door, the space which they had barely vacated. The second bullet smashed the car window above them, shattering it into tiny pieces and the third one hit a secret serviceman who had started running towards Janet and Susan. The latter rolled sideways with the Vice-President in her arms, shielding her with her body.

Chain launched himself at King Arthur, causing him to lose balance and they both fell heavily to the ground. As his gun rolled out of his hand, King Arthur turned to look at Chain with hatred blazing in his eyes. He viciously kicked Chain in the stomach and stood up again.

He hadn't taken two steps when C.I.D. agents and secret servicemen opened fire on him. He felt the bullets smash into his body as pain tore through him. Then, King Arthur crumpled slowly to the ground.

C.I.D. agents hurriedly helped Susan, Janet and Chain to their feet. Chain went over to gather Susan in his arms while Janet was immediately surrounded by secret servicemen. Bakari and King Musyoka made their way towards Chain and Susan who were both looking at King Arthur, dying on the pavement.

"Thanks," King said simply his voice husky. Then he quickly turned away and hurried over to his mother.

Chain and Susan watched the blood oozing out of the Professor's body, taking with it the last threat to the nation. Kenya was safe once again. King Arthur was dead and the Round Table was gone.

In the distance, Vice-President Janet Musyoka hurried into the Parliament building. It was budget day and there was a speech to be read.